RANDOM HOUSE

LARGE PRINT

BLOOD OATH

Also By Linda Fairstein
Available from Random House Large Print

Deadfall

Killer Look

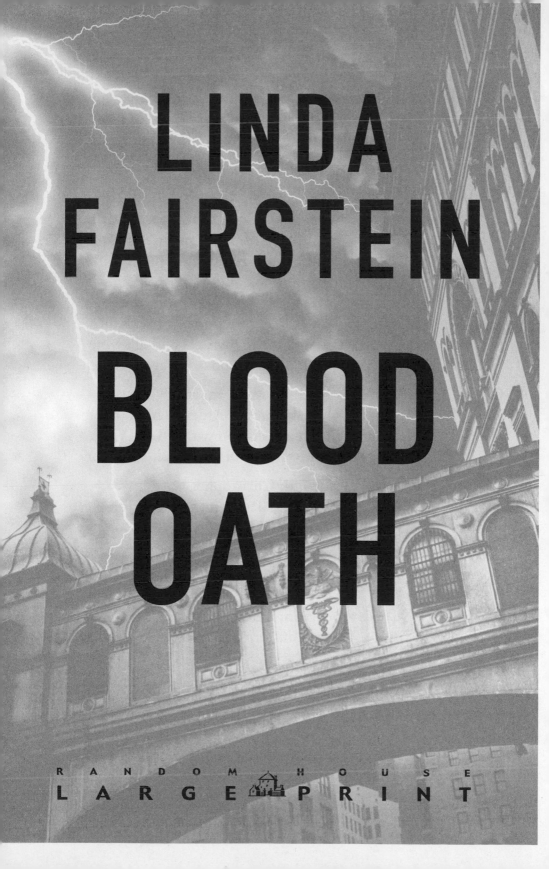

LINDA FAIRSTEIN

BLOOD OATH

R A N D O M   H O U S E
LARGE PRINT

Copyright © 2019 by Fairstein Enterprises, LLC

Published in the United States of America by Random House Large Print in association with DUTTON, an imprint of Penguin Random House LLC, New York.

Cover design: Christopher Lin
Cover photographs: © Getty Images (US) Inc.

The Library of Congress has established a Cataloging-in-Publication record for this title.

ISBN: 978-1-9848-2756-2

www.penguinrandomhouse.com
/large-print-format-books

FIRST LARGE PRINT EDITION

Printed in the United States of America

10 9 8 7 6 5 4 3 2 1

This Large Print edition published in accord with the standards of the N.A.V.H.

FOR JESSE AUSUBEL

Brilliant scientist, visionary leader,
treasured friend

And his colleagues at the Rockefeller University,
who use their creativity and genius every day
to make our world a better place

Very few of us are what we seem.

—Agatha Christie

BLOOD OATH

ONE

"Back from the dead, are you, Ms. Cooper?" the judge bellowed from the bench as I let the courtroom door close behind me.

I forced a smile and walked to the front row, taking a seat next to Helen Wyler, one of the young lawyers in the Sex Crimes Prosecution Unit.

"What's the matter?" Judge Corliss asked. "Cat got your tongue?"

There were only twenty people in the large room. There was the law secretary assigned to Corliss, who was sitting beside him, scribbling notes in her log; the clerk, who was at his desk to the left, pretending to fumble with the day's calendar; the stenographer, who had rested his hands at his side when Corliss started to yell; a defense attorney sitting at counsel table, looking over his shoulder and laughing at me; and the defendant himself—on trial for first-degree rape—fixated on the pretty face of the young law secretary who was working with the judge. The others, except for the jury and my colleague, Helen, had probably been corralled by the defense attorney to pretend to be family members interested in the outcome of the trial.

I raised my hands to my sides, palms up, and just shrugged at Corliss.

"Looks like I lose my bet, Alexandra," the judge said, standing up on his raised platform and pulling back his black gown—hands on his hips—expecting everyone would admire his fit torso and his bespoke shirt with monogrammed cuffs. "You're going to cost me fifty bucks."

"I'm so sorry, Alex," Helen said, leaning closer to me as she whispered. "I didn't want to bother you on your first day back in the office, but Corliss is totally trying to steamroll over me and I don't have the experience to stand up to him."

"Pay attention to me," Corliss said to me. "Not your sidekick. Ms. Wyler will get it right one of these days, with or without your help."

Now the defendant's entourage was engaged, too, trying to figure out who I was and why the judge was spending time and energy on me.

"Fifty large, Alexandra. I bet three of the other judges in the lunchroom you'd never set foot in this building again."

I poked Helen in the side so that she would get to her feet and address Corliss from her proper place, within the well of the courtroom.

She stood and pushed through the low wooden gate, taking her place at counsel table.

"May I have ten minutes with Ms. Cooper?" she asked.

The defendant—a serial rapist who specialized in attacking teenagers—put his head in his hands and groaned.

"You can have ten, Ms. Wyler," Corliss said, "so long as I get fifteen."

"The witness room is empty, Your Honor," Helen said. "We'll just go in there."

"I'm first," Corliss said. He motioned to me with his forefinger, telling me to approach him so we could have a private conversation. "And you'll stay right where you are, Ms. Wyler."

I ignored his summons and walked to the prosecution table, which was stacked high with trial folders and papers. Helen stepped back briskly, as though moving away from an out-of-control car coming in her direction.

"Why the silent treatment, Alexandra?" Corliss asked.

I turned to the stenographer, who had recorded the testimony at several of my trials. "Lenny, let's go on the record, please."

"Who's giving the orders in here? Somebody make you a judge while I wasn't looking?" Corliss asked. "Lenny, why don't you go help yourself to a cup of coffee?"

When Lenny stood up to leave the room, I turned my back to the bench and started to retrace my steps.

"Whoa, whoa!" Corliss said. "Let's slow this down, Alexandra."

Raymond Santiago looked up, leaning over past his lawyer to check out the minor commotion. His right hand moved instinctively to his groin, where he seemed to like to keep it most of the time, when he wasn't stalking his victims. What Santiago's lawyer referred to as his client's hypersexuality was likely to be on constant display for the jury.

I swiveled again. "I'm happy to talk to you, Your Honor," I said. "I want everything we say to be on the record. That's why I didn't answer when you first called out to me."

"Stick around, Lenny," Judge Corliss said, motioning to the stenographer to sit. "Ms. Cooper wants on the record, we'll give her on the record. Like I was saying, she's just back from—"

"I wasn't dead, Your Honor," I said, smiling at him. "Sorry to disappoint, but I wasn't even on life support."

The Honorable Bud Corliss liked to bully young assistants like Helen Wyler. He would shut down the stenographer and launch verbal arrows at the prosecutors, each one tipped with a poisonous comment about his or her skills. Sometimes, if his target was an attractive young woman, he'd add a remark about her anatomy. Then, if she chose to complain to a superior about the comment, there were no traces of Corliss's bad behavior in the transcript.

"I guess you really dodged a bullet, in the most literal sense," he said, sitting in his high-back leather chair and adjusting his gold cuff links. "I mean, the night your late lamented boss was shot in the head just a few feet away from you—dodging **that** bullet."

This was a conversation I didn't want to have in front of strangers—no less a perp charged with seventeen counts of rape and aggravated sexual assault.

"Strike that word 'lamented,'" Corliss said to Lenny, editing his own remarks. "Not everybody got broken up about the forced retirement of Paul Battaglia after a few too many terms in office, did they, Alexandra?"

"The district attorney mentored me, Your Honor," I said. "He put me in charge of the Special Victims Bureau a dozen years ago. I had nothing but respect for the man."

"Let me ask you something," he said, leaning forward and putting both elbows on his blotter. "I have a few questions about what happened that—"

"Judge Corliss, this is neither the time nor place," I said. "You've got jurors waiting for the testimony to resume, my colleague is anxious to complete the People's case by the end of the week, and the defendant—well . . ."

"What about him?"

"Mr. Santiago probably needs to get some medical attention for that itch in his groin he keeps scratching throughout our conversation," I said.

"This might be a good time to give him a short restroom break and throw him some calamine lotion before I have Ms. Wyler add in a count of masturbating in a public place."

"Good to know you haven't lost your sense of humor, Alexandra," Corliss said as Santiago's inexperienced court-appointed lawyer struggled to find grounds for an objection. "Ten-minute break, ladies and gentlemen. Let's clear the courtroom."

Court officers handcuffed the prisoner and took him out to the holding pen that serviced the thirteenth-floor trial rooms. His hangers-on—impervious to my comments—wandered out into the large corridor that ran the entire length of the enormous building.

I sat at counsel table with Helen Wyler. "What do you need?"

"I've made a terrible mistake, Alex," she said. "I don't think I'll get my first two victims back here if Corliss declares a mistrial."

"What have you done?" I asked.

"The fifteen-year-old who testified Friday—the one who was raped on the rooftop at Taft Houses?" Helen said.

"Yes, I remember." I knew the case well. Helen had indicted it before my leave had started almost three months earlier—after an incident that was unrelated to the murder of the district attorney.

"On cross this morning, she admitted texting

me six or seven times before the trial began," Helen said, slouching lower in her chair.

"Did she?"

"Yeah. Yeah, she did."

"But you didn't turn the texts over to the defense?"

I could see Corliss out of the corners of my eyes, pacing back and forth, trying to catch a fragment of our conversation.

"The texts weren't significant to the case facts, Alex," Helen said to me, stopping to bite her lip. "Graciela was just asking if she had to see Santiago in the courtroom and about how terrified she was to be within twenty feet of him. That kind of stuff."

The perp had grabbed the girl as she got off an elevator to go to her home in the projects, holding a knife to her neck to force her to the roof, where he raped her repeatedly for almost two hours.

"That kind of stuff, as you call it," I said, as calmly as I could, "is still Rosario Material. The defense is entitled to every one of those texts, Helen. You know that as well as I do."

"They got away from me," she said. "They were coming in at all hours of the night and somehow they just got away from me."

"So you didn't print them out?" I asked. "You didn't save them?"

"Graciela's emails, yes. The defense has them all. Her texts—well, I just forgot."

The New York Court of Appeals had mandated the disclosure of all of a prosecution witness's prior recorded statements in a ruling in the Rosario case, many decades ago. Each new form of social media ratcheted up the number of ways a nervous witness could communicate.

"Corliss knows?" I asked.

"Yes, because of her answers on cross," Helen said. "He's threatening to strike all of Graciela's testimony. Maybe even declare a mistrial. I'm screwed if he does that. She'll never go through this again."

"How much time has he given you?"

"Until tomorrow morning," Helen said, avoiding eye contact with me and lifting her head to stare at the light fixtures on the ceiling. "But that won't help because they don't exist. I deleted them."

"Have you tried TARU?" I asked, putting my hand on hers, which was on top of a pile of her notes. "They're wizards."

The NYPD's Technical Assistance Response Unit was a small, elite force of detectives responsible for all investigative tech support and the most complex computer forensics.

Helen shook her head. "I was too embarrassed to tell the SVU detectives last night. I just assumed it was a lost cause once I hit Delete. I've never worked a matter with TARU."

"Focus on your case," I said, standing up. "Where's your phone?"

"Top desk drawer."

"It won't be there when you get downstairs, but you'll have it back tonight," I said. "These TARU guys can retrieve stuff that's gone off into the Twilight Zone. Nothing ever gets fatally lost in the ether. Tell Corliss you'll have what he wants by morning."

"Shouldn't I ask for an adjournment?"

"Call your next witness, Helen," I said. "Raymond Santiago has preyed on young girls for the last time. Just don't let Corliss beat you down along the way."

I stepped away from her and waved to Corliss. "Thanks for giving me the time."

"Now I get my fifteen with you," he said, tucking his thumbs into the front of his leather belt, the sides of his robe pushed back, and striding down the three steps from his bench to walk to his robing room. "C'mon, Alexandra."

Helen Wyler was on her feet, apologizing to me for putting me in the judge's scope.

"It's okay. But don't you ever do what I'm about to do," I said. "The man's a pig. Don't let him bully you into being alone with him."

"But you—"

"I had my first felony trial in front of Corliss a dozen years ago," I said. "My entire team were guys—really good guys. You've met them all. My knees used to wobble when he demanded that I come into his robing room to discuss a plea deal or a procedural issue. So my pals swore that if I ever walked out with any of the judge's dandruff on my suit, they'd know I'd been too close to him and they'd take him down."

Helen laughed.

"Thanks for your concern," I said, "but at this stage in our relationship, Corliss doesn't have any real interest in me—and he certainly lacks the balls to take me on."

I followed him into the small cubicle behind the courtroom. There was a wooden chair and desk and two more chairs for visitors. Bud Corliss was staring out the window, looking down at the traffic on Centre Street.

"You've had a rough autumn," he said, his back to me. "First the kidnapping, and then the shock of witnessing Battaglia's murder."

"It was a pretty miserable couple of months, but I'm back on my feet, Judge," I said. "And I didn't mean to be rude when I came into your courtroom, but I just wasn't ready to throw this all out in front of Santiago and his crew."

I was being polite now, more for Helen Wyler's sake—and the salvation of her case—than my own.

"You ready for the grind?"

"You know I love it. My friends and family have been great, and my shrink is amazingly solid. Nobody seemed to like me when I was whining and needy, so I might as well do the one thing I know how to do."

Bud Corliss turned around to face me, half

sitting on the radiator cover below the windowsill. "You think they got the right guys? I mean, Battaglia's killers?"

"I do." I had been involved in that investigation up to my eyeballs.

"There were so many rumors floating around," Corliss said.

"Most of them were groundless and stupid, but you know how that goes," I said. "Some of them even had **me** as a conspirator in his murder."

"Then there's all the gossip about you running to take his place."

"That's just what it is, Judge. Gossip," I said, laughing with him. "You've known me a long time. Do you think I have the temperament for politics?"

"You'd be easier on the eyes than that mean old bastard you worked for," Corliss said, tiptoeing toward the line that he had crossed so many times before, as he looked me up and down, from the ankles to the crown of my head. "And your perfume smells a lot better than his foul, cheap cigars."

I took a step toward the door. "I'll miss the cigars, actually. That smell wafting my way always gave me ninety seconds' warning that Battaglia was coming to my office to needle me about something."

"There was also talk about you and that detective—Mike Chapman—eloping to the Vineyard together."

"Eloping?" I said, reaching for the door handle.

"That's one I hadn't heard. Way too many rumors for me in one day. Be good to Helen Wyler, Judge. She's well on her way to becoming an outstanding trial lawyer."

"About rumors, Alex," Corliss said, walking toward me and pressing his hand against the door to keep it closed, "you're going to hear something about Janet and me, and I'd just like to be sure you're in my corner."

I didn't know what he was talking about, and my expression gave that away.

"So word hasn't reached you yet?" he asked.

Bud Corliss was better known for his infidelities than for the legal reasoning in his opinions. His wife, Janet, had inherited a substantial sum of money from her father and added to it with a successful career as an interior designer sought after by Manhattan socialites and bicoastal movie stars.

"Which word would that be?"

Corliss had carried on a two-year affair with one of the women in my office that had prompted Battaglia to move her to the Appeals Division, to avoid the conflict of trying cases in front of her lover. The DA had used just about every favor owed to him to keep the entanglement off Page Six of the **New York Post.**

"Janet's unstable. I've tried to get help—"

"Look, Judge," I said, "this conversation is making me terrifically uncomfortable. I'd like you to take your hand off the door so I can quietly go on my way."

"A drink, then? One night this week?"

"That's not in the cards," I said, shaking my head. "Not happening. I don't know Janet well, but I'm not stepping in the middle of whatever you've got going on."

Bud Corliss removed his hand from the door. "This stays between us, Alex, because I might need your help, your advice."

"I'm listening."

"Janet told her best friend something," Corliss said. "She was desperate, I guess, and you know what these times are like."

"Her best friend writes speeches for the senator, doesn't she?" I asked.

"Yes, and that's the friend who's encouraging her to go public."

"What—with the fact that you've been unfaithful again?" I said. "I'd hardly call it breaking news."

Bud Corliss had both hands on his hips. I could see the gold cuff links and Patek Philippe watch that Janet had given to him, catching the sunlight that beamed through the dirty window of the robing room.

"That's all in her imagination, Alex," he said. "Janet has cried 'wolf' so many times that even her friends don't believe her."

I turned the knob and tugged on the heavy oak

door. "When you're ready for my help—and to tell me the truth—give me a call."

"I'll make it quick, then," Corliss said, his jaw tightening as he spoke the words. "Janet's claiming I hit her."

I spun around to face him, with barely a foot separating us.

"You hit your wife, Judge? And you're coming to **me** for help?"

"You know the reasons women claim this kind of thing," he said. "You know how people exaggerate when a marriage seems headed for the rocks."

"Did you hit her?" I asked, pushing against the door with my shoulder and backing into the dark, narrow hallway that led to the public corridor. "Because that's really all I need to know. And if the answer is yes, Bud, then you'd better get yourself a lawyer and not a prosecutorial stooge to try to hide behind."

"You're talking to me like I'm a common criminal, Alex," the judge said, holding his arms out to his sides in apparent disbelief. "Harvard College, graduate degree from Oxford, Columbia Law School—law review, in fact. I left a partnership at Dewey to come on the bench. I'm not some street thug you can threaten with a prosecution."

"Wife beaters come in every shape and size, Judge," I said. "Too bad you live in Bronx County, because it's out of my jurisdiction. Is that where you threw the punch?"

"I didn't punch—"

But I wasn't in the mood for mealymouthed excuses, so I cut off Corliss at his first hint of a denial. "After three months away, there'd be nothing like a domestic violence case to whet my appetite for a guilty verdict."

TWO

I opened the door to my office and smiled at the unexpected sight of Mike Chapman sitting in my chair with his feet propped up on my desk.

"What a nice surprise," I said. "If you're here to check on me, Detective, you might be pleased to know that I'm back in the saddle again and loaded for bear. Felony bear."

I started toward the desk to circle round and plant a kiss on top of Mike's head of long, dark hair, but he put up his hand to stop me. There was a time when we had to keep our personal relationship under wraps in order to continue working cases together, but since my kidnapping earlier in the year, there were no more secrets from any of our colleagues.

"You've got a visitor, Coop," Mike said. "Save the Romeo-Juliet bit for after hours."

I turned my head and saw a young woman sitting on the corner of the couch closest to the office door. Her face was expressionless, without the trace of a smile nor the tears or tension of distress.

"Hello," I said. "I'm Alexandra Cooper."

She nodded her head, avoiding eye contact with me. She probably knew, from Mike, who I was.

"This is Lucy Jenner, Coop."

Mike was staring at her, as though waiting for her to react to something.

"Hi, Lucy," I said. "Good to meet you."

It was never good for anyone to meet me in my professional capacity as a Special Victims prosecutor. Something bad had happened to put each visitor within my orbit.

Lucy was silent.

"Maybe we ought to make Lucy comfortable in the waiting area," I said to Mike. "My paralegal can get her a soda and something to eat while you fill me in."

"I wouldn't recommend that," Mike said. "My peeps tell me Lucy makes Usain Bolt look like he's dragging his feet on the way to the finish line. She's lightning fast."

"I've got nowhere to hide any longer," Lucy said. "I've stopped running."

There was no point in my pushing buttons yet.

"You two are way out ahead of me on this," I said. "Want to let me know why you're here?"

I had run the Special Victims Bureau for more than a decade, handling and overseeing sexual assault cases, domestic violence matters, child abuse, and murders related to those crimes. Mike Chapman was a first grade detective assigned to Manhattan

North's elite Homicide Squad. Sometimes our work overlapped, but this meeting was completely unanticipated.

"I told you about Ms. Cooper," Mike said to Lucy, removing his feet from my blotter and offering me my chair.

I shook my head. If I sat on this side of my desk, I'd be closer to my visitor—with no official-looking piece of government furniture to separate us.

Lucy Jenner tried to size me up by staring at me, as if that would give her an indication of whether what Mike had told her fit with my physical appearance, for whatever that was worth.

I turned the wooden chair that normally faced my desk in Lucy's direction and sat down on it. "I guess whatever Detective Chapman said to you about me or my job didn't put you at ease coming here. Maybe I can help with that."

"Whatever."

"I'm a prosecutor, Lucy. I handle cases that are—"

"I know what you do."

"Then would you mind if I ask you some questions?"

She shrugged her shoulders. "Everybody else does. Go ahead. Maybe I'll answer yours."

Not even a full day after returning to work and already my professional life was settling back into a familiar rhythm.

I turned to Mike. "What's the endgame here?"

People didn't go to their doctors, leave out the

most important symptoms, and see whether the guy was smart enough to guess the illness just by having the patient in the room. Why did so many witnesses come into my office and refuse to open up to me, expecting me to play "What's the Crime?" with them?

"You're going to tell us," Mike said. "That's why we're here."

"Have you two been working on something together?" I asked.

"For about two hours," Mike said. "Brooklyn South Homicide called me this morning. The lieutenant asked me to go over there to meet Lucy. Bring her to you. Let you figure out what to do."

I turned to square off with Lucy. "That's a start."

"He said he'd call and bring you up to speed," Mike said. "I'm just doing the delivery."

"Laura wasn't at her desk when I came down from court," I said, referring to my secretary. "I have no idea if there are messages."

"And the Brooklyn squad was in a frenzy about a headless body of a runner found in Prospect Park, so maybe the Loo just got hung up."

"Good excuse," I said. "I assume you have some role in a murder investigation, Lucy, if that's what took you to the Brooklyn South Homicide Squad. Why don't we start by talking about that?"

"Yes, I was a witness," she said. "That was ten years ago, when I was fourteen."

Lucy Jenner. Twenty-four years old. I was actually getting facts to work with.

"But the killer was only caught recently? I mean, just now?"

"No, ma'am. He was arrested back then."

I looked around at Mike. "Did you ever consider fast-forwarding so I have some idea of what I'm dealing with?"

"Lucy wouldn't say anything at all to the detectives in Brooklyn," he said. "And I hit a brick wall, too, trying to get started for you. She insisted on talking to a woman."

"I can honor that request," I said. "But when you walked into the police station this morning, you wouldn't even tell anyone why you were there?"

"That's not true," Lucy said. "That's not what happened. I got arrested last night. That's how come I wound up with the cops. I didn't walk into the station. I didn't want anything to do with the police."

I softened my tone. "Why were you arrested?"

Lucy didn't answer.

"Would you rather speak to me without Detective Chapman in the room?"

"He's been nice to me so far," she said. "He can stay."

"He's been nice to me, too," I said, smiling at her. "For a very long time."

Lucy's expression didn't change.

So I asked again. "Why did the police arrest you?"

"Because I stole things. Clean clothes to wear and food and stuff."

"Yesterday? You were caught stealing things yesterday?"

"No," she said, shaking her head. "Five years ago. Last time I was in New York."

"When you were eighteen?" I said sympathetically, thinking how sad it was that she had to steal just to get basic necessities, especially at such a young age. "That's crazy."

She looked up at me and cocked her head, as though she was trying to tell if I meant what I had said, or if I was going to inflict more damage on her.

"Lucy was driving her father's car last night," Mike said. "Taillight was busted, so uniformed pulled her over. They did a name check and the old warrant—a Manhattan warrant—dropped from five years back."

"And they brought her in instead of giving her an appearance ticket?" I asked.

"Cuffs, fingerprints, mug shot—the whole nine yards. The original charge was a felony."

"Grand larceny," I said, smiling at her. "So you stole a **lot** of clothes and a good bit of food."

"I didn't know a soul in the city, ma'am. Except the man—the man who hurt me—and he wouldn't give me anything."

"Do you mind if I go back and write down some information about you?" I asked. "Get some details to put this all in perspective?"

I wanted to get to the part about the man who hurt her.

"Are you keeping me locked up?" Lucy said.

"I think the detectives suggested you come to my office so I could get the Manhattan arrest warrant cleared, then get you out and on your way. They had no jurisdiction to do that in Brooklyn."

"Then ask me what you want."

I went to my desk and got a clean notepad from the top of the pile. Mike handed me a pen.

"Lucy Jenner," I said, sitting down again. "Twenty-four years old. What's your address in Brooklyn?"

"I don't have an address."

"Well, then. Your father's home."

"He's dead," she said, looking down at a spot on the floor. "My father died last spring."

"I'm so sorry."

"You couldn't know unless I told you," she said. "I hardly knew him. I only came back a few days ago, when my half brother told me I could have the car and some money he left me."

"Were you raised by your mother?"

"When she was alive," Lucy said. "Till before the murder case, when she got real sick. Before the murders happened and before the trial. Then I went off to live with her sister."

"Where? Where were you born?"

"Chicago."

"Would you tell us something about your family?"

She leaned her head back on the couch. "Like what?"

I needed to connect the young woman sitting in front of me—eyewitness to murders, teenage thief, and now orphaned adult who seemed rootless and ill at ease—to a background that would give context to what brought her into my office.

"A bit about your parents—who they were and what they did—and who you can be with now."

"Be with?"

"I want the judge to dismiss this warrant from six years ago, okay? I want to do that as soon as possible, and in order for that to happen, I have to be able to answer questions the judge will have, so he knows that your life has changed from that time."

"It's changed all right," Lucy said. "And it'll get worse before it ever gets better."

"Mike and I can try to fix that," I said. "Can you tell me about your mother?"

I was hoping some memory would emerge to bring a smile to her face.

"She was a teacher," Lucy said. "She taught math in an elementary school in our neighborhood. But she was sick for as long as I can remember. So sick that she had to quit working by the time I was eight or nine."

"That's hard."

"She was white. I know you didn't ask me that, but people say I look a lot like my mother, except for being just a little bit darker."

Lucy's skin was a very pale shade of brown—tawny and warm. She had a beautiful face—almost heart-shaped—with fine bones, framed by jet-black hair that hung to her shoulders.

"Did your father live with you?"

She sat up straighter now. "He never married my mother, and he left by the time I was three years old. He moved home to Brooklyn, and back in with the wife he'd been separated from when he started dating my mother."

I let her keep talking.

"My half brother is four years older than I am. Our dad and his mother were from Barbados."

I was hoping that Lucy could give the judge her brother's name as next of kin. That would add an element of stability to my application to dismiss the warrant. "Are you staying with your brother while you're here? Is that an address we can use?"

"Not advisable, Ms. Cooper," Mike said. "Rodney Jenner lives in a real flophouse, according to the cops who brought Lucy in."

"My brother doesn't want me there anyway," she said. "Not with his girlfriend and his two babies."

"Where, then? Where have you been living?"

She squinted, like she was trying to think of an answer.

"Try the back seat of a twelve-year-old Toyota with a burnt-out taillight," Mike said. "Casa Toyota. Short on closet space, but then so are most apartments in this city."

Lucy didn't seem the least bit upset by that description.

"That won't work," I said. "We can do better for you, I'm sure. Do you plan to go back to Chicago soon?"

Her shoulders hunched up—her expression still blank—as though a shrug answered everything.

"**Can** you go back, Lucy?" I knew that was a different question than **would** she.

"Yeah. My aunt Hannah has room for me. Hannah Dart. She lives in Winnetka—one of those fancy Chicago suburbs. It's my cousins who don't have much use for me."

"It would help if you give me all her contact information," I said. "We can use your aunt's name in court as long as I can call her first to get her to agree."

I moved my chair a few inches closer to Lucy, our knees almost touching.

"Would you tell us about the murders you witnessed?" I asked. "Mike's better at handling homicides than any ten detectives I've ever met."

"The murders aren't the problem," Lucy said. "They were solved. That bastard's still in jail."

"The cops took Lucy from the precinct," Mike said, "up to the Homicide Squad because when they ran her name check in the system, it came up on the old Homicide investigation—the one she was a witness in."

"But those murders must have something to do with whatever your issues are, Lucy," I said. "Won't you please take us that far?"

"Lucy wouldn't give the lieutenant the time of day," Mike said. "He told me that she saw some old photograph hanging on the wall in the station house and kind of freaked out."

"That's not a crime, is it?" she said, slumping down and crossing her arms. "Freaking out?"

"A photograph of what?" I asked. "A mug shot? The perp who committed the murders?"

Lucy almost managed a laugh. "Not a mug shot, Ms. Cooper. Not even close."

I needed to find a way in, to penetrate her icy veneer. "Will you talk to me about the man who hurt you? Tell me what he did?"

"There's no point in that, ma'am. No one ever believed me when I spoke up."

"Try one more time, please," I said. "It's my job to believe people who've been hurt."

"Then how come you've been away from your job for three months?" she asked. "Did you stop believing?"

"Sorry, Coop," Mike said. "I'm the one who told Lucy that you're just back to work."

I didn't take my eyes off her face as I steadied myself to speak to her. I didn't often reveal my personal story to witnesses in my office. "Because I got hurt, too. I know what it is to be scared to death, to have someone treat me so badly I didn't know how I'd ever recover from it."

Lucy met my stare head-on. "I bet you got believed, didn't you?"

She nailed me on that one.

"Yes. Yes, I did," I said. "And that helped me a lot."

She smirked at me, and I ignored it.

"Why don't you tell me what you witnessed all those years ago?" I said. "Can't we start with that?"

"I'm sick of telling that story."

"Well, Mike and I have never heard it."

She kicked her left foot back and forth, as regularly as a pendulum, while she considered answering me.

"Did the case involve anyone in your family?"

"No, ma'am. Nothing like that."

"Was it here, in Brooklyn?" I asked, thinking about the photograph on the wall in the station house that had spooked her.

She shook her head.

"Chicago, then?"

"Nope. First time I ran away from my aunt's house," Lucy said. "Iowa City."

"Whoa. That's hours from Chicago," I said. "And you were only fourteen years old. How did you get there?"

"I took a bus. Three hours is all."

"Alone? Did you run away alone?"

"No way. I was with my friend Austin."

"Your boyfriend?" I asked.

"That's not what I said, was it?" Lucy asked. "He was just a good friend, from my old 'hood. He was sixteen, so I trusted what he told me. We took the bus to go meet up with his cousin Buster, who lived in Iowa City."

"How did that go?"

"It was fine at first. Buster's mother was happy to see Austin, and she liked me because I helped with the dishes and the laundry."

"I'm glad she liked you," I said. "But your aunt must have been upset."

"She upsets easy. Always will," Lucy said. "Everything was okay—Buster's mother kept my aunt in touch and all that. It was summertime, so she couldn't fuss about me missing school, and the three of us used to hang out in the park. Hickory Hill Park. We didn't do anything wild. Just listened to music and met up with friends of Buster's."

"So it's not either one of them—Austin or Buster—who hurt you?"

Lucy shook her head from side to side. "They were my friends."

Her luminous hazel eyes looked as though they were filling with tears.

"What happened, Lucy? Can you tell us that?"

She bit her lip, showing emotion for the first time since we had started talking.

"They're both dead because of me," she said.

I reached out to put a hand on the knee of her jeans.

"That can't be the reason."

"It is," Lucy said, jerking her leg to the side and raising her voice. "It's because of me they were murdered."

"What did you do, Lucy?"

"I look white, Ms. Cooper. That's what I did," she said. "There was this madman—really a madman—who was going around the country with his AK-47. He was shooting at people, killing people he didn't even know."

"Austin and Buster?" I asked. "This guy shot them?"

Lucy nodded as tears rolled slowly from her eyes to the tip of her chin.

"He shot them because what he saw was two black guys hanging out with a white girl," Lucy said, talking so fast now she had to pause to catch her breath. "In Hickory Hill Park, on a ball field, at six o'clock at night, without so much as saying a word to us."

"A sniper, right?"

"Yes," Lucy murmured.

"Killing black men in a public park," I said.

"I told you that."

A madman going around the country, she had also said. "And the same guy killed a man in Salt Lake City for the same reason, didn't he? For jogging with a white woman."

She nodded.

"In Liberty Park, right?"

"Yeah," Lucy said.

"And an interracial couple playing tennis in Grant Park in Portland, Oregon," I said, pulling from memory the facts of a landmark federal case, tried by two prosecutors using a novel legal theory.

"You know Lucy's case?" Mike asked.

I held out my left arm in his direction to silence him. I had her talking now and I didn't want her to stop.

But Mike's comment triggered Lucy to realize I remembered her trial. "You know about it?"

"I know of it," I said, trying to keep her calm. "From casebooks and newspapers. The same guy even tried to kill a man in a park in Manhattan. Fort Tryon, up near the Cloisters museum."

Mike nodded.

"Every prosecutor in the country learned about it," I said. "It's historic."

Lucy wiped the tears off her right cheek with her fingers and stretched back her head so that she could look up at the ceiling, avoiding eye contact with me.

"The sniper was a murderous white supremacist,

Lucy," I said. "It's not because of you that Austin and Buster were killed."

"I was sitting on the bench, so close to Austin that pieces of metal shattered and flew into my neck—from the bullets," she said, rubbing the left side of her neck.

Shrapnel, I thought to myself. I remembered that from the media coverage, too. The teenage girl who was almost another casualty of the big-oted killer.

"So he's the man who hurt you," I said, jamming the pieces of the puzzle together faster than I should have done.

"I told you no. I already said it wasn't him."

"Sorry. I just assumed—"

"I don't even remember the pain from the shooting," she said. "Nothing can bring back Austin and Buster, but at least that racist asshole will never see the light of day again."

I was sitting bolt upright now, focused on Lucy but trying to figure out what we could do for her as the past seemed to be conflating with her present state of rootlessness.

"Look, Lucy," I said, "we can't make any of that go away, but we can certainly try to improve your situation. Dismiss your warrant, find you housing, get you counseling. We can do all of that."

"I want **him** to leave the room," Lucy said, pointing at Mike as her manner changed completely.

Her entire mood had shifted and her anger seemed suddenly palpable.

Mike laughed and ran his fingers through his thick hair. "An hour ago I was your best friend, kid. Now you're booting me out of here?"

Lucy was stone-faced.

"Why don't you check with Laura?" I asked him. "See if there are any messages I need to know about. And go to Helen Wyler's office and get her cell phone out of her top desk drawer. Call TARU and tell them I need an overnight download of every text she's had from her complaining witness in the last three weeks."

"Two to zip in favor of my exit, and you're giving me grunt work to do as well," Mike said, pushing back from my desk and walking to the door. "See you later."

I waited until the door closed tightly behind him.

"Is this better for you, Lucy?" I asked.

"Maybe," she said. "I don't know yet."

"Is there something you want to tell me?" I said. "Just me?"

"What are you going to do with the information, if I give it to you?"

"I can't give you an honest answer yet. That's just because I don't have a clue what you have to say."

"I told people before," Lucy said. "I told them five years ago, the first time I came to New York, but nobody did anything about it. Now it's probably too late."

"Try me, Lucy," I said. "The lieutenant who met you in Brooklyn earlier today obviously thought it was something I might be able to help you with. Why not try me?"

She looked toward the closed door, and I was afraid she was going to get up and walk out.

"I'm sick of reading these stories in the papers every day, all these women talking about shit that happened to them twenty years ago," Lucy said. "Nobody even doubts them the way people turned their backs on me."

This conversation was picking up intensity as Lucy got to the reveal. It wasn't about the post-traumatic stress of witnessing the murders of her friends or about cleaning up the warrant that had been held over her head for five years. Somewhere in this nightmare of a life story, there was a sexual assault that hadn't been credited when Lucy tried to report it.

"Well, it's my turn now," she said, stabbing the center of her chest with her forefinger, over and over again. "Me, too, Ms. Cooper. Me, too."

THREE

"How far did you get with Lucy after I left the room?" Mike asked.

"She shut me down pretty quick," I said. "I think she's testing me, to see if I'm really going to do the right thing."

"How so?"

"She said she was hungry and tired and felt dirty and had nothing more to say to me until I kept my word."

"Your word? Lucy's challenging that?" Mike said.

"She wants her old case dismissed, and I said I could do that."

"Where is she now?"

"Maxine is glued to her," I said.

My paralegal had worked with me for three years since graduating from college. She was as good as any prosecutor at evaluating cases and she had a heart of gold that made her a favorite of the survivors who passed through our offices.

"I set them up in the conference room with strict orders to Max not to let Lucy out of her sight. Laura ordered in sandwiches and drinks, then walked over to Broadway to buy some clean underwear and a couple of outfits at the Odd Lots discount store."

"What's next for Lucy?"

"A hot shower in the executive ladies' room, a change of clothes, and a nap."

"Then you'll have another go at her," Mike said.

"Over and over, till I get the story," I said. "How'd you do with Helen's phone?"

"The tech guys are on it. No big deal. They'll pull up those texts later today and have the phone back to her before midnight."

"Good. I'll let Helen know," I said. "Meanwhile, get on the phone to Brooklyn South Homicide and have someone take close-ups of all the photographs on the wall that Lucy might have seen. Email them to me and let's see if she can pinpoint the one that set her off."

"You think—?"

"I think maybe the reason she turned on you is that once she decided to tell me about the man who assaulted her—instead of telling any of the detectives at the squad—chances are it's because she saw a photo of someone she recognized. Maybe one of the cops on the case," I said. "It's not very hard to connect those dots. Likely the guy she freaked out about had a badge and you've got a badge. Could be as simple as that."

"A cop?" Mike said, glaring at me with his fists balled up against his waist. "Where are you going with this now, Coop? You're saying some cop raped a fourteen-year-old kid, just because she's going all weepy on you? You **do** believe that's why she wanted me out of your office, don't you?"

"Something set her off in the station house, didn't it? An old photograph, probably cops from that command."

"Yeah," Mike said. "I'll tell you why she got set off. The reality that a warrant was dropping that would keep her in the slammer for a few days. Have you checked her story with the aunt yet? And what do you really know about that case she testified in? Why would the NYPD have been involved?"

"The killer's name in Lucy's case is Weldon Baynes. Welly, he called himself, if you want to see what I 'really' know about it," I said, crossing my arms and sitting on the edge of the desk. "He was from Athens, Georgia, before he set out on his odyssey to kill black men, including her companions, Austin and Buster."

"Where did his overload of hate come from?" Mike asked.

"You've known enough bigots. Baynes was probably taught to hate his entire life, I'd guess. I don't know what the psychobabble was about his history, or I just don't remember that. All that's certain, I think, is that he wanted to start a race war—ignite some local fires and hope they'd spread across the country."

"But always targeting black men with white women?"

"Always. The couple in Fort Tryon Park had just left the Cloisters museum. They wcre both graduate students in art history at Columbia, not lovers," I said. "You know how deserted it can be up there on the Heights."

Mike and I had handled a murder case that involved the Cloisters early in our professional partnership. The museum housed a spectacular collection of medieval art that had been gifted to the city, along with the parkland of Fort Tryon, by John D. Rockefeller, Jr.

"That pair just got lucky?" Mike said. "I wasn't working Homicide then. Maybe that's why I'm not calling it up."

"Those two got very lucky, and that's an understatement. The sniper took several shots but missed the young man completely and got away clean. He was only linked to the other murders by the bullets, which the FBI compared because of the location—a public park, again—of the attempted murder."

"So NYPD cops were assigned."

"From our Hate Crime Task Force, with some experienced Homicide cops thrown in by each of the cities, including us, who partnered with FBI agents. Call Lieutenant Peterson—he'll tell you who was on the national team from our force," I said. "Get some names and we'll try to match them to the photos from the Brooklyn squad room."

"You think I'm snitching on some detective who's probably retired to the Outer Banks by now, enjoying his pension and sucking on his second margarita this very minute, when we don't even know what this kid's story is? When she's calling the shots and you're eager enough to fall for that," Mike said, running his fingers through his dark hair, rather than pounding his fists on my desk. "Get yourself another rat, Ms. Cooper. Get yourself some misfits from Internal Affairs."

I walked to my chair and picked up the phone. "I'll run down Lucy's story," I said. "I promise you that. Right now, though, she has the benefit of the doubt."

"Of course we give her the benefit of the doubt, once she opens up and tells her story," Mike said, headed for the door. "But you know I'm not going to start attacking men—cops, no less—who haven't been accused of anything."

"It's my job to get that story, and I have to use whatever tools are available to do so," I said. "Lucy reacted to something she saw in a photograph? Then I need to see that photo, too."

Mike's hand was on the knob, his back turned to me.

"And you, Detective Chapman, are a mandated reporter of child abuse under the Family Court Act of the State of New York," I said. "Walk out my door and you'll be in very hot water."

"The only two temperatures you know, Coop.

Very hot and boiling," Mike said, facing me again. "That's why you'll never be district attorney. You've got no thermostatic control for your attitude adjustment."

"I'll never be DA. because it's a job I don't want. Going around to all those party clubhouses and making deals or promises that an honest prosecutor shouldn't make. Rubber chicken dinners and christenings and bar mitzvahs for the kids of high-rolling donors every weekend? I couldn't stand a life like that," I said. "That's why I'll never be DA."

I held up my forefinger to my lips. I had dialed information in Illinois to find a number for Lucy's aunt.

"Don't try to shush me up by lifting your finger," he said. "That's rude."

"You're really steaming, aren't you?" I said, waiting for the directory assistance robot to connect me.

"Nothing like a rush to judgment, is there?"

"Hey, it's you who brought Lucy Jenner over here to me. So that I could help her, the way I remember it."

The ringing was interrupted by an outgoing message on an answering machine, asking me to leave the reason for my call. "Hello? Hello. My name is Alexandra Cooper, and I'm trying to reach Hannah Dart. I'm an assistant district attorney in New York City. There's nothing wrong—nothing at all—but we're just trying to help find residential placement for your niece, Lucy Jenner."

Mike had turned his back to me and was shaking his head.

I paused. "Lucy gave me your name as next of kin, and if you could get back to me as soon as possible, and let us know that she is welcome to stay with you for a while, it would allow us to—to—well, to get her on her way."

I ended the call with a thank-you and left both my office number and my cell.

"What if the aunt says no?" Mike asked.

"Then I get to plead with whoever the judge is about tossing the warrant and letting her out anyway. I think the circumstances of her original victimization will trump some nonsensical petty thefts," I said. "Are you making that call to Brooklyn for me?"

"You get the facts first."

"You've suddenly got a dog in this fight, Detective Chapman?" I asked, pushing back from my desk. "You have a thing for this white supremacist?" I asked. "Welly's your man?"

"Don't be a jerk, Coop. I brought Lucy here to you because I agreed with the lieutenant that you might be able to help her. You're the one who's dreaming up some story about a cop—or maybe some cop—when you haven't done anything to verify where Lucy is going with this story."

"I know that she's alone in this world, so far as I can tell, and she was trustworthy enough for the feds to make a case stand up with her help when she was just a kid."

"Let me go down the hall and get her," he said. "If she makes sense, I'll do whatever is right."

"Let her sleep for now," I said, throwing my hands up in the air. "Truce, Detective. I'll give the aunt two hours to return the call. It'll take that long for the Trial Division assistant to draw up the papers on the warrant. The aunt sounds responsible enough, according to Lucy, to give me some background and perspective."

"See you in two, then," Mike said, checking his watch before he opened the door.

"Where are you going?"

"My job is to catch murderers, Coop, or don't you remember that?"

FOUR

"Where are you?" I asked, just after the door slammed. I had dialed the cell phone of Mercer Wallace, an SVU detective who was Mike's best friend as well as one of mine. "I mean right this minute?"

"In Catherine's office, just across the street. Prepping for next week's trial."

"How fast can you get over to me?"

"Hang up and you'll see."

I opened my desk drawer and took out the NYPD's phone directory. It listed every precinct and specialty squad, as well as the names of the commanding officers.

I dialed Brooklyn South Homicide and waited for the number to ring ten times, before the call was picked up by the desk officer in the local precinct two flights downstairs.

"This is Alexandra Cooper, Manhattan DA— Sex Crimes Unit," I said. "No one's answering in Lieutenant Creavey's office. Have you got a uniformed officer you can send upstairs to get a message to the sergeant or any of the guys? There's some urgency to it."

"No, ma'am. I'm afraid the best you can do is leave word with me."

"But—"

"We had a male jogger down in Prospect Park this morning. No head. I'm talking really down, Ms. Cooter."

"Cooper."

"The entire squad is out on the case—looking for suspects as well as for the head," he said, chuckling in the way that only old hairbags do who've been on the job for so long that they've lost the ability to filter their black humor from their conversations with civilians. "Most of my uniforms are crawling around the park, too. Good day to rob a bank."

"I'll keep that in mind. Thanks anyway," I said, hanging up the phone.

Laura had returned from her shopping trip with a sandwich for me, which I nibbled at while I waited for Mercer.

I walked to her desk in the anteroom outside my door. "What's up with Lucy and Max?"

"I've never seen anyone so happy to have showered and put on clean clothes," Laura said. "Lucy told me she was up most of the night. So she was devouring her turkey sandwich between yawns, and anxious to put her head down for a while."

"Could you find someone to give Max a break

every now and then? Line up a few of the other paralegals."

"Not a problem," Laura said. "What time are you expecting to go to court on Lucy's warrant?"

"Whenever the clerk calls and tells me our papers have been docketed. I doubt it will be before six or seven this evening," I said. "I'm expecting Lucy's aunt to return my call, and TARU to get back to me once they have all the texts off Helen's phone."

"Got it," Laura said. "Have you thought about assigning someone else to do Lucy's arraignment?"

"I'm going to handle it. Of course, I need someone to represent the other side, since Lucy was technically brought in as a defendant. So I'm about to call the Legal Aid supervisor to ask her to stand up on the case to represent Lucy when I offer to drop charges," I said. "The time it would take me to explain the reason we're moving to dismiss to anyone else, well—it's just easier for me to do all the talking."

"I understand," Laura said.

"Why did you ask? Did Mike tell you to back me off away from Lucy Jenner's arraignment?"

Laura Wilkie liked to think of herself as Miss Moneypenny to Mike's James Bond. They flirted with each other constantly and I think she secretly harbored a wish to take on some dangerous foreign mission with him. This afternoon I was in the mood to send them off together to someplace far away from me.

"Not a word from Mike. Cross my heart," Laura said with a smile. "It would just be a favor to me."

"A favor? You don't want me to spend twenty minutes at an arraignment?" I said, patting her on the back as I stepped away. "Stop mothering me."

"Well, this could go into night court, and I just don't think you need that your first day back."

"Get a grip, Laura. I'm here and I'm firing on all cylinders."

I heard footsteps and smiled at Mercer as he stepped into the doorway. "Who are you firing at? Anybody I know?"

"That could happen," I said. "Was Catherine through with you?"

"I'm as prepped as I can be."

"Great," I said. "I'd like to pull you into a new matter. Come on in."

I called out to Laura as we breezed past her. "Velvet gloves with Lucy when she wakes up. Get her whatever she needs or wants and tell her I hope to have it all wrapped up for her by evening."

"Fine by me."

I didn't have to say any more to Mercer than the name Welly Baynes. Mercer had grown up in Queens, where his father had worked as an airline mechanic for Delta. He was one of the first African American detectives to make first grade, and had married a colleague named Vickee Eaton, who had risen through the ranks to a high-profile position in the department's office of public information.

"Welly Baynes," he said. "That man is evil incarnate. I thought he just liked to kill. I never heard any rape allegations."

"No. Not that. For all the hate he dumped into this world, he didn't do any of that, I don't think."

I explained how Lucy had come to be in my office earlier in the day, and what I had been told about her reaction to a photograph in the Brooklyn squad room.

"Mike can't get you what you need?" Mercer asked.

"He wants me to get the facts straight, get the allegations from Lucy before I start trolling old photos for a rogue cop," I said. "He didn't want to rile up Lieutenant Creavey unless we have a viable witness, but Lucy is reluctant to tell me the story before I keep my promise to dump her warrant."

"Can't be hard to pull up who was on the Hate Crime Squad back then," Mercer said. "I can help do that."

"I want the photographs, or at least I want good copies of them, so I'm ready to get specific when I talk to Lucy later. I want all the investigative tools available to try to make her case."

Mercer picked up my landline phone and dialed the squad number. When a cop answered, Mercer identified himself and asked him to transfer the call upstairs.

"It's ringing," he said to me.

"Be prepared for the headless jogger excuse."

"Yeah, it's already on the news. Full-on machete job," Mercer said. "Very rough justice."

Someone picked up the phone on the other end.

"Mercer Wallace. Manhattan Special Victims. I'm looking for Creavey."

Whoever was in the Brooklyn office recognized Mercer and they exchanged greetings.

Mercer covered the mouthpiece with his hand and told me that Creavey was on his way from the park to a presser at city hall. "Tell Detective Walsh—Jerry—what you want."

He passed the phone and I asked if he could take snapshots of the photographs on the squad room wall. Maybe in Creavey's office, too.

"Which ones do you want? He's got the president of the United States and the police commissioner hanging over his desk."

"Not those," I said, curbing my annoyance. "Those team shots with cops and agents in them. You know the ones."

"Whoa," Walsh said. "You don't know Creavey very well, do you? He's got this whole feng shui thing going on. Moves his photos around whenever he gets bored looking at the same old shit. I wouldn't even take pictures of them without asking him."

"Why don't you call him on his cell and ask?" I said.

"Loo's kind of jammed up today," Walsh said.

"A phone call, Jerry," I said. "My whole case might turn on a photograph you've got there. I'm not going to move them. I'd just like you to take photos of them."

Mike was right. It wasn't going to take long for me to get from being very hot to a boiling temperature.

"Stay tuned," Walsh said. "I'm putting you on hold while I reach out to him."

Ninety seconds waiting for Walsh to get back to me seemed like an hour.

"Lieutenant Creavey said he had a message for you, Ms. Cooper."

"Really?" For a second I thought I was going to get what I wanted.

"Yeah. He said if it's about some photographs that young lady he sent over to you saw last night—"

"Those are the ones."

"Creavey said to get yourself a search warrant, Madame Prosecutor."

"What?" I responded, trying to keep my cool.

Of course Creavey had seen Lucy Jenner react to someone's picture on the wall of his squad room. Maybe that was part of his motive in shipping her over to me.

"And the lieutenant said you ought to start with some probable cause in order to do that, but then I'm preaching to the choir when I tell you that, aren't I?" Jerry Walsh said, with a sharp edge in the tone of his voice. "The first thing you need is evidence of commission of a crime. Get all that, and then come on back with your search warrant."

FIVE

"Catherine called. She's counting on you for dinner tonight," Laura said when I opened my door and stepped out of my office with Mercer. "At Forlini's. She said she asked you yesterday."

"I knew I was supposed to tell you something," Mercer said, snapping his fingers. "I'm in, too."

Forlini's Restaurant, behind the courthouse on Baxter Street, had been like an annex of the DA's office for more than fifty years. Judges, cops, and prosecutors ate many of their lunches and dinners in the joint, assistant district attorneys and their adversaries waited out jury verdicts at the bar, and all of us drowned our sorrows there when cases went the wrong way.

"Sure," I said, although my focus was on getting Lucy's story from her before she spun out of control or shut me down. "Has Mike phoned?"

"No."

"Is Lucy awake?"

"Not yet. Max is making calls to find the complaining witnesses who swore out the original complaint against Lucy, outside the room where she's napping," Laura said. "Not a peep."

"What are you thinking?" Mercer asked.

"That Mike's right. That I need to have this conversation with Lucy sooner rather than later," I said. "If Creavey thinks I'm investigating a cop, I'll have the whole department in an uproar against me, and for all I know, it's just a wild guess I made."

"Let me see what I can pull up on the Internet about Welly's case—see if the investigators' photos come up, and print them out for you."

"Print out the Feebies, too," I said. "You can use Max's desk. Nothing would make Mike happier than if the bad guy was a fed and not a cop."

Laura gave me the rest of the messages. I put them to the side and looked up the number again for Hannah Dart. This time when I dialed, she answered.

"This is Hannah."

"Ms. Dart? It's Alex Cooper again. From New York," I said. "About Lucy."

"Is she all right?"

"She's fine. She's sleeping now, but she's fine."

"Sleeping? It's the middle of the day," Ms. Dart said. "Is Lucy in trouble?"

"No, she's not in trouble. Why do you ask that?"

"Well, you're calling from a prosecutor's office, aren't you?"

"Yes, but that's because I'm trying to help Lucy."

"Help her? How?"

"Ms. Dart, I'm thirty-eight years old, and I was just a year out of law school when Weldon Baynes shot Lucy's friends," I said. "But I remember the shock and horror of those crimes."

My statement was met by silence, before an icy response.

"If Lucy hadn't run away from home—**my** home—those kids would still be alive and her head might have stayed on straight."

Hannah Dart might have exactly what I needed to know about Lucy's head to get her story.

"That man was a stone-cold killer, Ms. Dart. Nothing that you or Lucy did could have altered his path."

"Can we make this quick, Ms. Cooper? If my daughter walks in the house and hears me talking about Lucy, she's likely to rip the phone out of my hand."

The cousins who didn't like Lucy Jenner. She was obviously right about that.

"It's your niece I'm calling about, Ms. Dart. If I'm not mistaken, you're her only blood relatives," I said. "You might want to care about how she is."

"She's got a father. Let him start to care."

"Lucy's father is dead. That's why she came to New York."

"Why? Then where has she been staying in the city?"

"Well, actually, I don't know the answer to that question," I said. "I thought perhaps you could fill in some of the blanks."

"Why is she in your office?" Dart asked. "There can't be a good answer to that."

I sighed and gave a short explanation. "Five years ago, when Lucy was in New York for a brief period, she may have stolen some food and necessities. I'm trying to clear that warrant—which seems mighty unimportant compared to her role in the murder case."

Hannah Dart's voice seemed to soften. "Everything pales in comparison to what Lucy experienced, and to the death of those boys."

"Then you'll help me?"

"What happens if I do?" Ms. Dart asked. "What happens if the judge agrees to let Lucy go?"

"Well, I was hoping you might be willing to take her in for a while," I said. "Let her live with you."

"Lucy's not a minor, Ms. Cooper. She can make her own way," Dart said. Whatever had briefly melted the ice was gone. Her voice was again as cold as the words she uttered. "That would be good for her."

I stifled my anger. "When was the last time you saw your niece?"

"Five years ago, Ms. Cooper. Right before she took off for New York."

"You can remember that so precisely because—?"

"Because it was my birthday. June twenty-second," Dart said. "Easy to remember because she spoiled the entire evening for my family. Something about wanting to go to New York to see one of the people who had handled her case—"

I took a deep breath. That part fit with the bits that Lucy had told us.

"—and when I disapproved of that, she simply left the house in the middle of the night."

"There might have been a good reason for her to want to make that trip," I said. According to the little that Lucy had revealed to me, she had a score to try to settle.

"Well, if there was," Dart said, "Lucy didn't think it necessary to tell me. She simply stole the money for the bus trip from my briefcase before she left."

"That wasn't smart."

"I could forgive that easier than the fact that she stole a ring I had given to my daughter for Christmas."

"A ring?"

"If you've got **my** Lucy Jenner with you, then you'll see the ring," Dart said. "It's a thin gold band, with the words 'LOVE, Mom and Dad' inscribed inside. She wears it on her pinky. Took it right off my daughter Callie's nightstand, in the bedroom they shared, when she left for New York."

I was racking my brain to think if I had noticed any jewelry on Lucy's hands.

"It's been five years, Ms. Dart. She may not have that ring anymore."

"Last time Lucy posted a picture of herself on Facebook a couple of months ago, it was still there on her finger. Makes my daughter crazy mad," Dart said. "I can bet everything I got that there are three things Lucy won't part with till she's dead."

A dark thought, but I wanted Hannah Dart to speak again.

"That little gold band, a handkerchief that her mother embroidered for her just before she died—which is the only thing of my sister's that Lucy was left with—and a two-dollar bill that her grandfather, my father, gave to her when she was ten," Dart said. Then she added, "For good luck. He always said the Jefferson two-bucks was for luck. That's why Lucy won't let go of it."

Grandpa Jenner might have been surprised to know that the rare bill had not proved all that lucky for its recipient.

"You're telling me that this girl has been through every kind of hell I can imagine, and she's still hanging on to things? To material things?" I asked.

"Those three things are her only connections to what once was a family—that each represent people who loved her very much," Dart said. "They're what gives me a spark of hope that there's some humanity left within her."

"But even so, you won't consider bringing her

in from the cold?" I said, borrowing a phrase from le Carré.

"Callie idolized Lucy," she said. "Lucy's three years older than my daughter, and was so bold and so strong that Callie thought everything Lucy did was worth looking up to. Till she stole that little gold ring and ran off."

She paused for a few seconds. "If she's ready to apologize to Callie, and if she still really has that ring to return, I'll give it some thought."

"Ms. Dart, you said that Lucy's head isn't on straight. Exactly what did you mean?"

"Why? You think it's right to steal from family?" she asked. "To lie and steal, then come back here, looking for mercy?"

I thought of the young woman's life and how every part of it had been fractured. A mother she seemed to adore who died way too young, a man who fathered her but played no role in her life, friends murdered in her presence for hanging out with her, and quite possibly a law enforcement official in whom she had put her trust at such a critical time in her life who might well have betrayed her.

"Stealing is one thing," I said. "Can you tell me what Lucy has lied about?"

"How long have you known my niece?"

"Today. I just met her today."

Hannah Dart laughed for the first time. "Well, that goes a long way to explaining things to me.

She can suck you in like a riptide going out to sea, if you let her."

It didn't sound like Lucy would be welcomed back to Winnetka any time soon.

"There's the front door opening now. My husband or one of my girls," Dart said. "I'm afraid I'll have to cut you off, Ms. Cooper."

"May I call you tomorrow?" I said, anxious not to lose the only connection to Lucy Jenner's past that I had.

"I'll get back to you when I can talk," Dart said. "But you watch yourself, Ms. Cooper. That girl is the most manipulative creature I've ever met."

It was my turn to be silent. My gut was churning.

"Lucy has the face of an angel," she said, "but she's got the soul of a viper, too. You can go to bat for her like you're telling me you are, but I'm warning you—you're doing so at your own risk."

SIX

"Would you please try to get Mike on the phone?" I said to Laura as I headed past her desk to find Max.

I pounded the hallway down to the executive lounge where Lucy was resting—my too-high heels for the kind of day it had become clicking on the floor like the steady beat of a metronome. Max was still at the desk outside the door, keeping herself busy with paperwork.

"Is Lucy wearing any jewelry?" I asked.

"Not that I recall," Max said. "I can open the door and look."

"Better still, did the Brooklyn cops voucher any of her property?"

"Yeah, it's here with the arrest report."

I grabbed the arraignment folder from the desktop and flipped through the paperwork.

There was a voucher listing the possessions taken from Lucy Jenner for safekeeping while she was in custody. I scanned the list. A driver's license, a MetroCard, a train ticket receipt from Washington,

DC, to Penn Station in Manhattan, dated a week earlier, one gold band with an inscription on the inside, one cotton handkerchief, and eighty-two dollars in cash. The breakdown of the denominations showed that one of them was a two-dollar bill.

"Any of the other paras loose this afternoon to do something for me?" I asked.

"I'll find you someone."

"Great," I said. "Laura can Xerox the voucher and I'll write a note requesting the release of this stuff from the property clerk at headquarters."

"You mean after Lucy's arraignment?" Max asked.

"I mean right now," I said. "I might need some of those items to coax her to open up."

"Okay," Max said. "And I've got good news for you. I've been trying to reach the complaining witness who owned the clothing store in Tribeca where Lucy did her shoplifting."

"And?"

"It went out of business seven months ago."

"Who signed the complaint?" I asked.

"The owner," Max said. "I'm running her down but it's a very common name."

"That accounts for more than seventeen hundred dollars' worth of the larceny, right?"

"Exactly."

"How did Lucy get it out of the store?" I asked.

"She wore it," Max said.

"Wait a minute. She **wore** a small fortune in clothes out of the boutique?"

"She went into the dressing room, took all her clothes off, and put on three layers of silk underwear. A thong and two pairs of panties, three bras, a camisole under a long-sleeved silk blouse—de la Renta, of course—and leather leggings," Max said. "Then she put on her own baggy jeans and sweater over the good stuff, and walked out with a stolen leather jacket tossed over her arm, carrying a Longchamp tote."

"Sensors set off alarms?" I said.

"Nope. Lucy carried one of those devices that removes the sensors," Max said. "They were all on the floor in the dressing room when the saleswoman went back in to clean up."

"Was that the call to 911?"

"Yes. But she didn't get very far. She was only half a block away, in a gourmet food shop, stuffing the tote bag full of pricey cheeses and fancy chocolates."

I leaned against the wall and tapped the back of my head against it. "It doesn't exactly sound like a street kid's survival kit, does it?"

"Nope," Max said. "Sounds to me like she was pregaming a sexy soiree by treating herself to some tempting new affair-wear."

"How about the food shop?"

"Still in business. The manager who swore out

the complaint affidavit is now the owner," Max said. "But Lucy never made it out of the shop."

I reached out and tapped her on the crown of her head. "Thanks, Max. Now I've got a plan after all. We can get this dismissed without even bringing up the sensational case at the hearing, and I shouldn't be the one who appears in front of the judge on the matter."

"Overkill, right? It'll call too much attention to Lucy if you show up on a grand larceny warrant."

I started back toward my office and Max followed. "I'll get someone to have the case tossed. Five years, no witness anymore on the underwear heist," I said with a smile, "and Lucy never actually stole the food because she didn't set foot out of the premises. No other criminal record, there's really nothing to hold her on."

"What's next?" Max's short legs were straining to keep up with my long paces.

"I'll get Kerry O'Donnell up here. I think Lucy will really like her," I said. "Wake her up in a few minutes, I'll make the intros. Then I can slide across to Forlini's, keep my date with Catherine for a quick bite, and once the case is dismissed, I'll spend the evening getting to the bottom of Lucy's story."

We had reached Laura's desk.

"What about a place for Lucy to stay tonight?" Max asked.

"Call Safe Horizon for me," I said. The organization was the best and biggest victim-advocacy nonprofit in the country and partnered with us regularly. "See if there are any open spots in their Streetwork program. Lucy qualifies on every level."

Safe Horizon ran domestic violence facilities that were far more sophisticated and safe than city shelters; child advocacy centers that co-located pediatricians, social workers, prosecutors, and detectives under one roof to ease the process of disclosing abuse for underage kids; and the Streetwork Project, designed to engage with homeless youth—up to the age of twenty-five—to offer stability and options, whether the cause of the homelessness was abuse or rejection or violence.

"Good idea," Max said. "It offers everything to get Lucy back on her feet while we work with her. Meals, showers, mental health services."

"Counselors instead of jailers, young women and men in like circumstances," I said. "And a strictly observed curfew."

"Would you please call Kerry O," I said to Laura, "and ask whether she can come up to my office?"

"Sure."

Mercer was sitting in the chair opposite my desk when I walked back in. "Did you get Aunt Hannah?" he asked as he spread out a stack of paper in front of himself like a deck of cards waiting to be cut.

"That's not exactly going to be the homecoming I was expecting," I said. "Lucy's got a tendency to snatch what doesn't belong to her—and also to lie."

"Ouch!" Mercer said. "Just when we were counting on some truth telling."

"What did you find?"

"Tons of online media about Welly's cases," Mercer said. "I printed out a copy for each of us. The first set is about Lucy's friends—the two victims."

He passed me some printouts from the **Des Moines Register** in the first week after the murders. Buster's and Austin's school photos told the story without words—heartbreaking images of Buster taken at the end of the school year just weeks earlier, and Austin pictured with a big smile with his regional-winning school softball team, in pinstripe uniforms.

"Here's Lucy," Mercer said, handing me more pages.

I looked at the close-up of her mournful face as she walked out of the police station from her first official interview, clinging onto the arm of Buster's mother. She had spent four days in the hospital for her injuries.

"Lots of stories about Lucy being a runaway and such," Mercer said. "I'll take them home tonight and read the whole thing. I haven't even downloaded the crimes in the other cities yet."

I flipped through the section about Lucy and came to a stop at an article dated eight months later. The federal prosecutors had been successful in their motion to consolidate all the cases, and the trial venue had been set in Salt Lake City.

On the front page of the **Deseret News**, before the start of the trial, was a photograph of four detectives standing on the courthouse steps. Mercer leaned in and tapped the picture, which bore the caption: NEW YORK'S FINEST IN SEARCH FOR JUSTICE.

I squinted at the small print to read the names.

"Do you know any of these guys?" I asked.

"Mostly old-timers," Mercer said. "A lot of years of investigative experience in that quartet. The two on the left are Hate Crime unit, one dead for five or six years now, the other one retired to Scottsdale."

"And these two?" I asked, pointing to the other pair.

"Major Case Squad at the time, not Homicide. The tall guy at the end is a lieutenant in the Robbery Squad now. That leaves Manny Cabela. He worked for months at the dig at the Twin Towers, on his own time, like so many other guys. Manny died two years ago of 9/11-related lung cancer."

I put my hand to my face and rubbed my eyes. The enormity of the World Trade Center tragedy would haunt all of us forever, and was still claiming lives to this day—most of them cops and firefighters.

"You've got to slow this train down, Alexandra," Mercer said. "I'm willing to believe there's something this girl wants to tell you, but people's lives—"

"I know that," I said. "I get it."

"There are reams of articles about these crimes and about the trial," Mercer said. "It was covered by every newspaper in the country. It will take you all week to catch up with them, and yeah, just maybe some little factoid in a feature story by a beat reporter will help you get to the bottom of this. But most important is that you sit down and talk to Lucy nice and calm tomorrow—"

"Tonight. I'm starting with her tonight."

"Suit yourself," Mercer said, shaking his head at me. "Nobody promised me that if you took a little time off these last few weeks, you'd be any less stubborn when you came back to work."

"Anything else in this stack I should be aware of?" I asked, getting to my feet.

"Two more photos, way near the bottom of the pile," he said, sorting through them for me. "This one was taken on the steps of city hall with the mayor greeting them, when the guys returned from Salt Lake after the trial."

It was the front page of the **New York Post**, headlined ALL'S WELL THAT ENDS WELLY—GUILTY VERDICTS PUT END TO GUNMAN'S RACE WAR.

"This is the kind of shot that could have been hanging in the station house," I said. "This is the sort of thing that could have set Lucy off."

"Sort of, could have, might have, maybe did," Mercer said. "I'll check out whether any of these guys even had a connection to that precinct or squad. If not, there are too many other news stories that would earn heroes a place on the wall."

"One more?"

Mercer pulled it out of the pile.

It was a photo taken after the trial, on the court-house steps in Salt Lake. The back row were detectives from every city represented in the prosecution case, standing together as the symbol of law enforcement victory. Below them—a much shorter line—were the survivors who had witnessed the killings. Lucy Jenner, the shortest and youngest of them, was on the end of the line. I picked up the page to give it a closer look, and saw that Manny Cabela's hand rested on Lucy's shoulder.

"Now, don't go reading tea leaves," Mercer said. "That touch is just a momentary act of compassion, okay?"

My door was open but Kerry O'Donnell knocked anyway. I smiled and waved her in.

"Did I hear someone say the word 'compassion' in Alex's office?" she asked. "Or has an impostor slipped in, in your place?"

"You've got me back."

"That's happy news. What do you need from me?"

I gave her the shortest take on Lucy's case—not the history of the Weldon Baynes murders, but the possibility that she was going to disclose a past sexual assault to me, once the warrant was cleared. No drama. No need for me to show up in court.

"Let me introduce you to Lucy—she's with Max—and Max will give you all the facts you need for the judge. Short and sweet."

"I don't know about the sweet part," Kerry said, "but I'll call you when it's done."

"I'll be right here. I'm having dinner with Catherine and Mercer across the street," I said. "Don't tell Lucy, but truth or consequences begins this evening."

We walked down the hall together. Max and Lucy were chatting with each other. Lucy looked better rested, and comfortably dressed in clean jeans and a pale blue turtleneck sweater.

She liked Kerry, which I had counted on, and she was happy about the news that they would go to court shortly to have all the charges dropped.

I told her about Streetwork and gave her the printout that described the program. She was pleased that she was going to a place with other young people who were as rootless as she, and no longer being held or confined to the Toyota in which she'd been living.

"What about my stuff?" she asked.

"What stuff?" I feigned ignorance of her personal treasures.

"My cash," she said. "My MetroCard, and the things I had with me that the cops took."

"I'll have that back in my office by the time Kerry brings you upstairs, okay?" I said. "The property clerk's office is just down the street at headquarters."

That would ensure her return to me after the judge let her go.

I watched as Kerry and Lucy set off toward the elevator.

"Okay if I take off now?" Max said. "It's five forty-five."

"Of course," I said. "I've got to go soon, too. Thanks for everything. Did Lucy talk about anything I should know?"

"Chitchat only. I wasn't planning to step on your toes and talk about the case."

"I count on you to keep me up to speed," I said. "I want to take you to lunch on Friday to thank you for covering my tail while I was off."

"Don't be silly," Max said. "That's my job. See you tomorrow."

I went back to my office so that Mercer and I could close up for a couple of hours to go to dinner.

"No more calls, ladies and gentlemen," Mike said. He had returned—much to my surprise—while I was down the hall with Lucy and Kerry. "No more calls, folks. We have a winner!"

"What—?" I started to ask.

"Hold your horses, blondie. Mercer tells me that Ms. Lucy's aunt claims that she has loose fingers and lying eyes. But first, I just want you to know that the NYPD has done its job again."

"Which job?" I asked.

"The slightly distressed bowling bag found beneath the seat of an empty Q train on Ninety-Sixth

Street an hour ago—proving the validity of the motto 'See something, say something'—contains the very severed head of the Brooklyn jogger who ran his last mile this morning in Prospect Park."

"Have they got a name?" Mercer asked.

"They do now. Seems to be payback for a shoot-out in a social club last weekend," Mike said. "They should be able to put their hands on the killer pretty quick."

"That'll lighten Lieutenant Creavey's spirits," Mercer said. "Identify the dead man and know who the killer is in the space of the same day."

"Now all Creavey has to make him miserable," I said, "is me."

SEVEN

"You're telling me that Lucy's aunt won't take her in?" Mike said.

It was six o'clock. Mike, Mercer, and I were leaving the building, turning off Hogan Place onto Baxter Street. Forlini's was a short walk away, behind the courthouse and across the street.

"Not yet. I'll keep trying. She has a few conditions and I'm figuring that if Lucy is willing to work with me, we can meet them."

"I thought for sure she'd end up in the Gray Bar Hotel for a few nights," Mike said, tossing his thumb in the direction of the city prison building—the Tombs—which was attached to the courthouse.

"No, we've got no hold on her. So I'll send her to Streetwork and hope she engages long enough for them to try to hook her up with benefits and figure out where she wants to settle for the next while."

"Didn't your shrink tell you to start back up slowly when you returned to the office?" Mike asked.

"Can't go any slower than a case that's ten years

old," I said. "Maybe I jumped the gun this after-noon, but Lucy's happier now that she's getting freed, and I think we'll do fine going forward."

Mercer pulled the handle on the heavy red door at the entrance to Forlini's. I walked in and turned right to go into the bar.

The minute I entered the room, the crowd of fifty or sixty of my friends who'd been waiting for my arrival burst into shouts and whistles, a few Bronx cheers, and the occasional "Surprise!" My hand flew over my mouth—I had no clue this was coming—as I looked from face to face at the pros-ecutors, detectives, defense attorneys, and staffers who had packed into the long room to welcome me back.

Max and Laura—both of whom had left un-usually early—were laughing and waving at me, happy to have pulled off their surprise. I nodded and waved back.

Just about every member of the Special Victims Bureau was in the bar—except for Kerry, who had accepted her mission to handle Lucy's dismissal with a poker face and no complaints.

Paper signs were taped to the walls above the narrow booths. KID COOP IS BACK, FRAGILE: HANDLE WITH CARE—written in red marker but with a big black **X** through the letters—and several others saying COOP FOR DA—DEWAR'S AGENT.

Catherine pushed forward through the group to

put her arms around me. "I know how you hate surprises, but we all wanted to do something for you."

"Well engineered, my friend," I said. "How can I mind something as cheerful as this?"

Kerry would text me when she was back in my office and I would swap my barstool for my desk chair.

Mike was calling over my head to Dempsey, the longtime bartender, and ordering drinks for us, and for anyone who wasn't already holding a glass. I was sidestepping my way through the rowdy group, greeting everyone I hadn't seen on my first day back at work.

Toasts were spontaneous and irreverent and totally in keeping with the black humor of the work we all did. The murder of the district attorney, Paul Battaglia, seemed like a distant memory—though I had been at his side when he was shot—and people were already joking about who would inherit the mantle of the big job.

An hour into the festivities, Mike moved in behind my red leather stool. "You'd better eat something if you're going to work on Lucy after this."

"One drink, Detective, and I'm nursing it." I was also nibbling at some of the jumbo shrimp that was on a platter at the bar. "My shrink insists that I go back to being myself."

"Well, that would be a six-pack of that smooth amber liquid, wouldn't it?"

"I'm still on the job. I'm counting on you to keep the bar at my place open until I get home later."

"Hey, Demps," Mike called out, "would you tune that TV volume up for me, for **Jeopardy**?"

I looked at my watch and saw that it was getting close to eight P.M., and wondered how much longer Kerry would have to wait to be heard by the judge.

"Listen up, everybody," Mike shouted to the women and men who were still hanging around. "Mercer, Coop, and I have been betting on the Final Jeopardy! question for a dozen years. I gotta interrupt the festivities for a few minutes, and you're welcome to watch. Winner takes all and the loser buys a round for everyone."

Our good friends had been through this routine with us. Mike didn't need a clock to know when it was 7:55. He found the closest TV set at the morgue, in the public relations office at DANY, in our favorite restaurants, or stepping over the bodies of the deceased at crime scenes.

Alex Trebek was about to do the reveal on the final category.

Mercer had grown up with world maps all over his room because of his father's job at Delta, so he was an expert in geography and all related subjects. Mike had studied military history at Fordham and knew more about wars, battles, generals, and the horses they rode in on—ancient and modern—than anyone I'd ever met. And I had majored in

English literature at Wellesley before deciding to go to law school at the University of Virginia and devote my career to public service. Give me a Brontë sister character's name or a quote from Anthony Trollope and I'd wipe the floor with General Custer's spirited bay, Dandy.

Trebek stepped to the side of the giant blue board, and the small group of hearty revelers still left at Forlini's gathered in closer to us.

"The final category tonight," Trebek said, repeating the phrase twice, "is 'Southern Discomfort.'"

I turned to look at the friends behind me for moral support. Nobody could guess any better than I. It seemed likely to involve geography, which favored Mercer, unless it was a trick turn of phrase. I'd be fine if the reference was to writers like Harper Lee or Truman Capote or Flannery O'Connor, each of whom had elements of disquiet in their work.

"I'll go twenty," I said.

Mercer was quick to double my bet.

"Feeling good about yourself, m'man?" Mike said to him, slapping his back. "I'm in for that, too. In fact, I'll double down on your number."

Some of the guys were clapping for Mike, admiring his bravado.

My iPhone buzzed and I pulled it out of my pocket. It was a text from Kerry. "All clear. Headed for your office."

"Let's just get this done," I said.

"Don't be a bad sport before the fact," Mike said.

"Tonight's Final Jeopardy! answer is 'Two Southern colonies loyal to England in Revolution.'"

"Totally misleading title," I said, scrawling an answer on my napkin in desperation.

"Sucker," Mike said to me as he and Mercer both wrote answers.

"Kerry's waiting for me," I said, turning over my napkin, raising it over my head, and waving it around so the troops could see it. "What was Georgia and that other place?"

"Dead wrong, Ms. Cooper," Mike said, sweeping the money in front of me closer to him. "The Battle of the Rice Boats in the Savannah Harbor—kind of like the Boston Tea Party—pulled those Georgians right into the cause."

"Take all I've got," Mercer said, leaning in with a laugh. "I figured all those Georgia and Carolina convicts were loyal to the king because he promised they could sail home after they served their time over here."

"Penal transportation, Mr. Wallace. It suited the Brits just fine before the Revolution," Mike said. "Actually, it was Maryland that received more felons than any other colony, and it would appear that very few of them ever returned to the Mother Soil."

Before Trebek announced the winner, Mike turned his back to the TV and told our pals the winning question, "What are East Florida and West Florida?"

Trebek had just told the viewing audience that there were no winners this time, so Mike gloated even more obnoxiously.

"Those were British colonies?" I asked. "Seriously?"

"You bet, Coop. Founded in 1763," Mike said. "So just leave your money where Dempsey can see it—'cause this round is on you—and get on with your work."

"You want me with you for this talk with Lucy?" Mercer asked.

"If her mood has changed, she might let you sit in," I said, picking up my bag and high-fiving Dempsey. "It's worth a try, if you don't mind."

All my colleagues knew that I had a rule that a victim was never interviewed without a witness to the statement in the room as an observer. There were so many nuances to these cases—cases that were eventually made in a courtroom by the detail extracted from memories—sometimes no matter how remote in time the occurrence of the crime. Every prosecutor had to deal with the survivor, when prepping for trial, who startled one of us with an "I never said that!" or "You must have written it down wrong."

Mercer and I said our good-nights—stopping to thank Catherine for putting the welcoming surprise together—as we wiggled our way out to the front door. Mike was at my heels.

"You've got Mercer to do this, right?" he asked.

"Yes. Stay and enjoy the rest of the evening."

Mike moved ahead of us and pushed open the door. "See you at home, blondie. Don't use all your energy up on Lucy."

I stepped down and looked left, down Baxter Street, toward the back of the courthouse.

There were three or four cars with flashing red lights and a commotion of some sort, right beside the entrance to the Tombs.

"Stay put, kid," Mike said as he and Mercer started to run toward the pack of people gathered around the vehicles. "Might be an escape."

I didn't follow them but walked out into the middle of the street to see if I could get a sense of the problem. It was obvious why the traffic had been cut off because the first set of flashing lights was an ambulance, not a car.

I broke into a trot. Whatever had happened must have occurred while we were in the bar, less than half a block from the Tombs.

Mike was standing over the shoulder of an EMT who was giving CPR to a woman who was lying on her back on the ground. He was yelling at the ten or twelve rubberneckers to stand off and give her air.

"What happened?" I asked Mercer, trying to get close enough to see.

"Don't know."

"Was she shot?" I asked. There were so many people with licensed guns who worked in and around the building—cops, prison guards, court officers, and then there were the perps, who carried them anyway—that shootings were more likely to happen on this street than any other.

"Can't tell."

Now the second EMT was working over the victim's mouth and chest while the first one pulled a wheeled gurney closer. I could see the woman's slender legs—bare feet, low-heeled shoes taken or kicked off to the side—but not her face.

"Let's move on this," the first EMT said. "Let's load her."

The second man sat back on his heels, ready to get up and lift her onto the gurney.

That's when the woman's legs began jerking violently. They were out of sync with each other, flailing like a chicken whose head had been cut off. She was making guttural noises, as though unable to speak, and as the EMTs lifted her and raised up the gurney, I could see that she was foaming at the mouth.

I was trembling at the sight of the woman, who appeared to be beyond medical help, before I was even aware that I was. I watched the foam on her lips and cheeks turn to liquid and run down the side of her face, then down her neck while she shook uncontrollably.

One of the EMTs standing opposite me positioned the gurney closest to the doors of the ambulance, while the second guy and Mike got ready to hoist the rear end and push it inside.

"I'm Homicide," Mike said. "Let's get her in and I'll ride with you."

"Thanks," the EMT said.

I could finally see the woman's face as the gurney was raised and loaded into the bus—police shorthand for ambulance.

"My God," I said to Mercer, grabbing his wrist and clinging to him. "It's Francie Fain."

I reached for the open door and stepped toward it. I had known Francie—a talented former prosecutor who was a defense lawyer now—since I'd started in the DA's office.

Mercer grabbed me by both shoulders and held me in place while Mike vaulted himself up next to the gurney and reached for the door to shut it as the bus began to move, sirens blaring.

"Don't let her die, Mike. Please don't let her die!"

EIGHT

I was leaning against the side of the enormous courthouse, beneath the shadows of the Bridge of Sighs.

"Compose yourself, girl," Mercer said. "What makes you think you can put out every fire, no matter what the cause?"

"I'm counting on the medics to deal with that end of things," I said. "I wanted to go with her, just to hold her hand. Give her some comfort."

I knew what it was like to be alone when the darkness of some unforeseen trauma envelops you.

"I'll bet you she was walking to Forlini's, to my little party," I said. "She probably just finished up in court and was on her way over."

"Those convulsions would have happened to her no matter where she was headed, don't you think?" Mercer said, pulling a handkerchief from his pocket to pass to me. "Has she been ill?"

"No. Nothing wrong with Francie. She ran a 5K race in Central Park last week," I said, "and before that she flew overseas to go to that conference at

Oxford on gun violence. I was supposed to debate her there. She said the best thing about my—my, uh, situation—was that I couldn't show up and butt heads with her."

I blew my nose into Mercer's handkerchief and wiped my eyes.

"Text Mike, please, to keep in touch with you while I'm interviewing Lucy," I said.

"That's one thing he doesn't need to be told."

I looked overhead at what was known as the Bridge of Sighs, the covered walkway with iron bars on its small windows that connected the criminal courthouse to the Tombs. Those criminals not set free—as Lucy Jenner had been—were condemned to cross that bridge to be taken to their cells in the city prison.

"What if it's a head injury?" I said, still staring up at the old structure, built nearly a century ago and named for its counterpart, the Venetian Bridge of Sighs, which was built in 1600. "What if Francie was mugged or assaulted here? Every kind of scumbag hangs around the courthouse after release, looking to score."

"Trust the docs on this one," Mercer said, encouraging me to move along. "The EMTs weren't looking for injury. They were just trying to stabilize her. Keep her airways open."

"But right here, at this spot," I said. "Isn't that ironic?"

"How so?" Mercer said. He towered over me at six feet four inches, leaning his head back to see where my finger was pointing.

"Bridge of Sighs," I said. "You know, Venice?"

"Yeah. The limestone arch that crosses the Rio di Palazzo—"

"Separating the convicts from the Doge's Palace," I said. "Condemned prisoners sighed as they took their last look at Venice through the stone grillwork of the bridge."

"And when this courthouse was built," Mercer said, "the skybridge you're looking at was named for its Venetian ancestor. Before the state began to use the electric chair, there was a gallows right here at the Tombs. This really was the last bit of earth the condemned men saw."

I squinted at him. "C'mon. A gallows, in nineteenth-century Manhattan?"

"At least fifty prisoners were hung right here where we're standing. Executed beneath the Bridge of Sighs. Maybe that'll get you moving along on your way."

I started to walk toward Hogan Place, the entrance to the DA's office, following a step or two behind Mercer.

"You should have a team from Major Case check on who Francie's clients were, especially today and tonight," I said. "Maybe someone she represented didn't expect to do the bridge walk, didn't expect to be kept in the slammer. Could be an unhappy thug or cohort who followed Francie out of the courthouse as payback."

"Did that shrink put you on psychotropic meds?" Mercer asked, cocking his head to look at me. "Your imagination is more vivid than ever."

"No drugs," I said, laughing at him. "I told her the only thing that brought on panic attacks anymore was the thought of no Dewar's at the end of my workday. And that soothing drink is contraindicated for drugs."

"Let's wait and get ourselves a diagnosis on Francie, and that will tell us whether it's a police matter or not."

Mercer put his gun on the table next to the metal detector, and the security guard waved us both through.

The building was usually still after eight o'clock. Lawyers hunched over their desks planning the next day's cross-examination, detectives being prepped for testifying at hearings or trials, paralegals helping with research on issues that had arisen during the day. The hallways were long, dark, and airless. The late-night work was often intense, and the quiet hung heavily throughout the corridors.

We got off the elevator on the eighth floor and headed for my office.

I turned the corner and was surprised to see Lucy

Jenner standing behind my desk. The top drawer was open and she withdrew her hand from it the second she caught sight of me.

"What are you doing?" I asked, shocked that the young woman would be brazen enough to go through my things. "Where's Kerry?"

"Bathroom, I guess," Lucy said, without a hint of embarrassment, as she slid the drawer back into place.

"There isn't any money in my desk," I said, angry that someone we were trying to help would take advantage of me. But it had happened so many times before that I had learned to use the drawers as they were intended—for pens, papers, and legal pads, not my wallet. "There's nothing of value."

"I was looking for a key," Lucy said, answering me but staring at Mercer. "Who's he?"

"Stick with the key for a minute," I said. "A key to what?"

"Ms. O'Donnell said you got my stuff back. My cash and my personal stuff," Lucy said. "I need to have those things before I leave."

"Kerry told you where they are?"

"Nope. But the paralegal who brought them from police headquarters told us that she locked them in Laura's desk."

"What do you mean by 'told us'? Told **you**?"

"Well, I overheard them talking to each other,"

Lucy said. "I want my things and I want to go to this Streetwork place where you said I can live for a while."

"That's half the deal," I said. "Let's switch places and you sit down over here. We haven't finished talking, you and I. I made good on my part."

Kerry came back in the room. "Everything okay?"

"Thanks, Kerry," I said. "Lucy's been on a scavenger hunt for the key to Laura's desk."

Kerry reached into her pants pocket and pulled out the key, handing it to Mercer, who was closer to her than I was. "You've got really good hearing, Lucy Jenner, if you picked up on that conversation. And I'd stay out of Ms. Cooper's drawers. She keeps a mousetrap in the second one on the left. The last witness who tried to look for something that didn't belong to her had her finger snapped in half."

Lucy Jenner stared at me with new respect. "You did that to someone?"

Kerry answered instead of me. "That's the third time it worked on nosy witnesses. Two teenage girls—just a month apart from each other—got their digits crushed down to the knuckles. But they reattached the top joint of the most recent one at Bellevue. So you just sit down and do whatever Ms. Cooper tells you to do. She doesn't suffer fools—or dissemblers—"

"Dissemblers?" Lucy asked. "What's that?"

"Thanks for all the time, Kerry," I said to her

as she backed out of the room with a wave. "The mousetraps with those little steel teeth on the clamps work so much better than flypaper, don't you think?"

"What's a dissembler?" Lucy asked again.

"Don't worry," I said, forcing a smile. "It's not what you are. It's late. It's late for all of us, so why don't we get started?"

"I asked you who this man is and you didn't answer me," Lucy said.

"Here I was, silly enough to think that if I got your warrant dismissed and set you free of the criminal justice system, you might warm up to me a little bit and appreciate that we're going to help you," I said, pulling out my chair and taking my position behind my desk. "All of us. This is Mercer Wallace. He's the best Special Victims detective I've ever worked with, and he's one of my closest friends."

"Did you really think that by bringing a black man in to question me instead of that Chapman cop, I'd fall for it?"

"Mercer's here because I need a partner on every case," I said, trying to keep my temper in check. "I'm bringing in the best SVU cop in the business, and that has nothing to do with his race. Now, sit up and let's get to work."

Lucy shuffled in her chair and played with the buttons on the cuffs of the new shirt she was wearing.

"I've had a lot of hours to think about what I said to you this morning," she said. "You know, about what happened to me."

"I'm sure you have," I said. "You've had time to rest and clean up and get some new clothes—and lots of time to think, to pull yourself together for me. I'm ready to get this done."

Lucy looked down and fingered the material of her shirt and pants. "Can I keep the clothes you bought me?"

She wasn't my first witness to seem to be as interested in the new things—free threads—as she was in the business at hand.

"Compliments of the City of New York," I said. "Are you comfortable now? What I want you to do is trust me. I'd like you to start back all those years ago and tell me the story of what happened to you."

Lucy glanced around to look at Mercer, who had taken a seat behind her, near the door.

"Pretend he isn't even here," I said. "Mercer's just an observer."

He was there to back me up on every detail that Lucy was about to reveal. Mercer was protection for **me** at this point.

"I'm going to ask all the questions for now," I said. "So if there is anything you want to know before we begin, anything that will make you more comfortable, you can ask them right now."

Lucy wiped her hand back and forth across her mouth. "My things. Can I have them?"

"When we're done," I said. I was trying to find the perfect pitch for the tone of my interrogation, somewhere between firm—helped in that regard by Kerry's anecdote about the mousetraps—and compassionate.

Lucy Jenner pouted.

"The best I can figure, the man who took advantage of you was involved after Buster and Austin were killed, am I right?"

No answer.

"What I mean is, I won't make you go through all of that again at this point in time, okay?" I wanted to lower the emotional content of the interview. "You choose the way you want to tell the story. I want you to try to relax. I'm not taking any steps until you're one hundred percent on board."

Lucy's chest started heaving. It was obvious she was getting upset, and she refused to make eye contact with me.

"I can't do it," she said, looking down at some place on the floor between my desk and her feet. "I thought I could, Ms. Cooper, but I just can't. Not because I don't want to, but I just can't."

"This morning you said you had told people five years ago, when you were here in the city. People who didn't believe you and didn't do anything about it."

Now Lucy had twisted her head to the side and was gnawing at a hangnail.

"I didn't say that," Lucy said. "I told you I tried."

"Tried what?"

"Tried to tell people."

I knew she had said that she had told people. Now she was backing off from that statement, proving my need to have Mercer present.

"Like I said to you then, Lucy, try **me**." I was leaning in toward her, trying to make the conversation as easy and intimate as I could.

Her chest heaved again as she exhaled and wiped a tear from her eye. "I can't do it, Ms. Cooper. I can't do it now for the same reason I couldn't do it then."

"Sure you can," I said. "These are different times—you said that yourself—and I'm here to work my tail off getting some kind of justice for you. You've come through so much in your young life that even though I've known you for just a few hours, I don't think there's much you can't do. What's the reason you're saying that?"

I pulled a Kleenex—a staple of my trade—from the box on my desk and passed it to her.

"Please, Lucy. Give me the reason."

She wiped her eyes and her cheeks and balled up the tissue in her fist.

"If anything worse happens to me than what I've been through," she said, "I won't be able to take it."

"Don't talk that way, Lucy. Let's see what we

can do—together," I said, curious that she was worried about something bad that could happen— something she didn't have the fortitude to endure. "Have you ever tried to hurt yourself?"

She was still sniffling as she pulled up one of the cuffs and showed me the scars of several marks where she had cut herself on her inner wrist.

I had seen scores of self-inflicted cuts on young women. These, like many others, looked superficial. They looked like an effort to call attention to herself, but not really to endanger her.

"If you trust me—and Mercer—there'll be nothing anyone can do to hurt you. Do you understand that?"

"I understand what you're saying, Ms. Cooper," Lucy said. "That doesn't mean I believe it."

"Who are you afraid of?" I asked. "The man who hurt you?"

"Yeah. Exactly. The man who raped me. He didn't just hurt me, he raped me."

I had been waiting for Lucy to use that word. Rape. She hadn't said it earlier in the day, and though it seemed to me to be the issue, she needed to speak it out loud and not have me guess at it.

"We put rapists in prison, Lucy. That's what Mercer and I do."

She had shredded the tissue in her hand, so I gave her two more.

"The reason I've never been able to tell anyone is that the man—my rapist," Lucy said, catching her breath, "my rapist threatened that if I ever said anything about what happened, he'd personally make sure he'd find me and find a way to break my spirit. To break me completely—whatever was left of me."

I tightened my lips and tried to find the right approach to reach her. "Whoever he is, Lucy, he can't be that powerful. Nobody is. You're got strength and courage you're not even aware you have."

Lucy pushed her chair back. She was defiant now. "He is powerful, Ms. Cooper. And beyond that, he made me swear not to tell."

"He obviously made you do a lot of things you didn't want to do," I said. "You were a kid, Lucy. Don't be afraid now of things that scared you then. Swearing to a rapist that you'd protect his secret is not a pledge you have to keep. Bring him to justice and I promise you that not even he can break your spirit."

"It was more than a pledge I made to him," Lucy said, hesitating for several seconds. "It was an oath. He said it was every bit as sacred as a religious rite—a promise to God."

"But, Lucy—" I started to say.

"He had a razor blade, Ms. Cooper. He cut his hand with it," she said, "and then he cut mine."

This time when she offered her hand to me, she opened her fist and showed me her palm. There was a scar across it, from the base of her index finger to the opposite corner where the palm joined with the top of her wrist.

"He mixed our blood together and made me swear never to tell," Lucy said, rubbing her palm.

"I don't know what will happen to me if I break that pledge, she said, pausing again. "It was a blood oath."

NINE

I got up and walked to Lucy, who stood up as I put my arms around her slender shoulders and squared her off to face me.

"That's a whole lot of mumbo jumbo," I said, urging her to look at me and listen. "A blood oath has no meaning in this day and age. It's just superstition, and the kind of irrational belief a man like that would use to twist you into knots when you were most vulnerable."

"He told me that it was a religious thing. Break it and my soul breaks with it."

"Are you religious?" I asked.

"No," Lucy said. "My mother gave up going to church when she found out that she was going to die and leave me all alone. I had no reason to believe in God after that."

"Sit down, please," I said to Lucy and then turned to Mercer. "Get in this with me, will you?"

The huge detective with the gentlest touch of any I knew walked forward and kneeled next to Lucy's chair.

"The power of blood oaths is mythical, Lucy, not real," Mercer said, talking softly, as though there was someone else around to hear him. "Princes and knights would shed their blood in ancient times, according to oral histories, swearing to protect their people from foreign conquerors."

At first she ignored him, but that was hard to do with Mercer.

"Mafia mobsters used that term," he went on, "to command the loyalty of new recruits, just like gang members still do. It's the stuff of Samurai legends you see in movies—scenes that are meant to make you cringe when blood is drawn."

Lucy tilted her head and looked at Mercer.

"It's vampire stories and gothic novels—and even in the pages of those things, when the good guy is ready to shed the influence of the bad guy, he or she just renounces the oath."

"Renounces it?"

Mercer stood up. "You abandon the covenant," he said, brushing the palm of one hand across his other as though he was ridding them of dirt. "Mobsters and gang members and Samurai and vampires—it's okay to be afraid of them. But you're not bound by any covenant a rapist swore you to. Over and done, Lucy Jenner. Let's us go bring this bastard to his knees."

Lucy looked from Mercer's face to mine. "How do I renounce a solemn oath I made?" she asked. "Will you help me?"

"There was nothing solemn about it," I said. "You tell me you want to break it? Consider it broken."

Mercer reached for a piece of paper on my desktop and grabbed a felt-tip pen.

"Write it out for me. That's more formal," he said. "That'll work in court, if you want to show it to the judge."

He had picked up on the childlike qualities Lucy exhibited, despite the street smarts she had been forced to develop by her lifestyle. He sensed that she needed something that was as visible to her as the razor cut on her hand.

She bent over the paper and wrote for a minute, then handed it to Mercer, who read it aloud.

"'I, Lucy Jenner, break the covenant I made with my rapist on August twenty-third, the year I turned fourteen, in the John Wayne Motor Inn, in Iowa City.'"

"Is that okay?" she asked, placing her hands under her thighs and sitting on them.

"It'll do fine," Mercer said. "Let's have Alex sign and date it."

He passed the paper to me. I was already agitated. What business would I have making this a case if it happened in Iowa City?

"You sure that's the name of the hotel?" I asked as I added my signature with the date and time. "John Wayne?"

"He was born in Iowa City," Lucy said, smiling

at me. "I know he got to be a movie star cowboy, but he was born in the Midwest."

I had a legal pad in front of me. I was used to the balance of establishing rapport with the victim through eye contact and paying careful attention to the facts and details. But some of the specifics had to be noted contemporaneously so that they didn't get lost in the bigger picture.

"I don't want to keep calling him 'the man' or 'the rapist,'" I said. "Are you ready to give us his name now?"

Lucy was warming up to Mercer. I think she liked the way he had given her the permission she had long wanted to abandon the oath that had silenced her.

She picked her head up, looking at him. "Later. I'm almost there."

"That will help," I said. "Do you remember the first time you met him?"

Lucy nodded her head. She had been a severely traumatized teenager when Austin and Buster were murdered, someone had come along to be part of her recovery team, and then betrayed her. Asking if she remembered how and when and where she first met her rapist was like asking me if I remembered my first root canal. I couldn't forget if I wanted to.

"Let's give him a name for now," I said. "Just so we can refer to him."

"Jake," Lucy said. She hadn't paused for a second to think about it.

"Jake?" I asked. "Is that what you actually called him—or did you just pick that to use with us to-night?"

"That's what he wanted me to call him," she said, seemingly attaching no significance to the name. "He didn't want me to use his real name."

"And that wasn't his nickname?" I asked.

"It was his middle name. I mean, I didn't know it back then, but one time a few months back, I Googled him and saw that his middle name is Jacob."

Jacob. Jacob. Jake. Jake. I thought of the photographs of cops and FBI agents that Mercer had printed out for me. I didn't want to stop Lucy now that she was talking. I could look up each one of them later, if she still balked at naming the man, to find the elusive "Jacob."

I scribbled "Jake" and "Jacob" and "J." on my pad, although there was no chance of my forgetting it.

"And you remember the first time you met Jake?" I prompted.

Lucy bit her lip and nodded again.

"Would you tell us about it? Would you tell us where it happened?"

She rocked her body from side to side.

"I met Jake here," she said. "I met him in New York."

Bingo, I thought to myself. I might have jurisdiction after all. I did nothing to give away the fact that her answer pleased me.

"What were the circumstances, Lucy?" I said. I wanted to draw her out and have her give us a narrative. I didn't want to pick at and pull for every fact. "Why were you here and who were you with?"

"After Austin and Buster were killed, there was an FBI agent assigned to my case," she said. "Assigned to me."

"Do you remember his name?"

"**Her** name, actually. Her name is Kathy Crain," Lucy said.

I wrote that on the pad. Lucy stretched up to see what I was doing.

"It's Kathy with a **K**, not a **C**," she said, correcting me. "She became, like, as close to me as anyone had been since my mother died. She sat on me like a hawk, watching me real carefully."

"So you didn't get hurt," Mercer said.

"I guess so. It was like she didn't want me out of her sight," Lucy said. "I was at my aunt's house part of the time, and in some different hotels and motels when we had to go to Iowa City to work on the case."

"But Agent Crain—Kathy—was always with you?" I asked.

"Yeah. Always," Lucy said. "Sometimes they sent a relief agent in when Kathy had days off."

"But always a woman?"

"Yeah," she said. "Kathy was bodyguarding me at my aunt's house—my aunt really hated having an agent living with us—when we got the news that Welly Baynes had been caught."

"That must have been a huge relief," I said.

"It was. But it couldn't bring back Buster and Austin."

"Totally right. But it would stop Baynes from killing anyone else," I said, and from trying to eliminate an eyewitness, like Lucy.

"That's what grown-ups kept telling me, but it didn't make me or their mothers feel any better."

"What was the next thing that happened, after you heard Baynes had been caught?"

"That's when I found out about the trip to New York," she said.

"Why New York?" I asked. "What was the trip about?"

"There was this whole team, this task force," she said. "You probably know that. They'd been going all over the country, all over to interview people to see which cases were the ones that Baynes did."

"Yes, I remember."

"They were from lots of places," Lucy said. "All the cities where murders happened, but most of them were from New York. Detectives and federal agents."

Mercer was still behind Lucy, off to her side, out

of her direct line of sight. As he listened to us talking, he was looking through the pile of news clips that he was holding on his lap, beneath his pad.

"Agents," I said. "Lots of FBI guys, I'm sure."

Mercer nodded. We'd been looking for photos of cops, but maybe Jake was an agent. That could make sense, too. And the picture on the precinct wall might have had the task force teammates all together, including the feds.

"You and Kathy flew to New York?" I asked.

Lucy smiled at that memory. "That was the good part. I'd never been on an airplane before, and I'd never been to the city, so all of that was really exciting. Best of all is that the government paid for it—my plane, my hotel room, my meals, and all that. Kathy took me to a Broadway show and to the Museum of Natural History."

"I'm glad you have good memories, too," I said. "Where did you meet Jake?"

Lucy bowed her head and started swinging her legs back and forth. I had wrenched her out of the happy parts of her trip to get her to give us what Mercer and I wanted.

"He came to the meeting at FBI headquarters," she said.

"Twenty-six Federal Plaza," I said, staring at Mercer over Lucy's head.

"I don't remember the address, but it was a tall office building with a ton of security around it."

"Sorry. I didn't expect you to remember," I said. "I was just trying to get some facts grounded. I can always reconstruct that. Actually, that building is just a few blocks away from here."

I could see why I had made Mike so angry. It wasn't that he didn't want justice for whoever had hurt Lucy—cop or no—but I had jumped at the idea that the bad guy was a cop, when it just as easily could have been a fed.

"I spent an hour or so with the guys who had been assigned to my case," Lucy said. "Kathy, too. They just wanted to separate me from the people from the other cases, so we didn't mix up our stories."

"I do that all the time," I said, keeping my tone casual and friendly. "It's a good policy. We all think we can remember things perfectly, but once someone else says, 'Oh, she was driving a blue car,' a lot of witnesses fill in the blanks of their own recollections without ever meaning to."

"Yeah, Kathy told me that's what it was about," Lucy said. "Anyway, the main FBI guy was the one who began to ask me questions. Sort of like this, starting with my background and stuff, and then going on to—you know, to ask about what I was doing with Buster and Austin."

"How many people were in the room?" I asked.

Lucy pulled her hands out from under her thighs and counted on her fingers, closing her eyes to re-create the scene. "Me, Kathy, the guy doing all the talking," she said. "Actually, when he got to the day of the shooting, he made the other cops leave the room."

We must have been getting closer to my target.

"That's good practice, too," I said. "The only one he needed in there with him was Kathy, because she knew everything you'd said up until that point."

She was biting one of her nails. "That's about when Jake came into the room."

I was waiting for this moment, but I was still startled when she introduced him into the narrative.

"I stopped talking, because I hadn't seen him before," Lucy said. "Kathy knew him really well. She got up and they kissed each other on the cheek, and then she told me his name—his real name, like kind of formal—and said they were old friends."

Mercer had put down his papers and was as riveted by Lucy's words as I was.

Lucy paused and smirked. "Kathy told me I could trust him with my life. She told me how lucky I was that he was my team leader."

"Then what hap—?" I began.

Lucy interrupted me. "The four of us talked for a few minutes, then he told them it was time to take a break, to leave us alone for a bit so he could get to know something about me. One-on-one. Things that weren't in the police reports."

"Did Kathy go?"

"Yeah, she said she'd bring us back some coffee," Lucy said. "She said this work was all about trust. We'd have to get to trust each other."

"And the man?"

"The first thing he said to me—Kathy was still there, so she can tell you it's true—the first thing he said to me was how easy it was to trust girls with hazel eyes," Lucy said, putting her hand to her mouth. "He had this great big smile, and he was just a foot away from my face. He said I had the most beautiful hazel eyes he'd ever seen, and that the two of us were going to do just fine together."

Shit. The grooming began the moment he laid eyes on his victim.

"Did you say anything?" I asked.

"No," she said. "He did all the talking at first. 'Lucy, we're going to be spending a lot of time together. And you can count on the fact that I'm going to be the best friend you've ever had.'"

She paused. "I didn't have many friends, with Buster and Austin gone. I was sort of glad to hear him say that."

I bet she was.

"That's when he told me I could call him Jake. Not in public, not in court, but that would be our secret name when I wanted to tell him something private."

This time I took a deep breath. "Jake. Okay, that's his nickname," I said. "What else did he say?"

"'Call me Jake, Lucy,'" she repeated. Then she dropped the bombshell. "'I'm going to be the prosecutor for your case.'"

TEN

A cop had been my first guess as the bad guy. Gut reaction, because of Lucy's panic in a police station, but the wrong one. Then I had figured a federal agent. I had failed to look at one of my own as the villain—a prosecutor. There were powerful men with dark secrets hiding in plain sight everywhere.

"How stupid of me," I said, pounding my fist on the desktop. "How narrow-minded and short-sighted."

"Zachary Palmer," Mercer said, flipping through the news clips until he found one of the cops and agents posing with their lead prosecutor. "Zachary J. Palmer."

We had let Lucy Jenner take a break—wash her tearstained face and get a soda from the vending machine.

"Jake," I said, throwing up my arms. "Nobody ever calls him Jake."

I grabbed the paper from Mercer's hand. "No doubt there's a photo like this on the wall in the station house. Palmer's Posse is what they called his team. He was the architect of the brilliant plan to join all Welly's local crimes to mount one federal case."

"How did he—?"

"Zach," I said, rambling on. "I've known him forever as Zach. First as a fed and then as an adjunct professor of Con Law at NYU—I guest lectured for him several times—and then as a liaison between the Justice Department and Homeland Security, and now—"

"Take a deep breath, Alex," Mercer said. "We can deal with this. And now what's he doing?"

"Zach is on the mayor's Anti-Terrorist Task Force," I said, "doing pretty much what he pleases. Making contacts with the top dogs at every law firm and hedge fund, flying off to Paris and London and Moscow and Jerusalem to meet with those special NYPD units in each of the foreign cities. Raising his political profile while he trolls for campaign donations and promises of help from American expats and Russian oligarchs—that's what I would call his full-time job."

"Nice deal."

"All mostly a cover while he positions himself to make a run for office."

"What off—?" Mercer said, shaking his head from side to side as the obvious answer dawned on him.

"District attorney of New York County," I said, almost in a whisper. "Can you believe the irony of this? Zach dancing circles around me, always ready to shove a shiv in my back if I got in his way, and meanwhile, Lucy Jenner walks in my door with a backstory that might blow him off the map."

"Have you seen him recently?"

"Zach made all the right noises when I was down for the count," I said. "Called and offered to stop by and visit. Wanted to make sure I was getting the counseling I needed."

"Sure he did," Mercer said. "Something he could use against you if you decide to run—emotional instability and dependence on drugs."

I crossed my arms and tossed back my head. "And always that same inappropriate language about the physical appearance of all the professional women he came across."

"You?"

"Fortunately, he spared me his compliments."

"Maybe he recognized you wouldn't tolerate them."

"Hindsight's a wonderful thing," I said. "If I had shut down every inappropriate comment I heard in this office since I've been bureau chief, I would have probably changed some behavior, don't you think?"

"You'd never have had time to get any work done, if you'd been like that," Mercer said. "Besides, how do you separate it all out? You've got a team of forty lawyers whose business it is to talk about penises and vaginas and whether a touching was consensual or not. You all make a living bouncing case ideas off each other—whose private parts were where and how did they get there? It's not as though you work in a bakery, kneading dough. I'd expect the language to be different here."

"I'm not exactly blind to the offensiveness of it all," I said. "Accepting all the dark humor and bad jokes."

"Started as a cop thing," Mercer said. "That's life on the job."

"There was a time not that long ago that I went in to see Battaglia," I said. "One of the bureau chiefs was harassing a young woman in my unit. Total asshole. Married guy."

"The worst ones usually are."

"He was stalking her after work, leaving notes on her desk that were disgustingly suggestive, refusing to give her good cases unless she met him for a cocktail. Then the touching began."

"The tired old mashing at the Xerox machine?" Mercer said.

"That and the overdone elevator crush and the supply closet jam-up."

"I bet Battaglia didn't give a damn."

I looked up at him in surprise. "How'd you figure that? He liked to think of himself as such a great feminist."

"Generational thing, I'm sure. Battaglia was from the days of the 'good ole boys' just having a little fun."

"Dead on," I said. "He told me that Jimmy was

just going through a midlife crisis when I went
to him with the story. That we all needed to ignore him till it passed. So of course we transferred
the woman out of Jimmy's bureau, and double of
course, she's a star. Midlife crisis, my ass. Jimmy K
is just a pig."

"The victim always loses," Mercer said. "Did
you tell him about any of your own shit? Lipsky
hitting on you big-time, showing up at your apartment door with his load on, when you were supposed to be helping him with his summation on
that double murder case your rookie year? Frank
Roper trying to tackle you to the ground after that
black-tie dinner at the country club?"

"Sometimes it's better for me to fight my own
battles," I said. "All those years of ballet lessons
helped me develop a swift knee hoist to the groin.
Frank's tuxedo pants split down the seam and I
don't think he ever looked in my direction again.
Not so much as a glance."

"Sounds like Frank," Mercer said.

"This is an office with five hundred lawyers and
another thousand support staff," I said. "What per-
centage of them have been on the receiving end of
harassment or assault, and who do they go to when
it's one of us who's the abuser?"

The Special Victims Bureau had a hotline phone
right down the hall from my office, but I doubted
my own colleagues would use it.

"I may have just landed a prosecutor with felony habits, and you know they rarely strike once."

"One vic at a time, Coop. Take 'em as they come to you."

"For now, I can't shake the image of Zach Palmer—distinguished federal prosecutor—climbing into bed with a teenage witness."

I had a ticking time bomb—Lucy Jenner—almost ready to come back into my office and tell me things about Zach Palmer I didn't want to know. But I had planted myself firmly in this quicksand up to my neck and was not about to crawl out because the possible perp was law enforcement, too.

"No more assumptions," Mercer said. "Lucy has to paint this picture for you."

"It gets worse," I said, ignoring his comment but thinking of my own predicament. "I'm having a drink with Zach tomorrow night. His invite, to discuss the race. He's pretty sure that if he makes it clear that he's raised the money already and has the community—and the Reverend Hal Shipley—in his pocket, I'll realize running would be wasting my time and energy."

"You keep saying you're not going to run," Mercer said. "Maybe it's time to let Zach Palmer think otherwise. Game him for a while."

"My head is spinning," I said, lowering myself into my chair. "This is the moment I always told myself it was time to go in to talk to the boss."

"Get your 'do the right thing' speech from him?" Mercer said. "Is that what you need?"

"Yeah, but the boss is dead," I said, spinning my chair away to face out the window into the dark of night. "I don't have a boss right now."

"You've got a conscience, Alexandra Cooper. That old windbag Battaglia didn't have anything to do with the settings on your moral compass."

I could see the streetlights below on Baxter Street. I was hatching a plan and could feel a grin growing on my face.

"You hear me?" Mercer asked. "Keep your date with Zach Palmer."

"I fully intend to," I said. "There's a vacancy in the front office, so no one to tell me I can't."

"Turn around, will you? Look me in the eye," Mercer said.

I swirled the chair slowly.

"Now, that expression on your face is a real shit-eater," he said, pointing right at my mouth. "Exactly what is it you're thinking? Are you getting out ahead of me with a plan?"

"Just a work in progress," I said. "I'm getting my Jake on."

ELEVEN

My desk phone rang and I answered it. "Alexandra Cooper."

"Chapman."

"How's Francie?" I asked. "Where are you?"

"I'm at Bellevue," Mike said. "She's critical, Coop, but the docs are working on her like she's the only ER admission tonight."

"Look, Mike, I was telling Mercer that maybe she was attacked by—"

"Stick to the law," he said. "There were no signs of injury to her head, and the marks on her legs and arms were from flailing because of the seizures— she got completely scraped up on the cement sidewalk. They're doing every kind of brain scan and test imaginable."

"Are you with her?"

"Back off, Coop. I rode in the ambulance, but she had no idea who she was or where she was, so forget about me," Mike said. "And now she's inside for all the tests."

"But you're staying with her?"

"The nurses want to know where her family is."

"Her mother lives in Texas, in an assisted living facility with a full-time companion," I said. "There isn't much other family. See if you can get a Legal Aid supervisor to find her next-of-kin contact."

Lucy was back, carrying a can of root beer and some red licorice from the vending machines. She knocked on my open door and I waved her in.

"I'll get on it," Mike said. "Are you making any progress?"

"A ton of it," I said.

"How big of an apology can I expect?" he asked.

"Super-size," I said. "Gotta go, though."

Mercer walked to the door and closed it.

Lucy sat down again and started gnawing on a Twizzler. "How late are you going to keep me here?"

"Till I get the answers I need," I said.

"You know this guy, don't you?" she said.

"I've met him. I'm not close to him, if that's what you're worried about."

"What I'm worried about is that if I start doing this, and Jake finds out about it, and then you back off 'cause you know what a big deal he is," Lucy said, "then I'm screwed."

Mercer spoke, behind the girl. She didn't turn her head to look at him. "There's one place Alex has more power than anyone else," he said, "and that's the courtroom."

She was staring me down. "You don't have more power than the judge."

"Depends on the judge," I said. "But I don't back down off cases, once I've made up my mind to take one. That's why I'll be so demanding of you when I start the questioning."

"Demanding what?"

"There's only one thing you can do wrong, Lucy, and that's lie to me. No matter what I ask, you can give me an answer or you can tell me that there are specific things that you don't remember, but if you lie to me—about the least little thing—our deal is done."

"Little things?"

"Yes, because at the end of the case, when the jury gets instructions about how to decide on the evidence, the judge tells them that if they believe you lied about anything—**any**thing at all— then they can discard all of your testimony. Not just the lie, even if you think it's a meaningless part of things—but **all** of it."

"Why would anyone lie if they were raped?" she asked.

"That's a really good question, and Mercer and I wonder about it all the time," I said. "People don't usually lie about the crime but about some of the details leading up to it. Sometimes they minimize things they did with the bad guy—the man who raped them—because they figure I'll think worse of them if I know everything they did."

"Like what?" she said. "Tell me like what?"

"So many things," I said. "It can be that they

drank too much but don't want me to know they did. Or that they did drugs with the guy, so they're afraid I'll have them arrested for smoking weed or snorting coke."

"Would you?"

"No," I said. "And sometimes it's about something sexual that happened between them and the bad guys. Some girls don't want me to think they made out with a man or took off some of their clothes, because they think I'll get the idea that they wanted to have sex with him."

Now Lucy was looking at me with greater interest. "So if I let somebody touch me—touch my breasts or something like that—it doesn't mean I was asking to be raped, does it?"

"Not at all," I said. "Not for a minute."

"All right," she said. "I think I understand. You can ask your questions."

I took her back to the day she first met Zach Palmer, spitting distance away from here at 26 Federal Plaza.

"How long were you alone with Jake that time?"

"I'm not sure," she said. "Probably fifteen or twenty minutes until Kathy came back with coffee."

"Did you know his real name?" I asked.

"Oh, sure," she said. "It was all Mr. Palmer this and Zach that, depending on how well people knew him. They all wanted me to understand what a big deal he was, so I'd appreciate what he was doing for me, I guess."

"When you were alone with him—while Kathy went out—did he discuss the case with you?"

Lucy shook her head in the negative. "Nope. Not ever when we were alone, other than to ask me if I was scared about getting shot, like Austin and Buster did," she said. "He just started then by telling me he needed to know everything there was to know about me—even the most personal stuff—which seemed kind of nasty."

"Actually, Lucy," I said, "I do the same thing. I like to tell my witnesses that I need to know as much about them as the very best defense attorney—the person representing the man on trial—could find out if he hired a private eye."

She sneered at me. "Why do you guys say that?"

"Because we can't have any surprises when you're on the witness stand at the trial and I'm behind the prosecutor's desk in the well of the courtroom, twenty feet away from you. By then it's too late for me to prevent the other side from asking questions that have nothing to do with your case."

She seemed to be focusing on my words, trying to absorb them.

"So in that first meeting, did he tell you why he wanted you to call him Jake, instead of his proper name?" I asked.

"He told me that our relationship was going to be different than that of all the other agents and cops," Lucy said. "That he would ask me about things that no one else needed to know, so he promised to keep any secrets I had to himself and not to share them with others or make them part of the case file."

"Secrets from Kathy Crain, too?" I asked.

"Especially her," Lucy said. "Jake said Kathy told him she had taken the place of my mother, and he knew that every teenage girl likes to keep secrets from her mother."

"Pretty savvy of him," I said. "That's not a crazy view of a typical mother-daughter dynamic. What else happened in that first meeting?"

"I'm not sure," she said, looking away.

I wanted to prod her memory a bit, without leading her. "Did he ask you personal questions?"

"I don't remember," Lucy said, expressing her annoyance with me. "You can't expect me to remember everything he said to me."

"You're absolutely right. I'm just trying to figure out when you say you're not sure, if it means you actually don't remember or you're just not ready to tell me something yet."

"Is it okay not to remember something?"

"Sure it is," I said. "A lot of this happened a very long time ago. But the more I make you go over things again and again, the more details that will come back to you."

Memories were likely to flood back in, whether Lucy wanted them to or not. Mercer and I knew how many painful episodes were repressed by survivors, and yet the imprint of the criminal behavior was so dominant that it didn't take much to bring them back to the surface.

"When Jake was alone with you in the FBI offices, did he touch you?" I asked, speaking calmly, in a soft voice.

She thought for twenty seconds.

"Like, in a bad way?" she asked.

"In any way," I said. I'd be the judge of what was good touch and what was bad.

"I mean, he hugged me," Lucy said. "That's all. He asked me a bunch of questions about Austin and Buster—how close we were to each other and general stuff like that."

Mercer and the guys in my unit had hugged women, too—sometimes to comfort them, sometimes in celebration after a trial victory. But the Me Too movement had made us more careful about the way we interfaced with our victims. There would be no more hugging from this point on.

"How close were you to Austin and Buster?"

"Jake wanted to know if I'd ever had sex with either one of them," she said, her annoyance on full display. "He said that would come out at the trial if I had, so he wanted to start with that information, to see whether I'd trust him with it."

"What did you tell him?" I asked.

"They were just my friends, those guys. No, I'd never had sex with them," Lucy said. "I was fourteen years old. I'd never had sex with anyone."

"You told that to Jake?" I said. "Just like you're telling me now?"

"Maybe I used different words, but that's what I said."

"And did he respond?" I asked.

"That's when he pulled me toward him and hugged me," Lucy said. "Nothing bad, I swear it. Just like a big bear hug. That's when he said we were going to do fine together. 'The prosecutor who'd never yet lost a case to a jury,' Jake said to me, 'and the truth-telling virgin with hazel eyes.'"

TWELVE

Catherine texted me and the incoming alert interrupted my talk with Lucy. I stepped out to Laura's desk to answer her, shortly after nine P.M.

"Spoke to Mike just now," she wrote. "He asked me to confirm that Francie was on her way to Forlini's to surprise you at our party."

"Was she?"

"Yes," Catherine responded.

"Any more details?"

"No. She was a no-show. Now we get why."

"Talk to you tomorrow."

I went back to my desk and apologized to Lucy for interrupting her. I wanted to move the story along. I could fill in Jake's foreplay in the next interviews, but before we broke for the night, I wanted to see if there was criminal conduct.

"How long did you stay in New York on that first trip?"

"Three days."

"Did you see Jake again that week?"

Lucy put her finger to her lips as she thought

about the answer. "No, but I saw Mr. Palmer a few times, if you know what I mean," she said. "I never saw him alone, so it was always 'Mr. Palmer' in front of the other lawyers and agents."

"That's good, Lucy. That's really good that you can make the distinction between the personal interactions and the ones with the legal team. That kind of careful thinking is very helpful."

She liked being told she did something well. She blushed a bit and smiled at me.

"Any other instances of touching while you were in New York City?" I can't believe I found myself hoping that something inappropriate had happened within my jurisdiction.

"He hugged me is all," Lucy said. "Mr. Palmer did. I mean, in front of everybody, in just a friendly way. Sort of each time the day was over."

Lucy must have been starved for affection. No family around, no good friends, and now suddenly a cadre of people with voices—lawyers who spoke for the most vulnerable population—suddenly they were looking out for her, too.

"When did you see him next—Jake, or Mr. Palmer?" I asked.

"It was in Portland, Oregon," she said. "Kathy and I flew out because the trial was going to be held in Oregon, for all the guys who were murdered by Welly."

"What happened there?"

"Nothing. Nothing at all," she said. "We were

going to begin the preparation for trial, but then the judge did something that Mr. Palmer didn't like."

"What do you mean?"

"A ruling, is that what you call it?" Lucy asked. "The judge ruled against something the team wanted to do, so Kathy and I flew back to Chicago. There was never a trial set in Oregon."

I made a note on my pad to research the background of the prosecution's case, city by city, crime scene by crime scene. Media clippings would help me establish where Zach Palmer was at any given point in time.

"The next time?" I asked.

"I was going to all these places," Lucy said, "even though they had nothing to do with my case. Next was Utah. Salt Lake City."

As in Portland, a man jogging in a park had been gunned down.

"Mr. Palmer had a hearing of some kind," she said. "He wanted me to be there—'in the wings,' he called it—in case the judge wanted to hear evidence of a similar kind of crime."

"Did you testify?" I asked.

"Nope," Lucy said, shaking her head. "But I did spend some time with Jake. Alone time."

"Exactly what was that," I said, "and where?"

"It was springtime, I know. May or June, I'm pretty sure," she said. "Kathy and I flew out to Salt Lake City from Chicago and got in on a Saturday night, really late. I was supposed to get together with some of the agents at the courthouse on Monday morning."

"Where did you and Kathy stay?" I asked.

"Same place as everyone else," she said. "Some big hotel that gave government rates, Kathy told me. Anyway, on Sunday morning, Kathy wanted to go to church, which was the last thing I wanted to do. I remember a whole bunch of agents were going to go with her."

"'Mr. Palmer wants to spend some time with you,' Kathy said. That was okay with me, 'cause I knew we had work to do," Lucy said. "She told me to meet him in the lobby at eleven."

"Okay, and—"

"Wait. Wait," Lucy said, holding up her hand at me. "Kathy also said all that stuff you tell kids when you're going out and leaving them with a babysitter, you know? 'Do whatever Mr. Palmer tells you to do. Don't talk back to him like you used to do with your aunt,' she told me. 'Just do whatever he wants.'"

Child abuse cases often started that way. So did situations with members of the clergy or with schoolteachers. The party placed in the care of the abuser was always told to obey his orders, often too young to understand the forbidden nature of the conduct. Do whatever he wants. I had heard those instructions more times than I could count.

"Did you meet with him at eleven?"

"Yeah, I did."

"Did you stay in the hotel, or go somewhere else?"

"I met him in the lobby, just like Kathy told me to," Lucy said. "We sat on one of the sofas in the huge room and talked a bit, just about how I was doing back home and how I was dealing with this case hanging over my head."

"That sounds like it was fine."

"It was," she said. "And I thought it was going to be even better when he told me he had a surprise for me."

"Oh, what kind of surprise?" I asked.

"Now it was Jake talking to me, if you know what I mean."

I nodded my head.

"He told me that he had rented a car so he could show me around the city, take me out to the Great Salt Lake. Let me be a kid for the day and not a witness, is how he put it."

"Just you two?"

"Yeah. Just me and Jake," she said. "We walked out to where the valet parking guy was, and when he saw Jake, he ran down to the lot and came back to the front of the hotel with a car—a Mustang convertible, a red one."

When Lucy grinned at me, I couldn't help but smile back.

"That was one of the best days ever," she told me, emphasizing the word "best." "Here was this really smart man who everybody respected and listened to, and it seemed like all he wanted to do was to let me have fun."

Zach certainly had developed a gift for the perfect predatory setup.

"I was wearing jeans," Lucy recalled. "In fact, we were both wearing jeans. He had ordered some food from the hotel and brought a couple of towels and said we were going to picnic."

I hid my facial expressions well. I was used to doing that whenever survivors told me their stories. I couldn't be judgmental of choices they had made. I knew that Lucy Jenner had just boarded an express train that would go off the rails and wreck itself before too long, but I understood what those hours of freedom must have represented to her.

"Did Palmer tell you to call him Jake that day?"

"Yeah, but he didn't have to remind me," Lucy said, trying to imitate him when she spoke. "'Forget I'm the United States Attorney. Now I'm just your buddy Jake. We're not talking about trial prep or learning about the law, we're just hanging out and being friends.'"

She paused for a few seconds. "And you know what, Ms. Cooper? That worked for me just fine."

"Was this supposed to be a secret, this day trip?"

"Jake turned it around on me. He said that **he** was the one who would get in trouble if all the church mice on his team thought he was goofing off," Lucy said. "That made sense to me. He told me our picnic would have to stay between us so he didn't make the agents mad that he was joyriding while they were praying for Welly's victims."

Another well-planned grooming device—each step gradual and each one completely calculated—by Zach Palmer. He let Lucy think she was protecting him rather than keeping her own secrets from Kathy Crain.

"I have to ask you, Lucy, whether there were lots of other things that you kept from Agent Crain before you started going places with Jake?"

She bit her lip and gave the question some thought. "I didn't go to very many places or do many things without Kathy, or whoever was standing in for her when she was off duty," Lucy said. "I kept a lot of my thoughts from her, a lot of the things I was feeling, but she knew everything that I did."

"Were you dating anyone during that time, after Buster and Austin were killed, but before the trial?"

"Now, that's a really stupid question, Ms. Cooper," she said, laughing and wagging her finger at me. "Did you ever know a boy who wanted to put the moves on anyone who spent day and night with an armed guard? He'd have to be crazy."

"One thing I can promise you is that before you and I are done, I'll have asked a bunch more stupid questions," I said, holding my hands up in the air, in surrender. "Fourteen's a tough age. You must have wanted a social life?"

Zach Palmer would have relied on that fact in his approach to Lucy, targeting her isolation and her emotional neediness.

"I wanted a lot of things I couldn't have," Lucy said. "They weren't any of Kathy's business, as nice as she could be."

"Tell me about the picnic, okay?"

Lucy described the ride out of town to the Great Salt Lake in the red convertible. It was such a unique experience in her young life that she recited specifics that left no doubt they were real. Jake's conversation had nothing to do with the law and everything to do with eliciting personal information about Lucy's interactions with family and friends—dead or alive.

I knew that I could retrieve all the data from those conversations on another day.

She talked about her reaction to seeing the vast lake. Although she had spent a lot of her youth in the general area of Lake Michigan, everything about this journey evoked different sensations.

"There are islands inside the Great Salt Lake," she said.

"I've never been there," I said. "Did you see any of them?"

"We drove to one called Antelope Island."

"You drove to an island in the lake?"

Lucy grimaced and slapped her thighs with both

hands. "Why do you doubt everything I say?" she asked. "What's that about?"

I apologized again. "I'm not familiar with what you're talking about. I didn't mean to be rude."

"There's a bridge to the island. I think they call it a causeway," she said. "If you don't believe me, you can Google it."

We were both getting tired and I understood that she had every reason to be cranky.

"I believe you, Lucy. And then?"

"There were beaches on the island. Lots of white-sand beaches everywhere, and the water really sparkled in the sunlight. We walked and we walked until we found one that had nobody on it, and Jake spread out the picnic."

I waited while she cleared her throat.

"He had the hotel kitchen make all this delicious food," she said. "Grilled chicken and coleslaw and an avocado salad—I'd never had an avocado before. I didn't even know what it was. There were brownies and chocolate chip cookies. And we ate with real silver forks, and napkins made of cloth that had the hotel's name on it."

"Sounds really good," I said.

But Lucy could envision that afternoon in her mind's eye, and she was barreling forward without waiting for questions.

"It wasn't like I needed another reason to stay close to Jake, but he gave me one," she said. "He asked me how many black people I'd seen since I got to Salt Lake the night before. I thought about it and told him only two—one of the maids in the hotel and the kid parking cars."

"How about the agents?" I asked.

"There were a couple of black guys on the team, but they hadn't made this trip," she said, "and the number two prosecutor was white, too."

"But—" I said, trying to interject something.

"Jake just went on telling me how lonely it was for him on the road, traveling to all these places where there was still such prejudice and so many bigots, trying to prosecute crimes that were all about race and hate," Lucy said. "And he told me that it was going to be lonely for me, too, even though my skin wasn't as dark as his. That I needed to know I could always rely on him, I could always come to him, and we would get through this time together."

It was impossible for me to speak to Lucy about race the way Jake had. I saw his point and couldn't challenge it.

"Then Jake got to his feet and stretched out his hand to me," Lucy said, with a lightness she had lost moments ago. "'Come with me, Lucy,' he said. 'We're going into the water.'"

"Really?" I asked.

"'Jake,'" I said to him, "'I can't swim, Jake! We can't go in the water!'"

Lucy was shaking her hands back and forth, like she was shooing the spirits away.

"But he pulled me to my feet and started

running to the edge of the sand. 'It's okay, Lucy. I know you told the agents in your first interview that you didn't go to the park that day to swim, because you didn't know how. But nobody can sink in this lake. The salt will keep you on top.'"

Her countenance changed again, and she was somber. "'You've got to trust me, girl,' he said. 'I promise you'll be fine. Didn't I tell you that relying on me was all I needed you to do? You trust me, and I'll do the rest.'"

Lucy paused and took a sip of her soda. "Jake had me by the hand and I waded in the water up to my ankles. Warm water, but I was shivering with fear, just by the thought of sinking to the bottom."

"I don't blame you," I said.

"'You're going to have to walk into where it's deeper,' Jake said. 'Up to your waist at least, and then you're going to lean back and I'll hold you up with both my arms till you see for yourself that you can float.'"

Lucy put her elbows on my desk and rested her head in her hands. "I looked all around for other people—not for help or anything—but to see if they were really floating. But all I could see were the gulls—dozens of them—flying over my head."

"Did you try to do it?" I asked.

"You're not judging me, are you?" she said, looking up at me.

"There's no reason for me to do that. You didn't do anything wrong." It was fourteen-year-old

Lucy Jenner who wanted that answer from me. A fourteen-year-old on a semi-deserted island in the middle of an enormous lake, and in the stranglehold of a thirtysomething-year-old federal prosecutor.

"That's when Jake stopped me," she said.

I swallowed hard, relieved that Zachary Palmer might have come to his senses.

"I mean, he stopped me for a minute. That's when he told me there was one more thing I had to do," Lucy said. "He told me my jeans were too heavy—the fabric, I mean—and that I'd better take them off before I got in any deeper."

"What did you—?"

"Jake said just to be on even ground with me, he'd take his off, too," she said.

Now I was ready to put **my** head in my hands. The next step in cementing the predator's grooming process—getting naked with his prey.

"So we both took off our jeans, Ms. Cooper, and threw them back onto the beach," Lucy said. "I walked out a foot or two, till the water covered my knees, to where Jake was standing."

"What were you wearing then, Lucy?" I hadn't wanted to interrupt her narrative—there was really no need to at this point—but I also didn't have the stomach tonight to hear what he did to this child. I was hoping to slow down the introduction of any sexual abuse.

"Panties. Just white cotton panties and my T-shirt."

"A bra?"

"No. No bra."

"And Jake?"

"Just his underwear," she said. "White ones, too. You know, the kind that are tight, not baggy."

"What happened then?" I asked.

Lucy looked up at the light fixture over my head. "Jake kept saying 'trust me'—over and over again as I walked toward him. Five times, maybe six, he said it. He held out his hand and pulled me closer to him, then sort of cradled me in his arms until I was on my back, floating on top of the salt water."

"And then?" I asked, waiting for something bad to happen.

"I floated, Ms. Cooper," Lucy said, almost triumphantly. "I'd never learned to swim and I'd been afraid of anything deeper than a bathtub my whole life. But I trusted Jake, just like he told me to do, and there I was—in the middle of the Great Salt Lake in Utah—floating on my back for almost five minutes."

"That must have been a great moment for you," I said.

"Yes, it was."

"And Jake," I said, "he didn't take advantage of you while you were in the water, with just your underwear and T-shirt on?"

"No, ma'am. We got back on the beach and I was kind of like giddy from my first swim—or whatever you want to call it. I was even over the embarrassment of being without my pants on."

"He didn't try to touch you, or kiss you?"

"Oh, he did kiss me," Lucy said. "Just right here on the forehead, just sweet, not sexy or anything."

"Nothing else you want to tell me that happened at the beach?" I asked, putting the first leg of an **X** through the word "UTAH" that I had scribbled on my pad as a possible site for the sexual abuse to begin. It looked like I was wrong, that Jake and Lucy were still in the state of foreplay. "Nothing sexual?"

Lucy leaned back in the chair and rubbed her eyes. "I'm not sure if he meant to do this or not," she said, "but when I bent down to pick up my jeans, Jake held me by the waist with both hands, from behind me."

She stopped talking, and I waited.

"It felt like he was rubbing himself against me—against my bum, my rear end. His penis was hard, Ms. Cooper. Real hard," Lucy said. "I just froze and held still for like half a minute or so, maybe a little longer. Then Jake let go and he said something I couldn't understand. I wasn't even sure if he was talking to me or to himself."

Lucy wouldn't look at me again, but she seemed determined to finish her story. "I felt something running down the back of my leg. Something sticky and warm, that mixed with the salt from the lake that had stuck to me."

"That sticky, warm stuff," I said. "Did you know what it was?"

"Not that day, I didn't," Lucy said. "I didn't know for sure until I met up with Jake again in Iowa City—until he raped me in the John Wayne Motor Inn."

THIRTEEN

A steaming-hot shower at the end of a difficult day usually cleared my head. But my mind seemed as fogged up as my bathroom mirror when I stepped out to towel myself off at eleven fifteen that night.

I slipped into a navy blue negligee and walked to the den, where Mike was pouring my favorite Scotch over a mass of ice cubes. I sat on one end of the leather love seat and waited for him to settle in on the other end so that I could put my feet in his lap.

"Why did you leave the hospital?" I asked.

"The docs will be running neurological tests all night," Mike said. "Francie will either be in the neuro lab or the ICU. There was no reason for me to hang around."

"I can't bear to think that she's all alone," I said, taking my first sip, "and do **not** tell me she isn't aware of that right now."

"Someone from her office should be there by now. They'll have her covered."

Mike reached over to grab an envelope that was on the coffee table in front of us. "This was in Francie's briefcase, which the medics picked up," he said. "One of the nurses asked me if I knew who to give it to."

He handed it to me. It was addressed to Ms. Hamilton Burger, which made me laugh in spite of Francie's current status.

Francie loved to call me Ms. Burger, referring to the hapless prosecutor in the Perry Mason television series, who only won three cases in 271 episodes of the show.

I opened the envelope and took out the store-bought greeting card—which featured a colorful picture of an empty life-preserver floating on a calm sea.

Inside, Francie had written in bright red ink **BURGER'S BACK!** at the top of the page.

Dear Alex—I've got so many perps lined up, waiting to meet you now that you're back on your feet. Let's go to trial together before you get your mojo in full gear. Why not give some deserving felon a break?

I tried to throw you a lifeline when you went missing, but all your crew had you covered. Can't stay long at the party—just a hug, if I can plow through that horde of prosecutors. Call me tomorrow and let's have lunch.

Missed you at the conference at Oxford. Awesome stuff. I'm thinking of taking a new job and want your advice.

Most sincerely, except for the part about wanting to try a case against you.—Clara (Francie) Darrow

I rested my head against a cushion and bit my lip. "God, how I'd love to call her tomorrow and have a great gossipy lunch, like we always do."

"Miracles happen," Mike said.

"At Bellevue?"

Bellevue was the country's oldest public hospital, founded in the 1730s for patients from nearby poorhouses, on the East Side of Manhattan. It had become a level one trauma center—and its one hundred thousand ER visits a year saved more patient lives than I could count. I wouldn't choose to go there for an elective procedure, but it was the first place medics and cops took people with gunshot or stab wounds, car crash injuries, major burns, and extreme cases—like Francie's—in which there was an issue of immediate survival.

"You bet," Mike said, reaching for Francie's card. "Talk to me about Lucy Jenner. Tell me how you're going to attack the case."

"I'm formulating my investigative plan," I said.

"How did you get Lucy to Streetwork?"

"Mercer drove her there. They held it open past midnight to let her process in."

"Is she coming back for more of a pounding from you tomorrow?"

"I gave her the day off," I said. "She needs to get into the drill at the program."

"What do you mean?" Mike asked.

"Streetwork counselors do all the social service work with their residents. Get them valid ID, offer them medical services so they can have proper exams, start to advise about job possibilities and eventually housing options," I said. "I want Lucy to get started with all that. Public benefits, too, so she gets whatever income she's entitled to."

"You really think she'll show up on Wednesday?"

"I do."

"Not because she's reliable, right?"

"Not at all for that reason," I said. "But so far, Mercer and I have believed her, which seems to give her a bit of hope. And secondly, we were all so tired by the time we quit for the night that she forgot to ask for her personal belongings again, and I forgot to give them to her."

"She'll be back," Mike said. "You're right about that, when those things are all that someone has in the world."

"Her aunt was pretty direct about Lucy's ability to manipulate and to lie. So far, she seemed credible in her abuse allegations, but I didn't like finding her hand in my desk drawer when we walked back in my office, so we'll use the day to verify the parts of her information that we can check on."

"Sensible."

"Besides, I didn't want to pry any more information out of her before I had my sit-down with Zach. The less I know going in about any criminal allegations against him when he talks to me, the more likely it is I can keep the case."

"Did you say sit-down?"

"I'm having a drink with him tomorrow evening," I said. "To talk about the special election in the spring to fill Battaglia's job."

"I can't believe you're keeping that meet."

"It's a chance I'll never have again, and Zach requested it himself. He can't scream entrapment."

"You're sure he raped Lucy?"

"She's used the word, but I stopped the questioning tonight before she described the act. So far, I have a statutory sexual abuse in Utah," I said, thinking of Jake rubbing his penis against Lucy's buttocks after their float in the lake, "and no crime in New York."

"So you're just chumming for his shark bite right now?" Mike said.

"I've got all the predatory grooming," I said. "Kind of textbook."

"You and Mercer are always talking about grooming. We don't have any of that crap in Homicide. You just point the gun at your target and shoot it. What's it supposed to mean, and can you use it in court?"

"You bet I can," I said. "You know how Battaglia

taught us to write our closing arguments first whenever we took a case to trial? Know where you want
to take the jury at the end of the People's case, then
go back and structure your prosecution that way."

"People of the State of New York against Zachary
Palmer," Mike said, reaching over with his vodka
to clink my glass. "You've already got a closing?"

I pointed to my head. "It's rolling around up
here."

"Give me the section on grooming."

I cleared my throat and took a slug of Scotch
this time, sitting up straight. "Ladies and gentlemen of the jury, grooming is the process by which
a perpetrator draws a victim into a sexual relationship and sustains that criminal relationship in secrecy," I said to my imaginary twelve jurors, then
turned back to Mike. "Cloaking the relationship,
hiding it from everyone else, is a key element of the
procedure. It's what allows the perp to ensnare kids
into this private world in which they become willing actors in what we would call abuse."

"Give me the steps," Mike said.

"The first stage is targeting the victim," I said.
"The molester is looking for the most vulnerable
child—emotionally needy, already isolated in some
way, and especially if they have little or no parental
oversight."

"Enter Lucy Jenner."

"Stage two is getting all the information possible about the child," I said. "A big part of this is

mixing with the responsible caretakers while giving off warm and carefully attuned attention."

"So Lucy's caretaker was an FBI agent," Mike said.

"You got it. One parent was dead and the other not the least bit involved in Lucy's life. Agent Kathy Crain was the caretaker—smart and expertly trained, and already an admirer of Zachary Palmer, with all his concerns and smooth moves. An obtrusive pervert, an awkward interloper—that kind of guy would arouse suspicion, but a stealth groomer never reveals himself to the caretaker."

"I'm getting it," Mike said.

"Third stage. The guy is filling all the needs that have been wanting for this child. Everything from gifts—new clothes, special trips, lavish picnic lunches—and I would bet the farm that I'm going to hear about more things in two days—to special attention, even affection. It's little wonder that the giver becomes idealized to the child and assumes a much greater importance in her life."

"Is all this premeditated?" Mike asked.

"Aren't most murders?"

"Yeah, but this takes some real skill to pull off. Any jackass can pull a trigger."

"Which brings me to stage four," I said. "Our guy has built up this relationship to the point where he can arrange time alone with his prey, which reinforces their special connection."

"And the sex?" Mike asked.

"Stage five, Detective Chapman. Once the abuser has established his victim's trust in him as her ultimate protector, and he has created an emotional dependence, then comes the sexualization of the relationship."

"Just right to it?" Mike said.

"Usually, there's some desensitization. They talk about intimacies with others, if there have been those, or he takes photographs. But do you want to know what one of the most popular methods is?"

"Sure I do."

"Swimming," I said, raising my glass in the air. "Behaviors like swimming together, which seems like a perfectly benign thing to do."

"Yeah, it does but—"

"This is where I nail the jurors," I said. "Think of it, a kind of sport that most kids like, that involves taking off your clothes together."

"But Lucy couldn't swim," Mike said.

"Jake knew that from the interviews in her file. That was part of his information-gathering about Lucy, and it's what made the Great Salt Lake ideal as a secret trip for just the two of them."

"Just take your clothes off, lean back, and float in my arms," Mike said.

"Then on the way out of the water, he rubbed against her buttocks until he ejaculated."

"She didn't say that, did she?" Mike asked.

"She was fourteen years old. I can make 'warm and sticky' into a recipe the jury will understand."

"But will that hold up in court? It wasn't his penis touching her body," Mike said. "He had his tighty-whities on and she had underwear."

"You're going back fifty years, Detective," I said, rolling my eyes at him. "You need that refresher course in sex crimes I give twice a year at the academy. Sexual abuse no longer requires skin touching skin. That's ancient law."

As much as Mercer loved working with survivors who needed the extra measure of compassion a great SVU detective brings to his or her work, Mike preferred the emotional detachment of his dead victims—no hand-holding needed, no legal nuances involved.

"All right," he said. "Stage five takes trust up a level to sexual contact."

"Exactly. And the final stage is maintaining control of the child over a prolonged period of time," I said. "Secrecy and the possibility of being blamed for cooperating with the perp are his two most powerful tools—short and long term.

"The relationship is as knotted and twisted as the abuser wanted it to be from the outset. If the kid thinks of ending the relationship, she knows the gifts and trips and special attention will end. Lucy knows there are people in her life—like Kathy—who always expressed such admiration for Zach, and like her aunt—who will blame **her** for engaging in the conduct. And she knows that exposing what she and Jake have been doing would not only humiliate her in the face of everyone else, but perhaps it would make her even more unwanted than she has been to this point."

"'Unwanted,'" Mike said. "Now, that's an ugly word. A teenage girl—virtually an orphan—finds herself ensnared in the web of a cunning predator. Not only is she vulnerable for that reason, but she's the star witness in a murder prosecution, and the perp is the puppeteer pulling her strings. Use 'unwanted' and that jury will be eating out of your hand."

"Do you understand the grooming process better?" I said.

"Yeah," Mike said. "Especially when you seal it with a blood oath."

Mike's cell phone vibrated and started twitching on my glass-top table as though it was alive.

He picked it up. "Chapman."

He listened to someone—I could hear a woman's voice speaking to him—before he answered.

"No, ma'am. I wasn't at the hospital on official business," he said. "There is no case. I'm just an acquaintance of Ms. Fain and we happened to be passing behind the courthouse when the medics were working on her."

Mike listened again.

"I can't answer that, but I'm here with one of her best friends."

Mike passed the phone to me. I put down my drink and introduced myself to the woman, who was the head nurse just starting her midnight shift at Bellevue's Neuro ICU. I told her I was a prosecutor in charge of special victims' cases, hoping that would add gravitas to the fact of my friendship.

"Are you related to Ms. Fain?" the nurse asked.

"No. No, I'm not. Just a good friend."

"Are there any relatives I can contact?"

"Her mother's in a nursing home in Texas," I said. "She's got advanced Alzheimer's, and Francie has no siblings. Isn't there anyone who's arrived from her job, from the Legal Aid Society?"

"Not that I'm aware of," the nurse said.

"I'll make some calls." It didn't matter that it was close to midnight. I had an emergency contact list for all the supervisors in the criminal division.

The nurse had a catch in her voice, as though she was holding something back from me.

"I'm looking for someone who knows whether Ms. Fain has a will," she said.

I clasped my hand to my mouth as she went on. "Ms. Fain is on life support, and we need to know whether she has a DNR if things take a worse turn tonight."

"Just a minute," I said, and covered the phone while I spoke to Mike. "Will you go into my office and look for the Legal Aid directory, please? Francie's on life support and they need to know if she has a 'do not resuscitate' order."

"Keep it together, Coop," he said, getting up from the love seat.

"I'll get on this right now," I said to the woman on the phone. "May I please have your number so I can call you back when I find one of her colleagues?"

The nurse gave me her name and the number at the nurses' station.

"Does this mean—this putting Francie on life support—does it mean the doctors know what's wrong? Is there a diagnosis?"

"No one's sure yet," she said. "It's still a puzzle. But brain disorders are very complicated and Ms. Fain has only been here a few hours. Please give us some time."

"I appreciate that," I said, nervously running my finger around the rim of my drinking glass. "I'm a good friend. I was supposed to see her tonight."

"We'll do our jobs on this end," the nurse said, "and the best thing you can do for us is find out where her papers are and who she has designated as her health care proxy."

"Certainly."

Francie was two years younger than me—maybe thirty-six or thirty-seven. What if she hadn't done a will or named a proxy yet?

"May I ask you, Ms. Cooper, might it be as simple as her husband or boyfriend that we should be looking for?"

"Francie isn't married," I said. "There's no boyfriend in the picture either."

"Then I suggest you find me someone to step in

as soon as possible," the nurse said. "There are important decisions to be made—and there are **two** lives at stake."

"Would you say that again?" I asked. "Did I understand you correctly?"

"There are privacy rules, Ms. Cooper. I've already said too much, and whatever happens, you didn't hear it from me. I'm just trying to stress the urgency here."

"I know all about HIPAA," I told her. "So let me be the one to say it to you. Francie's pregnant, I take it."

The nurse didn't respond, but she didn't correct me either.

There was enough need for urgency to save Francie's life. But apparently, the scans had revealed she was also carrying a child.

FOURTEEN

"There's a woman here to see you," Laura said, opening the door to my office wide enough to put her head in. It was shortly after nine A.M. "No appointment, and she'd prefer not to give me her name."

"Am I going to need protection or does she look sane?" I asked, covering my mouth as I yawned.

I finally reached Quint Akers, the chief of the Legal Aid Criminal Defense unit, around midnight. Quint was the man who had hired Francie years back and knew her well. He promised me he would go to the hospital himself, immediately, and continue to reach out to the lawyers on her team to see who knew her best.

I hardly slept at all, worried about Francie Fain's sudden flip from partygoer to patient on life support. And then there was the startling news of her pregnancy, which meant I had been way out of the loop on her private life—more so than I realized.

When I could get the image of my friend, mid-seizure and frothing at the mouth, lying on a city sidewalk out of my mind, I fretted about Lucy Jenner and how she would come out of this ordeal—even if we could prove a case. She had once trusted a prosecutor whose betrayal had cost her the last decade of her life. I wondered how she would fare in my hands as I tried to structure a cold case with no physical evidence.

"The woman looks about as sane as you do," Laura said, "on a good day."

"I deserved that. Send her in," I said. "And see if Max can sit in with me."

Two minutes later, Laura opened the door again and both Max and the woman entered.

"Good morning," I said. "I'm Alexandra Cooper."

"I don't mean to be rude," the woman said, "but I'd like to talk to you alone."

"My paralegal is an essential part of all my cases," I said. "She's as silent as the grave."

The woman flashed a look at Max but then focused back at me. "Thank you, but it just won't work for me," she said, turning on her heels to leave the room. "Stand on ceremony one time too many and the blood will be on **your** hands."

"Ceremony? What are you talking about? Whose blood?"

The well-dressed woman stopped at the door and glared at Max.

"Would you mind, Max?" I asked.

"No point in an unnecessary bloodletting if I'm

the one who's making the difference," Max said, as unflappable as always. She left the room.

First, Lucy Jenner yesterday and now this woman—it seemed like the ncw trend was demanding a private audience with me.

"Thank you, Ms. Cooper," the woman said, taking the chair opposite my desk. "We've never met, but you'll understand the reason I'm here."

I was stone-faced. I didn't like anyone playing games with my time.

"My name is Jessica Witte," she said.

"And your best friend is Janet Corliss, wife of the judge," I said, recognizing the name but not the face of my visitor. "You're a speechwriter for the junior senator."

"That much is all true, but I'd like to keep the senator out of this," Witte said. "She doesn't know I'm here."

"How about Janet?" I asked. "Does she know?"

"Of course. But if she sets foot in this courthouse, where her husband works, word will shoot through the building like wildfire."

"You're very well known, too," I said.

"My words are, Ms. Cooper. But speechwriters are invisible, so I don't expect I'll attract any attention by coming to 100 Centre Street. Our words are front and center, but we stay out of the limelight."

"What is it you want to discuss?" I said.

"Janet is looking for advice about what to do,"

Witte said. "She trusts your judgment and your discretion, and suggested I do the same."

"Does this concern her marriage?"

"It does."

"You need to understand that I work with Judge Corliss," I said. "One of my lawyers is on trial before him this week. I think it's best I turn you over to one of the other assistant district attorneys in my unit."

Jessica Witte put her hand out on my desk to stop me from getting up. "It's your guidance that Janet wants."

"I'm not in private practice, Ms. Witte. The best I can do is recommend some lawyers who can help her."

Jessica Witte shook her head. "You don't get it, do you? Bud Corliss—without his judicial robes—is a violent man. Are you afraid to take him on?"

"I'm fearful of bears and mountain lions and rattlesnakes," I said, thinking of the recent invitation from a law school friend to recover from the trauma of my kidnapping in the wilds of Montana, at his ranch. "Taking on guys who subject women to abuse? Squaring off against them in or out of court doesn't frighten me much at all. It's what I do."

"Fine," Witte said. "Then do it."

"Let me get a few things straight. The Corliss residence is in Bronx County, am I right?"

"Yes, they have a home in Riverdale."

Riverdale is an affluent community in the northwest corner of the Bronx, where many Manhattan businessmen built country estates a century ago.

"If you plan to tell me about events that occurred in another county, I'd best refer you to the Bronx DA's office."

"Janet keeps a pied-à-terre in Manhattan," Witte said. "She inherited it from her father. It's where Bud prefers to stay when he's sitting in this county."

"I didn't know that," I said.

"And you probably don't know that he threatened to kill her."

"We're getting into very serious territory here," I said. "Is Janet willing to come forward and tell me this herself?"

Jessica Witte hesitated. "She wants to know what the consequences will be if she does that. Janet wants to know if your office will prosecute Bud."

"First of all, I can't answer that without knowing specifically what the conduct has been," I said. "I also need to know if there are lawyers involved— any kind of matrimonial action in progress. And lastly, it may be that because Judge Corliss is sitting in Manhattan's Criminal Term, we might have to have a special prosecutor appointed in another county."

"It really sounds like you're ducking responsibility on this one," Witte said.

"Why in the world would I do that?"

"What's the difference if Janet plans to file for divorce? What if she has a lawyer for that purpose?"

"Perhaps no difference at all," I said. "But maybe you know that allegations of domestic abuse sky-rocket during matrimonials. Real ones, of course. And false ones."

"I can't believe you even mention the word 'false' to me," Witte said, snarling at me like a caged wildcat.

"Then why don't you tell me what happened?" I said, leaning back in my chair and steepling my fingers. "Did you hear the threat that the judge made? Did Janet happen to tape it?"

I was always hoping for corroborative evidence to back up the word of a witness. The law didn't require it, but jurors responded better to the existence of something in support of a complainant's word.

"The threat wasn't verbal, Ms. Cooper. It was physical."

What did Corliss tell me yesterday, before my day exploded with Lucy Jenner's story? That I would hear rumors of an assault on Janet—perhaps that he had hit her.

"What did he do, exactly, if you know?"

"Of course I know," Witte said. "Janet's my best friend. They were in the apartment in Manhattan. Bud came home late, claiming he'd been at work till after ten P.M. Janet accused him of infidelity—

she has a bit of a drinking problem and was probably intoxicated, but he's been terribly unfaithful."

There was nothing to be gained by my telling Jessica Witte that I was well aware of his philandering.

"Janet raised her voice and began to yell at Bud. She admitted that to me," Witte said. "But then he did it. He put his hands on her neck—on her throat, actually. Bud choked her. He actually choked her to make her shut up."

I had dozens of questions. What happened after that? Had the judge ever done this to her before? How long was he holding her throat? How was she able to free herself, or did he just let go? But I wanted these answers from the victim, not from her well-meaning best friend.

"That's terrible," I said. "Did Janet have any injuries? Did she go for any medical treatment?"

"She wasn't injured, and she was afraid to go to a doctor because her internist is Bud's doctor, too, so she was certain there'd be no assurance of confidentiality," Witte said. "It doesn't matter, Ms. Cooper. Choking is a crime, whether there are injuries or not."

"My staff deals with that every day of the week, I promise you."

Choking had been a crime in New York State for less than a decade. Prosecutors and advocates—my team—had fought for years to have strangulation added to the penal law because it had usually been ignored as a separate charge of criminal conduct for lack of injury or evidence—yet it was often a strong indicator of a more violent intention by the perpetrator. A man willing to stop the flow of oxygen to his victim—face-to-face—suggested he was capable of far greater violence.

"I wrote a lot of the senator's speeches on domestic abuse, Ms. Cooper," Witte said. "When a man places his hands on a woman's neck, it's really the ultimate form of control and power."

"I'm glad to have the senator in our corner," I said, doubting that Witte's speech research made her much of an expert on the issue. "But now we have to find a way to keep Janet Corliss safe. When did this happen?"

"About two months ago," Witte said.

"Did she continue to live with Bud after that?"

"What was she supposed to do?"

"I'm not second-guessing her at all. My question was not meant to be a criticism of Janet," I said. "She's the rare DV victim who is fortunate enough to have a second residence. I thought perhaps she might have kicked him out."

"Don't you dare blame Janet Corliss," Witte said, wagging a finger at me.

"I'm not in the habit of blaming victims," I snapped back at her. "What is it you want me to do?"

"Janet wants to know if you can come to her office, instead of interviewing her here."

"I've made exceptions like that before for a wide variety of reasons," I said. "I still think it makes more sense for me to send one of my lawyers who hasn't had a professional relationship with the judge, rather than go myself."

I flipped the pages of my daily calendar—still a book I kept on my desktop. "It's already Tuesday and my week is pretty full. That's another good reason to bring in someone else. I'll supervise, of course. Does Janet want an order of protection in the meantime?"

"I don't think that's necessary. Bud knows that she told me about his attack, so he's been pretty well behaved the last couple of months."

I took one of my cards from my desk drawer and passed it to Jessica Witte. "This has my cell number on it. Janet's welcome to use it 24/7 if she has any problems," I said. "She'd be wise to keep it in a place Bud won't find it. It might set him off again to know she's been in touch with me."

Witte took the business card and jammed it into her wallet. "But you can't tell me what would happen if she presses charges?"

"There are too many details I don't know at this moment," I said. "First-degree strangulation, which causes severe injuries, is a felony with mandatory state prison time. Fortunately for Janet, that isn't what you described. If this is the misdemeanor, without injury, there's less likelihood the judge will go to jail. But you wrote the speeches, so you probably know all the distinctions."

Witte was so into her own importance that she didn't take my comment as a dig.

"I'll get back to you about Janet's decision," she said, rising to her feet. "She wants you to know that she's writing a book. It's a novel, but it's sort of about her marriage, and—well, Bud's bad conduct off the bench."

I tried to hide my displeasure. Everyone I knew thought they could write a book. This sounded as though it was likely to fuel the flames of the Corlisses' relationship.

"Tell Janet we'll need to see the manuscript, as far as she's gotten."

"It's just fiction, like I said."

"The manuscript may still be relevant," I said, jotting a note on my pad about the book.

When Jessica Witte opened the door to leave, Laura buzzed me on the intercom. "I've got Quint Akers on line one for you."

"Quint," I said, putting the phone to my ear, "any news? Any improvement?"

"No change at all, but I want to thank you for calling me last night," he said. "It was the right thing to do. I sat with Francie till this morning, talking up a storm—telling war stories and gossiping about our mutual friends—and telling her how much her friends adore her. The docs say you never know what someone in her condition can hear."

"I gave myself a light day at the office," I said. "I'd like to run up for a visit."

"They've moved her, Alex."

"Moved her? Where?"

"To New York/Cornell Hospital. It's got a world-class neurology department."

York Avenue at Sixty-Eighth Street. "I can be there in half an hour."

"No visitors. They won't allow any. Not till they figure this out."

"Did you find out if there's a will?" I asked.

"I've got Francie's phone and we're going through all her contacts, but there doesn't seem to be a trust and estates lawyer or anything connected to making out a will," Quint said. "Young and healthy and everything to live for. The kind of thing even lawyers put off. You got one?"

"Yeah, I actually do." After my first unexpected encounter with someone who wanted me dead, I figured it made good sense to have a will. "What are you going to do about a health care proxy, in case there are decisions to be made?"

"I'm putting together a troika," Quint said. "I don't think anyone should have sole responsibility under the current circumstances. The prospect of what might have to be done is pretty overwhelming."

"You're staying on it, I hope."

Quint Akers had lots of backbone and keen in-telligence. "Yeah, I will."

"Who else are you pulling in?" I asked.

"I've already got Francie's best friend from the trial group, who's been with her since they joined Legal Aid," Quint said. "She's spelling me at the hospital, in case they let anyone back in to see Fran-cie during the day."

"Is there a chance I could be the third one, if you don't have a firm commitment from anyone else yet?" I said.

"Are you serious?" he asked.

"She was on her way to a party for me when she collapsed," I said. "And she wanted to have lunch next week. I feel very—sort of connected to her right now."

I didn't want to tell him that I knew more about her medical condition than I had a right to, nor that she was thinking of leaving her job at Legal Aid. I wanted to do something for her instead of just feel helpless about her condition.

"I think it's a crazy idea, Alex. I mean, suppose we have to make a life-or-death decision," Quint said, "and you're a person who's been an adversary of hers for the length of her legal career."

"That's bullshit, Quint."

"It's the truth. That's what you are. I mean, sup-pose some long-lost relative turns up with a point of view that you oppose, and finds out that your best connection to Francie is that you objected to almost everything she ever said in a court of law?" Quint asked. "I don't need controversy."

"Get real," I said. "She's been my friend for a very long time. Who's your third collaborator going to be? The new man in her life? Do you think he doesn't have a horse in this race?"

Quint took a few moments before he spoke again. "What new man? What are you talking about?"

I guessed the medical staff at New York/Cornell wouldn't tell Quint about Francie's pregnancy until he had officially been granted status as her health care proxy. He didn't seem to know any more than I did at this point.

"Just do what you have to do, Quint," I said. "I'm backup for anything Francie needs."

"Don't hold out on me now," he said.

"I can't help you. I'm the one you don't trust, just 'cause I sit on the other side of the courtroom."

"You know why I won't have you in on this, Alex? 'Cause you're unstable," Quint said. "That kidnapping rocked you. You may be back at your desk, but you're still out to lunch so far as I'm concerned. Just play back this conversation in your head, will you? You're bonkers."

"Troika, my ass," I said. "I have a steadier hand than you ever will, and a keen sense of devotion to my friends. So I hope you use better judgment than you're claiming to have now when it comes to saving Francie's life."

FIFTEEN

Max was back in my office fifteen minutes later.

"Do we have a plan?" she asked.

"I've split up my 'to do' list," I said. "Can you handle half of it for me?"

"Sure."

"Start with Streetwork. Ask them to report in to you twice a day, starting today, about how Lucy Jenner is responding to their efforts."

"They're not going to snitch on her, you know," Max said. "They're advocates and counselors and therapists who'll be working with her."

"I'm not looking for a snitch. I trust their work completely. But I want intel on whether Lucy's co-operating with their efforts to get her on her feet, and trying to make sure she doesn't go AWOL"

"What else?" Max said, nodding her head and writing everything down on a legal pad.

"I'm giving you the SOL laws to brief for me," I said. "Statutes of limitations for prosecuting sexual abuse of an underage girl in Oregon, Utah, and

Iowa for starters. The ages and requirements are likely to be different in every state."

"Am I looking for forcible assaults or statutory?" Max asked.

"I still don't have the details of each encounter yet, so you might as well search for both," I said.

"Lucy was fourteen when she met Zachary Palmer?" Max asked.

"For the time being, with an entire legal staff surrounding us, let's continue to refer to him as Jake."

"Sorry."

"Don't be silly," I said. "It's a unique situation and we'll have to make up rules for this as we go along."

"Fourteen?" she asked again.

"That's what she says. But her aunt makes her out to be an unreliable storyteller, so I'll spend a few hours today trying to run down some of her claims against him. The things she told me last night," I said. "See if we can corroborate her recollections with dates of hearings and local news clips—so we can match up her whereabouts, her age at the time—all that kind of thing before we move on to hotel records. Start with information in the public domain before we try to get it some other way."

"But suppose we need subpoenas? Who's our go-to person for sign-offs on them or the use of government search engines and any expenses we incur?" Max said.

"Me."

She squinted and looked me in the eye.

"No, really," Max said.

"Battaglia's dead and the front office is in complete turmoil. This is only my second day back at my desk, but it's pretty obvious," I said.

"You should be reporting to someone, Alex. It's safer that way."

"The special election is almost six months away, in April. All the executive assistants and super-titled special counsel designees are tripping over each other to sit closest to Paul Battaglia's empty throne."

Max had always been solidly in my corner.

"So who do you trust in this scramble for power in the pecking order above me?" I asked. "Pat McKinney?"

McKinney, the chief of the Trial Division, had a tortured history with me. Although technically higher up in the chain of command and above me in rank, he resented that Battaglia had urged me to skip over him to report directly to the DA. McKinney was sour and stubborn and would do almost anything to thwart an investigation I led.

"Never," Max said.

I reeled off four other names to her.

"It's kind of like the Seven Dwarfs in the inner

sanctum," she said, responding to my list. "Dopey, Lazy, Grumpy, and Dweeby."

"Which one of them has ever handled a rape investigation?" I asked.

"Not one. But the weight of all this doesn't fall on your back alone if things go terribly wrong, once you've run it up the ladder," Max said.

"Things have gone terribly wrong for Lucy Jenner since she was fourteen," I said. "There are so many loose rungs on that ladder in the executive wing at the moment that I'd rather take the hit and avoid it. Besides, I certainly don't know if Lucy has every detail right—memories can occasionally take strange detours over time. But I believe the broad strokes of her story."

Max just looked at me and nodded.

"Don't worry," I said with a smile. "You can always say 'I told you so.'"

"I'm ready to run with this," she said, turning to leave the room. "Pile on anything else you need."

The day was a mix of the usual things—phone calls from detectives and witnesses wanting updates on their cases, meetings with assistants in the unit to help strategize about upcoming trials, helping Laura handle the flow of walk-ins who wanted interviews about assorted criminal events, and trying to get deeper into the facts of Lucy's case.

Mercer showed up an hour after Max left the

room. He brought me another large cup of black coffee and sat down across from me.

"How goes it?" he asked. "What do you know about Francie?"

"Quint Akers is running the show," I said, leaning back in my chair. "He's cutting me out of things because he thinks I'm mad."

"Mad what? Mad at **him**?"

"Nope. Mad, as in unbalanced," I said, blowing on the hot dark liquid. "You've been through this whole post-kidnapping thing with me, Mercer. Am I unbalanced?"

"You serious?"

"Dead serious."

"Your hands are steady as the Rock of Gibraltar holding that cup of mud you're about to drink," Mercer said. "A month ago, you were trembling like a hummingbird."

"I feel good," I said. "I think people are sticking me with a label."

"Prove them wrong. Take a slam-dunk case away from one of the kids and stand on your own two feet," Mercer said. "Be top trial dog again."

I poked my finger at the stack of Lucy's paperwork on my desktop. "Stay with me on this one. I'd rather reestablish my bones with a gnarly mess like this case."

"Always with you," he said. "Find anything yet?"

I had the bag of items the police had taken from Lucy and vouchered. "Illinois driver's license, with a Chicago address," I said, handing it to him. "She lied about her date of birth on it. Makes herself twenty-two, two years younger than she is, according to the facts we know."

"I wonder when that started," Mercer said, jotting down the info on the license. "The lying about her age, I mean."

"Will you try to get a birth certificate?" I asked. "If we make a statutory case, then everything relies on her age—down to the month and the day—since she was moving around from state to state in prep for Welly's trial."

"No problem. Public record, probably Illinois, right?"

"Probably," I said. "And see if Kathy Crain is still an agent. She'll be a critical witness in this, if she hasn't been brainwashed by Jake along the way. I don't want to make any contact with her yet, but we need to know who's available if this picks up any speed."

Our lists grew and grew throughout the next few hours, and we stopped only to eat the sandwiches we ordered in.

At three o'clock, Laura buzzed me on the intercom. "Line two, Alex. I've got Zachary Palmer."

I froze for a second, looking like a deer in the headlights with all of the evidence of Palmer's split personality laid out on my desk. Then I shrugged as I looked over at Mercer and picked up the phone.

"Alexandra Cooper," I said.

"Madame Prosecutor. It's Zach," he said. "How are you doing?"

"All good. And you?"

"Top of my game," Zach said.

"Glad to hear it. Are we still on for a drink?"

"Something's come up that's going to make me late," he said. "Can we change it to dinner instead? Eight o'clock."

"I can do that," I said. "How about Patroon? It's my favorite steak place, and they make a fine cocktail."

"Good idea," he said. "We can put a little bit of meat on you. Fatten you up, Alex."

"Fatten me up? What, for the kill?"

"Oh yeah," Zach said. "I'm just looking to slaughter you at the polls next April, if you go that far. That's why I'm trying to rattle some of the skeletons in your closet now."

I seemed to be surrounded by people who were counting the chinks in my armor, but I had every reason to believe that Zachary Palmer's closet had more skeletons in it than my own.

"Rattle away, my friend," I said. "Game on."

SIXTEEN

Mike and I were driving up Third Avenue toward East Forty-Sixth Street, where Patroon was located, squaring the block so that he could park in front.

"What did Zach Palmer do in the Weldon Baynes case that was so unusual?" Mike asked.

"Back at the time of Baynes's rampage, Zach was a civil rights lawyer for the Department of Justice," I said. "He had always been a political activist, with a great record at NYU Law School. When the double murder happened in Salt Lake City, the attorney general assigned Zach to prosecute the case."

"You mean, just that one case?"

"Yes, that's how it started," I said. "But when he looked at the big picture, it was obvious that Welly Baynes was a white supremacist who had terrorized the country by going around shooting blacks, especially when they associated with white people. He did the same thing with Jews."

"Jews? But he didn't get tried for that in Utah," Mike said.

"Not then. Because Zach was smart enough to hone his issue down for the purpose of getting leverage for the trial," I said. "Look, Baynes even shot the white guy who published **True Hustling** magazine, because he printed articles showing interracial couples having sex."

"That guy who was paralyzed? Still in a wheelchair?"

"That's the one. Also a different issue and a separate trial," I said. "But in putting together the Salt Lake case, Zach came up with a novel theory. Instead of a murder case, he found an unusual statute that made it a federal crime to kill people—because of their race—in a public park."

"So the Civil Rights Division got to handle these cases," Mike said. "That's why Zach was able to bring in other incidents, like Lucy's."

"Yes. He was successful in arguing that the cases be joined—since he had federal jurisdiction in all of them—and tried together, in Salt Lake City."

"So he dragged Lucy all over the place with him—wherever there were pretrial hearings and opportunities for him to keep her close," Mike said.

"And everybody in her life—from her aunt to Agent Crain to the Palmer's Posse team—thought he was watching out for the girl and taking great care to prepare her for the rigors of her testimony," I said.

"The bastard fooled a lot of people," Mike said, checking the time on his watch. "You're way early."

"I figured this gives us a chance for the **Jeopardy!** question," I said, "and also a chance for Stephane to find me the quietest table so I can record the conversation."

Mike slammed his foot on the brake and the car jolted. I braced myself against the dashboard. "Record Zach Palmer?"

"Don't say it. I'm nuts, right? Join the parade."

Mike reached across me and grabbed my tote from the floor of the car, beneath my feet.

"Bad guess. You're not even warm," I said as he rummaged through it.

"Where's the recorder?" Mike said, having lost every trace of his characteristic humor. "You can't tape a lawyer, kid. You've refused to do it with sleazebag after sleazebag whenever I've asked you to."

"This is different."

"Yeah, it's different," Mike said. "Because **you** want to do it. That's the only thing that makes it different."

"Oh, no," I said. "The rules have changed."

"You always told me that taping another lawyer would smack of trickery," Mike said, turning in the driver's seat so that he was facing me. "That lady and gentleman lawyers wouldn't behave like that to each other. That—what was it—the New York City Bar Association forbids it, and you didn't want to be sanctioned by them."

"You just said it yourself. Zachary Palmer is apparently everything but a gentleman. He had a sexual relationship with his star witness in a federal case," I said, "and she was under the age of consent at the time. And I don't even know yet, but some of the contact may have been forcible."

"What about ethics, Coop? Did you throw them out the window with your good judgment?"

"The bar association woke up to the fact that everyone has the ability to record conversations with commonplace devices like phones," I said.

"Then put your phone on the table and go to town," Mike said.

"Zach's likely to check me out on that," I said. "He's not stupid. He'll play with my phone and tell me he has to make a call."

"Then skip it."

"The ethics rules now say a lawyer is permitted to tape another lawyer in pursuit of the common good—and you can bet the good is on my side. I'm wired up for a super-clear recording I can use if this case goes forward."

"Where's your recorder?"

"It's a professional hookup, Detective," I said, sitting up straight, my shoulders back and my breasts standing at attention. "The tech guys in the DA's Squad put the teeniest device possible—a micro-camera with an audio recorder—right inside the top button on my blouse."

"That, kid, was one stupid fucking idea," Mike said.

He reached over, holding my shoulder with one hand, and using the other to rip the top button off my pale pink shirt.

SEVENTEEN

"**Bon soir,** Madame Cooper," Stephane said, looking a bit surprised as Mike and I stepped into the dining room. The suave Frenchman had been the maître d' at Aretsky's Patroon since the day it opened twenty years ago. "I have your reservation at eight P.M. You're a bit early."

"That's right," I said. "We're intentionally early. Mike and I are going to go into the bar until my guest arrives."

"**Bien sûr,**" he said. "I think you know the way."

The cozy bar was at the right rear of the restaurant. I walked ahead of Mike, adjusting my blouse so that the missing button wouldn't be noticed.

I asked the bartender for some sparkling water, figuring it was better for me to be totally sharp during my face-to-face with Zach. Mike ordered a Tito's vodka martini straight up, with a twist.

We sat at a small table in the corner, in direct line of sight of the small television mounted above the impressive row of single-malt Scotches.

Mike held out his hand to me to return the

button. "Sorry, but I'm trying to save you some embarrassment."

I took the small object and threw it in my tote. "No hard feelings. You have to do what you think is right," I said. "But you'll be entirely to blame if Zach says anything I'd want to have as evidence."

Mike laughed. "Don't get all snarly and start sniping at me for de-buttoning you," he said. "I was just looking out for you. Do you want me here for this meeting?"

"No, but thanks. I just want Zach to see that I have you at my back, in case he thinks I'm weak-kneed," I said. "I'll just greet him, introduce you, and then you can head out. I'm sure he'll ask me a ton of questions about you."

"You plan to play him that you're interested in succeeding Battaglia?"

"I'd be crazy not to until I know what happened to Lucy," I said. "He'll be the front-runner unless I can prove he's a predator. It makes sense to see who else wants to get in the race. I just want to slow him down a bit until I know what the entire field of candidates looks like."

"It's okay that Zach knows that—that—I'm—"

I reached over and took hold of his hand. "Say it, Mike. You can say the **L** word, can't you?"

He ran his fingers through his hair. He was having a hard time suppressing his smile. "That I'm living with you?"

"Wrong **L**, you coward. Living with? Try again."

"You're the one who doesn't like public displays of affection," he said, starting in on his drink and changing the subject. "Is that why you don't want to get into the race? Because you're living with a cop, instead of someone more suitable to your background? You think your opponents would slam you for going down low in your private life instead of waiting for Prince Charming?"

"Michael Chapman, what's this sudden inferiority complex?"

"Look at you, kid. Wellesley College, University of Virginia School of Law, a trustafarian doing public service while your old man's fortune keeps you living high on Park Avenue, slipping off to your Vineyard getaway, dressing in Escada, and dining at the best joints in the city," Mike said. "Why would you be hanging out with me?"

My father, Benjamin Cooper, met my mother, Maude, when she was a nurse working in the same hospital where he started practicing medicine. I was still a kid when he and his partner invented a tiny plastic device—the Cooper-Hoffman Valve, as it came to be known—which is still used today in every heart operation worldwide that involves valve replacement. I loved my job, and was able to comfortably remain in the public sector because of the trust fund my parents had established for my two older brothers and for me.

"Because I love you," I said. "It's really simple. I love your courage and fearlessness—the way you go into the darkest places of the human soul and come out with guys who should never walk among us again. Who else does that but a terrifically smart and strong Homicide detective?"

Mike's late father, Brian, had been a great detective before him, and was thrilled that Mike chose to go to Fordham College and pursue his interest in military history. But shortly after Mike graduated, Brian died of a massive coronary the same day he turned in his shield and gun.

"That's all I know how to do," he said.

I went on. "Did you ever think that you might be my Prince Charming?"

Mike stirred the vodka with his finger. "That would mean you've hit rock bottom, blondie, and that's after going through a load of guys who've auditioned for the job."

"Nobody but you would have had the patience to get me back on my feet."

"Frankly, you were a pain in the ass the other way," Mike said, getting up to ask the bartender to put **Jeopardy!** on the screen.

We sat at the small table in the bar area for another fifteen minutes, just talking about how we were going to spend the next couple of fall weekends. There was a sweetness to this side of Mike when we were alone together, and I didn't want to sacrifice it to a political career that would threaten to rip us apart.

He spotted the Final Jeopardy! section before I

did and called out to the bartender to turn up the volume.

Trebek stepped aside to reveal the category, which was a single word on the big blue screen: Monsters.

"We should both be good at this one," Mike said, putting his twenty dollars on the small tabletop.

"You like horror movies better than I do," I said, matching his bet.

"**Creature from the Black Lagoon,**" Mike said. "That's my favorite. Man taking on the Gill Man in his own element."

"I can't even watch it. When I saw it as a kid, it was probably another month before I'd get in a bathtub again. I'm stuck at twenty bucks."

"Here's tonight's Final Jeopardy! answer," Trebek said. "'Age of the author who created the Franken-stein monster.'"

Mike groaned. "A question about literature disguised as a mysterious monster."

Then the longtime host of the show laughed and said, "Of course, you'll have to know who the author was to know this one."

"What's your answer, Detective?" I asked.

"You've already swallowed the canary, haven't you? Gloating doesn't become you," Mike said, "in case you thought this was a good look. You know this dude Trebek makes ten million dollars a year to stand here for half an hour a day asking trivia questions?"

"Best guess," I said, walking two fingers across the table toward the forty-dollar pile. "Changing the subject is a real tell that you're clueless."

Mike threw up his hands and then took a hit of vodka. "Who was—who was the man who wrote Frankenstein?"

"Such a bad answer," I said, "and so sexist to boot."

"What?"

I took the bills, held them with both hands, and snapped them tight before stuffing them in my tote. "**Frankenstein**—also entitled **The Modern Prometheus**—was written by Mary Shelley," I said, "when she was eighteen years old. Eighteen. Can you imagine?"

"What a misspent youth you had," Mike said, "with your nose in a book all the time."

I leaned forward. "Very apt character for this moment. Do you know what Victor Frankenstein's last words were?"

"Nope. Go on," Mike said. "Show off, why don't you? There's no one else here but me, but all that knowledge squeezed in behind your eyebrows must hurt to carry around."

"It only hurts when I can't impart my wisdom to you," I said. "'Seek happiness in tranquillity,'" I said, quoting the fictional scientist who created the monster, "'and avoid ambition.'"

"What's your point?"

"I don't need to do anything but my work and

to be with you. No playing politics with people's lives," I said.

"Hold that thought for an hour or two," Mike said, looking over the top of my head. "I think the man himself is here."

"Zach Palmer?" I asked.

"Keep your eyes on me," Mike said. "Stephane is directing him this way."

Zach came up behind me, leaned over and put his arms around me—in a way that suggested too much intimacy. "'Alexandra Cooper, for the People,'" he said, in a low voice, doing his best to imitate me. "How many times have you uttered that phrase standing in the well of a courtroom, striking fear in the hearts of your adversaries?"

"I hope fear was never the operative word, Zach," I said, shaking myself loose and standing up to exchange kisses on the check.

"Oh, that old search-for-the-truth thing," he said, reaching out to shake Mike's hand. "You must be Mike Chapman."

"I am."

"How do you like my opposition research?" Zach asked. "I'm ahead of the curve, don't you think?"

"You usually are," I said, grinning at him, despite the fact that my stomach was roiling at the idea of him oozing what he thought was his charm on a teenage victim.

"So if you're the guy for Alexandra, Detective,"

Zach said, pointing to his own hand, "how come you haven't put a ring on it yet?"

"I'm just waiting for her to ask me, Mr. Palmer," Mike said. "Coop always leads when we dance, so I'm just being patient until she kneels down and proposes."

"Oh, he'll be good on the hustings, Alexandra," Zach said, wagging a finger in Mike's direction. "Those women voters will love that you're the alpha dog and Mike follows your lead. It wouldn't work so well in Queens or on Staten Island, but the ladies in Manhattan will eat up your moxie."

"You're making too many assumptions, Zach," I said. "About the race to fill Paul's seat, that is."

"Then let's talk," he said.

"Sure. Let's go to our table."

I got up and went to the entrance of the dining room. Stephane saw me—in that seamless, fluid movement of a great maître-d'—and came toward us. "Your table is ready, madame."

"Are you staying for dinner, Mike?" Zach asked. "Because my body man can join us, too."

"Body man?" I said.

"You've got to jump into the action, Alexandra. Every politician has a body man who's the top aide, sticks by his side," Zach said. "That's how it's done these days. Seems like you've got some catching up to do."

"I'm a lot of things," Mike said, "but I am not about to be Coop's body man."

Mike said good night and headed to the exit.

I followed Stephane to our table, nodding at some of the regular diners I knew from frequent visits to the restaurant as I wound my way through the tables to a quiet corner banquette near the front window.

As Mike walked away, an attractive woman, younger than me, maybe thirty-four or thirty-five—passed him, coming in our direction.

"Are you all set, boss?" she asked. "Shall I wait for you in the car?"

"Thank you, Josie. We'll be about an hour," Zach said. "This is Ms. Cooper, by the way."

I tried not to stare at her, but I couldn't place our connection. She was as tall as I was—about five foot ten—but more wiry. Her auburn hair was swept up in a ponytail, and she was dressed all in black. Her face looked so familiar to me.

She smiled and waved at me. "Hi, I'm Josie Breed."

"Alex. Alex Cooper."

"Josie worked with me at Justice," Zach said. "She was an agent just out of Quantico but handled some of my big cases. She's tough. Smart, fearless, and tough."

Of course. Josie was one of the young agents standing on the steps of the Utah courthouse after the conviction of Welly Baynes. I had seen her picture yesterday—several versions of it—in all of the news clips about the trial. She must know Lucy Jenner, too.

"Nice to meet you," I said. "We'll have to talk sometime. I bet you've had some fascinating experiences."

"You'll be seeing a lot of her," Zach said. Then he winked at me. "Leave it to me, Alex. There's no rule against a body man being a good-looking girl."

EIGHTEEN

I sat down and straightened my blouse, trying to cover the pull in the cloth where my button had been.

"One bit of advice, Zach," I said, smiling at him as I spread my napkin on my lap. "Bad times to call a thirtysomething heat-packing former Feebie a 'girl.' I'm sure she's a formidable young woman."

"I know it's your job," he said, "but this Me Too bullshit isn't going to last through next spring. It's just a moment in time, before everybody goes back to doing what they used to do."

I looked up at Stephane as he apologized for interrupting to take our drink order. His gracious interruption saved me from responding to Zach's stupid remark in a fit of pique. "Dewar's for you, madame? And for you, sir?"

"Let me have a Hendrick's gin martini, straight up with olives," Zach said, "and then give us a few minutes to talk before we make our dinner decisions."

"**Bien sûr,** monsieur."

"So how are you feeling?" Zach asked, putting on his best sincere face.

"Good. I'm really good. I love being back at work and I think I've managed to put my kidnapping in the rearview mirror."

"I'm happy to hear that," Zach said. "I was getting really mixed reports about how you were dealing with the post-traumatic stress."

"Maybe you're asking the wrong people."

"Is it the meds keeping you steady? All those antianxiety drugs do wonders for people these days."

"I'm off the meds," I said. While they were the right option for some people, Zach was probably hoping to use the fact that I had been dependent on them for his campaign prep, figuring I might further unravel along the way.

"Good. Good for you," Zach said. "They help some people a lot and others get totally fucked up by the chemicals."

Stephane placed the drinks in front of each of us, and Zach lifted his glass to say "Cheers."

"Tell me what it is you want to talk about," I said.

"You were always pretty direct, so let's get to it," Zach said. "On December 1, I'm going to declare that I'm running for Battaglia's seat in the special election next April. There are a lot of dark horses—none quite as dark as me, which is pretty much to my advantage—so I'm making the rounds to see where they all stand."

"Who have you got on your list?"

"So far, I'm figuring the clowns in the executive wing of your office will duke it out among themselves, and the last man standing will jump in. Maybe McKinney, maybe that other spineless guy, Spindler. Has either of them told you?"

"I haven't seen much of them. Today's only my second day back, and neither of them were on my short list of visitors."

"I figured the attorney general would make the power grab," Zach said, "'cause there's not a soul in this state can tell what an AG does when he goes to work every day."

I laughed. "You're right about that."

"But then he—that great champion of women's rights—got caught up by four broads claiming he had them role-playing S and M bondage games in the bedroom, so he's out of my way," Zach said. "Actually, I began licking my chops when he took his big fall."

"Who else?"

"There's a partner at one of the boutique criminal defense firms who's made a fortune representing a drug cartel," Zach said. "A graduate of your office, about ten years before your time."

"Name?"

"I'm not dealing in names yet," Zach said. "No point giving him any allies before he makes a decision. But he's really vulnerable."

"Just because he represented drug dealers?" I asked.

Zach leaned in to me, stirring his martini before holding the glass to his lips. "More because I have so much negative stuff on him—personal stuff—that he wouldn't be able to run for dogcatcher by the time I'm done leaking it to the press."

"And women?" I asked. "It's long overdue to have the first woman in this job."

"Look, there's a retired judge who ran twice against Battaglia and lost both times," Zach said. "She didn't even pull twenty percent, so I don't think she's jumping in again."

"There are others," I said. "I can think of three or four women who'd be great at the top. Stars, each of them."

"I'm thinking you're the lady law that everybody is watching," Zach said, reaching his hand out to put it on top of mine. "I don't want to make a move until I know what you're doing."

I shook it free and picked up my glass. "Why me?"

"Where do I start? Name recognition," he said. "Every time you pick up a tabloid newspaper in this town, you're putting some pervert behind bars—hear me out—and that's a good thing. You'll have the Women's Bar Association, maybe even the DEA and PBA, too."

The Detectives Endowment Association and the Police Benevolent Association made big noise endorsing candidates, but all their members lived in outer boroughs or the suburbs.

I was mildly amused. I had never stopped to

think of groups that might rally behind me if I made the run. "Go on," I said, smiling broadly. "You're beginning to make it sound easy for me."

"When's the last time you checked online for New York City women's groups?" Zach asked. "Women in Finance, Women in Real Estate, Women in Film, Women in Fashion, and so on. That's before I even tally the advocacy groups who think you walk on water for your victims work."

"Are you cutting this down by gender? No men for me, except the cops?"

"Too many women to count before you hook some men on board, Coop," Zach said, sitting back and grinning at me.

"How about we turn this around? You've been raising money already," I said. "I hear from all my friends at law firms and corporate headquarters that you've been spreading your charisma all over town. And of course, you're deep in the pocket of that unholy man of the cloth—Reverend Hal Shipley."

"That fat fuck? Whoops, excuse my language, Alex, but that fat fraud will buy every vote he possibly can if I give him the cash," Zach said. "You know that as well as I do."

"I could have guessed it, but you make it crystal clear."

"I'll deny I ever said it," Zach said, patting his jacket and pants pocket, top to bottom and back up again. "Damn, I think I left my phone in the car and I have to check on something. May I borrow—?"

"Of course," I said, reaching into my tote and passing my phone to him after unlocking the password.

Like I told Mike, I knew he'd check whether I was recording him if he veered off the reservation.

He put his reading glasses on his nose, opened the phone, and looked at the phone setting. He dialed a number and spoke to someone for less than ten seconds, just saying he'd be late. All a ruse, I was sure, to double-check on whether I had recorded him.

Zach handed the phone back to me. "The mayor is Reverend Shipley's puppet, and now the Rev wants to expand his political empire. The only thing I agree with him about is that with the disproportionate arrests of black and brown citizens in this city, it's time for a candidate of color to be DA."

"So you'll be Shipley's puppet, too?"

"Hell, no. I'll rip those strings off as soon as I'm elected," Zach said. "That man's a fool. A corrupt fool."

"Don't you have to live in Manhattan to run for DA of this county?" I asked. "Aren't you still in New Jersey?"

"I guess you had no reason to know, but my wife and I split," Zach said. "We'd been having an on-and-off thing for years. It was just time for me to go."

"You have a place?"

"A fine apartment in Sugar Hill," Zach said.

During the Harlem Renaissance of the 1920s, a wealthy community of African Americans built homes in a northern neighborhood of Hamilton Heights that came to be known as Sugar Hill, reflecting the sweet life the neighborhood provided. Willie Mays, Duke Ellington, and W. E. B. Du Bois were among the prominent residents. It would be a proper political launching pad for Zachary Palmer.

"There are some beautiful homes in Sugar Hill," I said. "So I know you wanted to talk skeletons, Zach. Why not get started?"

He held his arms up in the air. "Just doing my due diligence, right?"

"Maybe it will help me make my decision. I'll tell you what," I said, acting playful for a purpose. "Give me your hands."

I held mine out in front of me. Zach just raised his eyebrows and looked at me.

"C'mon. Just do it. When I was a kid, my friends said I had a knack for seeing the future," I said. "Maybe I can tell if you've got rising political fortunes—or not. C'mon. Put them right here."

My palms were facing up when he placed his hands on top of mine. I rested them on the tabletop, in the middle, and slid mine away from underneath.

I picked up his right hand and turned it over, running my fingers over the skin.

"Wait a second, Alexandra," Zach said, trying to pull away. "Palm reading?"

"I think it's as reliable as political polling these days, don't you?"

"You can't be serious," he said.

"See this," I said, pointing to the line that went from his pinky across to his index finger. "This is your heart line, Zach. And it's really strong. So maybe you left your wife, but your love life is great."

"Whatever you say."

"Then there's the head line—this one that runs across the middle of your palm. The fact that it reaches over here to your ring finger means you're smart—but we knew that—and that you have great potential."

"Just what I'm trying to tell you," Zach said, pulling his hand away.

But what I wanted was to see whether Zach Palmer still bore the scar of the blood oath he had made with Lucy Jenner, and now I knew there wasn't a trace of it on his right hand.

I grabbed his left hand, but he balled it up into a fist and wouldn't turn it over.

"Humor me, Zach," I said. "Just let me see your fate line for a second."

He picked up his martini with his right hand and gave me his left.

"See that?" I said. "Your fate line intersects with your life line."

"What, pray tell, does that mean—other than that I'm really hungry?"

"If I remember my ninth-grade wizardry, it's telling me that your career is going to be very much affected by your emotions. That you've got great potential but you're short-tempered, too. And then," I said, peering down as though I was studying the imaginary lines and scrunching up my nose, "there's something in your past that troubles you."

Zach looked at me and sneered. "You must have the wrong guy's palm, babe," he said, pulling back again. "Don't tell me I have to add witchcraft to your résumé when we prep for debates."

I felt like Lucy had punched me in the gut for sucking me into her story—or at least the part of it that described their blood oath in an Iowa hotel room. If there was something in Zach's past that troubled him, it hadn't left a scar on his skin.

NINETEEN

"I'm going to begin by putting my experience up against yours, to give you a reality check," Zach said. "You're a one-trick pony. Prosecutor for your entire career. Putting people behind bars is all you do."

"My team has exonerated more men who've been falsely accused than all the innocence projects in the country put together," I said.

"I was an assistant United States attorney for a time, with a much greater scope than you've had. Then I went on to Justice, before teaching Con Law at NYU."

"You obviously thought well enough of me to ask me to lecture for your classes, year after year."

"Yeah, and you gave the same lecture every time," Zach said. "Just added a few new war stories is all you did. I went back to Justice and was the liaison to Homeland Security."

Both of his hands formed a giant circle in the air.

"I get it, Zach. You're global, not that people

voting to get criminals out of their neighborhoods care much about that fact in their local prosecutor."

"Oh, they **will** care, Alex. The specter of 9/11 still hangs over this city like an albatross wrapping its wings around the neck of a drowning man," Zach said. "I'll bring up my Homeland Security experience in a post-9/11 city every chance I get."

In between pressing me about how many times I'd been overturned on appeal and the record of the office on minority hiring, he ordered a steak and I opted for Dover sole. We both needed a strong second drink.

"What were you doing with Paul Battaglia the night he was murdered?" Zach asked.

"You know what?" I said. "I'm still not really sure how he wound up on the steps of the museum. It was a setup by the guy who wanted him dead."

"The anti-Coops will be picketing with copies of the headlines that blamed you for his death."

"They'd be wrong," I said.

"Are you ready to relive it?" Zach asked "Or will it look like you put on some sexy pantyhose and your highest heels to step over his still-warm corpse to take his place? The people who voted for Battaglia for six terms will be shocked to find out that in the end, you really had no respect for him."

"He was a complicated man."

"Then there's your love life," Zach said, smiling at me again. "I seem to think voters like women who haven't climbed in and out of bed with a lot of guys. Maybe you should have stopped along the way to rock a cradle."

"Off-limits, Zach."

"I'd like to help you, but nobody can stop the rumors that are out there." He started ticking off names of men I had dated, whether or not I'd been intimate with them.

"What did you do? Have a GPS on my ass?" I asked, stopping for a double swallow of Scotch. "How about we turn those tables on you?"

"Take your best shot, Alex, but I just don't think you have it in you to be tough enough to throw mud at any of the candidates—especially me. It's not your style."

"I'm a quick study when I put my mind to something," I said. "How long were you married?"

"Six years. Amicable split. The ex is totally in my corner," Zach said.

"Kids?"

"Fraternal twins, a boy and a girl."

"You left them, too?" I asked.

"Joint custody. They're killer cute," Zach said. "Gonna be great on the campaign trail."

"Did you ever sleep with one of your students, Zach? At the law school, I mean."

"I like your style, Alex. Starting right at the jugular," Zach said. "Only the one I married, is the answer to that."

"How about the women you worked cases with?" I asked. "Ever hit on a colleague on your trial team?"

"That's taking me way back," he said. "Are you counting mutual attraction, or who hit first?"

"I'm trying to count any breathing being who might suddenly stand up and shout out what you did to her and when," I said. Then in a mocking, breathy voice, "'There I was, pounding out my closing argument late at night in my office, when I heard a knock on the door, and it was Zach—'"

"Not my MO, Alex," Zach said, almost chuckling. "I never knocked. I just eased on in the door, if you know what I mean."

"Josie Breed?" I asked.

"No way," he said. "No test-driving the body man."

"Agents? Agents in general, when you were out on the road, working some of your high-profile magic?" I said. "It's lonely going from town to town, I'm sure."

"You don't know half of it."

"Kathy Crain?" I asked. "Wasn't she out on the road with you, back in the day?"

"Special Agent Katharine Crain," Zach said, looking at me over the lip of his drinking glass. "Now, that was a fine woman. You knew her?"

"I—I, uh, met her somewhere—about two years back, maybe three. It must have been some kind of women-in-law-enforcement thing, and I know she asked about you," I said. "She wanted to know if I knew you or had any experience with you."

Zach's brow furrowed. "That's kind of weird. I thought Kathy had gone off the grid. Retired down south because she wanted to get away from the action."

He was definitely distracted by my mention of her name. I didn't know Kathy Crain, but she must be sitting on a gold mine of negative info about Zach, having observed him in such close quarters. It was her urging, in part, that put Lucy Jenner in his hands.

"Did Kathy talk about me?" he asked. "She worked a big case with me, for a very long time."

"I remember that. I think in this business we all remember what you did to nail that bastard Welly Baynes," I said. "You get total props for that conviction, and it will be a huge gold star for you on the campaign trail."

Zach nodded his head.

"Kathy, by the way, only had nice things to say," I said, "and, well, she mentioned what a rough time it was for all of you putting the Baynes prosecution together. Lots of bumps in that road. When I asked her to talk about them with me, she told me it wasn't the time."

"How long ago was that? I mean, when you had this chat with Kathy Crain?"

"Two, maybe three years ago," I said.

He was biting his lip and staring into his drink.

"C'mon, Zach. You look concerned," I said, teasing him. "You do it with Kathy Crain?"

"She was old enough to be my mother," he said, still thinking of something else, it seemed to me. Then he shook off whatever cloud had passed through his mind and smiled. "I don't do old, Alex."

"Aha! So all I have to do is keep my eyes open for the barely legals who show up at your rallies, huh?"

"What you sound like now is my wife," Zach said. "My ex-wife."

"Tough assignment," I said. "You remind me so much of Jake. Always sniffing around where he didn't belong."

Zach Palmer put down his glass and glared at me.

"What did you just say?"

"Trust me, it wasn't a compliment," I said, faking a laugh. "Jake—and looking for love in all the wrong places. That's all I meant."

"Jake?" Zach looked angry now, as he spit out words at me. "What are you talking about?"

"Don't go showing that mad face on the campaign trail," I said. "I'm not sure what kind of line I crossed, but I've come close to a major nerve, I think?"

"Kathy Crain," Zach said. "She was using the name Jake?"

I put out both hands in front of me. "Slow down, Mr. Palmer. You remember Jake Tyler?"

The wrinkles on his brow returned.

"I'm talking about Jake Tyler, the guy I used to date," I said. "The NBC newsman—you know, he was third string for Brian Williams and Lester Holt. I introduced you to him because he did a really strong profile of you when you were at Justice."

"Sure. Your news jock," he said.

"Yes, the guy who cheated on me with that actress who was found dead on Martha's Vineyard. Isabella Lascar—murdered while she was staying at my home," I said. "With my lover. Jake Tyler. What you said about yourself just reminded me of my own lousy experience with an unfaithful man."

He was examining me with his deep brown eyes as though he could measure my truth-telling by letting them bore into me.

"You're free to use that story if I run against you," I said. "It's bound to have every woman in the room sympathizing with me."

"Here's the deal, Alex. I wanted to meet with you tonight to convince you not to run, okay?"

"You're doing a fine job so far," I said. "You're hurling those slings and arrows at me like I did something wrong."

"You did pretty well yourself," Zach said. "Look, I want to be district attorney of this county for all the right reasons. The perception of justice in this town is completely skewed, and I've got the chops to get things fixed. Get the low-level criminals out of jail, stop prosecuting black and brown men for misdemeanors that white guys don't get picked up for, reform Riker's Island—which is a hellhole right now."

"You think I don't care about those things?"

"I'm here to make a deal with you, Alex."

"You rip me to shreds and then you say you've got a deal to offer me?" I asked. "Not likely."

Zach was laser-focused again. "Stay out of the race, which is going to get ugly."

"Why are you so sure about that? Just because you're going to stir things up?"

"No, not for that reason," Zach said. "You know as well as anyone, this position is like a lifetime appointment. No term limits, and every DA we have stays in for six or eight election cycles."

He was right about that.

"It's the only job I want—the cap in my career— and this election will be my sole chance to secure it. I'll be eighty years old by the time someone your age hangs up her hat and walks away from the job, if you were to get it. It's a pretty powerful position, and I'm the right man to control it."

The waiter set our plates down in front of each of us. I had lost most of what I thought was my appetite.

Zach sliced into his steak as easily as he had tried to cut up my character. He chewed for a minute before speaking again.

"I'd ask you to be my number two when I win," he said. "My executive assistant DA. Basically run the show, do all the internal decision-making, be as innovative for the rest of the office as you've been for sex crimes."

"That's what you're offering me?" I asked. "Where will you be?"

"Up front, dealing with the mayor as well as the mudslingers."

"I'm not interested," I said.

"Is it the number two thing that sticks in your craw? Do you really need to be the one who's on top?"

"What I need is to do something that I care about, working for someone I respect."

"I'll pretend I didn't get what you meant by that last line," Zach said. "The respect part. Try me. I think we'd do well together."

There was a chill that had fallen over our dinner table. I took a few bites of the delicious sole, but the conversation confirmed to me that Zach wasn't fit for any kind of public office.

We managed to talk about issues that interested both of us—where we thought Battaglia had lost his footing in the last year of his life, what needed to be updated in the criminal justice system, how hard it must be to manage more than five hundred lawyers who need to do "the right thing" every day of the week.

"Do you have time for coffee?" Zach asked.

"No. I'm going to stop off to visit a sick friend."

"Can we drop you somewhere?"

"No, thanks. I'll grab a cab."

I put my credit card on the table to split the bill with him, and Zach put his hand on top of mine. "I'll clean up my act, Alex. Put a lid on my loose tongue and slow down with the skirt chasing. You know that."

"It may be a bit late."

He reached into his jacket pocket and took out a business card. "This has all my contact information," he said. "Think about some of this stuff I threw at you, if you need any help making your decision. And let me know if you hear anything about others who plan to jump into the race. We'll have to start collecting signatures on petitions pretty soon."

I picked up the card. "Zachary J. Palmer," I said aloud. "What's the J for?"

Zach rubbed his eyes. "Jacob."

"Really? No wonder you got twitchy when I said the name Jake. You must have thought I was talking about you."

"No such thing."

"Nobody ever called you Jake?" I asked.

"Only my grandmother, and she's been dead a really long time."

"I know I've heard someone refer to you that way," I said. "Maybe it was the agent—Kathy Crain. The one who worked with you on Welly's case."

Zach pushed back from the table and stood up. "Then she'd have been mistaken is what I'd say." His teeth were clenched and his expression was sour. "And you'd be advised to stay out of my way and stick to what it is that you do best."

TWENTY

"New York/Cornell Hospital, please," I said to the cabdriver. "I'd like to go to the entrance on East Sixty-Eighth Street, just off York Avenue."

He pressed the meter and headed north on Third Avenue without saying a word.

It was only a ten-minute ride to the enormous medical center. At nine forty-five in the evening, there was very little traffic on the streets.

I texted Mike that I was going to stop by and check on Francie, hoping for the chance to squeeze her hand or stroke her forehead if the nurses would let me in.

The security guard at the front desk, probably near the end of his eight-hour shift, seemed tired and uninterested.

I showed him my DA's office ID and gold badge—just like a detective's badge but without any corresponding juice—and asked for the Neuro ICU.

"Take the F elevator bank to the third floor and follow the signs."

I thanked him and walked down the corridor.

Most visitors were gone at this late hour, but several walked by me as the elevator doors opened and discharged some glum-looking folks.

When I reached the third floor, I pushed through several sets of double doors until I reached the nursing station for Neuro ICU.

I could see in the glass-walled sides of the first three cubicles. Patients in them were attached to an array of monitors that beeped and blipped. One nurse was bedside and another was standing at the station, noting something on a chart.

"Good evening," I said. "I'm sorry to interrupt you."

"No problem. How can I help you?"

"I'm here to see Francie Fain," I said. "I'm not family, and I know it's late, but she's a dear friend and I was just thinking you might let me in for a minute to whisper some encouragement in her ear."

"Just a minute," the woman said. "Let me talk to the other nurse. I just came on to cover while one of them went to have her dinner."

She walked to the door of the cubicle and I heard her say Francie's name. The second nurse shook her head as they both walked back to the station.

"Is she the one who flatlined earlier?" the first nurse I talked to said. "Before I got here?"

Dead? She couldn't possibly be dead.

"No," the second nurse said, running her finger down the list of patient names, then looking up at me, still talking to the other woman. "The flatliner was a man. Delivery guy without a helmet thrown off his bicycle and crushed his skull."

She flipped the top page of papers on the clipboard.

"What's this Francie Fain to you?" she asked.

"I'm a friend. A close friend," I said. "We worked together."

"Ms. Fain was transferred out of here at two P.M. today," the in-charge nurse said, reading from the sheet of paper.

"To another floor?" I asked. "Does that mean she regained consciousness?"

She put the clipboard down and brought Francie's name up on the computer.

"No. There's no change in her condition."

"Can you please tell me what room she's in?" I said.

The monitors in the second cubicle began to beep rapidly and both women looked up at the overhead screen. The in-charge nurse pointed and told the temp kid to check on the patient. Then she kept tapping on the keyboard, but looked puzzled each time an answer came up.

"Ms. Fain isn't here."

"What do you mean?"

"She was signed out of the hospital," the nurse said.

"But she's in a coma, or she was this morning," I said, a nausea growing in my stomach. "She didn't walk out on her own steam, I don't think."

"You'll have to check with hospital administration when they open tomorrow," the nurse said. "We've got our hands full up here tonight, as you can see."

"But she was a patient in this unit, right?" I asked.

"Yes, it looks like she was a transfer from Bellevue."

"What else does it say about her?"

"Look, ma'am, Francie Fain is gone, okay? I can't tell you anything else."

"I'm not asking to see her medical records," I said, trying not to let myself get shrill. "Nothing privileged. But surely there must be the name of the person who signed her out or authorized her discharge?"

I reached back in my tote for my badge and ID.

The nurse scowled at me and told me to come around to look at the computer screen. "Maybe this will mean more to you than it means to me."

A piece of letter-size paper had been scanned into the system, separate from the medical records:

"I hereby accept responsibility for the treatment of Francie Fain, upon her discharge from Cornell Hospital."

It was dated at one P.M. today.

The signature line read "Keith Scully," and below it, "Police Commissioner of the City of New York."

TWENTY-ONE

"How the hell am I supposed to know?" Mike asked.

"You can certainly find out," I said, standing at home at my bar, pouring Scotch over a glass full of ice cubes. "You can make some calls now."

"It's eleven thirty at night. You think I'm calling the commissioner at this hour when we don't even know what we're looking at?"

"Francie was spirited out of one of the best hospitals in the city, in extremely dire physical condition, in broad daylight, at the direction of your boss. The least you can do is see what Vickee knows about this."

Mercer's wife, Vickee Eaton, was also a detective, assigned to the office of the deputy commissioner of public information. There was little that went on in the inner sanctum at headquarters that she wasn't aware of.

"Why don't you do that yourself?" Mike asked. "Let go of the Dewar's bottle before you shatter the glass with your grip, and pick up your phone."

"I tried Vickee from the cab but she's not answering," I said. "Probably because she sees that it's me calling."

Mike took out his phone and dialed Vickee's cell. "Going straight to voice mail."

"I'm reading this right, aren't I?" I asked. "Francie didn't have a seizure. She's the victim of some kind of crime, which is why Scully signed the release order."

"Apparently so," Mike said. "But the one thing I'm sure of is that she wasn't raped, which takes you out of the equation, professionally. So can you power down a bit? The commissioner doesn't leak. And he's got no reason to talk to you."

"She's still my friend," I said.

"Francie was on her feet, walking to Forlini's one minute, and on the ground with—what?— some kind of severe head injury the next. Clothing intact, except for her shoes."

"You were with her in the ambulance," I said. "You must have seen something that suggested a beating or strike to the head?"

"What I saw doesn't mean a damn," Mike said. "The EMTs didn't notice any signs of external injury. What's the name of that Legal Aid supervisor? He may have a cluc."

"He doesn't," I said, sitting down on the floor of the den, wearing an old denim shirt of Mike's, taking another long sip before stretching my legs out to try to relieve the tension in my back. "I called him, too. Quint didn't get stuff done fast enough to be named her proxy and pick the two others to sign off with him on medical care, before the commissioner got whatever dramatic news it is and kidnapped Francie."

"Keith Scully doesn't kidnap people," Mike said, resting his bare foot on my stomach. "You should be the last person to use that term loosely."

"Well, Francie's gone and no one knows where," I said. "It's terrifying, actually."

"Pod people," Mike said, sliding off the sofa and onto the floor, running his hand the length of my leg.

"What?"

"Maybe the pod people took her," Mike said, trying to lighten the mood. "**Invasion of the Body Snatchers**, kid. Your inventory of horror film trivia is pathetic."

"I've never been into horror," I said. "Well, maybe Frankenstein and Dracula, but not sci-fi."

"And I've never been into Francie," Mike said, rolling over to put his mouth against mine, before speaking again. "Something about women who like to rip me apart in a courtroom, try to make me look like an idiot in front of the jury, and then apologize and say they were just doing their job."

"When I'm a defense attorney, I won't do that to you," I said, kissing him again. "I promise."

"You're not serious," he said. "You've gotta stay

on the side of the angels, Coop. I expect you to die with your prosecutorial boots on."

I turned on my side and rested my elbow on the carpet so I could pick up my glass and drink a bit more. "I'll be hanging out a shingle if Zach Palmer turns out to be the next district attorney. As much as I want to keep doing violence-against-women work, I won't stay if he's elected."

"Don't you think his chances rest on you building a case with Lucy? That could decide his fate—as well as yours," Mike said. "Did you open a grand jury investigation today?"

"No. No, I didn't do that," I said. "If he suspected I was onto him at dinner tonight and asked if anyone was 'investigating' him, I wanted to be able to say no with a clear conscience."

"Half-clear, anyway."

"I'm going to start the investigation tomorrow," I said. "I'll go into the grand jury first thing so I can begin to subpoena documents for the relevant dates. Help nail down a time and place. I haven't even gotten to ask Lucy the details of what happened."

"Did Zach say anything interesting?"

"He's a pig," I said. "And he doesn't even try to hide it. His language, his attitude about women, his hunger for the job—at the expense of dragging out the dirty laundry of anyone who plans to oppose him."

"Did Lucy's name come up in the conversation?" Mike asked. He leaned over to pull up my shirt and kiss my abdomen.

"No way was I going there," I said. "But I skirted around it, talking about the agent who sort of babysat Lucy, and pretending I'd met her at a conference. The woman named Kathy Crain."

"Why?"

"I just want to get him thinking about what he's done," I said. "Guilt is a powerful motivator. I'd love it if he fell on his sword and backed out of the race."

"Wishful thinking," Mike said. "He's already dreaming of his name chiseled in stone over the entrance to the building. What else?"

"Well, Jake. I talked about Jake when Zach gave me his business card," I said. "I pretended to be surprised that his middle name was Jacob."

"Sounds like you didn't hold your hand as close to your chest as you might have," Mike said. "You weren't there to tip him off, you know."

"I think it was fine," I said. "You can listen to the tape if you come to the office tomorrow."

"Tape? I ripped that recorder right off your blouse, kid—for your own good—or don't you remember?"

I sipped my Scotch and then smiled. "You're always telling me not to be so impulsive," I said. "But this time you were way off the mark."

"How so?" Mike said, sitting up straight.

"The tech guys were concerned that when I chewed on my food it might interfere with reception on the recorder if they placed it too close to my mouth," I said. "So they concealed the mini device in the third button down, not in the top one," I said. "Not in the one you snagged."

"You actually recorded your conversation with Zach Palmer, despite what I told you?" Mike asked.

I pointed at the spot on my chest where my cleavage started to show—the point where the recorder had been.

"Why not?" I said. "You think only detectives earn the right to go rogue?"

TWENTY-TWO

"Good morning," I said, standing in front of the room of twenty-three grand jurors, arrayed before me in two semicircular rows of ten people, and three beyond them—one of whom was the foreman. "My name is Alexandra Cooper."

This was the first case I was presenting to them since returning from my leave of absence. It was essential for me to get started in the grand jury. I couldn't issue subpoenas without the signature of the foreman, nor did I have the power to compel witnesses to talk to me, while they could be summoned to appear before the grand jury with ease.

I slipped in ahead of my colleagues who were in the adjacent waiting room with witnesses for their own cases—cops and civilians—who would testify in expectation that the jurors would return an indictment, which was required in all felony cases in New York State.

Some jurors were still reading newspapers and noshing on bagels or egg sandwiches. A few were attentive, spotting a lawyer they hadn't seen before, and looking me over in my navy blue pinstripe skirt suit, ready to hear the charges.

"I would like to open an investigation into the matter regarding John Doe," I said. There was no point naming Zachary Palmer before I had proof certain that he had committed these crimes.

"At this time, the charges include rape in the third degree and sexual abuse in the third degree," I said. I had opted to start with statutory crimes rather than the far more inflammatory first-degree forcible rape charges that Lucy had alluded to when she visited New York six years ago.

I was used to what happened when jurors heard the word "rape." Newspapers were flattened on the wooden panels in front of each chair and the breakfast food was bagged and put beneath their seats. It always got the full attention of everyone in the room, but I hadn't expected the hands of four women jurors to shoot up in the air the instant I stated the crime.

"I usually prefer questions after the presentation," I said, "but I'm happy to come to each of you and take them individually."

There was no point tainting the panel with comments from any of the jurors, so I climbed the three steps to get to the first woman.

I leaned in close to her and asked her what she wanted to tell me.

"Look, I've going through a rough patch since last year, with all this Me Too business," the woman said. "I had a bad experience with a guy when I was in college, twenty years ago, and I'm finally dealing with it in therapy. I just don't think I'm the right person to sit on a case like this."

"May I ask you, was the 'experience' you're referring to a sexual assault?" I asked.

"Yeah," she said, "at least that's what I think."

"Did you report it to anyone at the time?"

"No. No, I just wrote it off to having too much to drink," she said, "and now it kind of haunts me."

"Would you like to speak to someone who works with me? We have so much experience handling these circumstances," I said. "Do you think that might help?"

"It didn't happen here," she said. "It happened during my junior year abroad, in Italy."

"I'd still be happy to set you up with one of my lawyers, or a counselor."

"I just don't want to hear about somebody else's rape, do you get it?" she said, raising her voice at me.

"Understood," I said, straightening up. "I don't intend to present any testimony in the next few days, so I'll talk with the foreman about excusing you."

I hadn't expected this amount of fallout from the onset of last year's movement. I needed sixteen of these twenty-three jurors to constitute a quorum to hear the case, and they were beginning to drop like flies.

Jurors 8, 14, and 19 all had similar reservations about sitting, and one of the male jurors—

number 2—wanted to be relieved of his duty because his teenage daughter had been the victim of a date rape.

I returned to the front of the room. "Thank you all for your candor. Today, I'm just opening the investigation without any witnesses, so perhaps you can regroup and make a decision about who will participate before I return next week."

I left the grand jury room and closed the door behind me, handing my charge slip to the warden who controlled the proceedings.

"You look shell-shocked," he said.

"It's the first rape case I've presented in months, and I'm down almost a quarter of the panel."

"The world is a different place," he said. "You'll have your hands full."

"I already do," I said. "See you next week."

I walked down the ninth-floor corridor, stopping at the DA's Squad tech office to drop off my blouse.

"How'd it go?" the lone detective asked me.

"I'll know as soon as you make me a copy," I said. "Mercer will be with me, so just call and we'll pick it up when you're done."

"Looks like your blouse is ripped," he said, holding it up to me. "Did your target get frisky with you?"

"Not the target," I said with a chuckle. "Just a wardrobe malfunction on my end. See you later, and thanks."

I jogged down the flight of stairs to my office.

Mercer was talking to Laura at her desk, and I could see Lucy sitting opposite my desk.

"Any problem when you went to pick Lucy up this morning?" I asked Mercer.

"None at all. She seems to like Streetwork."

"That's a relief," I said. "Did Vickee mention anything about Francie Fain, and the fact that Scully signed her out of Cornell yesterday?"

He shook his head. "She tried to snoop around after she picked up your message last night, but the commissioner isn't playing games. There hasn't been a single press inquiry, so he told Vickee she gets no information about Fain unless a reporter sticks his or her nose in for a story."

"Something's wrong with that picture," I said.

"There are so many private facilities for people with head injuries who are—well, who are slow to make medical progress," Mercer said.

"Yeah, but it's not usually the police commissioner who has them committed."

"Between us for now, the Major Case Squad has grabbed the video surveillance cameras behind the Tombs," Mercer said. "Vickee knows that much."

The entrance to the garage where buses brought prisoners from Riker's Island to the courthouse for their appearances was adjacent to the Bridge of Sighs—the point where Francie collapsed. Cameras were there to capture any unusual behavior, record the license plates of Correction Department buses—arrivals and departures—and record escape attempts.

"They must already know what's on them," I said.

"No one seized them the first night," Mercer said, "because Francie was a medical emergency. Once they got word from the docs yesterday that something else is going on, they hauled in the videos and hopefully watched them last night. Can you keep that news to yourself?"

"Of course," I said. "At least it gives me some hope someone can solve this."

"Be thankful it's Major Case and not Homicide," Mercer said. "It means your friend is still alive."

I bit my lip and shook my head, picking up my messages from Laura's desk and walking in to greet Lucy.

"Don't you look spiffy," I said to her. "You've got a new wardrobe."

She smiled at me. "It's awesome at Streetwork," she said. "I've already met some really nice people, and nobody thinks I'm weird for being there. Nobody questions why you're alone or what got you there."

"I'm happy to hear that," I said. I asked Lucy about her accommodations and her counselors, how many meals she had yesterday and whether they had given her pocket money to get around with. Then it was time to get started.

"We've got some more critical work to do today, so I hope you're ready."

Lucy looked at Mercer's face and then back to me. "I don't have a choice, do I?"

"You've made terribly serious allegations. I think we better press ahead and see where they lead us."

"You promised me I could have the stuff that was taken from me by the police."

"Sure. We're going to talk about what you had with you when you were picked up," I said, asking Mercer to get the manila envelope that contained Lucy's vouchered belongings from Laura.

He placed it in front of me, and Lucy leaned in over my desk, as though to reach for the items.

"Slow down," I said. "Some questions first. Is this your driver's license?"

"Yeah."

"I mean, a real one," I said. "A valid Illinois license."

"Sort of real," she said.

"Lucy, did you pass your test?" I asked. "Or did you buy this on the street?"

She hesitated, but not for as long as she did two days ago when she didn't want to give me information. "On the street. Back in Illinois."

"And on here," I said, holding it up with one hand, "you lied about your date of birth, didn't you?"

"Not a big lie," Lucy said. "I made myself younger. People are always nicer to homeless people when they think they're kids."

"Whose address is this in Chicago?"

She was picking at her nails. "I don't remember."

"Try harder."

"I still don't remember."

I passed the license over her head to Mercer. "Would you run that address for me, please?"

"I don't really care," she said. "The guys at Streetwork are hooking me up with brand-new ID. I don't need that."

I held up the MetroCard. "Where did you get this?"

"In the subway."

"Did you know that each MetroCard is stamped by a computer system, so we can tell the date of purchase and how it was bought?"

It wasn't taking long for Lucy Jenner to slip into her petulant loner mode. "I found it on the ground, okay? I didn't say I bought it."

I was on to my next exhibit—an Amtrak ticket receipt from DC's Union Station to Penn Station in Manhattan. Her aunt was right. Lucy was a facile liar, even about the little things. I didn't know what consequences this would have for the big picture.

"Did you find this, too?" I asked. "This train ticket? Or did you really use it?"

Mercer stepped out from behind Lucy's chair and sat on the desk, facing her. "Do you get the point yet that Alex and I are trying to help you?" he asked. "Do me a favor and save your attitude for someone else."

"I haven't got an attitude," she said. "I don't like to be picked on."

"And Alexandra doesn't like to be lied to," Mercer said. "Did you really go to Washington?"

"Yes, I did. I took a bus there from Chicago."

"Why?" I asked, speaking gently and encouraging her to trust us. "Why did you go to DC?"

"I was staying at this shelter in Chicago—it was really a dump. One day I went to the library to use a computer," Lucy said. "You can do that at the public library in most places."

"Yes, in New York, too. It's a great resource."

"My advocate at the shelter was pushing me to get a job."

"What kind of work had you done in the years before that?" I asked.

"I was a nanny for a while, for a really nice family," Lucy said.

I wasn't surprised that she couldn't or wouldn't remember the name of the people for whom she had worked. I wanted to check her out with them, but I would come back to that another time.

"And I waitressed a lot," she said. "Local restaurants, diners, small hotels. So this day, at the library, I saw an opening for waitresses at a big hotel in Chicago, that even offered them housing—like a dormitory—to live in."

"Sounds good," I said.

"I emailed them right there from the library, because I knew I could come back and check that computer in a day or two to see if they were giving me an interview."

She was sitting up straight, seemingly proud of herself for getting that far.

"I like that, Lucy," I said. "What a good idea. Do you remember the name of the hotel?"

I was getting all the detail I could, hoping to confirm nonessential facts, as a way of gaining reliance on the important ones.

"Yeah," Lucy said, the corner of her mouth turning up in a grin. "The Palmer Inn, on Lake Michigan. A big old fancy Chicago hotel."

"A very famous one," I said. "Good for you."

Now she leaned over and took her water bottle off my desk and drank from it.

"Except I never went there to interview, 'cause the name of the place reminded me of Jake. You know, Jake Palmer. So as long as I was sitting at a computer, I Googled Jake, as Zachary Palmer."

She looked up at me for more approval, but I was silent. I didn't know where she was going with this.

"I wanted to see him again," Lucy said. "I mean, not to hook up with him, if that's what you're thinking. I wanted to confront him—if that's the right word. I wanted to make him pay for what he did to me."

There was no reason for me to comment on her intentions.

"What did you learn by Googling him?"

She started to count facts on her fingers. "First,

that he'd become a really big shot as a lawyer, mostly because of my case. Second, that he'd had all these important jobs. Third, that he had a wife and kids somewhere near New York, so I didn't want to go there and take the chance of messing them up, too. Fourth was that he was the—what's it called— keynote? The keynote speaker at a big conference in England that week, and for sure I couldn't get there to see him."

She was clutching her pinky between her fingers. "The fifth thing was that he was going to be in Washington the following week. Talking about Homeland Security," she said. "At the Hilton Hotel. Open to the public."

"You had a plan?"

"Yeah. I'd just go show up at the Hilton and wait for him to finish. Sandbag him after his speech, kind of like how he sandbagged me."

Not undeserved.

"Who paid for the bus ticket?" I asked.

"Got the cheapest one. Midweek, late at night," Lucy said. "Sixty-four dollars."

"I asked who paid for it."

"They were glad to see me go at the shelter," she said. "The manager loaned me some money. They trust me—I'll pay it back."

"Did you see Zach Palmer—Jake, to you— in DC?"

"Nope, I waited for hours, but the speech was

canceled on account of some terrorist threat. Rich, isn't it? He's supposed to speak about security and someone phones in a threat. That's when I called my half brother and he told me I could come to Brooklyn and get my father's car."

"So you took the train."

"I know you're going to ask me. It was forty-nine dollars," Lucy said. "I just stayed in the station overnight, asking people for money."

"Begging?" I asked. "Do you mean you were begging for money?"

"Begging, yeah. It's not hard to do when you're my age and kind of desperate. And you can always count on a nice police officer to give you the last ten bucks, especially when you're in a train station," she said, smiling at Mercer. "They're happy you're getting out of their town anyway."

"Did you come to New York," I asked, "to make another stab at finding Jake, or to see your half brother?"

"Both, to be honest with you," Lucy said. "I got to Rodney's house first, because he had things of my dad's to give me, and I figured he'd let me stay a while. But the cops got me before I could find a way to get to Jake."

I had the three more personal objects in the manila envelope, and I kept my hands on it while I talked to her.

"Mercer and I are going to work our tails off to

help you," I said, "and one of the ways we're going to do that is to double-check every single thing you tell us."

"You don't believe me?"

"I think you're quick to make things up if something looks bad for you, so if you want a jury to believe your story about Jake, every other thing you say has to be true. Where you stayed in Chicago, how you got the money for the bus to DC, whether there was really a canceled speech at the Hilton— get it? Every little thing."

Lucy was furious. "None of those things have to do with Jake raping me."

Mercer stepped in. "You're right, but they have to do with how Alex—or a jury—can trust you."

"Let's just do a hypothetical," I said. "Suppose Mercer and I take you at your word for everything you say about Jake—about Zachary Palmer, who really is quite a big shot now, just like you called it."

"Yeah."

"Suppose we don't doubt a thing you say, and then six months from now, Jake's lawyer has you on the witness stand, cross-examining you."

"I'm probably not going to like that," she said.

"Nobody does," I said. "But I can protect you if you're telling the truth. I can object to all the irrelevant things his lawyer tries to go at you for. Like, how did you buy a bus ticket to DC and how did you pay for a train ticket to New York?"

"Those things are true."

"So let me give you another example," I said, standing up, coming around the desk, and practically getting right in Lucy's face.

"Suppose Jake takes the witness stand, in his own defense."

"Yeah. I've seen that on TV."

"Suppose I get to the part where I'm going at him hard for the way he convinced you to be with him, to do everything he asked you to do, and most especially to keep quiet about him all these years."

Lucy flapped her hands before resting them on the arms of the chair. "He'll just deny it all. Why am I bothering?"

"You've already testified for the State," I said, "and I had you walk in front of the jury box so that each one of the twelve jurors could see the scar across the palm of your hand."

She clasped her hands together and then ran the fingers of her right hand along the line of the scar in her left palm.

"Go on," she said.

"Do you remember the O. J. Simpson trial?" I asked. "Ever see that on TV?"

Lucy gave me a blank stare.

"The prosecutor made the famous murderer put on the glove they claimed he was wearing, but he couldn't get it on his hand."

I was thinking about how the jury went on to acquit because the glove didn't fit, but what had been current events in my life was some kind of ancient history to a twenty-four-year-old. It may have been the trial of the last century, but it was nothing to Lucy Jenner.

"Never mind," I said. "Here's my point. The jury sees your hand, your deep scar, and hears you tell them that it was the sign of your blood oath with Jake."

She tilted her head and looked at me. "Yeah?"

"Then it's his turn, if he chooses to testify."

"He gets to choose if he does or not?" Lucy asked.

"That's right," I said. "And if he wants to, if he's able to deny all this or prove you told a lie—even a little one—then his lawyer gets the chance to let the jury see his hands—right up close. The twelve jurors might choose to disbelieve everything you've told them if you're wrong about that."

I was fresh off looking at Zachary's palms— both of them—the evening before. Neither one bore a scar.

"What if," I said, lifting her chin to make her look at me, "what if there's not a scar on either of his hands?"

"So what," she said, twisting her head away from my hand. "It was ten years ago. Maybe I don't remember everything as perfectly as you want me to."

"You don't have to be perfect," Mercer said, his deep voice calm and steady. "But you have to be honest."

Lucy Jenner put her elbows on my desktop and

buried her head in her hands. "I'm trying. I haven't wanted to think about this—to go back to that moment—for the longest time, and now you're making me do it."

"I know you were cut," I said, "but sometimes people cut themselves when they're in emotional trouble. Was it that?"

"Don't be so stupid. There was no other reason to cut my palm, except Jake made me."

"And him, what did he do?" I asked. "Take yourself back there, Lucy, as painful as that is to do."

Her eyes were shut tight and the first tears began to fall. She was reliving an encounter with her assailant.

"Jake told me we had to seal my promise with a blood oath," she said. "He took my hand and ran his blade across it."

"Then what?" I asked. "Then what did he do?"

Lucy's eyes were still closed. She had willed herself back to the John Wayne Motor Inn in Iowa City. "Jake cut himself, too, but it was on his fingertip. He cut open a bit of his forefinger."

"You saw him lots of times after that," I said. "Is there any kind of mark or scar on his finger?"

Lucy closed her eyes and put her fingers in her ears, as though to shut me out.

"Lucy," I said, pounding my fist on my desk to demand her attention.

"I'm thinking about it. Can't you just leave me alone?" she asked.

"That's the one thing I can't do."

Slowly she took her fingers away and opened her eyes. "Yeah. Yeah," she said. "Jake had cuts on his forefinger and his thumb."

"Cuts?" I asked. "More than one?"

"Sometimes when we were with other people, and they'd start to ask me questions—you know, the agents and cops—he'd hold that finger up to his lips, like he was shushing me. Reminding me that I had made an oath not to talk about us."

"Did he bleed, too, when he cut your palm?" I asked. Maybe that would help her recall what he did to himself.

"Yes, yes, he bled. He grabbed my hand and traced his blood along the slice in my palm with his forefinger," Lucy said. "He mixed his blood with mine, I swear to God. And then he undressed me, and then he made me have intercourse with him."

TWENTY-THREE

"I was so busy checking out his two palms, I never thought to look at his fingertips," I said. "How stupid is that?"

"Don't beat yourself up," Mercer said. "And back off the girl, too. Don't make it too hard on her the next visit."

Lucy had excused herself to go to the bathroom and wash up.

"Time isn't with us on this. I've got to dig into her while we've got her."

I had called Max and she joined us in my office. "I haven't finished briefing it yet," she said, "but first degree in Iowa would be sexual contact with someone who hadn't reached her fifteenth birthday. Still, under sixteen, like Lucy, makes it a felony, punishable by up to ten years in prison."

It was too early to claim victory, but I liked the news. "Statutory limits?"

"Sadly," Max said. "Yes. Ten years. We need the exact date to be sure the ten years haven't expired."

"I opened in the grand jury today, so you can

prepare a subpoena for me when you have a chance," I said. "The John Wayne Motor Inn?"

"I've already checked, Alex. It's no longer in business."

"Damn it. Then we'll need some other way to confirm the date," I said. "Mercer, can you try for court records this afternoon?"

"Sure."

"I don't need to brief the Romeo and Juliet stuff, do I?" Max asked.

Statutory laws in most states didn't allow prosecutions of teenage boys for sexual contact with girls close in age, even though under the age of consent.

"Nope. Zach Palmer was never Romeo," I said. "He was in his thirties when he had intercourse with Lucy. How about Utah?"

Max checked her notepad. "Rubbing against Lucy, even over clothing, makes it the crime of Unlawful Sexual Contact, and there doesn't seem to be a statute of limitation problem in Utah."

"Thanks," I said. "Mercer and I will just try to get a bit more done today with Lucy. Then you and I can spend some time together figuring what's next."

I could see Lucy standing by Laura's desk, and I called to her. "C'mon back in."

I tried to be clinical and avoid prompting an emotional reaction from Lucy. I went over cities and towns in which Jake—she told us—had entered her hotel room, almost whenever Kathy Crain had an afternoon or evening off. Mercer was making notes, although most of the dates were vague and would require great good luck in tracking down any corroboration of them.

"Let's talk about Manhattan," I said, "the time you ran away from your aunt's house six years ago and came to the city."

"What's the difference?" Lucy asked. "If people don't care about what happened when I was fourteen, who'll care about an eighteen-year-old runaway?"

"Of course people will care," I said. "Stay with me for another hour. I'd like to know more."

Lucy told the story of that first bus trip again, and how she got caught shoplifting in Tribeca.

"You haven't told us why you decided to come to New York in the first place," I said. "Why did you risk running away from your aunt's home?"

Lucy took a deep breath. "Because he called me."

"He?"

"Jake," she said, "or Mr. Palmer is how my aunt knew him. He called her house to talk to me."

I perked up at the idea that there would be telephone company records of the call, if we could nail down an approximate date.

"Had he called you before that?" I asked.

"I hadn't heard from him since Baynes was sentenced, three months after the trial," Lucy said. "Jake had used me for what he needed, and then he just dropped me like I was garbage."

"Did he tell you why he was calling?"

"Sure," she said. "Sure he did. It was my eighteenth birthday. That's the reason he called."

"Jake remembered the exact date?" I said. That would make the subpoena process so much easier.

"He had it in his files from the investigation and trial, so why wouldn't he know it?"

"Do you remember the call?"

"Mostly all of it," Lucy said. "First, he wished me a happy birthday, when I didn't have much in my life to make me happy."

"Did you tell him that?"

"No reason to," she said. "He knew too much about me as it was. Then he asked me what I was doing, and I told him I was waiting tables and doing some office work—like answering phones—for my uncle."

"What else?" I said.

"Jake started cutting me off when I was telling him," Lucy said. "Like he wasn't really interested in me at all. He just kept repeating, 'So we're good, right? So we're good?'"

She stared at the floor. "I really wasn't sure what he meant by that—maybe that I had kept my promise not to tell? 'You're good with me, Lucy, right?'"

I nodded at her.

"Then he told me he had to go, and he ended the call, just like that," she said.

"That was it? Nothing about what he was doing or where he was?" I said. "What did you do?"

"Somehow I got past my aunt and went into the room I shared with my cousin, and I curled up on my bed and started to cry. Like really cry, the way I hadn't done in years."

"That's good for you, Lucy," Mercer said. "It's good to let it all out."

"So my aunt has this button on the phone," she said. "You can press it and it gives you the number of the last caller. Later that same night, I hit it, and it showed me a phone number from the 212 area code."

"Manhattan," I said.

"New York University Law School," Lucy said. "I called it the next day, but it was the main number, and I couldn't get an extension for Professor Palmer. The main office wouldn't give it to me unless I left my name."

"Did you keep trying?"

"No, I looked the school up on the Internet, and it said he was teaching there."

That was true. I had been one of his guest lecturers.

"I just decided to come here, to come to New York and kind of surprise him. I wanted to see him in person so that he couldn't hang up on me or just blow me off like he did on the phone," Lucy said. "I wanted to tell him something. I wanted to do it right in his face."

"Tell him what?"

Lucy took her time before she answered, full

of fire. "I wanted him to know that things really weren't 'good' for me, like he was asking. That it wasn't bad enough that my life sucked because I watched my two friends be slaughtered, but then Zachary Palmer—who everybody treated like he was a god—then he raped me. And he raped me over and over again."

She stopped for an intake of breath. "You want specific details, Ms. Cooper? You think I'd make this shit up?" she asked. "Tell me if this sounds real. That we'd be at dinner with the agents and all that, and Jake would always find a way to say he wanted to stop by his hotel room and go over the next day's testimony with me. Or that he'd take me out to dinner alone, and then have his way with me in the car on our way back to my room."

"It's okay, Lucy. Have some water," I said. "Mercer and I believe you."

"How about this? D'you ever do **this** with a witness? We'd be in my room—he'd send Kathy on a break with the other agents—and the local news would come on at ten o'clock," Lucy said, back in the moment again. "And Jake would get up to adjust the angle of the mirror on the wall so that he could watch himself having sex with me, and at the same time catch himself being interviewed on the courthouse steps."

I couldn't find words to adequately express my shock. I taught my prosecutors not to react physically to the descriptions accusers often gave. Some of them shut down when they saw that we were horrified by the perpetrators' actions. I simply let Lucy go on. The perp having sex with his victim while exercising his vanity and watching himself on a televised news feed. This was the kind of detail that would convince any jury of Lucy's truthtelling.

"Jake used to tell me he could win any trial because he was—what's the word—meticulous?" Lucy asked rhetorically. "He would save every scrap of evidence—every note or document or photograph. He took photographs of me. Lots of photographs."

"What kind of pictures?" I asked.

"The first ones were normal," she said. "Me doing everyday things—in his office, with Kathy at a restaurant, or in front of our hotel, riding in his car."

Lucy's eyes shifted to the ceiling. "Then he started taking ones of me with no clothes on, posing me the way he wanted me."

When she stopped for a minute, I asked questions. "Did he take them with a camera?"

"Nope. Just with his phone."

"Did he ever give you copies?"

"No, not even when I asked for them," she said, lowering her head and her voice. "He said that he took them so he could remember me when we weren't together anymore. Jake said the photographs would be evidence."

"Evidence of what?" Mercer asked.

Lucy got up from her chair. "You want to know what I think, or what Jake thinks?"

"You first," Mercer said.

"If I could get my hands on anything he had from that time, back when I was fourteen, I'd be able to take him to court and kick his ass."

"You're doing fine right now," I said. "What did Jake tell you?"

Lucy pursed her lips. "He told me that the photos, that the scraps of paper I wrote on that he kept, with dates and addresses and all sorts of names of people we came into contact with—he told me all of that would be evidence of our affair, if I ever went back on our oath."

"Affair?" Mercer said, looking as though he would put a fist right through Zachary Palmer's face.

"He told me it was a love affair—not a crime. It got to be so routine for him to have sex with me that he didn't even pay attention when I said I didn't want to do it or that I was afraid to be with him again," Lucy said, rubbing her palms back and forth on the legs of her jeans. "I didn't know it wasn't legal for a thirty-five-year-old man to have sex with a teenager. How was I supposed to know that?"

"What happened when you came to Manhattan—when you turned eighteen?" I asked.

"I took the bus from Chicago to the Port Authority, and then got directions for a subway down to Washington Square, where the law school is," she said. "Jake didn't have a regular office 'cause he wasn't there full-time, but I left him a note telling him that I was in New York. I signed my name and wrote my phone number."

"You have a cell phone?" I asked.

"Not now," she said. "I just use burner phones when I have the cash. But my aunt bought me a cell phone when I lived with her. I can give you that number, too. She cut it off when I didn't come home after a month."

"And Jake called you back?"

"The next day," Lucy said. "The day I went shopping and got picked up by the police."

I didn't want to stop her narrative by making her angry, but I didn't know why she was shoplifting undergarments that anyone would describe as "sexy."

"Silk underwear, a thong, leather leggings," I said, recalling some of the items on the police voucher. "Who were you planning to wear those for?"

In a flash, Lucy kicked my desk with the toe of her shoe. The loud bang startled me. "It's not what you think, okay?"

"Then help me," I said, thinking the assortment of clothing more suited an assignation than a confrontation.

Lucy looked away again. "I wanted to have the clothes to tempt him—Jake or Zach, whoever he was going to be when I showed up. I was afraid he'd turn me away before I could make him understand that he had ruined my life. Then I got arrested and the police took all the things from me. The things I wanted to buy."

The things she stole, but no need to underscore that.

"I called him the next day, after I got out of jail—I was still in my T-shirt and jeans—and told him what happened," I said. "He wanted to see me. He wanted to know what I said to the police."

"What did you tell him?"

"That I didn't tell the police anything. I think he agreed to meet me because he wanted to be sure of that."

"Where did you meet?" I asked.

"He had an apartment in the East Twenties," Lucy said. "I went there. And yeah, I know what you're going to say."

"I'm not here to be judgmental, Lucy. I understand your rage," I said.

"It was eight o'clock at night. He buzzed me in the lobby door with an intercom, and I climbed three flights," she said. "I was fighting back tears and shaking all over. Jake opened the door and I started to cry."

Mercer was off to Lucy's side, motioning to me with his hand, suggesting that I take things down a notch.

"He took my hand and brought me inside the

door, pulling me against him and giving me a hug—like a big embrace," she said. "I pushed back, but there was really nowhere to go. The thing that was strangest was that the apartment was empty. Not a piece of furniture in it, and just a bare lightbulb overhead."

"Why was it empty? Do you know?" I asked.

"Yeah. Jake was moving out that coming weekend," she said. "He was really anxious about whether I told the police about him—about what he had done to me when I was a kid—but I held up my hand to show him the scar and told him I would never forget our oath."

"Smart."

"Then he pushed me against the wall and started to kiss me," Lucy said. "I told him to get off."

"Did he?"

"He said he wouldn't let me go until he had a taste of me again. A taste of my skin."

"Why don't you stop for a while, Lucy?" I said. "You're beginning to tremble, just talking about him."

"I am? I didn't even realize that," she said, leaning back in the chair, her face streaked with tears and whatever makeup she had put on before coming to my office. "There isn't much left to say anyway. Jake pinned me against the wall with one arm across my neck, pressing so hard I could barely breathe. Then he unzipped my jeans and pulled them down. I was crying so hard and gasping for air that I couldn't stop him. That's when he unzipped his fly and exposed himself. That's when he raped me, Ms. Cooper. That time, by force."

I didn't care about professional boundaries when she was so distraught. I kneeled in front of Lucy Jenner and took her in my arms, encouraging her to let out all her pain and anger.

"I'll tell you why that apartment was empty, Ms. Cooper," Lucy said a couple of minutes later, wiping her eyes with the back of her hand. "It was three days before his wedding. His marriage to a student of his just a few years older than me. He was moving in with her."

There were no words I could offer in exchange.

"Jake left me there, curled up in a ball on the floor of the empty apartment. As he walked out the door, he thanked me for giving him such a great bachelor party. And he told me I could tell anyone I wanted about him, because no one would ever believe me."

TWENTY-FOUR

"Just don't be all full of yourself," Mercer said, "because you've got Zachary Palmer nailed on a first-degree rape that you can prosecute in this county."

"'Nailed' is an overstatement," I said. "But I think I have probable cause. I need to back up some of this information—like seeing if we can get the address of the apartment Zach lived in while he was teaching at NYU, and Lucy's cell phone records if she or her aunt remember the carrier."

We knew that Lucy needed a break from the intensity of the questioning. At one o'clock, Maxine came by to take her out for lunch, to a Chinese restaurant a few blocks away from the courthouse.

Laura ordered in sandwiches for Mercer and me as we continued to talk about what to do next.

"What's your plan?" Mercer asked. "Do you intend to tell Zach he's a target?"

"Not quite yet," I said. "I have to see if I can get a presentation together to get in the grand jury this term."

In New York County, grand juries sat for half a day, five days a week, for an entire month. But if an assistant DA couldn't complete a case within that time, he or she had to withdraw it and start all over the next month. I feared we were too close to the end of the term to get it done.

"Would you do it NA?" he asked.

Non-arrest, Mercer meant.

"I'd have to do it that way," I said, folding up the wrapper from my turkey sandwich to throw it out, taking a swig of my Diet Coke. "I'd be excoriated by the media for grandstanding or just trying to take down a political opponent if I dragged Zach out of a station house in handcuffs, and then couldn't make a case."

"But you have to give him notice, don't you?"

I got up from my desk and started to pace the length of my office, back and forth. "Yes. I have to give him the opportunity to testify in the grand jury."

"You want to step down from this and hand it to someone else?"

"Not a prayer of a chance," I said.

"You don't have to go mano a mano with him," Mercer said. "It's not a personal thing."

"No, but it would be a sign of weakness that everyone seems to be looking for in me, now that I'm back."

"Then you've got to stick with Lucy through thick and thin," Mercer said. "This kid has picked herself up from the ashes and managed to soldier on. You can't flip-flop on your decision to try the case down the line."

"When have you known me to do that?" I asked, putting my hands on my hips and squaring off with Mercer. "All I have to deal with is the fact that, like her aunt told me, Lucy's manipulative. She's lied in the past and she'll lie to us. That's the one thing we can't tolerate."

"Chill, Alexandra," Mercer said. "Let's start with your wish list."

I walked back to my desk and started writing on a fresh pad, as I spoke the order of play to Mercer.

"Decide how and when to tell Zach Palmer he's a target," I said. "Include an extra two days for him to get counsel, which will be a top dog like Lem Howell or Martin London."

"Damn," Mercer said. "That'll be a test of wills."

"Just be there to catch me if I fall," I said. "I can draft subpoenas today. I'll need all the police reports from Lucy's arrest six years ago. I'll need all the police and FBI reports from the Welly Barnes case—regarding Lucy and everyone else. Long-range issue will be mapping out the whereabouts of Lucy, Zach, Kathy Crain, and the other agents as they moved around the country."

"You think you can get that evidence admitted?" Mercer asked. "The stuff he did to Lucy in Iowa and Utah?"

"I have to get it in," I said. "It establishes the

entire chain of events for Lucy to come to New York and be victimized here. It's the reason Zach called her right before his wedding to see if all was good with her, making sure nothing would implode on his way down the aisle."

"Search warrants?"

"Dicey, at best," I said. "Lucy suggests that Zach might have souvenirs, like the photographs and notes, but that info is really stale at this point. He's moved homes—to marry and now to divorce—and has had offices in a variety of places. I'd have to develop that from other witnesses, if they come forward, or if he talks to me."

"What's your smoking gun going to be?" he asked.

I laughed. "I haven't found that yet."

"You need something incontrovertible," Mercer said, "to back up all the problems of time passed by and memories gone weak. You need the dude's DNA on an old pair of Lucy's jeans or a bloody knife of sorts."

"Keep on keeping on, Detective Wallace. I don't mind that you're dreaming," I said, "but I think we'll be doing this one bare bones."

"That may be," he said, "but any juror who doesn't melt when Lucy testifies would have to have a heart of stone."

Mercer and I had been through this too many times together to know that what we wanted for our witness wouldn't necessarily come to pass.

Some would see the early years of contact the way Zach described it to Lucy—as a consensual affair, even though she was below the age of legal consent.

Still others would blame her for all of it. The Great Salt Lake seduction, the runaway bus trip to New York, the shoplifting of lingerie meant best for a tryst, the fact that she tracked her predator down and willingly went—alone—to his apartment, and her failure to make a more timely outcry than this week, when she was picked up by police on an old warrant. I knew what kind of ugly defense could be mounted against these charges, and while it took me the trust of a dozen jurors to convict, it would only take one person who blamed Lucy to hang the rest.

It was two thirty by the time Max delivered Lucy back to us. They had eaten at one of the delicious little restaurants on Pell Street, and Max had walked her charge all around Chinatown to show her the sights—as well as to relax her.

"You did really well this morning, Lucy," I said.

"Does that mean you both believe me?" she said, lowering herself into the chair. "Are you going to arrest Jake? I mean, Zachary Palmer."

"We do believe you and at some point soon he'll be charged with these crimes," I said. "Let's just get a little more done today."

It was details I needed most, and any facts that could be corroborated by independent evidence. The law no longer required the latter, as it used to do, but jurors wanted as much of it as they could have.

I broke down the visit to Jake's apartment six years ago, second by second, word by word, and touch by touch.

Lucy was fading by four thirty and I understood why. "We can pick this up on Friday," I said, figuring to give her the next day off. "The worst is over, I promise you."

"How about my things?" she asked.

"You bet," I said. "Where were we? I'm keeping the fake ID and the MetroCard and the train receipt, okay?"

"How about my money?"

I counted out the eighty dollars and passed it to her. "Then there's this two-dollar bill," I said. "Very neat. You don't see many of those."

"It's my good-luck charm," Lucy said, taking the bill from me. "At least, I used to think it was."

"It will be again," Mercer said. "Hang on to it."

"Here's the handkerchief," I said. "It's got your initials on it, I see."

Lucy's aunt had explained that to me on the phone. I wanted to see if she confirmed the same story, but mostly I was getting to the ring, and whether Lucy would admit it belonged to her cousin.

The handkerchief was dirty and worn, but when Lucy smoothed it out, you could see the embroidered initials—**LJ**—made with lavender thread against the white cotton.

"My mother made this for me, right before she died," Lucy said. "I keep it with me all the time."

"That's a lovely keepsake to have," I said. "Then there's this gold ring. Where did you get this?"

"You're not going to like my answer," Lucy said, "but I stole it. It belonged to my cousin Callie. I guess I was just so jealous of her for having it that the night I ran away, I took it from next to her bed."

"Actually," I said, "I like that answer a lot. All we want from you is the truth, and that's what you told us."

I got up from my desk to walk Lucy to the door so that Max could accompany her back to the Streetwork facility. I was still holding the ring.

"Maybe you'll have the opportunity to give this back to Callie," Mercer said, pointing at it.

"Do you want to wear it now?" I asked.

Lucy shook her head. "When this is done, I'd like to try to mend things with my aunt and with Callie. It's safer in your drawer, I think."

"Smart idea," Mercer said. "We'll help you get back with your aunt when you're ready. That's the kind of thing I like to do."

Lucy was wrapping the handkerchief around her fingers as we walked toward Max's office.

"You'll probably think this is stupid," she said

to me, holding her hand up in the air, "but this is the handkerchief I used to stop the bleeding when Jake cut me."

"You mean—?"

"Yeah, ten years ago, when we made the oath. He nicked his fingertip and rubbed it into the bloody palm of my hand, like I told you," Lucy said. "When I didn't stop bleeding right away, I crumpled this up and made a fist."

I stopped in my tracks. "May I see it again?"

"Sure," she said. "If you look right over here, there's still some of the bloodstain on it."

"But you must have washed this hundreds of times."

Lucy laughed. "Not so many as you think. I didn't have a washing machine except when I was at my aunt's house, and mostly I've been afraid that the lavender threads—see how pale they are?— would lose all their color."

I was studying the faint pink tinge on a three-inch square of the handkerchief.

"Lavender was my mother's favorite color," she went on.

Then I pointed to the spot with my pinky. "You think this is blood?"

"I know it is."

"Yours, and maybe some drops of Jake's mixed in it?"

"Probably so."

"Did you ever tell him about this handkerchief, way back then? I mean, did you tell him that it was very special to you because your mother made it for you?"

"I could have told him," Lucy said. "But who knows if he'd remember?"

"Would you mind very much if I held on to this a little longer?" I asked. "I promise you I won't lose it. It could be a very important piece of our case."

"That old thing could be evidence against Jake?" Lucy said. "How my mother would have loved that. Do you think it's something about the blood?"

"Well, if I'd gotten my hands on the handkerchief ten years ago, we'd be looking for Jake's DNA mixed into that blood sample," I said, with a new lilt in my voice. "And even though this stain is there, it's sure to be contaminated by now."

"So it's no good?"

"It would have been ideal if you'd put it away right after you used it, and never touched it again until now."

"That would have been impossible," Lucy said.

"I like the reason you kept it with you. But Jake doesn't have to figure that out. For all he knows, you left it in a drawer at your aunt's house," I said. "I might even tell him that."

Lucy chewed on the corner of her lip. "I don't understand why it's okay for you to tell lies, but it's wrong for me to do it."

"Because I'm not going to lie to him, Lucy," I said. "But a bloodstained handkerchief that a prosecutor could threaten to submit to a lab for DNA testing will make for a powerful bluff. And I'm always game for a bluff."

TWENTY-FIVE

"You got the bloody knife?" Mike asked.

We were sitting at the corner table in the front room at Primola with Mercer, waiting for Vickee Eaton to arrive.

"Well," I said, "it's an old threadbare piece of cotton that seems to have some blood on it—degraded, to be sure. But it might be a way to start a conversation with Zachary Palmer about Lucy."

"You opened that door pretty wide when you met with him last night," Mercer said. "Talking about Kathy Crain and Josie Breed, dropping the Jake name on him—I'm kind of surprised you didn't raise his dander up. He's a fool, but he's not stupid."

"Did she let you listen to the tape?" Mike asked Mercer.

"Yeah. Alex got a lot out of the guy."

"Sounds like you missed the message about subtlety," Mike said, raising a glass to me. "It's hard to bluff when you start showing all your cards."

"That's not what I did," I said. At least, I didn't think that I had.

"The last thing you want to do is put him in a position to take action."

I raised my Dewar's and we clinked. "I'm the one who's poised for action," I said, reeling off the steps I needed to take before I headed into the grand jury.

"How about his elementary school disciplinary records," Mike said, pushing back from the table. "You going for them, too? Or you think you have enough to bury him with that list you just recited?"

"This will do for starters," I said, getting up to follow him to Giuliano's office, downstairs from the dining room. "C'mon, Mercer. Back me up."

The owner, Giuliano, had a small TV in his office, which he lets us use to satisfy Mike's addiction to **Jeopardy!** The three of us crowded in, standing room only, and waited for Trebek to announce the category.

"In case you've just joined us, tonight's Final Jeopardy! category is 'Astronomy,' folks. 'Astronomy.'"

"That doesn't bode well for any of us," I said.

"It'll still cost you twenty bucks to be in the game," Mike said.

"I'm good for it."

Trebek revealed the answer. NATIVE AMERICAN NAME FOR OCTOBER'S FULL MOON.

Then he went on talking while two of the contestants looked as puzzled as I was, and the third one began to scrawl a question on his screen. "That's right, folks. Each month's full moon has a particular name, and this month's October moon—coming up any day now—is the one we're looking for."

The annoying music played in the background while I scratched my head for the right question.

"What's the harvest moon?" Mercer asked.

"That would be wrong," Mike said.

"Isn't that September?" I said.

"Yeah, Madame Bluff. So what's this month?" Mike said.

"I give up."

Mike gave his reply, beating all three contestants. "What is the hunter's moon?"

Trebek consoled the three losers and came up with the same name as Mike. "That's right," the show host repeated. "Named by Native Americans centuries ago, because it's the time of year when sunset and moonrise are closest together, and the light at night is brightest."

"Prime time for hunters," Mike said, clicking off the television. "The tall grasses are gone, so the animals are more exposed than in summer, and the sky is bright all evening."

I followed Mike to the staircase. "And you know that factoid because—?"

"Book of common knowledge, blondie," he said, blowing me off with a toss of his hand. "Next week we'll have Zach Palmer in our sights, under an October hunter's moon. There'll be nowhere for him to hide."

When I turned the corner and rounded the long bar, I saw Vickee at our table. She got up to give her husband a warm embrace, and to exchange kisses with Mike and me.

Vickee was the daughter of a much-decorated detective and the wife of one of the very best men on the force. She knew what a high-stakes game she played in by working for the deputy commissioner of public information.

Mercer had ordered a glass of Pinot Grigio for her. She seemed so tense—taut muscles in her face and stiff body language—that I assumed she'd had a bear of a day.

"Everything okay?" I asked.

Vickee grimaced. "You first."

I let Mercer give her a quick update on our progress with Lucy and my conversation with Zach Palmer last night.

"I don't want to distract you from your goal," she said. "Sounds like you're making headway. But you need to know this."

"What is it?" I asked.

Vickee inhaled. "You've all got to protect me on this. There are only half a dozen of us who know it as of right now."

"Cone of silence," Mike said, raising his right hand, in far too light a response.

"I'm serious," Vickee said.

"It's Francie," I said, flattening my hands on the table. "It's about Francie, isn't it? Has her condition worsened?"

"Still critical," Vickee said. "No change at all. But the docs know what happened to her now, and it changes everything."

Vickee waited until Giuliano set the wineglass down in front of her with his customary **"Salute"** and walked away.

"Francie was poisoned," Vickee said. "That's what put her in a coma."

"But she was frothing at the mouth and convulsing," I said. "What kind of poison does that?"

"A pretty deadly one," Vickee said. "Francie's barely clinging to life. She was poisoned by a potent nerve agent—the most lethal one ever developed."

TWENTY-SIX

"How could that happen to Francie Fain?" I asked.

I wasn't challenging the facts, but I was ignorant of what kind of toxin had such violent effects. I imagined the result of ingesting poison would lend itself to a more tranquil death, like in the cozy mystery novels of Agatha Christie.

"I can answer that in three words. I can't get my brain around the Russian expression, but the translation is easy," Vickee said. "'Kiss of death.'"

"Am I supposed to know what that is?" I asked her.

"How's your Russian, Coop?" Mike asked, interrupting us. "'Kiss of death' is the English translation of the Russian poison used against Francie—the latest in a long line of deadly chemical weapons."

"A nerve agent, developed by the Russians," Vickee said. "An extremely powerful nerve agent. At four o'clock today I'd never heard of it, and now I'm practically an expert."

"Go back to your news stories," Mike said. "Think nerve agents as military weapons."

"Out of my reach," I said. "Help me."

"Remember your history? Tokyo subways in 1995? Someone released an odorless gas called sarin, which killed a dozen people."

"Sounds vaguely familiar."

"Sarin's a nerve agent," Mike said. "You breathe it in or it makes contact with your skin and you're dead in minutes. It's a weapon of mass destruction, which was supposedly stockpiled in Iraq in the nineties, and then outlawed by international panels of weapons inspectors."

"But Francie had nothing to do with—" I tried to say something but Mike was rolling over me.

"Fast-forward to 2017, when Kim Jong-un's brother was assassinated in the airport in Kuala Lumpur," he said, "by two women who smeared a nerve agent on his face. I think that one was called VX."

"You're talking military stockpiles and foreign dictators," I said. "This has nothing to do with Francie."

"Hear me out," Mike said. "After the Korean kill, there was that couple in England last year— the Skripals. They were Soviet ex-pats poisoned by the cutting-edge level of agents. Novichok—'the newcomer' is how it translated. It was developed for military use—probably ten times more potent than whatever they used before it. The bad guys applied it to the door handle of the house where the Skripals lived and were likely targeting the father, who'd been former KGB—a double agent. Both of them, father and daughter, touched the handle—just touched it—and they almost died."

"But Novichok had an indeterminate shelf life," Vickee said. "It can remain dangerous for years, once it's deployed. So this latest poison was developed for the one-time hit—not contagious, no lingering effects, no chance of killing people aside from the target. That's why the Russians have been calling it the Kiss of Death."

"Russian military nerve agents?" I said, protesting again. "That's ridiculous. Francie is a defense attorney for the indigent. Her being the target of the Kiss of Death makes no sense at all."

"Do you know Quint Akers?" Vickee asked me.

"Sure. Francie's supervisor."

"We talked to him late today—but we didn't tell him the diagnosis. He says Francie was in England a few weeks ago, and we know that places her not terribly far from where the Skripals were targeted."

"I can't believe you're talking about this stuff," I said. "I was supposed to be at that conference, too. It wasn't about espionage and spies and secret agents. That's absurd. It was an international symposium on violent crime."

"Scully thinks the English visit is a long shot, too," Vickee said, "but this newest nerve agent can work instantaneously when you touch it—or it can be absorbed more slowly into the bloodstream, depending on the method of delivery."

"Francie may have been collateral damage, right?" I asked. "That makes more sense than her being a target."

"It is what it is," Vickee said. "The medical experts are certain they have identified a nerve agent, and in all likelihood it was a direct hit on Francie. We're doing a clean sweep of Francie's apartment tonight, in case whatever toxin it is happens to be in something that's there—maybe even something she brought home from England—a gift or a souvenir that she just opened yesterday."

"Did those Skirpers—?"

"Skripals," Mike said.

"Whoever they are. Did they live?" I asked. "Did they survive direct contact with the nerve agent used against them?"

"Yes, but it's slow going. They were both in comas for weeks," Vickee said, nodding at me.

"Tell Coop the truth," Mike said. "Not everyone recovers. Some who survive these chemical weapons have permanent nerve damage, chronic weakness in the arms and legs, severe depression, an inability to concentrate enough to read or to write. These are deadly, dark drugs."

All this, and Francie was pregnant, too. Vickee hadn't mentioned that and I didn't dare ask.

"I told the commissioner that Francie wrote you

a note to hand off at your party," Vickee said. "That it mentioned something about a new job. Did you know anything about it?"

"That came as a total surprise. We never had the chance to talk," I said. "I'll make sure to give Mercer the note to get to you, for vouchering."

"The conference—did she have a chance to tell you about that?" Vickee asked.

"It occurred right after I'd been released from the kidnappers. No, we never discussed that either. My fault, because I just didn't focus on things that didn't seem life-or-death at the time."

Now I could kick myself for being so self-involved during my recovery.

"You have no idea what changes Francie was planning on making in her life?"

"I never thought she'd leave her job any more than I'd leave mine," I said. "She lived for her work."

"Like Coop said, does the commissioner think this poisoning was intentional?" Mike asked. "Isn't there a chance Francie Fain wasn't the intended victim?"

"There's a chance she wasn't, but like I said, this latest version of nerve agents isn't contagious," Vickee said. "Do you want to help?"

"Course I do," Mike said.

"Scully had to call the head of the FBI," Vickee said. "It's the feds who are going through Francie's apartment with our team. They're better prepared on the chem weapons response. But we need someone to look at the video surveillance tapes for the hours before and after she collapsed on Baxter Street. It wasn't an issue when we thought she was simply ill, but it's critically important now."

"I'm the man," Mike said.

"Great. I told the commissioner you were the perfect candidate to do this because you were there just after she fell down, and you rode in the ambulance with her," Vickee said. "We figured if we let Major Case guys do it, there'd be too many of them we'd have to tell about the nerve agent. But you—"

Mike poked her in the rib. "But me, I'm discreet, right?"

"You'd damn well better be the soul of discretion," Mercer said, tipping his glass and pointing it at Mike.

"Who'd want Francie dead?" I said, looking for comfort in my drink.

"Maybe a perp she represented?" Mercer said.

"The ones she got off are grateful," I said, "and the others are safely behind bars upstate, courtesy of my colleagues."

"Did she have a guy?" Mike asked.

I waited for Vickee to answer, to see what she knew about Francie's pregnancy—which would mean Keith Scully knew about it as well.

"We don't know exactly," Vickee said.

"You do know there's a rumor Francie was pregnant?" I said, unable to hold back any longer.

"I guess that news is out there already," she said,

nibbling on a breadstick. "My boss wasn't sure that her friends knew, so I wasn't going to mention it."

"I'm not certain that anyone else does," I said. "Sorry, Vick. I didn't mean to make you spill the beans. I just didn't want the fetal DNA to be over-looked, if it becomes an issue. It could provide a valuable lead."

"Scully's on it," Vickee said. "Francie's in real danger of losing the baby, and he knows what has to be done if she does."

There was not a ray of hope in this story, no matter how I looked at it.

"How do you not go public with this?" I asked. "If Francie wasn't the intended victim, there could be so many more people at risk. The perp—or perps—might try again until they get it right."

"Scully and the mayor are going back and forth on that," Vickee said. "It's been forty-eight hours since Francie went down, and no other cases have been reported. Scully thinks he's only got another twenty-four before he has to make a statement. The mayor disagrees with him, of course. I get the feeling he hopes this is a one-off that will save him a huge political headache if there are no other victims."

"What a coward," I said. "But that's nothing new for him."

"So there's only one thing we haven't talked about yet," Mike said, "and that is what the com-missioner did with the patient."

Vickee's back stiffened again. She didn't speak.

"We know she's not at New York/Cornell Hospital," I said.

"If you can trust us to tell us this much, and to ask me to screen the videos," Mike said, "you might let us know about the disappearing act the commissioner pulled."

"Don't put me in that position, Mike. Francie's getting all the medical attention she possibly needs," Vickee said. "And she's safer this way, too."

"Safer from **me**?" Mike asked, leaning back and putting his hands on his chest, in mock surprise. "I'm not the baby daddy, Vick. I'm not a suspect here. Let us in, will you?"

Vickee stood up and stared her husband down. "Mercer, I'm out of here, okay? I'm as concerned about Francie Fain as the three of you," she said, pointing her finger at Mike and then me, "but that's as far as we go tonight."

Mercer got up to join her.

"If you two think you can top the best scientists in this country researching this new drug and its antidotes 24/7, trying to reverse the symptoms and all that," Vickee said to the two of us, "I assure you I'll advise the commissioner that you should just jump in and go to the head of the class."

I'd never seen my friend this angry.

"And in case you think you deserve some kind

of award for having very special balls, Mike, 'cause they're what you're usually trying to show off," Vickee said, "let me just remind you they're no match for the brains of the five or six Nobel laureates who have been up all night working to keep Francie Fain alive."

TWENTY-SEVEN

"I've been to every hospital in Manhattan over the years, and most in the outer boroughs," I said to Mike as we settled in at home in the den. "I should be able to figure out who's got the best resources to care for Francie."

Rape victims were treated in most emergency rooms, and we worked closely with forensic nurse examiners and docs who prepared evidence collection kits during those exams—now a critical feature in most trials.

My colleagues and I had stood beside gurneys in ERs to interview witnesses when an arrest time was critical, we had visited patients in ICUs just to make a silent bond when a case was assigned, and we often sat with survivors who were hospitalized with other injuries as we worked on their cases.

"You want to start on the southern tip of the island?" Mike asked. "Or top down?"

"Bottom up," I said. "I've never seen Vickee snap like that."

"She's sitting on a powder keg," Mike said, "and we weren't much help."

"How about a drink?" I said, reclining on the sofa in a pair of leggings and one of Mike's shirts. I started to name the hospitals, drawing an imaginary map in the air. "Presbyterian Downtown, Beth Israel, Bellevue, NYU Langone."

"Not so much research at those," Mike said. "No Nobelists, I don't think."

"Cornell, St. Luke's-Roosevelt, Lenox Hill, Mount Sinai," I said, and by the time I had ticked off Metropolitan, Harlem, and Presbyterian Columbia in Washington Heights, Mike was cooling me down with a healthy dose of Dewar's on the rocks.

He fixed a drink for himself and sat down in an armchair across the room.

"You skipped a few."

"Specialty hospitals," I said, dismissing them in one breath. "Places she isn't likely to be. Ear, Nose, and Throat is mostly plastic surgery, which Francie doesn't need; Memorial Sloan Kettering is a great cancer facility, which is fortunately not her issue; Hospital for Special Surgery is orthopedic, and nothing was broken. Did I ever tell you when HSS was founded, it was called the Hospital for the Ruptured and Crippled?"

"You got that story from your old man, right?" Mike asked.

"Yes, like everything else I know about this

subject," I said. "Then there's Joint Diseases on East Seventeenth," I said.

"Never been there," Mike said. "No homicides, I guess."

"That one was originally called the Jewish Hospital for Deformities."

"Dr. Benjamin Cooper knows way too much about medicine."

I sat up straight. "Why didn't I think of that?"

"What?" Mike asked.

I grabbed my iPhone from the side table and dialed the international number for my parents, who were at their home in the Caribbean for the fall and winter.

"I'll ask my father," I said. "He'll figure this out."

It was an hour later on the tiny island of St. Barth's than our ten thirty P.M., but my father was a night owl, just like me.

"Dad?" I said when he answered the phone.

"Alexandra," he boomed back, enthusiastically. "Is everything okay?"

I had just spoken with him and my mother at length on Monday, assuring them that everything had gone well on my first day back at work.

"All good with Mike and with me, but we're puzzling out a problem in a case, and I thought maybe you could help."

"Just what a man wants to hear," he said, "that I might know as much as Siri."

"I like the sound of your voice much better,"

I said, "and I know how much you love me, so I expect you'll try harder than she would."

"I'll give it a whirl," my father said. "What's the question?"

"Let me put you on speaker so Mike can hear, too. We need help identifying a major medical research center in Manhattan," I said. "At least, Mike and I think it's in Manhattan."

"Oh, darling," he said. "I think you've given me an impossible task. Almost every major medical center in the city has a serious research arm attached."

"Some must be more outstanding than others," I said. "C'mon, Dad. What do you know about Nobel laureates?"

He laughed at me. "Do I need to remind you, Alexandra? I wasn't exactly a sore loser, but I never won one."

"I know you don't have a Nobel Prize, Dad, but you were given a Lasker Award, and that's pretty swell company."

The Alfred and Mary Lasker Award was given annually to living persons who made major contributions to medical science. My father and his partner had received the award for their work on heart disease more than twenty-five years earlier.

He ignored my compliment and asked me a question in return. "What does this have to do with sexual assault?"

"Nothing," I said. "Nothing at all. But someone I care about with a very rare diagnosis has been moved from New York/Cornell Hospital—shrouded in secrecy—to some kind of research facility, where there are something like five or six Nobel Prize laureates working on her."

"You should have started with that fact, Alexandra. It's a rather unique identifier," my father said. "A facility with twenty-two Lasker Award winners and twenty-five Nobel Prize winners, six of them current faculty."

"And it's medical, Dr. Cooper?" Mike asked.

"Entirely," he said. "It's the first institute for research in America, founded in 1901, exclusively dedicated to the scientific study of medicine."

"Where is it, Dad?"

"Right under your nose, Alexandra. Behind wrought iron gates, guarded by a security team to keep it private, on York Avenue, between Sixty-Third Street and Sixty-Eighth Street. The best-kept secret in the city."

I looked at Mike and shook my head. A five-block stretch of the Upper East Side that was a total mystery to me.

"The Rockefeller Institute," my father said, "complete with a sequestered twenty-bed hospital held in reserve for some of the most extreme medical cases in modern history. You'll find your six Nobelists in there—and probably your patient, too."

TWENTY-EIGHT

"I've seen a sign on the gates," Mike said. "Isn't it called Rockefeller University now?"

"Yes, but it was created as an institute and only changed its title to university in 1965," my father said. "There are no college students at this university, Mike. It's a pure research service, with a PhD program but no undergraduates."

"And it abuts New York/Cornell Hospital," Mike said, putting his hands together, reminding me that Francie had been on the north side of Sixty-Eighth Street just twenty-four hours earlier.

"That's true. But there's no relationship between them," my father said. "It's just a coincidence of location."

"Do you know anyone on staff there, Dad?"

"Afraid not, darling. If you can think of any other way for me to be helpful, I'm more than happy to try."

"Thanks, Dad. We'll keep you posted," I said. "Love you. Good night."

I sank back onto the sofa and picked up my

drink. "You're right, Mike. There's very little he doesn't know about medicine, but I'm not sure what this information gets us."

"Aren't you curious about what goes on behind those wrought iron gates, and why that Rockefeller Hospital would be a better place to treat Francie than where she was?"

"Yes, I'm curious," I said. "And if I stay up all night, I'll never get the connection between her and some military weapon of mass destruction. It's not that it matters where she is, but that she's alive and someone is trying to save her life. I'd just like to lay eyes on her for five minutes, and whisper encouragement in her ear."

Mike was using my iPad, apparently Googling something.

"Here's the website for Rock U," he said.

"What'll that do for me?"

"The head of security in every hospital in this city is usually a retired boss from the NYPD. Probably not a Nobel laureate, but a pretty sure way for me to get in," Mike said. "I'm looking up faculty and staff."

"The back door might be a better way in than the front."

"Director of security," Mike said. "Roger Murfee."

"An acquaintance?"

"Aces. Super guy," Mike said. "He was a lieutenant commander in Harlem for six years before he left to take this job, the bio says. We had our share of walking body bags out of the projects together, with Murf riding shotgun for me."

Mike seemed totally engaged in looking up his former colleagues who were guarding over Francie's facility. But the next moment, when he opened his mouth, his attention was back on her medical condition.

"Nerve agents work by disrupting the central nervous system. They kill by asphyxiation—or by cardiac arrest."

I couldn't speak. I just listened to Mike.

"If Francie had collapsed fifteen minutes earlier, sitting alone at her desk, cleaning up her papers after a long, stressful day in court," Mike said, "and not found till hours later—or in the morning—the assumption would have been that she had a heart attack."

"She's too young for that," I said.

"I bet you don't have any idea of her medical history, or the effect of pregnancy on it."

"I don't, but . . ."

"One of the things that makes Novichok and its progeny a level worse than earlier nerve agents is that they are designed to be untraceable," Mike said. "A woman keels over at her desk in the Legal Aid offices? She's got no family to advocate for her, to fight to get someone's attention in the system. Even with an autopsy, it's unlikely the medical examiner would find any sign of the cause."

"Francie's not dead," I said.

"She's at a hospital that seems to be the last resort for someone on life support, don't you think? If she doesn't make it, then the whole matter goes from Major Case to the Homicide Squad."

He stood up, took the glass from my hand, and rinsed it out in the sink of the wet bar. "Six A.M., Coop. Set your alarm. I want to check out what's going on. I have a feeling the commissioner is holding out on something he knows about all this."

"Then I'm coming with you," I said.

"Good," Mike said. "It may be your last chance to see Francie Fain."

TWENTY-NINE

"Is he expecting you?" the guard in the security booth at the Sixty-Sixth Street gate said to Mike, who had flashed his gold shield to the uniformed man.

"He'll be happy to see me. Let's just leave it at that."

We had walked through the two tall stone pillars that were topped with an elegant wrought iron archway, a typical design at the time it was built, more than a century ago.

Mike's answer didn't seem to raise any concern in the guard. "Well, you're early, but you might as well go on in," he said. "Just turn right at the Founder's Hall, at the top of the drive, and it'll be your next building on the left."

"Thanks," Mike said.

We walked uphill toward the five-story gray-brick building with limestone trim that had the name FOUNDER'S HALL carved above the entrance. It seemed to anchor the campus of the institute-turned-university, and was undoubtedly the first structure built there.

We turned right to reach the next building, almost as old as the main one, bearing its original designation: NURSES' RESIDENCE.

"This means we must be getting close to the hospital," Mike said, climbing the steps and opening the front door, shortly before seven A.M.

Instead of a residential hall, the first floor had clearly been turned into suites of offices. The first ones, to the left and to the right, were both marked SECURITY.

Murf's name was on a sign over the door to the left. Mike knocked but there was no response. He opened it and we entered, sitting down in the reception area, where Mike picked up a map of the grounds from a pile on the secretary's desk.

We began to study it but hadn't gotten very far when Roger Murfee came through the door.

"Well, well, well," he said, smiling at Mike and extending his hand. "It's sort of like a bad penny turning up. It had to happen sooner or later."

"I'm Alexandra—"

"Cooper," Murf said. "Special Victims. My guys had a ton of cases with you."

He was taller than Mike and lean, with a handsome face framed by short, slightly wavy blond hair and frameless glasses.

"Good to meet you," I said.

"Somebody asleep at the front gate when you got here?" Murf asked.

"Tinning the old-timers still works," Mike said. "The shiny badge opens a lot of doors."

Murf unlocked his door and led us into his office. "I've been here five years, without a scintilla of a violent crime. So don't change the odds for me, okay?"

"Just sniffing around," Mike said. "Looking for a body."

"Fresh out of luck. I don't do bodies anymore."

"Even before you hear my story?" Mike asked.

"I'll give you fifteen minutes," Murf said. "What do you want to know?"

"What is this place, and why is there a private hospital here?"

"Let me answer your question with a question. What do you know about John D. Rockefeller? I mean Senior, the original?"

"That he was probably the richest person in modern history," Mike said. "Founded the Standard Oil Company in the 1870s."

"And known for his philanthropy, too," I added.

Murf filled in all the gaps with a brief bio of John D.'s business and philanthropic successes in his very long life.

He went on. "In 1900, Rockefeller's first grandchild—his daughter's baby, Jack—died of scarlet fever. There was no treatment for the disease back then. The billionaire was devastated by the boy's death. He told friends that he had enough money to try to find a cure for both scarlet fever and infectious diseases like it."

"Sad story," I said.

"But it launched this incredible place," Murf said. "Within months, Rockefeller agreed to fund the creation of this new research facility dedicated exclusively to the scientific study of medicine—the nature and causes of disease, and the methods of treatment."

"Okay," Mike said. "I get the research part of it. But why a hospital?"

"His science advisers insisted on a small private hospital on the same campus," Murf said. "The research would be done in the laboratories, but the patients would be carefully selected from the general population of the city to receive the new treatments. There was no institute like this in the entire country."

"So the hospital is essentially a lab, too," I said.

"Yes," Murf said. "It opened in 1910, just before the height of the polio epidemic. So polio was one of the first diseases studied for treatment, along with typhoid and syphilis and pneumonia—which used to kill twenty-five percent of the people who contracted it."

"Can we see the hospital?" Mike asked.

"Sure. Sure you can," Murf said. "It's still in its original building."

"Still small, then," I said. "Still exclusive."

Murf got up from his desk. "Exclusive? Let's just say it's a club you don't want to join, although you'll have the most brilliant docs in the world working on you."

"You like your job?" Mike asked as we headed for the door.

"Best place in the world to be," Murf said. "It's like a mini precinct. We've got close to forty men and women, on duty 24/7. Two thousand people work here and about two hundred of them are grad students—PhD candidates. I've never been treated so well in my life."

"I get it," Mike said. "No perps on campus. No mopes to mess with you. They're all brainiacs, doing good for the world."

We turned left again and Murf pointed up over our heads. Three stories above us was an elevated bridge—once copper coated, now with a light green patina that made it stand out against the brick buildings on either end. It connected the third floor of the old Nurses' Residence with the hospital.

"Remind you of anything?" Murf asked.

I looked up and laughed. "You've got your own Bridge of Sighs," I said.

"You bet we do," Murf said. "The patients used to be wheeled over to the solarium in the Nurses' Residence, and their wistful glances out over the East River were often their last looks at the cityscape."

"Condemned men and women making that

final crossing on the bridge," Mike said. "Just like the Tombs. Just like the Doge's Palace."

I wanted to get that image out of my head. "Such prime real estate to build a medical institute on back then," I said. "Bordering on the river, I mean."

"By 1900, this thirteen-acre plot of land was left intact on Manhattan Island," Murf said. "It had been a family farm—the Schermerhorn Farm—since the eighteenth century, until John D. bought it. You should see the old photographs, with great views over the river and all the way out to Long Island."

Mike stopped to walk closer to the edge of the building, which hung out over the FDR Drive and the river. He turned back to join us and we continued on to the entrance of the hospital.

"You've got new construction going on," he said to Murf.

"Yeah, we're adding some new labs and offices. State of the art," Murf said. "These scientists have it good. They're sitting right on the river, above the Drive."

"They probably don't even know what they're sitting on," Mike said.

"What do you mean?" I asked.

"The FDR Drive was built after World War II," he said. "From landfill."

"Okay," I said.

"That landfill came from England, you know."

Murf looked at me and shrugged.

"This part of Manhattan is built with the rubble from the blitz of the city of Bristol," Mike said, putting his knowledge of military history to good use.

"That's crazy," I said.

"Not so crazy as you think. Our ships had been delivering supplies to England, in all the time leading up to the Normandy invasion. Specifically to the port city of Bristol," Mike said. "The ships couldn't come back empty. They needed to be filled with ballast. Something heavy had to go in the bilge to stabilize them, so they used the material from all the buildings—homes, factories, aircraft manufacturing plants, and even churches—that were destroyed by the Nazis."

"That will make my ride home feel a little different from now on," I said.

Murf had pulled open the door of the old Rockefeller Hospital to let us in. "Interesting factoid, Mike. But you never made your point. Exactly what are we looking for?"

"Coop and I are thinking you might have a patient here who might need our help—well, her help specifically when she wakes up out of a coma."

I let Mike put the weight on me. Every cop wanted to help when they thought a woman had been the victim of a rape.

Murf just stared. "But you want to see her now, even though she's not conscious?"

I phumphered for an answer. "We—uh, I just missed seeing her at Cornell, and now I understand she's been transferred here. It's the way I usually do things, just to get connected to my victim—and perhaps there's family around I could introduce myself to."

I got the feeling that Murf was too smart to buy into us completely.

"I don't get to make decisions about patients and who gets to see them," he said.

"Well, can you ask one of the nurses or docs about her? About her condition, and whether we'd be allowed in?" I said. "Her name is Francie Fain."

"They're not even going to tell **me** about her condition," he said. "HIPAA regulations and all that."

We had gotten off the elevator on the third floor. Although the bones of the building were old, the interiors had been completely modernized. I watched as Murf approached the nurses' station.

He leaned in and spoke with the only nurse at the desk, looking back at us to explain who we were.

Her stern expression didn't waver for a second. I could see that the corridor to our right had an open door, and that a physician in a lab coat was heading back to the desk.

But something the nurse said—without moving her head to either side—made Murf look in the opposite direction, toward the corridor entrance to our left.

"Look, Mike," I said. "There'll be no getting in that wing."

There was a sign posted over the closed door, with a single word printed in a large, bold font. It had to be where Francie Fain had been taken. All the sign said was QUARANTINE.

THIRTY

"Not a word to Mercer about our visit to Rockefeller," Mike said half an hour later when he dropped me at the courthouse. "He's likely to tell Vickee, and then Scully will be after my scalp."

He was on his way to headquarters to view the video surveillance tapes from Francie's last walk down Baxter Street.

"Understood," I said, getting out of his car and stopping at the coffee cart for two large cups of black coffee.

There was plenty for me to do to organize the presentation of my case against Zach Palmer. The harder task was to figure out how and when to tell him that he had better retain counsel and prepare to defend himself. Since it was already Thursday, I decided to wait until Monday to make that move.

"You must have been here awfully early," Laura said when she reached her desk almost an hour after I had settled in.

"You know the offer of a door-to-door ride from

Detective Chapman is always too good to refuse," I said, giving her a thumbs-up and a morning smile. "Try your best to keep the day quiet for me, will you?"

"That might take some magical powers that I simply don't possess," Laura said. "Are you taking calls?"

"Screening them carefully, if you don't mind."

Mercer wasn't far behind, with a third cardboard cup of coffee and a blueberry muffin for each of us.

"I want to apologize for my role in upsetting Vickee last night," I said.

"You ought to call her up and tell her," he said. "I'm not authorized to accept apologies on her behalf."

"I've already tried to call her twice, but she's just letting it go to voice mail."

"Vickee's walking a tightrope," Mercer said. "Scully's got her on a tight leash, and she knows she can't make you and Mike happy at the same time."

We got to work, dividing our chores on Lucy's case. I called her aunt to let her know that I thought we were making progress, that Lucy admitted to stealing her cousin's ring, and that she hoped to be reunited with the family when she was ready to leave Streetwork. Her aunt seemed pleased, and suddenly much warmer, to hear that news. I decided there was no reason to get into the fine points of the case against Zach Palmer at this point.

An hour later, Laura buzzed me. "I've got the judge's wife—Janet Corliss—on your first line. Do you want her?"

"Want her? Of course not," I said, "but I'd better take her."

I pressed the plastic button and answered the call. "This is Alexandra Cooper."

"Ms. Cooper? It's Janet Corliss."

"How can I help you?"

"My friend Jessica Witte was down to see you on Tuesday. You told her you'd consider coming to my office to meet with me—and, well, there's getting to be some urgency to it."

There was usually some urgency with most of the people I dealt with, and it was always part of my job to triage each matter.

"Would you be comfortable with next week, Ms. Corliss?" I asked.

"Next week? Did you say next week? I could be dead by next week."

"Then we'll deal with it right away," I said. "I've got a fabulous deputy. Perhaps Catherine could get to you this afternoon or tomorrow?"

"You're too important to do this yourself?" she asked. "Or are you in Bud's pocket, too?"

"Excuse me? Bud's pocket?"

There were moments that the burden of being a public servant weighed heavily on my tongue. I couldn't tell the woman what I really thought about her comment, her dig at my ethics, without causing her to try to climb the chain of command—though it didn't go very far up since Battaglia's death.

"Listen to me, Ms. Cooper," the distraught woman said. I assumed that the tension of her situation might have heightened the aggressive tone she took with me. "My husband just made an offer to a young lawyer to be his new law secretary. It's an important job, as you know, and the fellow who's had it for the last eight years is moving to the West Coast."

"I didn't know that. He's a smart kid and he's been a great asset to your husband," I said.

"So now he offers the job to a young woman," she said, "and I believe they're having an affair."

"I can only imagine how upsetting that must be to you, but it's not my territory, Ms. Corliss," I said. "I prosecute violent crimes. I don't meddle in affairs."

"This woman is the one we were fighting about when Bud tried to choke me, Ms. Cooper. Does that make it all a bit more relevant?" Janet Corliss asked. "I accused Bud of having a sexual relationship with her. He denied it, of course, but he put his hands on my throat because he got so angry."

"Yes, your friend told me about that, and we need to discuss whether or not you want to prosecute, which you're certainly entitled to do."

"I need to see you today," Janet Corliss said, screeching into the phone. "The woman Bud offered the job to has disappeared. She's a Legal Aid lawyer and her name is Francie Fain."

I almost gasped out loud. I was reeling at the mention of Francie's name.

"No one in her office has the faintest idea where she is," she went on. Janet Corliss took a deep breath and I flashed back to the note in Francie's briefcase, telling me that she was thinking of taking a new job and wanted my advice. I thought, too, of her pregnancy.

"Ms. Corliss," I said, trying to calm myself as I spoke, "Francie's a good friend of mine. It's entirely inappropriate for me to handle your complaint, as I'm sure you realize. I'm going to get the best prosecutor to come see you as soon as possible. Catherine Dashfer will call you back shortly."

"You'll regret passing me off to someone else, Ms. Cooper," she said. "There are things about my husband that you need to know."

THIRTY-ONE

"I get the feeling I'm kind of talking you down from a window ledge," Catherine said after five minutes in my office, listening to the complicated stories that had interwoven themselves since I was called up to Judge Corliss's courtroom on Monday.

"Truth? I was actually feeling like I was back to normal," I said to her. She was as solid a friend as she was a lawyer, and there was nothing I couldn't trust her with. "Suddenly, I'm back out with my legs dangling over the windowsill, and it feels better to be out there than where I'm sitting now."

"This **is** your normal, Alex," Catherine said. "Have you forgotten how we run here, in just a few short weeks? Bedlam, chaos, mayhem, and every now and then we just have a busy day. You're registering somewhere between bedlam and mayhem."

"Can you do some stroking of Ms. Corliss this afternoon?" I asked. "Call her and go up to her office to hear what she has to say? I'm worried that her domestic situation might truly be escalating this week."

"Pronto. I can go right after lunch, and take a paralegal with me."

"Smart," I said, passing her my notes with a wink. "Has Bud ever groped you? I mean, just making sure you don't have a conflict."

"Nope. I never tried a case in front of him, and I was warned off going into the robing room for plea discussions."

"Perfect."

"What do I need to know about Francie?" she asked.

"Janet Corliss is trying to make something out of her disappearance," I said. "All you need to know is that Francie is ill and has taken a leave of absence from Legal Aid for the next few weeks."

"Who do you trust in the Bud-Janet face-off?" Catherine said.

"Based on Bud's history, I'd go with Janet. But it sounds like a lot of balls are being thrown up in the air—some of them aimed at each other, and there may be a matrimonial split at stake, so I'm counting on you to ferret out the truth."

"Where will you be?"

"Mercer and I are going to dash over to One PP," I said. Police Plaza was the headquarters of the NYPD, and it was a short walk from the DA's office, ducking around the side of the federal courthouse. "Mike called just before you walked in. He wants us to see some routine video surveillance tape that may have captured something while Francie was on her way to Forlini's Monday night."

We both got up and walked to the door. Mercer was on Laura's phone, and I waited for him to hang up before we all walked down the corridor.

"Talk later," Catherine said. "I'll let you know what I think."

At eleven fifteen, Mercer and I were making our way to headquarters. When we reached the elaborate security screening, he placed his gun on the conveyer belt and I followed him through the scanning machine.

The commissioner and his retinue had offices on the fourteenth floor. We took the elevator upstairs and signed in, waiting for Vickee to take us to a conference room she had set up with three video screens lined up side by side on the wall facing the long wooden table.

"You getting anywhere?" Mercer asked Mike.

"Blind, I think."

"He's watched each tape about twenty times," Vickee said, "and I'm not sure we know any more than we did before we had them."

The three screens represented images captured by three different cameras along the route.

"Francie's office is at 60 Lafayette Street," Mike said, referring to some of the suites occupied by the criminal division of Legal Aid, "so she comes into the picture crossing over to walk past One Hogan Place."

Hogan Place was a very short block, renamed in the nineties for the great district attorney Frank Hogan, who served in that job for thirty-two years, even longer than Paul Battaglia. Because One Hogan was the entrance to the DA's office, there were security cameras over the doorway and on each end of the street.

"Check out the first screen," Mike said. He pressed the Start button and the grainy black-and-white tape rolled.

It was shortly before eight P.M., and the sidewalk had a good number of people—mostly staff, I assumed—walking out of our building as well as the one directly across the street. Francie entered the shot after about fifteen seconds, walking across Centre Street, from her office past the front door of ours.

Two or three times, she waved and had a verbal exchange with colleagues of mine, and once she stopped to plant a kiss on the cheek of another prosecutor.

"I've put pads in front of you," Vickee said. "You and Mercer can jot down names of anyone you recognize."

I picked up a pen and wrote down three names, which I'm sure would be an exercise in futility. "No killers that I see."

"I want names in case they saw something that had no meaning at the time," Vickee said. "We should go back to all of them."

"Second screen," Mercer said.

The next sequence picked Francie up in front of the steps of One Hogan, on her cell phone, placing a call and having a short conversation before hanging it up.

"You have the phone?" Mercer asked.

"Major Case did the dump," she said. "She was trying to reach a client on that call, but she just left a message on a machine."

When Francie reached the corner of the block to square the building and turn left on Baxter Street to walk to Forlini's, the screen darkened. Her figure became more shadowy and indistinct as she walked away from the stationary camera.

The third screen picked her up again at the intersection of the two streets—Baxter and Hogan Place—from a camera mounted high overhead against the side of the building.

The block was packed thick with blue-and-white patrol cars and black unmarked detective vehicles, some parked half on the sidewalk and others doubled in for long court arraignments or bookings.

"See her there?" Vickee asked.

Mike had obviously watched this earlier. Mercer and I both nodded.

"What's she doing?" I asked. "Why'd she turn, do you think?"

"Keep watching," Mike said.

Francie stood in place while someone approached her. It was clearly a person she knew, because she waited and seemed to be talking to him or her.

"Where did that guy come from?" Mercer asked.

"Why are you saying it's a guy?" Vickee said. "Watch again. I mean, maybe it is, but can any of you see any identifying features?"

The overhead angle made it hard to see anything at all about either figure. We knew the first one on the sidewalk was Francie Fain because we had seen her so clearly in the first two videos. Now she stopped and turned her head, as though someone had called to her.

The second figure emerged from between several cars that were parked tightly together. He or she was taller than Francie, who was about five foot seven in her mid-height heels, and was clothed in jeans and a dark hoodie-style jacket, with the hood covering the head and upper portion of the face.

"Slow it down," Mercer said.

We watched as the person eased into the camera's frame, having already called Francie's name. He or she continued walking toward Francie, although no one else was within range, and they could have begun to speak from that distance.

"Why change the speed?" Vickee asked. "Someone you think you know?"

"It's worth checking out," Mercer said. "You see any regulars, Mike?"

"I'm good but I'm not that good," Mike said. "Androgynous male white with flat head, at least five foot nine and—"

"Why did you say 'male'?" Vickee asked.

"Simple. You see him squeeze between the patrol car and that second unmarked number that's parked too close to it?" Mike said. "See where he puts his hand, how he cups it on the front of his pants below his belt, to protect his dick—sorry—his private parts from getting squished against the metal? That's a guy thing."

"That is so lame," I said. "It's not a guy thing at all. I do it, too. I put my hand down to flatten whatever I'm wearing so my jacket or dress doesn't get caught on the car grillwork. Totally gender-neutral movement."

Mike played that clip again, at least three times, but it didn't seem to solve anything.

"I don't see that person touching Francie," Mercer said. "Am I wrong?"

We all murmured in agreement.

"Okay," Vickee said. "Now Francie waves good-bye—we can't get it close enough to lip-read anything—and completes the turn onto Baxter Street, with Forlini's less than two blocks away."

The three screens went blank and were replaced by other videos from the rear of the courthouse.

Mike clicked on the first one, which was at the back door of the building. "She's walking alone again. She takes out her phone like she's going to make a call, but before she does, the same figure runs in her direction, seems to shout something to her."

This time the person in black seemed to jog back into view, cup hands to his or her mouth, and call out a few words before backing away out of sight.

"What's that motion Francie made with her right hand, when she spun around to look?" I asked.

"Seems to me," Mike said, holding up his arm to imitate the motion, "that she was either suggesting that the person wait for her, or that she was saying 'five'—you know, holding up five fingers."

"'I'll only be five minutes'?" I suggested.

We moved our attention to the second screen. The camera was poised on the south side of the walkway—the overhead Bridge of Sighs—pointing downward.

"Oh my God," I said, throwing my hand over my mouth.

Two people had passed Francie Fain on the sidewalk, both of them in suits and carrying briefcases. One had brushed her shoulder—maybe a little intoxicated from a post-work cocktail at a Baxter Street bar.

But it was the sight of Francie Fain that had brought me up short. In the thirty seconds it had taken her to get from the corner of Hogan Place to the back of the Tombs, she suddenly appeared to become dizzy, leaning against the side of the building for support.

"She's drooling, right?" Mercer said. "Drooling and shaking uncontrollably."

There was no one in sight. I just wanted to reach through the screen and steady my friend, find out what she had eaten or drunk or been injected with. I wanted to make whatever was happening stop.

"That man that bumped her," I said, "should we try to find him, too?"

"Male black. Gray or navy blue pinstripe suit, expensive briefcase," Mike said.

"Why did you guess he's black?" I asked.

"I'll run this one back," Mike said. "When he held up his hand, like excusing himself to your friend, I'd say he has dark skin."

"It's like a video Rorschach," Mercer said. "We're all looking at different things when the pieces start moving."

"You're right," I said. "I'm so fixated on Francie Fain that I didn't even notice the man put up a hand."

The last scene showed Francie in a full-on convulsion, sprawled on the ground and trying desperately to breathe as she thrashed from side to side.

"Would you pull up that first video of this group again, when she's turning the corner from Hogan Place onto Baxter Street?" I asked.

Mike stood up and came behind me, massaging my shoulders. "Hard to watch, kid. We know that."

"I want to see it again for a reason, Mike. You gave me an idea."

He went back to his chair, leaned over it, and restarted the video I wanted to see. When it got to the point at which the figure in black picked up a hand to cup his or her mouth and call out to Francie, I told him to freeze it.

"Now make it larger," I said. "Give us a close-up of the hand."

Mike zoomed in on the person, whose hand appeared from within the arm of the oversize hoodie when it was lifted to his or her mouth.

"That's a woman!" I said. "It's a woman who knows there are cameras all around these buildings, and has dressed and covered herself to conceal her identity."

All three of them were leaning in now to take a closer look.

"Something stuck out to me the first time I watched it, but I couldn't articulate it until Mike said something about the man's hands in the next frame," I said. "Check out the fingernails as the hand comes out of the sleeve of the jacket."

In the frozen blowup of the side of the left hand that was closest to the camera, the fingernails were long and slim, delicately shaped as though they'd been manicured.

"Cherchez la femme," Mike said. "That's putting a nail in a coffin."

THIRTY-TWO

"I'm not saying this is the person who brought down Francie Fain," I said, "but you've got to find out who she is and what she stopped Francie for."

"I'm with you," Vickee said.

"Get someone over to Francie's office and see who her visitors were on Monday, all throughout the day, until she left."

"I can do that," Mike said.

"We've been to her office," Vickee said. "Crime Scene went to both her home and her office in Hazmat suits and came out with everything that wasn't nailed down. It's all at the lab being processed."

"See if you can get a picture of Janet Corliss from somewhere," I said. "A judicial dinner photo spread or a column in the **New York Social Diary.**"

"We got perps in the society columns now?" Mike asked.

"I'm not saying she's a perp. She's just a little frantic—and quite possibly for a good reason," I said. "She has convinced herself that Bud and Francie were carrying on together. I'd like tech guys to try to compare Janet's height and body type and hands—if we can see them—to the woman in the video, just so we cover all the possible bases."

"You want us to pixelate Janet Corliss?" Mike said. "Sounds more like something her husband would do to a law clerk."

"Francie didn't seem afraid of the woman, whoever she was," Mercer said.

"Yeah, but we don't know what her relationship really is with either of the Corlisses," I said. "Could be they are all just friends, and the judge got a little more friendly than before."

"We've all got things to do," Vickee said, turning to leave the room. "Thanks for coming over to take a look at this."

"Could I talk to you for a few minutes?" I asked her.

"It's not necessary," Vickee said.

"I just want to apologize for my behavior—our rudeness—at Primola last night," I said. "You're the last person I'd want to push."

"Come for dinner when this is all behind us," Vickee said. "Logan asked why he hasn't seen you."

Vickee and Mercer's kid—my godson—was almost five years old. I had kept my distance from him when I was at the height of my PTSD period, but the invite to see Logan—to be back in the warmth of their home—meant Vickee accepted my weak apology.

On the way back, Mercer and I stopped at the deli to pick up sandwiches to eat in my office, then continued working on our case.

It was four o'clock when Laura told me that Lucy Jenner was on the phone.

"Lucy? All good?" I asked.

"I want you to talk to someone," Lucy said, sounding slightly off, as though she'd been drugged. "I'm passing my phone to my counselor from Streetwork."

"Ms. Cooper?" the woman asked, introducing herself by name. "I need to talk to you about Lucy."

"Is everything okay?" I asked. "She doesn't sound like herself."

"Well, she was involved in an accident today. I'm with her at Mount Sinai West, the old Roosevelt Hospital, right now. She's fine, medically. No worries."

"What's wrong? What kind of accident?"

"Lucy was coming from the library."

"The New York Public Library? Fifth Avenue, with the lions out in front?"

"Yes, the main one. Basically, she fell and got pretty scraped up, so we brought her here to be checked out."

"But it was just a fall?" I asked.

"Yes, ma'am. Sort of a fall."

"What was she doing at the library?" I stood up, pacing back and forth behind my desk with the phone cord trailing behind me. "Let me talk to her, please."

I would have to get the meaning of "sort of" from Lucy herself.

Lucy got back on the phone. "Can't my counselor tell you what happened?"

"No, no," I said. "I want to hear it from you, and I want to know that you're okay. Let's start with that. Are you—?"

"I'm okay."

"You don't quite sound like yourself."

"The doctor gave me something for pain, for my bruises."

"Bruises?" I said.

"I was at the library for a couple of hours, and then I walked to the subway station, to come back to the project."

"Which subway?"

She told me the location of the station on Sixth Avenue, at the far end of Bryant Park.

"I was standing on the platform, with this guy and this girl from Streetwork, and somebody was making a commotion. It's just that when people starting pushing and shoving, I was the one that got jammed in the middle, and I just fell."

"Fell? How did you fall?"

"Onto the tracks," Lucy said. "Onto the subway tracks."

"**What?**" I shrieked into the phone. "How did you get up?"

"Two guys. Two men who were standing there helped," Lucy said, sounding both weary and scared. "One jumped down and helped lift me up on the platform."

"Stay right where you are, Lucy," I said. "Mercer and I will be there as fast as we can."

"My counselor wants to take me back to Street-work, but she listed you as my contact on the hospital papers, so the discharge nurse made us call."

"Stay put," I said, jabbing my finger onto my desk blotter. "Don't talk to anyone except your counselor and the nurse. Mercer and I are coming to get you."

THIRTY-THREE

Mercer stuck the red flasher on top of his old Crown Vic and turned on the whelper. The combination of lights and sirens on an unmarked car always worked to move through traffic. We reached the hospital on Fifty-Ninth Street and Tenth Avenue in thirty-five minutes.

I ran in ahead of Mercer. Many of our rape victims were treated there because of its outstanding Sexual Assault Forensic Examiner program. I knew the way to the ER as well as to my own office, and found Lucy sitting on the side of a gurney, her counselor with her.

"Thanks for calling," I said to the Safe Horizon advocate who was standing beside Lucy. "Would you mind stepping out while we talk?"

Before I could pull the curtain around our cubicle, Mercer had joined me.

"I'm going to ask your permission to do this," I said to the girl, "but I'd like to put my arms around you. You look like you've been in a boxing match."

Lucy bit her lip and nodded her head. "That would feel good."

She didn't start crying until I held her against me in an embrace. "Let it all out," I said. "You've been carrying a load around for so long."

When she was finished crying and wiping her tears, I told her to sit down again on the gurney.

"What hurts?" I asked.

"Everything."

"Show us where you're bruised."

There were abrasions and lacerations on Lucy's hands, from trying to break the fall from the platform to the tracks. She pulled up her jeans legs to show us her skinned knees and calves. One side of her face was scraped and puffy.

"Stitches anywhere?" I asked.

She hung her head and spoke quietly. "No. Just black and blue."

"And bloody," I said, dabbing at the area around a Band-Aid on her forehead. "Things that will heal."

That was in sharp contrast to what Mercer and I were dealing with in regard to Lucy's time with Zach Palmer.

Mercer took over asking the questions. He made Lucy be specific about the time and the exact platform location, the names of her companions, and everything she observed around her.

"How crowded was the platform?" he asked.

"I don't know. It was sort of narrow where we

were standing, on the side of the staircase, but I didn't count the people."

"Were people pushing one another?" Mercer asked. "Or did you think there was someone pushing you in particular?"

"How could I tell that?" Lucy asked.

"Well, did you feel anyone's hands on your body?" he said. He was a gentle examiner, but firm and able to search out details.

"I was facing the tracks, looking out for the train," she said. "I didn't feel anything on my back, you know? But it was like someone cracked the back of my legs, not with a weapon or anything—well, maybe a shopping bag, but hard enough to make my knees buckle—and then all I remember is tumbling down."

"Where were your two friends?"

"Close by me, I guess."

"Did one of them do something to you, do you think?" Mercer said.

"No way. They were standing right beside me," Lucy said. "Plus, they're totally good people, in the same kinds of situations—without homes, without families—like I'm in."

"So no one was in front of you, and this probably came from behind," he said. "How many people got shoved off the platform?"

"Well, it was just me," Lucy said. "The men who helped me up, one of them just jumped. There was no sign of the train yet."

"Did police—?"

"Yes, police officers showed up right away. They took the names of the two guys, just so you know," she said. "And they brought me to the hospital."

"That's good, Lucy," Mercer said. "Just let the drug take over and relax you, and we'll talk about this more later on."

"I just want to ask you a few things," I said to Lucy. "Would you tell me why you were at the library?"

No answer.

"Lucy?"

"I—um—my orientation stuff doesn't start until tomorrow, so I had permission to go to the library. Well, not exactly the library, but to go out for a few hours this morning, so I went where two of the other kids from the program were going."

"Why did they choose the library?" I asked. "Or did you?"

"That's where a lot of the kids go—the ones like me that don't have phones and laptops and stuff like that. Don't tell on them, will you?"

"I won't tell on anyone," I said. "Mercer and I have one goal—and that's to keep you safe. Did you use a computer at the library?"

"Is that a bad thing?"

"Not at all."

"The program has library cards for us," Lucy said. "There are computers and laptops that the public can use there, as long as you have a card. For a lot of the residents at Streetwork, it's the only way to keep in contact with people in their lives. The Wi-Fi is free."

"Did you go there to contact someone?" I asked her.

She shook her head in the negative.

"Have you emailed anyone since you got here to tell them where you're staying in Manhattan?"

Lucy had seemed so unconnected from everyone in her young life that I hadn't given much thought to her being in e-communication with anyone.

She shook her head again.

"No one?" I asked. "Would you answer me out loud?"

"No one."

"Did you tell anyone where you're staying?"

"No," she said, rubbing her eyes and yawning. The painkiller was making her sleepy. "Not really."

I squatted beside the gurney to get her to look me in the eye.

"'No' is not the same thing as 'not really,'" I said. "Who did you tell?"

"You're not going to be mad at me, are you?"

"I'm too concerned to be mad, Lucy."

"Last night, when I got to Streetwork, one of the guys had a laptop," she said. "I don't know whether he was supposed to have it or not. But he let me use it."

"For what?" I asked. "What did you do with it?"

"So I—well, I just thought I'd check Facebook."

I rocked back and held on to the edge of the gurney. "Go on."

"It had been a long time since I'd been online, and I figured it would be good to let people know I was doing okay."

"People?" I asked. "What people?"

"Like Facebook friends, is all. I'm not even sure who they are at this point, 'cause I've been so out of touch."

"How many friends do you have? How many people read your posts?"

"Maybe twenty-five," she said. "Maybe thirty-five. I'm not sure."

"And did you tell them where you were staying?" I asked. "Did you give them the address of the program, or say anything about it?"

I didn't want her putting herself or anyone else there at risk.

"Nope. Nothing about Streetwork."

"That's really good," I said. "Did you say anything about being with Mercer or me, or coming down to the DA's office?"

I didn't dare ask whether she had used Jake's name.

"Of course not," she said, yawning again. "I wouldn't talk about anything like that."

"I'll get Max to pull up your post when I go in tomorrow," I said, "so you might as well tell me what you wrote."

"It's all kind of bland. Blah-blah-blah kind of

stuff," Lucy said. "And then I said I had a library card and I'd be going to the big library on Fifth Avenue tomorrow morning—I mean today—if anyone wanted to get online with me."

She had put it out there for anyone to find.

"Did anyone comment on your post?"

"Nope."

"Do you have a list of your friends?" I asked. "Can you give me all the names?"

"I have no idea at this point."

"There's a way to do it, Lucy. We'll get them off your site."

She curled her legs up beneath her and put her head down on the slim pillow on the gurney. "I'm really tired. Are you almost done?"

I was afraid that if Lucy had enemies—Zach Palmer or anyone else in her thorny young life—she was now being tracked on Facebook. I was afraid she had been pushed off the subway platform by someone who had been alerted by her innocent reference to the library, and then followed her to the train station. I was afraid that something she may have put up on the Internet would lead like a trail of bread crumbs back to the place I had thought would be her safe haven.

"It's the medication, Lucy," I said, trying to figure out what to do. "That's what's knocking you out. I want you to eat something and I want you to have a good night's sleep, so don't get too comfortable here."

"Can't my counselor just take me back to Streetwork?"

"You're not going there tonight," I said, running out of realistic options. "You're going to come home and sleep at my place."

THIRTY-FOUR

"I didn't tell you it was smart," I said to Mike two hours later. "It's necessary, that's all. Until I can get the full download on Lucy's Facebook information and go through all her friends and exactly what she's put up and out, she can't be at Streetwork."

Mercer and I had dressed Lucy in surgical scrubs that the triage nurse gave us from one of the supply cabinets. Her Safe Horizon counselor had given us a baseball cap, and when Mercer brought the car around to a side door of the hospital, Lucy walked out and ducked down behind the rear seat. Then he drove back around the block to pick me up in front of the ER.

"You think you fooled anyone?" Mike asked.

"I'm just hoping we did," I said. "At least no one saw me walk out the door with her, if anyone was watching."

Lucy was sound asleep in my guest room. It was eight thirty in the evening—I had been in no mood for **Jeopardy!**—and Mike had just returned to the apartment.

"What are you thinking of doing with her after tonight?" Mike asked. "I'm a pretty good bodyguard for the late shift, but I have to report to work tomorrow."

"We both do. Can you hold out a while on dinner and I'll order in a pizza when Lucy wakes up?"

"Sure," Mike said. "What about making her a material witness and finding a hotel room for her, with police protection?"

"I hate to resort to that," I said. "Hotels are where it all started with Jake. I doubt that atmosphere will add to Lucy's emotional stability. I now think I have to deal with him—Zach—in the morning, so I can start my grand jury case on Monday. Get Lucy's testimony under oath, and see if I can work a rapprochement with her aunt so she can go back there."

"Either way, kid, you need a team to guard her now that she's broadcast her whereabouts," Mike said. "Who are you going to ask for that?"

"Used to be I'd lay it all out for Paul Battaglia. Then he'd call the commissioner and get me whatever I wanted," I said. "I'm not sure now who to trust with Lucy's story and with my plans to make a case against Zachary Palmer."

"The commissioner himself," Mike said. "Scully respects your judgment."

"I can't count on that anymore. I made him pretty unhappy a few weeks ago, and also I can't count on the fact he won't tell Mayor DeBlowhard."

"Sooner or later, this is going to be news," Mike said. "Front-page news, top of the fold."

"Once I get the indictment against Zach—if I do—and unseal it, then Scully has to give me someone to partner with Mercer on the arrest."

"Mercer," Mike said. "Why can't he guard Lucy tomorrow? Do you need him for your conversation with Zach?"

"I'm going solo for that," I said, walking to the bar to pour us each a drink.

"In your office?" Mike asked.

"No. Too many ears and eyes."

"Not his office," Mike said. "He's probably got a trapdoor in the floor like a Bond villain. You'd be chum for some great whites he keeps in a tank down below."

"I've had that thought," I said. "No, I'll call him and pick a public place. Somewhere he can't start screaming at me when I take out the plastic baggie with Lucy's bloody handkerchief in it and pretend I've had it tested. Maybe a hotel lobby in Midtown, with a lounge area. Quiet, elegant, and for me, a feeling of safety."

"Use the Palace on East Fiftieth or the Four Seasons on Fifty-Seventh. There are ex-cop security guards all around both places, both have entrances on two sides, and neither one is far from his office."

"Good idea," I said.

We were watching an old movie on Turner Classics when Lucy walked into the den at nine thirty.

I stood up. "Glad you're back on your feet," I said. "Do you feel any better?"

"Nope. Everything aches."

"That's the way it goes with big bruises," Mike said. "They're supposed to ache. You'll feel better after you eat."

I ordered in a large pepperoni pizza and made sure Lucy drank plenty of water while we waited for dinner.

"Can I watch TV, too?" she asked.

"Anything you want," I said.

I left her in the den with Mike and went inside to call Catherine to see how her meeting with Janet Corliss had gone. My call went to voice mail.

A few minutes later, Mike came to my office to talk. "Have you thought about tomorrow?"

"I've been thinking about what you said and I think you're right after all," I said.

"Which one of my bright ideas did you like?"

"Kiss me," I said. "Then I'll tell you."

Mike leaned over and wrapped his arms around me, sealing the deal with a long, deep kiss—and then a second one.

"I'm calling Keith," I said, picking up my cell phone again from my desktop.

"As in the commissioner?"

"Look, Mike," I said. "I'll have to prepare him for whatever the grand jury does about Zach Palmer, maybe as early as tomorrow afternoon. And I'm ready to tell him that I know where Francie Fain is."

"You can't give up Vickee," Mike said, slamming his hand on my desk.

"I'd never give her up—you know that. Vickee refused to tell us," I said. "I can swear to that fact on a stack of Bibles. Just think of how many people I work with who are friends of Francie's. I bet even Judge Corliss knows where she is."

I turned my back to Mike and speed-dialed the commissioner's cell.

"Keith? I'm sorry, I meant to say commissioner. It's Alex Cooper here," I said. We had known each other long before we were chiefs in our respective departments. I'd slipped in his first name to remind him of that. "Sorry about the late hour."

"What have you got, Alexandra?" he said, with a hint of annoyance in his voice.

"Something unexpected dropped into my lap this week," I said. "At first, I didn't know what to make of it, but I've spent the last couple of days doubling down on the witness and she tells a monster story. I could use your help."

"Explain yourself. I'm not a mind reader," Scully said. He was clipped—more so than usual—but he was a man who didn't like people wasting his time.

"The perp is fairly prominent, so I think I should sit down with you and Vickee Eaton to prep you in case the grand jury returns a true bill next week."

"Who is he?" Scully asked.

"I'd prefer to tell you in person, if you've got time late afternoon tomorrow."

"Are you taking your lessons in etiquette from Mike Chapman these days?" the commissioner said. "You're asking for my personal involvement to help you with a case, but you're refusing to tell me who your target is?"

"I learned from Paul Battaglia," I said, thinking that might make Scully understand my maneuverings and be somewhat amused by my channeling of the late district attorney—a master of manipulation.

"It looked better on Battaglia," Scully said. "May the old bastard rest in peace."

"Tomorrow afternoon? May I come to One PP?"

"Yes," he said. "When are you expecting an indictment?"

"Next Wednesday at the earliest."

"Exquisite timing—to call me at ten forty-seven tonight when you're six days out," Scully said facetiously.

"There's a rather urgent piece of this," I said.

"How urgent?"

"You'll just have to trust me, Keith."

He paused before he spoke. "I used to."

"I'm back, operating on all cylinders," I said. "This isn't a Chapman operation—it's all Mercer and me."

"What's the ask?" the commissioner said.

"The victim," I said. "Twenty-four years old. A cold case and the crime's got great legs against a public figure, all of which I plan to be able to prove.

If we don't make a move next week, I expect before too long his name will be carved on the front of a government building in DC."

"Wasn't Battaglia's mantra that you can't play politics with people's lives?"

"I'm not playing anything," I said, as sharply as I could. "I've had my witness in a safe place for several days, but she went on social media yesterday, just in time for someone to push her onto the subway tracks this afternoon."

"I got that report," he said. "That's your vic?"

I had the commissioner's attention. "Yes."

"Where is she now? Back at Streetwork?"

"Too chancy," I said. "I have her at my apartment."

"Who's riding shotgun?" he asked. "Mike or Mercer?"

"Mike," I said, turning to look at him. He just shook his head from side to side, obviously displeased with my approach to the problem.

"And now you want to make her a material witness? Put her up at the Mandarin Oriental for a few grand a night? Massages and manicures included?"

"I'll ignore your sarcasm," I said. "A hotel is too rough, given her history. You'll understand when I fill you in tomorrow."

I braced myself for the ask.

"I have an idea, Keith, and you're the only person who can make it happen."

"What?"

"I understand that the safest place in town is

where you have Francie Fain," I said. "I want to get my vic into Rockefeller Hospital, for safekeeping."

He didn't speak.

"Word is out, and it's not leaked from your office, if that's what you're steaming about," I said. "We can talk about that tomorrow, too."

"I'm listening."

"You must have cops guarding Francie Fain 24/7, don't you?" I said. "You can get to her hospital room easily, on the East Side, but she's in a place most people don't even know exists."

"It's not going to work, Alex," the commissioner said. "We've got Fain in quarantine. I can't authorize that a healthy young woman goes into the same wing of the hospital as some kind of ruse in an unrelated case."

"That quarantine isn't medical," I said. "There's no contagion at issue with this so-called Kiss of Death nerve agent. You're just trying to isolate my friend Francie from a possible killer—and from the press."

"So what if I am?"

"That's exactly what I want to do for Lucy Jenner," I said. "I'm asking for the very same protection for my witness—for a week, max. For just one week."

"I'm not waiting till tomorrow to find out what you've got," the commissioner said. "Meet me at Rock U at midnight. The security office in the old Nurses' Residence. Bring the girl."

THIRTY-FIVE

Mike made a big deal of going out the front entrance of my building, as my friend Vinny, the doorman, helped him into his department car. He turned on the lights and sirens and sped out, going toward the West Side. If anyone was watching the apartment, he was sure to have been seen leaving by himself—rushing off to an imaginary crime scene.

Before he created the commotion, Mike had taken Lucy and me to the basement garage of my apartment, where we waited with the attendant for Mike to return, in a different car that he had swapped out with the nearby Nineteenth Police Precinct. He pulled down the driveway into the garage. I got in the front seat while Lucy got in the rear. We drove out slowly, made a full stop, and proceeded on our way.

The distance to the front gates of Rockefeller University was only a short one from my home, but Mike took such a circuitous route on the one-way streets and avenues of the Upper East Side that we didn't arrive at Sixty-Sixth Street for almost twenty minutes. Following him would have been more of a challenge than doing a Rubik's Cube in the same time allotted for the drive.

The guard at the front gate of the old institute campus came out to the car to check Mike's ID.

"The police commissioner's already at the security office," he said, waving us in. "You can park at the top of the drive."

"What did I do wrong?" Lucy asked as I opened her car door and walked with her on the path to security.

"Not a thing," I said. "But I need you to stay offline for another week."

"What's this place?" she asked, looking around the dark campus.

"It's called a university, but it's only for very advanced degrees in science. The labs and classes are in those newer buildings on the north side of the drive," I said. "They've got an old hospital here, too, and it might be a good place for you to be till your injuries are all healed."

"A hospital?" she said. "Because I had an accident at the subway?"

"Not a typical hospital," I said. "It's very small, and they're used to working on unusual cases."

Lucy seemed intent on believing that her fall from the platform to the tracks today was a random event. Maybe she couldn't cope with thinking it had been intentional, but I had to take steps until we ruled that out, and I didn't want to do anything to alarm her.

"I'm hardly injured."

"The docs were worried about the possibility of concussion," I said, "so they're just going to keep you here overnight and for observation tomorrow. Maybe the weekend, too."

"Will you stay with me tonight?" she asked, reaching to link her arm with mine.

"Sure I will."

The commissioner's aide, who was at his side every day, took Lucy from me and off down the hall to a vending machine to buy a soda for her. It had been years since Keith Scully interacted with a crime victim, and I wouldn't have let him press her under any circumstances. Fortunately for me, he wasn't a micromanager.

He, Mike, and I went into Roger Murfee's office, and Scully closed the door behind us.

"I take it that young woman is your survivor?" he asked.

"Yes."

"You say the case was cold."

"Not because your guys couldn't find the perp," I said, referring to the usual designation when investigations stalled and were later reopened with new forensic techniques. "That's not what I meant. It's an old case but only reported this week."

"Another Me Too, then," the commissioner said. "Who is it?"

"Public servant," I said. "Great track record as a prosecutor. This woman was his victim, when she was a witness for him in a case."

Keith Scully was a Marine through and through. He stood straight, his eyes narrowed, and his teeth were clenched, clearly expressing his disgust.

I gave him an outline of my case, leaving out all the detail and anything that would connect it to Zachary Palmer. I wanted him to understand the tortured route that Lucy Jenner had taken to get to this point.

"You sure you can nail this guy?"

"I believe her," I said. "That's what counts, isn't it? And Mercer and I expect to have a lot more by Monday."

"Corroboration? And don't tell me the law doesn't require it," he said. "You won't make a really old case without it."

I held my tongue. I didn't need any guidance on how to prosecute a rape case. My team had pioneered every innovative technique in the field for more than a decade.

"I'm on it," I said.

"You think someone pushed your kid onto the tracks?" he asked. "That would suggest your man knows you're coming after him."

"Coop doesn't believe in coincidence any more than I do," Mike said. "Could Lucy's fall have been accidental? Yeah, but neither of us think so."

"Look, Commissioner, maybe I was too heavy-handed when I met with him the other night," I said.

"You **what**?" Scully asked. "Which of my brainless big shots backed you up on that plan?"

"I did it entirely on my own," I said, holding up my right hand like I was taking an oath. "I hadn't started the investigation. I—I met with him because he wanted to talk politics with me. I'd made the date a week earlier."

Scully's hands were on his hips. "I hope you didn't step in it too deep, Alex. I hope you didn't open the door for, well—whoever he is."

"Let me tell him that he's a target tomorrow—I guess that's today now—and that he needs to pony up with a lawyer," I said, "and I'll identify him to you the minute I'm done with that meeting."

"The girl went up on social media without telling Coop," Mike said to Scully. "That could be what drew someone out of the woodwork. She's led a really rootless and somewhat dangerous lifestyle for the last six years and we don't know who else has a grudge—from her half brother to anyone else she might have scammed. That's why we need to stash her here. How can it hurt you?"

Keith Scully didn't like being out of the know. He turned his back to us and thought for a minute.

"Would you have told Paul Battaglia who the guy is?" he asked.

"I would have," I said. "I'd have had no choice."

Then he turned to face us again, smoothing his tie. "Then you'd damn well better tell me."

"I understand, Commissioner," I said, nodding my head. "I'm going to present evidence against Zachary Palmer."

Scully's expression didn't change. "You'd better act fast, Alexandra. He tells me he's the next district attorney of New York County."

THIRTY-SIX

"Good evening. Which one of you is Ms. Cooper?" the head nurse asked. Before Scully left, he gave his team orders to expect us, and they had alerted her desk.

"I am."

"Then the young lady with you will be identified as Patient Eleven," she said, typing something on the computer and printing out a tag, which she then fitted into a plastic wristlet. "I was told not to put a name or date of birth."

"Thank you," I said as she put it around Lucy's left wrist. "She's just here for observation."

"So I've been told. Will you please follow me?"

She led the two of us and Mike through the door marked QUARANTINE that we had seen the morning before.

This wing of the Rockefeller Hospital had eight small rooms. During a century of use for everything from scarlet fever to the Ebola virus, they had been upgraded and equipped for state-of-the-art medical care, but each one was still small, as determined by the old building's architectural footprint.

In the quiet corridor, two men were sitting on chairs outside a closed door, on guard. One was wearing the uniform of an NYPD officer and the other had on civilian clothes, with a windbreaker bearing the FBI seal on the front. I knew it was Francie Fain's room. Two others were backup at the far end of the hallway, where there was another door, about thirty feet away.

Mike went down to talk to them, to explain the addition of a patient, and then did the same to the two guards across the hall from me.

The nurse brought Lucy a hospital gown and I encouraged her to put it on. "You'll get a good night's sleep, and I'll be in the cubicle right next to you."

"Who are those men and why are they here?" she asked.

"They're looking out for a patient who's had a lot of problems," I said. "I don't really know more than that."

"Will you be here when I wake up in the morning?"

"Absolutely," I said. "Your only job is to have pleasant dreams."

Lucy squeezed my hand and said, "Good night."

Mike was waiting for me in the corridor. "If you're both good, I'll take off."

"It seems fine to me."

"You got these four guys babysitting you, and Murfee has a crew of nearly forty campus security officers, with many of them on at night," Mike said. "Scully said there are more than four hundred surveillance cameras on the Rockefeller campus. One hundred twenty years and not a murder on the grounds. So go to sleep."

I kissed him on the cheek and thanked him for getting us here. He patted me on the back and left the floor.

A second nurse—a young man about my age— came by to ask what I needed when he saw me leave Lucy and go into my cubicle.

"Nothing, thanks. I'll just sit and read for a while until I stretch out on the bed, if that's okay."

"That's fine," he said, turning on the standing lamp that was next to a chair in the corner. "My name is Billy—Billy Feathers—if you need anything at all."

He walked out and returned soon after with a pitcher of ice water and some plastic cups.

"Have you worked here very long?" I asked.

"Fifteen years."

"Long time," I said, putting down my book. "What brought you here?"

"Most people have never heard of us, but within the medical community—even internationally— we're known for doing amazing things. You know the reason the hospital was even included in the creation of the institute," Billy said, "was the idea that direct contact by the doctors with illness— really deadly illness—would ignite their intellectual curiosity—new facts that could lead to treatments."

"But you? You yourself?"

Billy leaned against the radiator under the windowsill. "My older sister worked for an NGO in Africa, about twenty years ago," he said. "She died there, in Mali, of malaria, even though she had been vaccinated against it."

He paused for a few moments. "Malaria parasites are quite complex genetically, so not all our vaccines are effective. Rockefeller was one of the few places doing research on the disease, so that started me in this direction."

"I can understand that."

"Malaria is one of Melinda and Bill Gates's causes, and Melinda's given millions to the university to further the work on malaria. Anyway, it's allowed me a purpose and a place to work to honor my sister's life."

Then Billy smiled at me. "If you're here a few days, I'll take you over to Flexner, to the fly labs."

"I expect to be here all weekend," I said. "What are fly labs?"

"Are you squeamish?" he asked.

"Let's just say I've seen a lot, and flies aren't a major problem for me."

"Flexner's one of the newer buildings on the north side of campus, where a lot of the laboratories are. It's where the mosquito rooms are," he said. "It's impossible to get in there, except I've got a pass I can use to swipe us in."

"Yeah, but what's there?"

"There are these small rooms within the labs," he said, excitedly, "that hold canisters of mosquitoes. Volunteers like me stick our arms into the canister, and the researchers see which of us they bit, and which they didn't. Flies, too. That's a really simplified way of putting it."

"I get the point."

"You work with DNA as a prosecutor, don't you?" Billy asked.

I was surprised he knew what my job was. "Yes."

"Did you know that it was doctors here at Rockefeller in 1944 who made the historic discovery that genes are made of DNA, not of protein or other substances? It's probably the most important scientific finding of the twentieth century."

"Are you sure?" I said. "I thought it was Crick and Watson."

"No, no," Billy said. "They discovered the double helix structure that makes up the DNA molecule, but our doctors here proved that DNA was the carrier of all hereditary information."

My respect for Rock U was growing by the minute.

"Ms. Cooper," he said, "Ralph Steinman was our doc who won the Nobel for creating the first experimental vaccine for the HIV infection. We still do a significant amount of research in the AIDS-HIV field."

"I want a tour, Billy," I said. "I can see your enthusiasm for the institute. But you must have better things to do tonight than educate me."

"I'm talking your head off," he said, getting up to go on his way. "There's no cure for that, I'm afraid."

"Thanks for everything," I said. "See you in the morning, if you're still on."

"Yes, I started at midnight and it's a twelve-hour shift."

I walked to the room next door and pushed it open to look at Lucy, who was sound asleep.

Although I had brought a tote bag with clothes for the next day and a nightshirt for tonight, I decided it was more appropriate to just lie down on the bed in my jeans and sweater. There were too many people on the tiny corridor to expect much privacy. I turned out the light and tried to get comfortable.

It was probably close to two by the time I fell asleep and six A.M. when a small commotion awakened me.

I opened the door to my room and looked out. The hallway was completely empty—none of the cops or FBI agents in place.

I ran out of my room in my bare feet—my heart in my mouth—and opened Lucy's door. I was relieved to see that she was still sleeping, oblivious to the noises I had heard.

I looked across the hallway toward Francie Fain's room. I thought about opening the door, just as the head nurse came back through the entrance to the wing with a doctor—his lab coat and stethoscope signaled his role—and one of the uniformed cops.

The nurse and doctor entered the room, and the cop stood next to the door, facing outward, not even acknowledging me.

I took a step forward and he held out his arm. "Go back to your room, if you don't mind," he said. "They don't need any help in here."

"But I'm—"

"We know who you are," the cop said. "Best if you return to your room."

I took a step or two backward and stopped when I saw Billy push through the double doors and rush toward Francie's room.

"What is it, Billy?" I asked.

"The doctors took the patient off life support two hours ago," he stopped to tell me. "She didn't make it. They said she didn't stand a chance. I'm so sorry you had to wake up to this, Ms. Cooper, but Ms. Fain is dead."

THIRTY-SEVEN

I sat on the edge of my bed for half an hour, my door open, listening to the noises that were made in the aftermath of Francie Fain's life. It was enough to wake the dead.

The beeping and clicking of all the monitors had ceased, but some of the heavy equipment was being taken out of the room and wheeled through the double doors, banging off the walls and sides of the entrance as it was shoved along by four chattering orderlies.

Members of the medical staff had been called in, perhaps from the adjacent wing where other patients were being cared for. They were talking among themselves, taking turns walking in to look at the patient, as though they were doing rounds on the deceased.

Normally, because Francie Fain had been in a hospital facility under the care of doctors, the sign-off by a medical examiner wasn't necessary. But when I heard Dr. Jonathan Mayes introduce himself to the uniformed cop, I realized the fact that this was a homicide required the presence of a morgue official.

I stood in the doorway of my room and waited ten minutes, until Jonathan reappeared from Francie's bedside, and came into the hallway, talking to the doctor wearing the lab coat.

They spoke for several minutes, then Jonathan went back into the room, reemerging with his briefcase and jacket.

"Hey, Jonathan," I said, thinking of both his medical expertise and his compassion. "I'm so glad you'll be assigned to do this postmortem. I'm devastated by Francie's death."

"Alex?" he said, taking the reading glasses off his nose. He had an English accent, although he'd lived in the States since medical school. "They didn't tell me you were on this one."

"I'm not. I'm—uh—I'm just keeping a witness company—totally unrelated. Not really a medical case, but we figured it would be a chance to use Francie's protection services for the next few days."

Jonathan grimaced. "Sorry to deprive you of that so quickly."

"That's the least of it," I said. "Scully's got us covered."

"I never met Francie," he said. "I don't think I've actually ever testified in a case she represented."

"You'd remember," I said. "I promise you that."

"I'm sure I'll see you soon," he said.

"May I ask a favor, Jonathan?"

"If it's about cause of death and all that, my friend, the answer is no. I'm under very strict orders from the chief medical examiner not to discuss this matter with anyone."

"Nothing like that," I said. "Francie's got no family here, and I have no idea what will be decided by Quint Akers or whoever gets to run the show, but I'd like to go in to be with her now for two minutes, just to say my own good-bye."

"Are you sure you want to do that?" Jonathan asked. "It's never easy."

"Francie was on her way to my welcome-back party when she was stricken—or whatever it was that happened," I said. "I think it's only right."

"That's not a problem at all, as long as you're up to it," Jonathan said. "The nurses are cleaning up the body now. I'll just tell them you'd like to come in when they're done."

"Thanks so much."

Jonathan did a quick turnaround in and out of Francie's room. "They'll be ready for you shortly," he said. "Do you need a steady arm to hold?"

I had been to the morgue scores of times in connection with cases I had worked over the years. I had recently spent an hour alone with the corpse of Paul Battaglia, after witnessing his assassination.

"I can do this, but thank you for offering."

Jonathan left, and when the nurses came out to motion to me to come in, I walked across the hall and stood beside the hospital bed.

I hardly recognized Francie, although it had been such a short time since I had seen her on the street the night she collapsed. From the injuries caused by her thrashing around to the EMTs' efforts to resuscitate her and finally to the tubes of the ventilator, I was not looking at the vibrant young defender I had sparred with so often.

The head nurse stepped out with the soiled linens, and only Billy was left at the foot of the bed.

"Will you think I'm crazy if I talk to her?" I asked.

"I do it all the time," he said. "It's good for you, I think."

"Hey, Francie," I said, biting my lip. "It's Mrs. Burger. Mrs. Hamilton Burger. God, I loved your note. And how I hate that I didn't get to put my arms around you one last time."

Billy had his head down, sort of pretending not to listen as I babbled on.

"We'll find him, Francie. We'll get whoever did this and I will send his ass up the river for you, 'cause I think this is one time you might favor that result."

I stroked her hair and tried to understand what had happened to her.

I lifted the edge of the hospital sheet that covered her and picked up her hand, wrapping it in mine. Rigor had not yet set in nor had the temperature of her extremities begun to chill.

I looked down. Her knuckles were bruised and

scraped from her convulsions after the fall onto the pavement of Baxter Street. I rubbed her palm, foolishly thinking it would have hurt her for me to put pressure on the back of her hands, where the discoloration was so severe.

"I'm going to miss you, Francie Fain," I said, stroking her fingers and bringing her hand to my mouth to kiss her fingertips. "I'm going to miss your sass and your smarts and your attitude and all you stood for. I'm going to miss every 'objection' you used to shout, whether you had cause to or not."

While I was talking, I touched something hard on the surface of her skin and turned her hand over to look at it.

On the palm of her hand was a scar. A long scar, from the base of her forefinger to the lower corner on the opposite side of her hand.

I breathed in and threw back my head.

"You took a blood oath, Francie Fain. A goddamn blood oath," I said aloud. "When the hell did you do that?"

THIRTY-EIGHT

"Can you find out whether the cops and feds are still going to be here for a few hours?" I asked Billy. "I'm just going to jump in the shower and clean up before I wake Lucy up. I don't want her to see any of this."

"Will do," he said.

I took my clothes down to the restroom at the end of the hall and showered there. I had a black blazer, white shirt, and black slacks to put on—a somber outfit for my meeting to drop the news on Zach Palmer.

But that was before I saw Francie's scar and was scrambling to rearrange my priorities for the day.

By the time I had dressed, brushed on some makeup, and walked toward my overnight cubicle, another cop and another agent—this time both women— werc standing outside Francie's room.

Billy Feathers saw me coming and pulled me to the side. "There's a new shift, with new officers, as you can see," he said. "Seven A.M. to seven P.M. Apparently, the police commissioner wants the body to stay here until this evening—or maybe even until tomorrow—and then she'll be transported to the morgue when he gives us the orders."

"Thanks so much," I said.

"The docs here want to take some tissue samples, too," he said. "Sadly, this is an opportunity for them to learn more about how your friend died."

"I wish I could tell you myself," I said.

"I know better than to ask questions," Billy said. "There's a century of secrets under this old roof."

"I bet there are," I said. "I'm expecting a detective named Mercer Wallace, who'll be hanging out with Lucy after I leave. Is there any place close by that won't have her staring at Francie's room all day?"

"For sure," Billy said. "There's a really lovely solarium for the patients—when they're well enough—if you head out that exit, just past the restroom you used. It's sunny and light, right overlooking the East River. There's a TV and lots of green plants—"

"I don't mean to be rude, Billy," I said, cutting him off. "I get it. Will you have a breakfast tray for Lucy, and can you bring it out there?"

"You get her up and dressed, I'll bring you each a tray."

I ducked into my room and dialed Mike's number. "She's dead. Now you've got yourself a homicide."

"I know that, kid," he said. "Scully had Vickee

call me five minutes after he got the news. And Mercer's on his way to you, to take Lucy under his wing. Sorry you had to be so close to all this."

"Why is he keeping Francie's body here all day?" I asked.

"Because he's going to have a presser this morning to announce the attack—the first attack in this country that we know of with this new nerve agent," Mike said.

"What'll that do now that she's dead?"

"The commissioner thinks it's smarter to pretend Francie's still alive—next door at New York/Cornell Hospital, where she was supposed to be—to see if it pulls any suspects out of the woodwork. The commissioner's hoping you can keep your yap shut and go along with the program."

"Anything that helps, of course," I said, "but I made a pretty dramatic discovery. I need you to get here ASAP and get back in Francie's room with a camera."

"Speak up, Coop. I can hardly hear you."

"I can't shout it to you. There are people I don't know in the hallway."

"Go."

"Dr. Mayes was here," I said. "He let me go in to be with Francie. I held her hand, Mike. I meant to just do it for myself, you know? To make **me** feel better, 'cause I sure as hell know that she didn't feel it. But when I had her hand in mine, I felt something raised on her palm. When I turned it over, there was a scar—a line cut diagonally across her palm, identical to the one Lucy has."

Mike didn't comment.

"Did you hear me?"

"Like you had a megaphone held up to your mouth."

"Will you tell Scully?" I asked. "Get someone in to photograph Francie's hand, bring it to Jonathan Mayes's attention so he can give us a medical opinion about what caused it, and figure out how to use that information."

"The second we hang up," Mike said.

"I've never met a successful sexual predator who stops at one victim," I said. "I should have thought about this possibility before."

"What's your plan?" he said. "Are you still going to call Zach and meet with him today?"

"Wild horses couldn't stop me," I said. "After I do a thorough background workup on the late Francie Fain, to see where her life intersected with Zach's."

THIRTY-NINE

Mercer and Lucy were set up in the solarium by eight A.M. He had a plan to talk to her about how and where she had spent the last six years, and whether she had made any enemies who might want to hurt her—lies, thefts, family discord with her half brother in Brooklyn. Anything at all. He had an IT guy ready to research all her social media contacts, too, to see if there was anyone on the list who might have been looking when she posted her New York City location.

Mike and I went directly to my office and got to work. I called Zach Palmer's number, determined to make an appointment with him before the news of Francie's ambush went out over the wires.

I left a message, asking him to meet me at two P.M. at either the Four Seasons or the Palace. I figured that by giving him a choice of hotel lounges, he wouldn't think I had planted any listening devices or backup men in advance.

At nine, reminding Mike that Francie had been a prosecutor before she switched teams, I called our

Human Resources director. "I need an old personnel file," I said to the guy. "Francie Fain. F-A-I-N. She worked here for four years—and left maybe six years ago."

When Laura came in, I barely greeted her before barking orders. "Would you pull up that profile the **American Lawyer** did on Zach Palmer last year, and see if you can find a complete bio of him anywhere?"

"I brought you coffee, too," Laura said, knowing it took three cups to get me on my way in the morning. "Sorry, Mike. I didn't know you'd be here."

"You're slipping, Moneypenny," he said. "I figured you'd anticipate my every move."

She was smiling so broadly she barely heard me thank her.

A new paralegal delivered Francie's personnel file ten minutes later and I buried myself in it.

"Okay. Francie was thirty-six years old," I said. "Two years younger than I am."

"And Zach?"

"Laura should have a printout of the article for us any minute, with specifics. He's forty-four, I think."

Francie's file read backward, after listing her DOB. She was a graduate of Cardozo Law School and Middlebury College. Neither of those was Zach's alma mater, nor would the eight-year age difference have allowed them to overlap.

"Here are the notes of the interview write-up for

this job," I said, reading from the recommendation of one of my former colleagues. "He makes a lot of the fact that she had a fractured upbringing and—"

"Fractured? What does that mean in DA-speak?" Mike asked. He had a toothpick wedged between two teeth, and he was chewing on it while he talked.

I skimmed the essay and flipped through other papers that included her references. "That woman in a nursing home in Texas—the one I said was her mother—adopted her," I said. "Looks like Francie's parents were killed in a car crash when she was seven, and then she spent time in a series of foster homes, in Northern Virginia, where the family lived."

"Go on," Mike said.

"It's really impressive that she pulled herself together," I said, turning another page. "One of her references says she ran away from foster care a couple of times, that she learned about court hearings when one of her foster dads had her picked up on a PINS petition."

Persons In Need of Supervision were kids under the age of eighteen who were chronic runaways or who consistently played hooky from school.

"Listen to this," I said to Mike. "'Francie's personal experiences gave her a particular empathy for the underdog, for the person who was never given a fair chance,' is what one of her law school profs wrote about her."

"It must have made her a powerful advocate

for victims of violence when she started here," Mike said.

"It did. And when she decided to put her talent to work for the accused," I said, "it made her just as determined to get her clients off."

I continued to read as I walked to Laura's desk, just as she was printing out some of the articles about Zach Palmer, and returned, handing them to Mike.

"'Ms. Fain,' the recommendation closes, 'exhibited a noticeable change in her attitude and in her adjustment to living a more meaningful life after entering a program the court directed her to participate in'—this part's in quotes, Mike—'as an incorrigible fourteen-year-old.'"

I stopped for a moment. "Imagine," I said. "Francie, incorrigible? I just can't."

I skimmed the rest of the letter, telling Mike the highlights. "Anyway, this thing was like Outward Bound, the guy says. It was called OVERCOME, and it sent problem kids like Francie into a national park for the summer with a small peer group and two leaders—hiking twenty miles a day with all their gear, pitching tents every night, cooking their own food over a fire they had to make."

"And you probably whined and moaned about having to practice for the swim team races every day at your parents' country club," Mike said.

"Hey, don't I always tell you how lucky I am?"

I was searching for the connection to Zachary Palmer but couldn't find it in the old personnel file.

Mike was studying the media pieces about Zach. "Middle-class family in the District of Columbia. Three older siblings. Mother a schoolteacher, father was retired military working as a civilian for the Department of the Navy in Anacostia."

He stopped chewing the toothpick and sat up. "'When Mr. Palmer was twenty years old,'" Mike read to me from the monthly legal periodical, "'between his sophomore and junior years at Harvard University, he worked as a counselor for a program run in the DC and Virginia courts for disadvantaged youth called OVERCOME.'"

"Grooming 101," I said, putting my papers down, riveted on the fact that we had located the missing intersection in the lives of Francie Fain and Zachary Palmer.

"Find someone needy, vulnerable, and fragile, isolate her from anyone who possibly still had an interest in her, and swear her to secrecy," I said. "I'm sure the well-meaning judge told young Francie to obey whatever her team leader told her to do."

"Into the woods seemed to be a perfect formula for our predator," Mike said. "And it made him an absolute pro by the time he encountered Lucy Jenner."

FORTY

I picked up the phone on my desk and dialed the commissioner's cell.

"Scully."

"Mike and I just found the link between Francie Fain and Zachary Palmer," I said, telling him what we had put together.

"Who else knows?" the commissioner asked.

"No one. We're alone in my office."

"Keep it that way," he said. "I've called a conference for noon. The story will be about the use of a nerve agent on a citizen in this city, and the fact that the victim is recovering and cooperating with us on the investigation."

"I understand."

"Do you still have a meeting with Palmer?" he asked.

"I've asked for one at two P.M., Midtown."

"You're not going without backup, Alexandra," the commissioner said.

"I appreciate that," I said. "You're right."

"We know how the nerve agent got into the

country," Scully said. "Again, this is for you and Chapman, but no one else. If it turns out to have anything to do with Palmer and be useful to you, I want you to have it from me."

"I'm ready for you."

"There was a bottle of perfume on Francie's desk," Scully said. "The nerve agent solution was in the perfume, so when she applied it, she essentially killed herself."

"A perfume bottle?" I asked. "How can that be? How did she walk out of her office and get three or four blocks away?"

"The quick answer is that this Kiss of Death poison can work in a couple of different ways. You need to understand this, Alexandra, so you don't go off the rails before we know the whole story."

"I'm listening."

"Basically, if Francie—or anyone else—inhaled the nerve agent, it would take effect in her lungs at once, causing them to stop working by interfering with the nerve function in all her major organs. She'd have suffered cardiac arrest, and if she had just collapsed at her desk, there's a chance no one would find the death suspicious."

"But she walked, Commissioner," I said. "She seemed fine in those videotapes."

"Because it's most likely that the perfume was applied to her skin—to the pressure points on her wrist and her throat. The agent operates more slowly that way, which allowed for Francie to be out on the street, almost reaching your party, by the time it was absorbed through her skin, yet no one else would be contaminated."

"Who gave her the perfume?" I asked, trying to control the anger in my voice. "Major Case took the Legal Aid visitors' log and we have no idea who got in to see Francie that day."

"Calm down," Scully said. "There was an empty bag in Francie's wastebasket. It had the box from the perfume bottle—the fragrance brand is a new one, called Duchess, if I'm not mistaken. We can't find the receipt, but it's possible that Francie bought it at the duty-free shop at Heathrow Airport when she was leaving England a few weeks ago. It's a brand that isn't sold in the States."

"Oh, Keith," I said, slipping into the familiar as I lost my patience with him. "Don't tell me you think Francie poisoned herself? That's absurd."

"The first uses of Kiss of Death as a murder weapon, like Novichok before it, have been on British soil," he said. "In the case of Novichok, some of it was sprayed on door handles to penetrate the skin of an unwitting man and his daughter."

"Yes, I know. The double agent who'd defected."

"But more recently, Alexandra, the nerve agent killed a couple of friends—not former spies, just ordinary citizens—who had picked up a bottle of cologne in a park and taken it home. They died days later, after applying it to themselves."

"So you can send out a recall of all the bottles of

Duchess that have been manufactured," I said, "on the chance that you've got a madman working in a perfume factory. Or you can tell Mike and me that we should go on looking for our killer. It's your call, Commissioner Scully. Your call."

FORTY-ONE

Two tech guys wired me up for my two P.M. meeting with Zach Palmer. He had responded to my call by midmorning, and chose as the setting the large lobby of the Palace hotel, which extended from East Fiftieth to East Fifty-First Street, with a comfortable cocktail lounge—open and completely visible to passersby—on the Fifty-First Street side.

Another pair of detectives from the DA's Squad drove me to the hotel—one man, one woman— and each waited for me inside one of the entrances, so that I remained in their line of sight. They were meant to be obvious to Zach, and I assumed they were. They were on board to protect me, in case my target didn't like the news I was prepared to drop on him.

Zach was already seated when I arrived. As I got thirty or forty feet away from him, Josie Breed— his so-called body man—turned her back to me and walked off to a darkened area beyond the concierge desk.

Zach had chosen a small round table with two wing chairs on either side of it as our setting. A bottle of sparkling water and two glasses were on the table. He didn't bother to get up when he greeted me.

"Now, really, Alexandra," he said, "what were you thinking by bringing along an entourage from the NYPD? I'm not about to take you down in the lobby of the Palace—or are you that insecure?"

"You've gotten me over my basic insecurity," I said. "Do you mind if I sit?"

"Help yourself," he said, flipping his hand over as he pointed to the second chair.

"I've got something very serious to talk to you about," I said, sitting down on the edge of the chair and putting a folder and manila envelope on the table between us, "and I want you to know that I'm wearing a wire. I'm recording our conversation."

"What's good for the goose, my friend, is good for the gander."

"Sorry?"

"You think you're the only one who can wire up?" he said. "I don't want to steal your thunder, but I can't for the life of me figure out why you lied to me the other night."

"Lied?" I asked. "Me?"

The last thing I wanted was to have this discussion turned around to make me the bad guy, especially preserved on tape.

"It's hard to trust someone who makes things up—fabricates conversations and encounters out of whole cloth."

"Tell me what you mean, Zach, so I can get on with our business."

"You told me that story about meeting a retired FBI agent named Katharine Crain, two or three years ago," he said, imitating my tone of voice. "Some gathering of women in law enforcement, going on and on about how you talked to her about my prosecution of Welly Baynes. So persuasive you were, so honest—why, you almost had me."

My mouth twitched nervously once or twice, but I hoped Zach hadn't caught it. I didn't want him in the driver's seat.

Lucy's handkerchief was in the manila envelope on the table in front of me, but it seemed less useful as I gathered that my first bluff had failed.

"Maybe I was mistaken about the agent's name," I said. "Maybe I—"

"Like I told you," Zach said, "Kathy Crain was done with the life. You know, the whole FBI thing. Off the grid is where I said she went when she retired. Seemed to me she wasn't going to any conferences, wasn't linking in with you law enforcement ladies, wasn't Instagramming her personal business to the rest of you. Chewing the fat over an old case, the way you told it—well, that just isn't the Kathy Crain I know."

"Then it was someone else," I said. "I made a mistake."

Zach leaned in on both elbows. "You've made mistakes all right, but I don't think this was one of them. This was just a mean-spirited lie—let's call it what it is. So I phoned Kathy Crain just to be certain, and your name didn't ring the first bell with her. And yakking with a stranger about an old case and about me? Well, that was no more likely to happen with Kathy than if you summoned J. Edgar Hoover to a ladies' lunch and really believed that he'd show up in a dress."

"I apologize," I said, nervously fingering the manila envelope.

"Just what is it you were fishing for?"

I hadn't meant to start my speech on the defensive. I needed to regain my composure and control.

"I want you to know that I've opened a grand jury investigation, Zach, and that you are the target," I said. "There's not much more I can tell you right now, but I suggest that you get a lawyer as soon as possible. You'll have to make a decision about testifying—maybe as early as next week—before I ask for a vote."

Zach looked as though he'd been gut punched by a heavyweight boxer, but then picked himself up and kept jabbing.

"You could have done this in a phone call," he said. "It's not like I needed to see you again."

"That seemed a bit cowardly on my part. I wanted to face you when I gave you the news."

"What do you think you have on me?" he asked. "You know you damn well better be right because this will look like nothing more than a publicity stunt when my PR team gets in gear."

"I have you so rock solid that unless you hire a wizard to defend you—someone who can make the testimony and evidence evaporate into thin air— you'll be lucky they don't name a prison wing for you, instead of a federal courthouse," I said.

"You're out of your mind," Zach said, taking gulps of sparkling water between sentences. "That's the first thing everyone's going to think, going to say about you. 'That girl has just gone and lost her mind.' And you already know that word has been on the street, since you went all batshit crazy—between being kidnapped and somehow entangling yourself in Paul Battaglia's murder. You'll just be that crazy girl who used to be a player."

"Undoubtedly, it will start that way with some people," I said, "but then I'll get to unseal the indictment and the charges against you will become public. The tide is likely to turn, not all at once, I expect. But some dogged reporter will see past your smarmy persona and begin turning over every rock he can find from the time you stopped bed-wetting until the minute you walk out of here, worrying

about who's left for you to call as character witnesses."

"What's the crime?" Zach said, pounding his
fist on the table. "What are you possibly alleging as
criminal conduct?"

"More counts of sexual assault than I can enu-
merate right now."

"Sexual assault?" he said, throwing back his head
and laughing—almost as though he meant it. "Do
I look like I need to force myself on a woman? Are
you insane? Do I look like I'm starved for sexual
attention?"

"You know that has nothing to do with this
issue," I said.

"Why? Just because I never hit on **you**? You feeling all left out and lonely, Ms. District Attorney?
Won't you sound all high-and-mighty when you
can say you never fell for my—"

"Zach," I said. "Cut it out, will you? I'm taping you."

"Then don't edit out the part about the night
after Battaglia was honored by the Oliver Wendell
Holmes Society four or five years ago," he said,
"when you were so tipsy that you were practically
falling off your chair, begging me to take you home.
Was that the Scotch whiskey speaking to me, or
was it my archrival, looking for some honey in all
the wrong places?"

"That never happened, Zachary Palmer. Don't

muddy this up by making it personal between the two of us."

"Oh, it is **so** personal. This whole thing is nothing but personal."

"You want to go on with your bullshit, Zach, or do you want me to tell you what you're facing?"

He paused, but he wasn't focusing on the problem I was dumping in his lap.

I lowered my voice. There weren't many people in the lounge, but the restaurant staff was watching this mini drama unfold.

"I was asking you about trying the Weldon Baynes case," I said. "I brought up the name of one of your most loyal agents, Kathy Crain. I even recognized your body man—Josie Breed—from the old news clips about the trial."

"What of it? I'm a hero to the Justice Department and to anyone who cares about hate crimes, about civil rights," he said. "I prosecuted a maniac who had killed people simply out of the horrible bias that drove his life. What's the part of that you don't understand?"

"Frankly, I don't understand the split personality, Zach. Who's Jake, and when does he come sneaking out from behind your zipper?"

"Jake? A childhood nickname is all," he said. "You've let yourself be tied up in knots by a manipulative little liar, and she has played you for a total fool."

I spoke each word slowly, keeping my emotion

in check. "You had a sexual relationship with one of your witnesses, during the Baynes trial in which she testified, at a time when she was below the age of consent."

"Don't be stupid, Alexandra," Zach said, pounding the tabletop again for emphasis. "I was a prosecutor, not a predator. You want the story? You want to know why you're wrong?"

"I'm not here to argue the facts with you today. I'm just telling you what you're up against," I said. "Have your lawyer call me on Monday. He can bring you in to my office and you can do queen for a day. You have a story? Tell it to me once you've got representation. Or I'll be telling it to the grand jury, my way."

"Do you have a witness? You have someone you think a jury will believe?" he asked. "Or do you have an emotionally disturbed kid who never quite matured properly because of the trauma she suffered, watching a double murder of her friends? A young woman who lies and steals and tries to suck you in and drag you under because she gets caught doing something wrong?"

I was mildly nauseous to hear the outlines of Zach's defense. His description of Lucy Jenner was very much like the one her aunt had given me. I believed that I had gotten beyond all that with Lucy, but every now and then I had second thoughts.

"Did you ever know what it's like to have a witness in a matter—or maybe it's just so unique to special victims' cases that you don't know—a witness so young or so inexperienced that she or he doesn't even know the language for sexual acts? Who can't describe the body parts because she or he hasn't yet learned those words?" I asked, reining in my temper and channeling the weight of my years of experience. "There is nothing more powerful than when that kid sits in front of a jury and brings the horrific event totally to life by recalling detail or description that just makes you **know** with every fiber of your being that she or he was subjected to that life-altering experience."

Zach fidgeted in his chair, but he was listening to me.

"Language doesn't matter, date and time and place don't matter, the fact that she or he may not even know then that what happened is a crime doesn't matter," I said, "because the retelling is so immediate, so ingrained in the memory of that child, and so vividly described to me and then to the jurors, that you know—you just **know**—and you know beyond a shadow of any doubt, that she or he is telling the god-awful truth."

Zach sat back in his chair and put two fingers to his mouth, taking a deep breath. Then he put his hands together and started clapping, a slow, steady round of applause, growing louder and louder, that had everyone around the lobby looking over at him.

"Is that your closing argument?" he asked,

smirking at me. "Is that the very best you can do? Because I will wipe the floor with your mealy-mouthed words. I will kick your ass right out of the well of the courtroom with that jibberish about someone's addled memories tugging at the heart-strings of the jury—speaking words that have not a scintilla of evidence to back them up. I swear that will happen. I swear you will live to regret the huge mistake you are about to make."

"You do? I'd advise you to think long and hard about what I'm telling you," I said, standing up and grabbing my tote. "You're on notice, Zach. Like I said, get yourself a lawyer and tell him to call me before I start presenting evidence next week."

"Rhetoric never convicted anyone of anything," he said. "You may think your highly prejudicial im-agery will carry you to the finish line in a case like this, but you haven't got a lick of evidence. And without that, you lose in the jury room, and you lose again in the court of public opinion."

I was standing beside the table. "Remember put-ting cases in the grand jury?" I asked. "Surely you remember how to do that?"

"Indeed I do."

"After I put in the first part of my case on Mon-day, and I leave the room, not planning on coming back in for a day or two, remember how the fore-man will ask me for a code name? A code name for the case I'm presenting, so the jurors can distin-guish it from others they hear in between?"

Zach didn't answer. He just cocked his head and looked at me.

"I can't simply say the word 'rape,' because we have dozens of those cases before the grand jurors every month," I said. "And I can't just say 'cold case' or 'Me Too,' because we have scores of them as well."

"What's your point?" Zach asked.

"I was thinking the code word I'm going to use to help the jurors remember my presentation will be 'blood oath.'"

Zach Palmer nearly dropped his water glass.

"Let the record reflect," I said, speaking to an imaginary court reporter, "that the defendant attempted to take a sip of his drink, but his hands were shaking so badly upon hearing the phrase 'blood oath' that the liquid spilled all over the table and onto his pants and the carpet beneath it."

"Get out of here," Zach said, putting the glass down and standing up to face me across the table. "Get out of here right this minute."

I reached for the manila envelope, and when I picked it up, I removed Lucy's handkerchief from it.

I held it at the corner by my fingernails and dangled it over the tabletop.

"You got the sniffles now?" he asked, staring at the old piece of cotton cloth.

"No," I said. "I prefer to think that I've got the bloody knife—the evidence you didn't imagine I'd come up with."

Zach tried to snatch it from me but I pulled back and held on to it. I lifted it again, close to my chest, steeling myself for the bluff.

"See that embroidered letter **L** on it?" I asked. "Lucy's mother gave it to the girl, just before she died. I'm on my way to the DNA lab with it now. That very pale stain just off the center is from the blood—the mixture of bloods, I should say—that Lucy wiped away from her hand after you cut her. And there's no statute of limitations—none at all—on the reliability of DNA."

FORTY-TWO

"Are you okay, Ms. Cooper?" one of the detectives asked me as we got back into the squad car for the trip downtown to my office. "You look shaky."

"I'm okay," I said, settling into the rear seat and looking over my shoulder to see if Palmer and Breed were coming out the same door of the hotel. "I'm hoping Mr. Palmer was more rattled than I am, or I wasn't all that effective."

"Ready to go?" he asked, pulling away from the curb before I could answer.

"Sure. But let's make a quick stop on the way."

"Commissioner Scully said we're to return you to One Hogan."

"I'll call and clear it with him, but let's stop at the DNA lab. I want to leave a piece of evidence there."

I didn't have to dial Scully. My phone rang before I could get it out of my pocket.

"How'd it go?" he asked.

"He denied everything—not that I expected

him to roll over," I said. "He'll probably pony up with a lawyer this weekend, and then we'll have a real dogfight."

"The tech guys will take the wire off you and make us each a copy," Scully said. "I'll let you know what I think."

"I've asked the detectives to make a stop at the Forensic Biology lab on our way back," I said, referring to the state-of-the-art center for DNA analysis—a branch of the ME's office—on East Twenty-Sixth Street.

"That piece of rag?" the commissioner asked. "That handkerchief is useless."

"I just want to run in there, in case Zach has his body man or anyone else following me, to call my bluff."

"In and out," Scully said. "No nonsense."

I held my tongue. "Of course not."

We pulled up in front of the building and I sprinted out of the car, showed my ID, and went to the sixth floor to my friend Noelle, one of the top forensic biologists in the country.

Noelle's desk was surrounded by staffers looking for answers from her.

I held up my hand and waved. "Got five minutes for me?"

She laughed. "Take a number, will you?"

"Happy to wait my turn."

Noelle stepped away from her desk and walked

to the window with me. "What have you got? Something that has to go to the front of the line, I'm sure."

"Consistency is a great thing," I said, smiling at her and letting her peek inside the manila envelope. "So this handkerchief is more than ten years old, and its owner has carried it around for most of that time, just in her pocket as a memento. Would you expect to find anything of value on it?"

"Yes," Noelle said. "A great many contaminants."

"But you'd test it for me, wouldn't you?" I asked.

"A handkerchief. Hmmmm. Looking for what substance?"

"This faint stain next to the embroidery might be human blood."

"No guarantees, but I can have this worked up."

I didn't want to suggest to Noelle that it might be a mixed sample. She was the pro, and submitting it without prejudice was the better way to go.

"For Monday?" I asked. I wanted to know if there was any chance of the stain providing evidence against Zach.

"I'll call you a week from today," Noelle said, walking back to her desk with the manila folder. "Fill out the paperwork."

"C'mon, pal. Rush it for me."

She rolled her eyes. "I'll see what I can do. No promises."

"I'll buy dinner," I said. "Anywhere you'd like. Just aim for something earlier than next Friday."

I scribbled out the necessary information on the forms and went back downstairs to the car.

The detective got on the FDR Drive and I was back at my desk at three thirty.

The tech guys came down and removed the wire, promising to make copies immediately.

My first call was to Mike, telling him what had gone on with Zach, and arranging to meet him later.

I reached Mercer, who was still at the hospital, hanging out with Lucy.

"She was going a little stir-crazy, and as a matter of fact, so was I," he said. "The nurses found me a lab coat big enough to cover me, and they gave Lucy a baseball cap. I covered her with a blanket and stuck her in a wheelchair, and we spent part of the day exploring the Rock U campus. Incognito, I think."

"You'll have to show me around."

"It's a fascinating place," Mercer said. "A whole bunch of new buildings to mix with the original ones. I'd say there are more geniuses per square foot in these five city blocks than anywhere in the world."

"That was kind of my father's point, too."

"We had lunch in the faculty dining room, no questions asked."

"Great. I'm glad you got her out," I said. "I'm going to spend the night again. Mike will keep me company. We should be able to get there by seven."

"I'm fine with that."

"Cops and agents still on the corridor?" I asked.

"Yes. Francie's body is still in the room—being guarded by cops and feds," Mercer said. "Scully hasn't let anyone in on his plan, but he must be cooking one up."

"Damn. I was just talking to him," I said. "I could have asked. Why do you say that?"

"In case you haven't heard," Mercer said, "the docs apparently took tissue from the embryo a few days ago, not knowing how long Francie would make it on life support."

"Francie's fetus?" I said, clutching my hand to my chest.

"Yes."

"So they've probably done the DNA," I said, my heart beating a little faster. "They'll be able to tell who the father is."

"When they have someone to compare the profile to," Mercer said. "Actually, I'm told Scully invited Quint Akers in to be tested."

"That's insane," I said. "Francie and Quint were never an item."

"The commissioner wants Quint to be the guinea pig, since he was her boss. To open the doors to other guys she worked with to be tested."

"He has no business making Francie's private life a hotbed of rumors at Legal Aid," I said. "I'll call him right back and tell him his methodology sucks."

"No, you won't," Mercer said, his biting tone coming right through my iPhone. "I have this story line deep-throated from Vickee. You have no business knowing any of it, so just forget about it."

"For Vickee's sake," I said, "I'll do my best."

"Why, you have a better idea?" Mercer asked.

"Every now and then I do," I said. "If it were my plan, I'd ignore the idea of an office romance with Quint. I'd dive right into the belly of the beast."

FORTY-THREE

I sat down on a bench in the rear row of the courtroom and waited for Helen Wyler to finish the questioning of her witness. It had only been a few days since I'd been summoned up to her trial to help her navigate the issue of discovery material that she'd neglected to turn over to the defense.

Bud Corliss spotted me the moment I entered. He sat up straight and glared at me for three or four minutes.

"Nothing further, Your Honor," Helen said.

"Ten-minute break," the judge said, stepping off the bench and motioning to me. "Come on into my robing room, Ms. Cooper."

I walked down the center aisle, stopping to assure Helen—and defense counsel—that my appearance had nothing to do with her case. One of the court officers ushered me in through the well of the courtroom and out the door behind the clerk.

"You got a problem with me, Alexandra?" he asked, lighting a cigar and puffing on it, with his head out of the window of the small room. "Has my wife been to see you?"

"Not yet, she hasn't," I said. "I thought I'd check on how the trial was going."

"You're right about Wyler," he said, not turning back to me. "Good lawyer. She's got potential."

"I'm also here because I think we have a friend in common," I said. "A friend who isn't doing very well."

"Doing well" was a perverse euphemism for "dead," but Bud Corliss wasn't supposed to know about Francie Fain's medical condition.

"We have a lot of friends in common."

"I'm terribly concerned about Francie Fain," I said. "I think you must be, too."

Corliss brought his head back in through the window so quickly he almost cracked it against the frame. "What do you know about Francie?" he asked.

"Nothing," I said. "I can't get any information, not even from the police commissioner. I was hoping you might know something."

He crushed his lit cigar against the windowsill before looking up, then balanced the stub on the edge of his desk. It had been years since smoking was allowed in city buildings. That legislation had slowed the judge down a bit, but hadn't stopped him.

"Who's been talking to you?" Corliss asked.

"No one. Not now," I said. "But Francie told me about coming to work with you as your law secretary, just Monday, my first day back."

Corliss's eyes narrowed as he looked at me. "You? She told you?"

I opened the Redweld folder. I had taken an eight-by-ten picture frame off my office wall. In the photograph, Francie and I were side by side, arms around each other's shoulders, after last year's softball game between Legal Aid and the DA's office women.

I passed the frame to Corliss. "I guess she never mentioned that we were good friends."

He held the picture with both hands, brushing off the dust front and back, then staring at it for thirty seconds.

"Francie's a fine young woman," Corliss said, handing it back to me. "I hope she accepts my offer."

"I—uh—I just wanted you to see that we're friends, which gave her good reason to confide in me—you know, about things."

"Things? What do you mean, 'about things'?" he bellowed. "What else beside the job offer was there?"

"Nothing. Nothing at all," I said. "But if you ever want to talk about her—about Francie, I mean— you can always give me a call. Like you, I just want the best for her."

"That's why you came up here?" Corliss asked. "Take a hike, Alexandra. I'm trying to finish up for the week with all this testimony and get out of here."

Bud Corliss didn't wait for me. He stormed out of the robing room, across the short hallway, and back into the courtroom. I heard the heavy door slam shut behind him.

I used a tissue to pick up the cigar stub from Corliss's desk. He was known to be cheap enough to put out the butts but leave what remained of them on desks or tables or the edges of book-shelves, to finish at a later time.

I dropped the half-smoked stogie into my Redweld and slipped out through the corridor that led to the elevator bank. I was back at my desk five minutes later.

Then I dialed Mike's number.

"Whaddaya got?" he asked.

"Something that stays between you and me," I said. "No Mercer, for the time being, or he'll get Vickee busted."

"Roger that."

"I've used up all my favors at the DNA lab," I said. "But I've got Bud Corliss's DNA—saliva on his cigar butt and touch DNA on a glass picture frame. I'll tell you where I'm going with it when I see you, but you have to get it to the lab for me as soon as humanly possible."

"Oh yeah? In regard to what?" Mike asked.

"The possible paternity of Francie's unborn child."

"Jesus, Coop. I thought you just meant the judge was using his tried-and-true inappropriate language on Francie. I didn't take it a step further than that."

"I'm not trying to blindside you," I said. "But I think I'm on solid ground."

"Who'd you use to collect the evidence—the butt and the picture frame—and where are they now?"

"I'm just back from Corliss's court part," I said. "The items are right on my desk."

"I'll shoot down to you and pick them up myself," Mike said. "But what are you going to do about proving the cigar came from the judge, and that he touched the frame, too? Who was your undercover, kid?"

"I did it myself, Mike. I **am** the chain of custody."

FORTY-FOUR

Mike left my office at five to voucher the two items and deliver them to the DNA lab. I closed up my office shortly after—taking as many of the Zach Palmer files as I could carry with me—brushing off offers from friends to go to Trial Bureau 50's TGIF weekly keg party and the wine tasting in the Child Abuse Unit.

I flagged down a yellow cab in front of the courthouse, putting my head back and closing my eyes for the slow ride uptown. The driver was fighting rush-hour traffic and the catnap was refreshing.

At my apartment, I dropped all my case folders on my desk, and went into the bathroom to take a steaming-hot shower. I was happy to be out of my work clothes, and dressed in a crisp white polo shirt and straight-leg jeans.

Then I packed a small sail bag with my cosmetics and clean underwear for the morning. By tomorrow, I expected the commissioner would work out an arrangement to move Francie's body to the morgue, change the bodyguard assignment, and help me figure a secure place to keep Lucy Jenner.

"Need a taxi?" the doorman asked as I walked toward him.

"Thanks, Oscar, but I need fresh air," I said. "I've been stuck indoors way too much all week, and I don't have far to go."

I was about ten steps away when I turned back. "When Mike Chapman comes by, would you tell him I'm stopping at PJ Bernstein Deli for sandwiches, and I'll meet him at the hospital?"

"You got it, Ms. Cooper."

The old-fashioned New York–style deli was between my Park Avenue apartment and York Avenue—the entrance to the hospital campus—on the corner of Third Avenue and Seventieth Street. I waited at the counter for the order of an assortment of ten thick sandwiches—enough for Mike, Mercer, Lucy, and me, as well as for Billy and others on the nursing staff.

It was a beautiful fall evening—mild and clear—and I knew there wouldn't be many of them left before cold weather moved in.

I walked past the entrance to New York/Cornell Hospital—thinking of my vain effort to get to see Francie there a few nights earlier, and kept going the extra two blocks south to the Rockefeller gates.

My name was on the security guard's list at the entrance booth. He checked my ID and watched me head up the short hill toward Founder's Hall, then off to the right to the hospital.

In the lobby of the hospital, there were now two officers stationed next to the front door, one a uniformed cop and the other a fed. I said hello to them and kept on going. I wondered why they had been added to the security detail and figured that Mercer would know.

I took the elevator upstairs and got off on the third floor. The hallways were still and dimly lit. I only passed one physician and saw three nurses between the front door and the quiet corridor where I had seen Francie's body this morning, in a small room, guarded by one federal agent and one cop.

Lucy's door was ajar. I tapped on it and pushed in. She was sitting on her bed with a stack of magazines piled up next to her, flipping pages of one while Mercer watched the news on television.

"How's everything?" I asked.

"Boring," Lucy said. "Totally boring."

"Glad to hear that," I said, smiling at her. "Nothing could make me happier than you having a boring day."

"Yeah, I was going to tell you that it's silent as a grave around here," Mercer said, "but then . . . well, that's exactly what it is."

I nodded at him. "I hope you're both starving," I said, placing the plastic bag filled with PJ Bernstein goodies on the tray table beside Lucy's bed.

"Where's Mike?" Mercer asked.

"He should be here soon."

"Do I have to wait for him to get here to eat?" Lucy asked.

"Of course not," I said. "What would you like?"

"Did you bring a turkey sandwich?" she asked.

"Several," I said, reaching into the bag and handing her the sandwich and chips, and a napkin.

"There's a vending machine down the hall," Mercer said. "I'll get some sodas. Just step out with me a minute, Alex."

Mercer took my elbow and guided me just outside the door. The two security officers looked up at us. Mercer turned his back to them and whispered to me.

"I'm not sure those two guys even know, but the docs removed Francie's body from that room—downstairs and out to the morgue—not long after you left for work."

"In a medical examiner's van?" I asked, surprised that Scully would tip his hand when he seemed so adamant about having a plan that involved Francie.

"Get real, Alex. How long could they keep a body here? She'd be decomposing and—"

"I get it. No more details needed."

"Scully used a hearse from a funeral home in Brooklyn," Mercer said. "Just made it look like a routine DOA going on her way."

"Yeah, but nothing about Rock Hospital is routine," I said. "And why is there still a cop and a Feebie outside that room if Francie's body is gone?"

"Because there's another body in there."

"**What?**"

"Keep your voice down," Mercer said. "About twenty minutes after you left, one of the docs and two orderlies came to the room with a gurney. They were all dressed in Hazmat outfits."

"Nerve agent gear, I guess?"

"Exactly," Mercer said. "They told the guards they were taking Francie for some tests, and the hallway had to be cleared. So the officer and the fed were chased back downstairs to the lobby, and the head doc took responsibility for the patient's—well—for the patient's safety."

"Francie's corpse was removed," I said, "and no one saw that happening."

"Correct. And now there's one of those ana-tomically correct vinyl dolls, brought in by the orderlies—all blown up and lying beneath a sheet in the room across the hall."

"Being bodyguarded, by officers who have no idea they're watching over a dummy," I said. "And you know this—let me guess—because Vickee told you?"

"Nope. I got it from the commissioner himself," Mercer said. "The cop and the fed are backup for us, to make sure Lucy's safe here. But we've only got twenty-four hours to decide what you're doing with Lucy, or he'll direct you to get a material wit-ness order to hold her in some crappy cheap hotel that takes the city's daily rate until she testifies."

"That's what we do with snitches," I said. "She'd be treated like a prisoner. Let's figure out something better."

He tapped my shoulder and told me to go back in and distract Lucy while he went to get the drinks.

When Mercer returned, Billy Feathers was with him, helping to carry the sodas.

"Thanks, Billy," I said. "You must have better things to do than this."

"Not a problem," he said. "I just came back on duty and it's my last shift of the week. Bad news is that you're stuck with me, because I can't go across the hall to the other wing."

"Why not?" I asked, before opening the door to the room.

"Serious case was brought in this afternoon," Billy said. "A man became terribly ill on a flight from Africa. Jamaica Hospital sent him to us. This time the quarantine sign is on the entrance to the other wing, and it's for real."

"What is it?" I asked.

Billy paused, then said the word. "Monkeypox."

"You're joking, right? That sounds like a name a kid would make up."

"It's nothing to joke about," Billy said. "It's a very rare, very deadly disease. Mostly in African populations, usually transmitted to humans by rodents, though it obviously starts in places with dense monkey populations."

"This man—?"

"He broke out with fever on the flight, and then the rash was visible by the time he made it through customs."

"Is it infectious?" Mercer asked.

"Yes, extremely so. In much the same way small-pox was, back before vaccines. It spreads through respiratory droplets from the patient—usually those are airborne—or from actual contact with his lesions. The last time we had an outbreak in the States was 2003."

"Oh my God," I said. "What are we exposing Lucy to?"

"This is what we do," Billy said, putting his hand on my arm to calm me. "This is the reason Rockefeller Hospital exists. Lucy will be fine—and so will all of us."

"But—"

"The patient is in isolation, in a negative air pressure room in the other wing."

"Negative air pressure room?" I asked.

"It's an isolation technique that we're equipped for, specifically to prevent cross-contamination. It's a ventilation system, with the patient all en-closed in plexiglass. Air is pumped into the room, but can't escape from it—it's sucked out by special pumps—so it prevents contagion from spreading."

I could feel my skin crawling already. "That really works for a deadly virus?"

"Don't freak out," Billy said, with a grin. "We use negative air rooms for Ebola and all the other

deadly poxes. It's a very effective technique to control and contain the spread of the infection."

"If that's supposed to make me feel better," I
said, "you've failed miserably."

"What's the deal?" Mercer asked. "Your Rock
docs have the cure, so the patient gets transferred
to you?"

Billy shook his head. "Sadly, there is no cure for
this virus. But that's what they're working on here
at the university, and we're uniquely equipped to
find it."

Mercer turned to me and held out a finger toward
my lips. "Not a word to Lucy about this."

Chills were running up and down my arms. I
wasn't squeamish. Medicine was too much a part
of my upbringing for me to worry about something
bad happening to me in a great hospital.

But the thought of our proximity to a deadly
virus with no cure spooked me and set me on edge.

"Make a plan, Mercer," I said, about to pull the
handle to open the door of the room. "We need to
get Lucy out of this place."

FORTY-FIVE

"Tonight's Final Jeopardy! category is 'Islands,'" Alex Trebek said, sounding flatter than usual—like he was as glad to get to the end of his week as I was.

Mike was taking bites out of his ham and cheese sandwich as though he hadn't eaten in days.

"Why do you all watch this show?" Lucy asked as the three of us crowded around her narrow bed and the show went to commercial break.

"Just to prevent Coop's head from swelling," Mike said. "She likes to think she knows a lot, so Mercer and I try to keep that in check by taking her money whenever she misses a beat."

Lucy looked up at me, furrowing her brow.

"He's pulling your leg," I said. "They both know far more than I do about anything that counts."

"Here's my twenty," Mike said, and now it was Mercer's time to up the ante.

"I'll see that and hit you for double," he said.

"You'll never get lost if you hang with Mercer, Lucy," I said. "He used world maps for wallpaper when he was growing up."

"If Coop's in for forty," Mike said, "I'll go for it, too."

"Reluctantly," I said. "Very reluctantly, but count me in, and if I win, I split the proceeds with Lucy."

She gave me a thumbs-up and laughed.

I took a few bites of my sandwich and washed it down with water.

"Tonight's Final Jeopardy! answer is," Trebek said, revealing the giant blue board, "'First colonized by the Dutch, home to the extinct dodo bird.'"

Mike high-fived Mercer. "We might just have a tie," he said. "What is New Zealand?"

"I hate to call you a loser, my friend," Mercer said, "but New Zealand was settled by the Polynesians, long before the Dutch ever sailed on in. The whole Maori culture was in place centuries before Europeans arrived. How about you?"

I looked at Lucy. "Any ideas?" I asked.

She shrugged. "The only dodo I ever knew about is the one in **Alice in Wonderland**, but there's no island connected with that."

"Good thinking," I said. I was happy to get her in the game. "I'd forgotten about him."

"None of you ever heard of Mauritius?" Mercer said. "What is the island of Mauritius?"

Trebek congratulated the winning contestant while Mike gathered our bills and gave them to Mercer.

"Where might that bit of land be?" Mike asked.

"About twelve hundred miles off the southeast coast of Africa, out in the Indian Ocean," Mercer said. "And it's those Dutchmen who killed off all the dodos, by the way, back in the seventeenth century, because the poor birds couldn't even fly."

"Flightless birds," Mike said. "Kind of oxymoronic, isn't it?"

Lucy had buried her nose back in a magazine, ignoring our chatter.

"Stop scratching yourself, Coop," Mike said. "You're giving me the itch."

Mercer was gathering up his things, getting ready to head out for the night. "I'll see you at eight tomorrow. I expect you two to come up with an idea."

"I'll walk you down to the lobby," I said, rubbing my left forearm.

"Did you rub against a pot of poison ivy on your way here?" Mike asked as I was about to follow Mercer out of the room.

"Just a psychosomatic thing," I said, not wanting to let Lucy know about the man with an incurable virus on the other side of the nurses' station. "Maybe it's just in my head that there's a mosquito lab across campus."

Mercer and I walked past the guards who were stationed outside the door of the dummy. "You're sleeping here?" he said.

"It seems to make Lucy more comfortable, and I guess I've got just one night to go."

"We'll figure it out," he said. "Clearer heads tomorrow morning."

"Where's your car?"

"Just before the entrance gates, in one of the campus parking spaces."

We walked down the front steps, and I took a deep breath of fresh air, reaching my arms up high and then bending down to touch my toes. I repeated the stretches three times.

"I feel like I'm tied up in knots," I said. "This was my first week back and it seems as though the stress level is higher than ever. The second week will probably have me in a straitjacket."

"Sometimes you make me laugh," Mercer said. "You've stared down death a lot of times, Alexandra Cooper, and here you are, getting some imaginary vibes about a disease you are no more likely to catch than—"

"Don't say it. I'm extremely superstitious, as you know."

I took a few steps forward and looked up at the sky. The campus was dark, but the city lights still made it impossible to see the stars.

"What are you looking for up there?" Mercer asked.

"One star," I said. "A lucky star, just to make a wish upon, like I used to do when I was a kid."

"Forget the lucky star," Mercer said. "You've got a full-on hunter's moon tonight."

FORTY-SIX

"Okay with you if I wander next door to my bed?" I asked Lucy, after the late news came on at eleven P.M. "I'm fading fast."

"It's been so long since I've had television in my own room," she said. "If it doesn't bother you, I'll probably watch a while longer."

"Suit yourself."

Mike was in the hallway, trading war stories with the cop sitting outside the room with the dummy corpse. When he'd first arrived, I told him about the swap for Francie's body—which the cop and agent didn't know, I'd been told—and also gave him the news of the newly admitted patient with the deadly African virus.

I stayed in my shirt and jeans and lay down on top of the bed, pulling the thin hospital sheet over me. The door was ajar and the light over my headboard was on. I was checking messages on my iPad.

About ten minutes later, Billy Feathers knocked on the door and asked if he could come in.

"Of course you can. I'm just resting," I said. "Starting to count sheep soon. Everything okay?"

"All good," Billy said. "We like it when the late shift is quiet. I've been asked to distribute some masks and caps and gowns—just a routine safety precaution."

He put down a handful of syringes on my night-stand and handed me the hospital gear.

I immediately forgot about the sheep. "What kind of precaution? Against the pox? You told me—"

"Nothing at all is going to happen to you," Billy said. "This is a hospital for infectious dis-ease, Alex. We take precautions. That's what we do. Human-to-human transmission of monkeypox occurs through contact with respiratory droplets, like I said. A particle discharged from a sneeze or a cough. But the droplets only travel a few feet—not the length of a corridor and not under the closed door of the quarantined wing. They're out of busi-ness within seconds."

"So why this?" I asked, holding up the white surgical mask and hospital-green cap that would tie behind my neck if needed.

"Worst-case scenario," Billy said, heading for the door with his arms full of masks, caps, and gowns.

"What scenario would that be?" I asked. "Poor Mr. Pox decides to escape from his negative air cu-bicle and come over to chat me up?"

"Don't flatter yourself, girl," Billy said. "He's not moving so fast—not even in your direction."

"And the syringes?" I asked. "What are those for?"

"You watch too much TV," he said. "Saline flush, that's all that is."

I knew from time around my father in hospitals that saline flushes were used to clear intravenous lines, to ensure that all the required medication had passed through, and to lower the possibility of blood clots.

"Another precaution?" I asked.

"Don't shoot me, Alex," Billy said, mocking my serious tone. "I'm just here to deliver them to the nurses' station."

"Billy," I said, getting up to go to the door. "Let me take Lucy's mask and gown. I don't want you going into her room to rattle her about things at this hour of the night."

"Rules are rules," he said. "I'll just set them down on her chair and go."

He turned to leave, forgetting the saline syringes. I'd give them to him when he returned.

I stood in the doorway and asked Mike to come back to my room. He held up a finger, telling me to wait. Both the cop and the agent he was talking to seemed riveted by whatever war story he had launched into.

When he walked into my room, his clothing was covered by green scrubs, and a mask was tied at his neck, but not pulled over his face. "Who do I remind you of?"

"Not a clue," I said.

"I'm thinking George Clooney," Mike said. "**ER.**"

I put my hand up to his forehead and laughed. "Fever, maybe? You do sound delusional, Detective."

"Made you smile, didn't I?"

"I'm thinking that maybe you should call Commissioner Scully and have someone pick us up and take Lucy and me—and you, Dr. McDreamy, if you're ready to go—over to my apartment right now."

"Now? It's almost midnight."

"Francie's at the morgue—"

"Her bodyguards seem a little dim about that fact," Mike said.

"And I'm not willing to expose Lucy to the chance of getting some incurable disease, from that monkeypox virus that's taken up residence down the hall."

"You're a little overdramatic, don't you think? The odds are—"

"Maybe so, but will you call the commissioner?"

"Anything you say, Coop. Is that the answer you wanted?"

I put my hands on Mike's shoulders and reached up to kiss his cheek. "That works with me every time."

He put his hand on the door and opened it so that he could walk out. I took a step behind him, to poke my head into Lucy's room and see if she had gone to sleep yet.

But the corridor had an eerie feel. For the first time since I'd arrived at Rock U Hospital, there was not a person in sight on this hallway. Both the FBI agent and the NYPD cop had left their posts at the same moment. Their chairs were empty. And no one was guarding the room where Francie Fain had died.

Mike ripped the scrubs off and grabbed my wrist. "Get in with Lucy and stay there," he said. "I'll be back for you both in five."

FORTY-SEVEN

Lucy was on the bed, knees drawn up and her arms around them, hooked on a rerun of a sitcom I didn't recognize. She didn't even notice that I had come into the room.

There was a soft knock on the door and I almost jumped at the sound.

"Who is it?" I asked, noticing that there were no locks on the doors.

"Billy," he said. "It's me."

Lucy turned her head for a minute but went right back to her show.

"Where's Mike?" he asked.

"He went down to the lobby," I said. "We can't figure why those two guards disappeared, and he's trying to find out who's on duty from the security staff."

"Oh, it's nothing serious," Billy said. "We told them they had to put the masks and gowns on— just like I told you—and since the shift change was happening, the two of them told us to give the gowns to the new team that's coming on now. They're in the restroom getting suited up."

I smiled with relief.

"Anyway, the reason I wanted Mike is because there's a guy at the front gate," Billy said. "You know, the entrance on York at Sixty-Eighth Street?"

"Yes."

"Well, security just called the nurses' station because he claims that he's Francie Fain's father—up from Texas—and he wants to come in to see her."

My nerves had already been jangling about our proximity to the pox. Now I was really jumpy.

"I'm pretty sure Francie's father is dead," I said. "It can't be her father, I'm certain of that. And what is anyone doing showing up here at this hour?"

"That goes on all the time when family arrive from out of town to see patients who aren't doing well. He knows she's on life support," Billy said. "He wants to see her before anything worse happens."

"Let me call Mike and tell him to hold the man down there at the gate," I said. "Find out who he really is."

Billy took his phone out of his uniform pocket. "I'll call the lobby and tell them to block him, too, in case he gets past security while you find Mike."

I ran ten feet down the corridor to speed-dial Mike from the privacy of my room.

"Yeah?"

"Where are you?" I asked.

"I'm on my way to the front gate."

"You know there's a man—?"

"Claiming to be Francie Fain's father," Mike said.

"Her father died when she was a kid," I said. "And her adoptive mother never married."

I suddenly had a thought. "What if it's Judge Corliss?" I asked. "He's old enough to be her father. He might be saying he's her dad just so he can get access to her room. We can't let him know about Francie yet."

"Why not?" Mike said. I could hear the street noise in the background. "It might be the perfect moment to catch him off guard."

"Hurry up, then," I said. "I'll be waiting for you in Lucy's room."

"I'd distance myself from Lucy, if I were you," Mike said.

"But why?" I asked. "She's so vulnerable in all this."

"Exactly. But the man identifying himself also asked if you were here."

"He **what**?"

"He asked the guard if you were sitting vigil with Francie."

If I hadn't been scared until this moment, I was suddenly terrified.

"If this man is looking for **you**, Coop, there are two possible reasons. He wants to do something evil to you, or he figures you've got Lucy in tow, here at the hospital. Either way, one or both of you are his targets. So find a way to split up as safely as you can. Backup teams are on the way from the nearest precinct. I'll have you both covered, I swear it."

"How do I make Lucy safe?" I tried to blow off the fear and be useful to my young charge.

"Figure it out, kid. Just don't stop thinking," Mike said. "It's what you do."

I bit my lip and tried to clear my head.

"Just stay low, do you hear me?" Mike said. He was breathing harder, as though he'd broken into a trot.

I was standing still but I was breathing harder, too.

"No one's supposed to know we're here, Mike," I said. "That was the whole point of choosing this location—this little old hospital that no one seems to know exists."

"Let me deal with this guy at the gate and then I'm coming back to take you and Lucy out," Mike said. "Your job is to keep your cool and do the right thing for Lucy. Then let's blow this joint."

FORTY-EIGHT

I couldn't leave Lucy alone. It was my fault we had her hidden here. I wanted to wait for Mike, but if this problem got away from him, I needed to be able to protect her, not abandon her.

I kept my phone in my hand and walked into her room. She was lying down on her side, still glued to the TV.

"Sorry to interrupt you, Lucy."

"Hmm?" she answered without looking up.

"We're going to be leaving here tonight, and going over to my place," I said.

"Why?" she asked. "Because that woman is dead?"

Her voice was as flat as if she was talking to me about the television schedule.

"How do you know about that woman? How did you find out anything about her?" I said, a bit too frantically for my own liking.

Lucy just shrugged. "Those guys in the hall sometimes talked too loud," she said. "It's a hospital. You've got to expect that sometimes people die."

She didn't seem to know there was any connection between the dead woman and herself. There weren't many people who knew—yet—that Zach Palmer had subjected Francie Fain to the same kind of sexual assault as Lucy, sealing her silence, too, with a blood oath.

"Mike's going to be here shortly," I said. "I'd like you to put your jeans on and your shoes, and get ready to go."

"But I have my own room in this place," she said. "My own TV. Nobody makes me do anything that I don't feel like doing here."

"I've got Netflix and Amazon Prime and a million stations you can watch," I said, raising the tone of urgency in my voice. "Please just do as I say."

Lucy reluctantly stood up, slipped into her jeans, and bent over to put her shoes back on.

Billy Feathers pushed open the door. "Did you get Mike?" he asked.

"Yeah. He'll be up as fast as he can."

"The guards should have been back here by now," Billy said.

We were looking at each other, both anxious and both confused about where the law enforcement security officers were.

"How do you feel?" Billy asked. "I mean about being here?"

"Lousy," I said. "I want to go and I want to get Lucy out of the hospital."

Lucy was dressed now, standing beside her bed and listening to us.

"Is there a back door?" I asked. "We could wait for Mike on the street."

"There's only the ambulance bay, and I can't operate that by myself."

"I can climb out windows," Lucy said, seeming more eager than frightened.

"I don't doubt it," I said. "But they seem to either face the front of the hospital building, or they hang out over the East River."

Just then, a voice came on the loudspeaker in the hallway wall just outside Lucy's room. We were all startled.

"Code Violet. Code Violet. I repeat, Code Violet in first-floor restroom."

I knew enough about hospital protocol to know that Code Blue was a critical medical emergency, Code Red signified smoke or fire, and Code Black usually meant a bomb threat.

Billy headed for the door.

"What's Violet?" I asked. "What does it mean?"

"A combative situation," he said. "It's not about a patient condition. Someone's fighting—or been injured."

"But the bathroom is where the two cops were dressing," I said. "And they're armed."

"Maybe they're hurt," Billy said. "I've got to help."

I grabbed Billy by both arms and squared off against him. "There are others to respond to that situation. You've got to help me get Lucy out of here," I said. "Think of a way. Any way that avoids the front entrance and the elevator and the stairwell that leads to the lobby."

Billy inhaled and rubbed his eyes. "I can get you both safely to the security office, I'm pretty sure."

"Without using the elevator?" I asked. "Without going through the lobby and the front door?"

I was as agitated as he was, but trying to stay solid for Lucy's sake. Someone had killed Francie Fain and was perhaps after me as well. Lucy would be the next link in the deadly chain.

"Yes," Billy said. "Yes, I'm sure."

"How will you go?" I asked.

"Out the far end," he said. "Opposite the direction of the elevator and the quarantined wing. We'll go across the Bridge of Sighs, to the old Nurses' Residence."

"You can get in?"

"I've got the key," he said, jingling the ring of keys on his belt. "Security's on the ground floor of that building."

"Code Violet. Repeat, Code Violet," the stern voice said, sounding a bit more urgent. "Code Violet on One West."

"Let's hurry," he said. "I want to get you out first, then go downstairs to help."

"If that's what you need to do, Billy, I get it," I said. "But I need to set up a ruse first, some way to hide Lucy as best I can. Someone may have figured out that I'm here, because of Francie, but Lucy has to stay out of sight."

"I understand," Billy said.

"Then let's cross the hall."

"What?" Lucy asked.

The corridor was still empty. I ran across and pushed open the door of the room where Francie Fain had been, when she was still alive and on life support. I motioned for Billy and Lucy to follow.

There was a form under a sheet, lying atop a gurney, which was supposed to be a double for the body of Francie Fain. I pulled back the cover, revealing the anatomically correct blowup doll that had been placed there instead.

I opened the closet door and stuffed the doll inside.

"Lie down on the gurney," I said to Lucy. "Stay as still as you can and close your eyes. It's better than staring at the sheet I'm going to put over you."

"Why are you doing this?" she asked.

"Because I don't know who's in this hospital right now, and I don't want anyone to see you," I said. "Now, lie down."

She did as she was told and I pulled the sheet up over her head.

I wrapped the long green scrubs around myself and tied a knot in the front. I covered my blond hair with a cap and put the mask over my nose and mouth.

"You take the lead, Billy," I said. "When I open the door, head as quickly as you can to the Bridge of Sighs. No looking back."

I pulled on the door and stuck my head out. There was still no one on the hallway. To my right was the elevator and the quarantined wing. To my left was the solarium and exit to the Nurses' Residence, which now housed the main security office three flights down.

The Code Violet calls had stopped. I had no idea whether someone had been hurt and the situation resolved or not.

"On the count of three," I said, and when I got to three, Billy pulled and I pushed the gurney out into the hallway, brushing the edge of one of the chairs that the cops had been sitting in and steering it to the right.

As we passed my room, Billy pulling the gurney from the front, I ducked in and grabbed the handful of syringes he had left behind, sticking them in my jeans pocket before I grabbed the foot of the gurney.

We had only thirty feet to go, and no one in front of us to block the route.

"If I don't go all the way with you, Billy," I said, "how else can I get out?"

"But you have to come," he insisted, turning his head to argue with me. "Both of you need to be safe."

"You've got to make Lucy safe with tonight's security team," I said. "That's where Mike will go to get help. He wants us separated."

If someone was following me, I didn't need to put Lucy in harm's way.

"I know there's a way down, but I'm not sure where it goes out."

"Down?" I asked. "What do you mean? Out where?"

"After we make the left turn here, the last doorway we pass after the bridge is a stairwell," he said, half-turned again to face me. "If you go down below the first floor—starting here on three—to the basement level, it's pretty rough but it will take you most of the way underground across the old campus, three blocks to the north."

"Rough?" I asked as we wheeled Lucy down the hall.

"It was built a hundred years ago. It's dark and narrow and filled with pipes overhead and on all sides."

"But you've done it? You can get through?"

"You and anyone else," Billy said. "About twenty feet in to the basement tunnel, there's a small door to the left—at a break between the pipes—which will take you one flight further down. Think of it as a submarine—incredibly narrow and low and dark. A sub-basement that tracks the path above it, only most people don't know it's there because it's unmarked."

"But you've been in it?" I asked, making sure it existed.

"Once only, five years ago," Billy said. "For an emergency tornado drill. But all we did was climb down the steps and go a few yards in, not the whole way, so I have no idea where that tunnel leads to."

"So that takes me to . . . ?"

"I wish I could be sure, Alex," Billy said. "It used to lead out to the river, in the early days, so hazardous materials could be loaded onto boats and floated away."

I was trying to absorb all of this. A sub-basement that sounded as claustrophobic as a submarine, leading away from this building but with destination uncertain, and once used for the transport of hazardous material.

"You promise me you'll stay with Lucy?" I whispered, hoping the young woman couldn't hear over the rattling of the gurney.

We had turned the corner, squeezed through the tall, leafy plants in the solarium, and rolled over the ghostly Bridge of Sighs. I took my last look down on the campus, to my left, hoping for a sighting of Mike, and then my eyes caught bright beams from the hunter's moon lighting up the East River to my right.

I saw the door that Billy wanted me to use. It

was just steps before the one that he would use to take Lucy to security.

Billy's hand was steady as he put the key in the door to the old Nurses' Residence and I gave the gurney one last push.

A voice behind us—a woman's voice—was yelling to us. I could hear her clearly although she wasn't yet in sight.

"Nurse! Hey, you! Nurse!" she screamed. "Stop, will you? I'm an agent, an FBI agent—you'd better stop right now."

I heard the door slam shut behind Lucy Jenner and Billy Feathers, and listened to him turn the lock. I stepped back and slipped into the adjacent stairwell, just as Billy had directed me to do, hoping that our pursuer didn't see me separate from Billy and the gurney.

I flattened myself against the wall, not daring to move. There were no locks on the stairwell doors. Hospital staff had to move around without being accidentally sealed off from one of the floors. I counted on the fact that our pursuer would occupy herself with attempting to follow the gurney, but that Billy and Lucy would lose her.

The agent went running to the door Billy had exited and pulled on it repeatedly, but it didn't give. Then she began banging on it, ordering him to open up, as she continued to pound on it and kick it.

I used the noise of her pounding as cover, to

allow me to circle down from the third-floor stair-well to the second, and on again to the first floor.

I had my hand on the basement door when I heard her shout, again in vain, "Shit, you damn fool. Open this door right now."

I knew I had heard that voice before. The frus-trated speaker was an FBI agent, albeit a retired one. Tough, smart, and fearless.

She was Josie Breed, Zach Palmer's body man.

FORTY-NINE

When the banging stopped, I heard footsteps running away from the door that Billy Feathers had taken Lucy through. Maybe Josie Breed was doubling back to check the patient's room, where the gurney now holding Lucy had been minutes earlier—the gurney that Josie thought was holding Francie Fain.

I was on the first floor of the stairwell, staring at the door that led to the grimy basement and the tiny confines below it.

I speed-dialed Mike and got him on the first ring.

"Where are you?" he asked.

"It's Josie Breed," I said, without answering his question. I was breathing heavily, almost gasping between words. "It's Zach Palmer's body man who's in here trying to hunt us down."

"I know that," Mike said. "She's Zach's assassin."

That single word was heart-stopping.

"Tell me where you are," he demanded.

"I sent Lucy off with Billy Feathers to security.

You've got to make them safe," I said. "What do you mean, 'assassin'?"

"Josie faked her way in tonight as an agent, just using her old badge and fake ID," Mike said. "She killed the other agent—the real one—in the restroom at the hospital. Shot her twice in the head when her back was turned, with a silencer to muffle the noise."

That attack had set off the Code Violet we'd heard over the loudspeaker, I thought, covering my mouth with my hand.

"Josie came there tonight to finish off Francie Fain," Mike said, "and then double the stakes by getting you. Getting Lucy, too, if you have her here with you. The perfect trifecta."

"I was so careful," I said, listening for any sounds from above, but hearing none. "How did she—?"

"That was Zach here at the gate, pretending he was Francie's father, to get them in," Mike said. "Josie had his back, before she figured out the better trick to get in by pretending to be an agent. And she saw you when you walked Mercer out to his car."

"So I brought this down on myself?"

"Josie also delivered the perfume bottle with the nerve agent to Francie Fain the day Francie was poisoned," Mike said. "Short story is that Zach and Francie ran into each other at that conference in England a few weeks back."

Of course they did, I thought. He had been in London on antiterrorist business. He'd be the first to know about the nerve agents that had been let loose by the Russians on British soil. I was furious.

"They don't sell nerve agents with the perfume at the duty-free shops at Heathrow," I said. "How did Zach get his hands on it?"

"Josie and her contacts in the evil empire," Mike said. "She had a mole in Putin's crew when she was legitimately with the feds. Now that the stuff is being used in England and Europe, she was able to smuggle out a small amount of the Kiss of Death poison."

How much was a small amount? How many people were still at risk, and was Lucy Jenner one of them? Was I? My head was spinning.

"Where are you?" Mike asked again.

"In the stairwell that leads down from the solarium," I said. I didn't tell him that my knees were shaking and that a terrible chill had seized me from head to toe.

"I'm almost there, kid," Mike said. "I'm coming to get you out. Just stay on the phone with me. Just keep talking so I know you're okay."

I held the phone away and listened for footsteps in the corridor above me, but heard none.

"But why would Zach want to kill Francie?" I asked. "Why, after all this time, and how do you know that?"

I could hear that Mike was jogging, his feet

pounding on the asphalt Rock U drive, coming up the hill from York Avenue, toward the hospital.

"Francie took advantage of the meeting in England to confront Zach about what he had done to her so many years ago," Mike said. "She even told him she was quitting her job to work for Corliss, and that she was having the judge's baby."

My trip to get the Judge's DNA hadn't been in vain. Small victory on this high-stakes night.

Mike kept talking to keep me with him. "Francie told Zach that she hadn't been able to have a relationship with a man in all the decades since he had molested her, but that she was ready to go public with her story now."

"And Corliss?" I asked.

"It seems to be that whatever his faults—and who knows how he really feels—that relationship, her first since Zach raped her, was completely consensual."

I slumped against the wall and rubbed my eyes with my free hand. "Poor, poor Francie," I said.

I looked up, thinking I had heard a noise in the corridor above me, but I was just nervous and on edge.

"How do you know this?" I asked.

"You're slow, Coop," Mike said. "You didn't even ask me the good news. We've got Zach Palmer in custody over at the Nineteenth Squad, and he's squealing like a stuck pig."

"Squealing—why?"

"You didn't think he was a stand-up guy, did you?" Mike says. "He's blaming everything on Josie Breed. Zach Palmer says silencing Francie—and Lucy—and you—was all Josie's idea. Zach says she's a natural-born killer."

I rested my head back against the wall.

"Hang tough, Coop. I'm close," Mike said. "I'm really close."

I wasn't imagining it this time. There were footsteps above me. I heard them, and they vibrated down the stairwell wall. The pounding began again on the door to the Nurses' Residence two flights up.

"So is Josie Breed," I said. "So is she."

FIFTY

I couldn't speak any lower than I was speaking. "The basement, Mike. Billy told me there's a basement."

"What? I can't hear you."

"I'm going to the basement. Come get me there," I said. "Find me. Find out where it lets out at the end and meet me there."

"Don't go down, kid!" Mike screamed at me. "Cell phones don't work in there, because of the old iron foundation of the hospital building. Stay where I can hear you. Stay where I can talk you through this."

I wanted to listen to Mike. I wanted him to know how much I needed him to get to me.

But the time for talking me through this escape was over, and I pressed the button that ended our conversation.

Josie Breed had stopped pounding on the door through which Lucy and Billy had fled to the safety—I hoped—of the security office. She must have realized that the adjacent door—not even knowing I had used it to exit—was possibly an alternate route that would get her there.

There was silence around me for almost a minute. Then I heard a couple of steps, and the sound of the heavy metal door creaking open above me.

My tracker entered the stairwell and stood still at the landing on the top, as though listening for anything that revealed the presence of another human.

I stopped breathing. I didn't move a muscle.

I looked down and saw that the bare lightbulb overhead had cast my shadow onto the dull gray paint of the hospital floor.

Josie Breed must have seen it, too. When she put her foot on the first step of the tall staircase, I heard the sound of the release of a round into the chamber of her handgun. I knew I was alone in what seemed like the most isolated place in New York City, in the company of a stone-cold assassin, who had me clearly in her sights.

FIFTY-ONE

I pulled open the entrance to the basement door and started to run.

My eyes adjusted slowly to the darkness around me, and I could see the seemingly endless stretch of pipes—water, heat, air-conditioning—painted red and yellow and blue to differentiate them.

There was nowhere to go but straight ahead, and Josie would be right behind me in a matter of seconds.

I saw the break in the pipes to my left—the one Billy told me led to an even more desolate hole deeper in the ground, and now obsolete.

I had three or four seconds to make the choice to enter it or not. I used one of them to look at my cell phone, and saw that it had no bars. Mike must have been right. I could think of a better use of the device that might even buy me some time.

I leaned over and placed my phone on the floor, and then slid it forward with one long stroke, so that it went thirty or forty yards down the passageway, careening off the sides with a noise that sounded like the discharge of a cannon in an enclosed space.

Just as I put my hand on the door leading to the sub-basement and stepped through it, Josie Breed entered the main basement area that I had just traveled through.

I held my hand against the heavy door so that it closed behind me without a sound.

She must have assumed the noise she heard—the phone traveling through the tunnel ahead of her—was my flight route. I could hear her walk past the sub-basement door, following the path of my abandoned phone.

I bent my head and started placing one foot ahead of the other along the claustrophobic subterranean path that Billy had described to me. It was an airless and dank tunnel, more than a century old. When I put my hand on one of the old pipes to steady my way forward, it felt as though a century's worth of cobwebs had accumulated here since John D. Rockefeller created his visionary scientific institute, and they were now all sticking to my skin.

There were occasional sounds, mostly coming from the basement above me. Perhaps it was Josie Breed as she walked, or the antiquated pipes that rumbled and shuddered as I made my way forward.

I couldn't tell the direction in which I was headed. The tunnel went straight for at least one hundred yards, then took a dogleg curve to the left, before twisting and turning in shorter fragments.

I was still somewhere under the original institute buildings, I assumed, but with no idea where—or how—this would turn out.

There seemed to be no breaks in the line of pipes as far as I had come, and no obvious egress from this stale tube.

Suddenly the noise of running footsteps overhead began—a single set—and it sounded like a wild horse that was thundering toward its master.

Something must have convinced Josie that my phone was just a diversionary tactic—maybe no footprints in the dusty basement above me?—and she was doubling back to figure out which way I had gone.

I cringed when I heard the subbasement door open behind me, far enough back and around too many bends in the passageway to offer a line of sight from Josie Breed to me, but it was clear I was no longer alone.

"Alex Cooper!"

Josie's voice reverberated through the tunnel and bounced off its walls and ceiling as though she had blasted my name through a megaphone.

I quickened my pace and kept on slinking ahead, unintentionally crunching an occasional cockroach with my sneakers.

"Alex!" Josie shouted. "Lucy Jenner! You're dead to me."

Maybe she hadn't figured out that Lucy had been taken to a safer place by Billy Feathers. I had no intention of answering her, no intention of letting her hear the desperation in my voice.

I hadn't expected a gunshot, not until Josie was close enough to aim her weapon at me. But she fired a round against the side of the tunnel to put the fear of God in me—and then a second one for good measure. As I listened to them ricochet off the concrete walls, I knew she had succeeded in her goal.

There were no bends in the passageway. Everything was at right angles, and each time I got close to the last part of a length of pipe, it looked like I had reached a dead end.

Every twenty or thirty feet, there was a recess built into the tunnel sides, each one large enough to step into and stand back inside, to be flush against the pipes that snaked along the wall. Once or twice I thought of doing that, but knew that once Josie Breed overtook my position, I would be no match for her gun if I tried to mount a struggle.

So far, by staying in the center course of this narrow track, each right or left turn had given me new hope of outrunning the madwoman who was giving chase.

I figured I had run more than half a mile, not round and round like a gerbil on its miniature treadmill but twisting through the underbelly of the original buildings, the three that fronted on the East River: Rockefeller Hospital, the Nurses' Residence, and Founder's Hall.

There had to be a point at which this tunnel once met the East River, where dangerous materials had been offloaded onto barges that carried them away. I had to be close.

It was time to take another chance.

"We're almost there, Mike," I screamed, knowing that Chapman was nowhere close to me and not able to hear this, but hoping that it would fool Josie Breed into thinking that he actually knew my whereabouts, and that he, too, was armed—and dangerous. "Lucy's up in front of me, okay?"

I paused, then added, "Josie Breed's behind us and she's got a gun."

Josie bought the story. She started talking straight to Lucy Jenner, not to me. My imaginary running buddy was her first interest.

"Lucy! Lucy Jenner," Josie yelled. "I'm here to rescue you from Alex Cooper, girl. Zach wants to make it all right with you. He doesn't want Alex using you, you understand? Zach wants to take you with him—take you somewhere you can be together, like it was before."

Suddenly, I was brought up short. I made a right turn and there was nothing in front of me but an impenetrable stone wall. Huge boulders were piled tightly against each other, permanently held in place by mortar that had sealed up all the cracks that once existed.

I was running my hands up and down the cold boulders. Rock U was perfectly named. I was caught between a solid wall of rock and the maniac hunting me down.

On either side of the wall were two of the recesses—each about a foot deep—the kind that had dotted the wall of the entire tunnel.

I felt inside each of them for some means of egress. There had to have been a way out of this lifeless tunnel when it was first constructed.

"That's a lie, Lucy," I said, turning my attention back to slowing Josie down. "Zach's been arrested. He was picked up at the entrance gate on York Avenue when Josie faked her way into the hospital."

I paused, but Josie's footsteps kept coming toward me. "Zach gave her up in a heartbeat," I said. "He told Mike that it was Josie who killed Francie Fain, and Josie who murdered another agent in the hospital tonight."

Josie Breed stopped in her tracks. She was still a hundred feet or so behind me, if I had to guess the distance. But her movement had ceased. It was dead quiet in the tunnel.

I felt around on the stone wall again, higher first, standing on my toes, and then bending over to feel around the bottom.

My hand came to rest on a series of metal latches—five or six of them—attached to a steel plate two feet wide by two feet high on the bottom half of the rock wall. It had to be the hole through which hazardous materials were once evacuated from the hospital grounds.

I dropped to my knees and started pulling at the bolts. They were rusted and covered in mold. I pulled my sweater off over my head and covered my fingers with it. They were already bleeding from my efforts to wrench the latches free.

"Lucy?" It was Josie Breed. "Can you hear me?"

I muffled my mouth with the sweater and raised my voice a register and answered, "Yes."

"You'll be okay, Lucy, whatever happens," Josie said.

"Stay by me, Lucy," I said. "Mike's got our backs."

I had opened each one of the bolts, and now I started pushing against the metal plate but not moving it.

I sat on the ground and faced the wall. I lifted my legs and kicked against the metal. By the third kick, I thought that I could smell a whiff of fresh air over the stench of the mold, and maybe even a hint of the water's scent from the river.

"Come right ahead, Josie," I said. "I've got a handful of syringes, filled with monkeypox virus."

"You're crazy, Alex," she said, sort of snorting as she tried to sound tough. "I've got a gun. And I don't even know what monkeypox is."

"I don't know how many bullets your gun holds—maybe six, maybe nine," I said. "And it reloads every time you fire it. So let's see. You fired two into the head of an agent, in the bathroom, and two a few minutes ago in the tunnel. Who knows how many before that. So are you ready to bet your next two or three against a deadly pox? Miss hitting Lucy on your first try and get only me? You're taking a chance, Josie. I wasn't Zach's victim, but Lucy was—so you need to get Lucy, or Zach's still going down for a very long time."

I could hear Josie Breed start to walk again, coming toward me, slowly and surely.

I took one of the saline syringes out of my pocket. I got back on my knees and turned my body. Glass syringes didn't exist anymore. I would have to crack one of the plastic casings to make my threat seem real.

I broke off the end of the saline syringe and threw it like I was launching a small missile in Josie's direction. I heard it land against the wall and splinter.

"There's your first dose of the pox, Josie. The droplets are flying out of that broken syringe and it's all around you," I called out. "There's no cure for it yet, but if they can find one anywhere, you're in the right hospital."

Josie was backing away now, that much was clear from the sound of her steps. "You're crazy, you know that? You can't kill me with some made-up pox."

"It's not made up, Josie," I called out. "It's a slower death than your nerve agents, but there's no antidote. Try not to breathe it in."

"You're breathing it, too," she shouted.

"I've got a mask on," I said. "No pox for me."

I didn't think I had stopped her, but I had

slowed her advance and given her something to think about.

I sat down again, facing the rock wall, and lifted both legs. I thrust them forward with every ounce of energy left in my body.

The metal plate gave way with a huge bang against the rock wall outside, below it. The noise echoed throughout the tunnel, and the cool night air rushed in behind.

Josie Breed must have heard the loud crash of the metal and felt the infusion of oxygen. I took advantage of that to let her think I had gotten Lucy out of harm's way.

"You're free, Lucy!" I shouted as loud as I could. "Run, Lucy. Good girl! Keep running. I'm right behind you."

But instead of sliding out through the opening, I got to my feet and pressed myself into the recess to the left of the stone wall. I pushed myself so far back in that the row of pipes was pressing into my back and thighs. I hoped that Josie would be looking straight ahead at the hole in the wall when she reached this point, not to either side.

Once more, Josie screamed Lucy's name as she started to walk in my direction. "Don't go, Lucy! Don't go!"

Josie Breed was running now. I pulled another syringe out of my pocket and removed the plastic cover from the tip of the needle.

I held my arm over my head, knowing I would

only have one chance to strike at Josie Breed, before she turned her gun on me.

When she got close to the exit hole—maybe ten feet away from me—Josie dropped down to crawl forward, almost flat on the ground, propelling herself ahead with her arms. Like me, she was probably assessing the means of getting out of the tunnel as fast as she could.

She was directly below me—on a path to her escape—when she noticed my feet off to the side of the hole. She had been creeping along with her gun in her right hand.

She gasped and looked up at me, shifting her weight to her left hand so that she could lift her gun and aim it at me. "Liar! You're a goddamn liar!"

I lunged at Josie Breed while she tried to stabilize herself. I stabbed her in the back of her neck with the syringe—as deep as it would go.

She howled like a wounded animal, dropping the gun and putting both hands to her neck to grab my weapon and try to remove it.

As she fumbled with the needle—which I had jammed in—and as she writhed in pain, I reached down to pick up her gun from the tunnel floor and stuck it securely in the rear waistband of my jeans.

"Help me," Josie said, grabbing at the needle over and over again, but unable to dislodge it. "Help me, please!"

I straddled her body and pinned both of her arms behind her back, tying them together with my sweater and knotting the sleeves three times. She wasn't going anywhere with the syringe in her neck and her arms restrained.

Then I pushed Josie's body to the side and sat down, leaning back with my feet in front of me. I slid forward, letting my legs drop over the side of the open hatch. I pulled myself up and ducked my head through the opening.

Ten feet beneath me was the solid seawall that protected the island of Manhattan from the roiling waters of the East River. Reinforced concrete—almost two feet thick—covered the debris that had once been, before the Bristol Blitz, the homes and churches and schools of an English city.

I twisted around and gripped the metal bolts that were secured ages ago into the rocks of the tunnel's foundation. My legs swung free while I summoned the courage to let go with my hands, and then I jumped off, landing on the concrete seawall beneath me.

The light of the hunter's moon, gleaming off the river, had guided me safely out of the tunnel that I feared would be my burial chamber.

FIFTY-TWO

I sat on the wall for fifteen minutes to steady myself.

By then, Mike and three uniformed cops—each with a large flashlight—had summoned officers to stop traffic on the FDR Drive. The four came charging over the lanes of the highway to help me down from my perch.

"You like it when you don't listen to me and you're still right, don't you?" Mike said, tousling my hair and kissing me on top of my head.

"I wasn't out to prove a point, Detective," I said, pressing my hand into his as we crossed back to the other side. "I didn't have a lot of choices."

"Seems like you made at least one good one."

"By the way, Josie Breed is right overhead," I said to Mike and the other cops, handing them her gun. "Sorry about getting my prints all over this, but I was kind of self-absorbed, trying to get it away from her."

"We'll manage just fine proving this belonged to Josie. And we know where she is," Mike said.

"Some of the crew from Emergency Services went into the tunnel the same way you did."

"Did they find her right where I left her?" I said. "At the end of the tunnel, needle in her neck and hands tied?"

"Bound up just like a Christmas present, kid," Mike said, "and ranting about some kind of monkeypox you infected her with."

"Aren't you the same guy who told me my bluffs didn't work?"

"This was one of your better ones," Mike said. "Josie's kind of freaked out, so they're examining her at Rockefeller Hospital, just to be sure."

"Is Lucy okay?" I asked as we walked around the campus wall to get back to York Avenue.

"She's doing just fine," Mike said. "Billy Feathers is her new hero."

"He's amazing, isn't he?"

"Mercer came in to be with her, and with Francie's case a provable homicide, we probably don't have to expose Lucy to a trial," Mike said. "Mercer and Vickee will take her home with them for a few days, till we straighten things out with her aunt. I think we've put Lucy's enemies out of business."

I burrowed my head in his shoulder, letting him wrap me in an embrace. Then he picked up my hands and put them to his lips.

"Sweet taste," he said. "The combination of blood and—what? A hint of rust, isn't it?"

"Throw in a serious dose of dust," I said. "Nothing that a shower and a strong drink won't wipe out."

"Let's walk another block to the Cornell ER," he said. "I don't want you in the same place as Josie Breed, but you need a tetanus shot for these bloody hands."

I nodded my head.

"How's Zach?" I said. "How'd he react to being confronted?"

"Still arrogant," Mike said. "Still claiming that his relationships were all consensual."

"A fourteen-year-old girl can't consent," I said.

"Don't argue your case to me, kid," Mike said. "Zach's a serial scumbag and I think your first two victims are just the tip of the iceberg."

"That was Josie in the Baxter Street video, wasn't it?" I asked. "What could she have possibly been saying to Francie?"

"All we can do is guess, unless she tells us," Mike said. "Maybe she was just making sure Francie got the bottle of perfume that she left on the desk—making sure she had used some of it."

"She probably lurked around till Francie collapsed, a few minutes later," I said.

"No doubt."

"What kind of hold could Zach possibly have on Josie?" I asked. "Why would she kill for him?"

"It turns out that Josie is Zach's half sister," Mike said.

"What?"

"Yeah, his father had an affair—resulting in an illegitimate kid—and that's Josie. Zach got her into the FBI when he learned about it," Mike said. "He's protected her all through her adult life, once he knew. She had some issues in the agency, which is why she was out so young, but he's always kept her cover and gotten her work, and she worships the ground he walks on."

I was shaking my head as we approached the ER entrance. "Accepting the fact that he raped young girls?" I said. "Willing to kill for him?"

"Must be a weak link in the DNA," Mike said. "There's a bit of sociopathic genetic material in both of them."

"And Bud Corliss is the father of Francie's baby," I said. "I guess DNA will confirm that tomorrow."

"That'll be the end of his very unhappy marriage, too," Mike said. "Catherine asked me to tell you that was bound to happen."

"Was it just yesterday afternoon that she met with Janet Corliss?"

"Catherine's on top of it," Mike said. "There's no doubt the judge put his hands on his wife's throat. She's completely credible. It looks like you cleared the bench of another once-powerful jurist."

"He was so verbally abusive to so many of my young lawyers," I said. "I can't imagine what it was like to be on the receiving end of his domestic rage."

The triage nurse had been told to expect me. One of the young RNs took me to a restroom to let me clean up before the doctor examined me.

I came out dressed in a hospital gown, scrapes and cuts on my arms and legs.

"I'm a mess," I said to Mike, holding out my hands for him to inspect, and then sitting on the edge of the gurney to wait for the doc.

"You're right about that," he said.

"You really called it when you said, '**Cherchez la femme,**'" I said.

"Yeah, but you're the one who figured out it was a woman under the hoodie. I just tried to woo you with my French."

"They might be the only three words you know," I said, reaching my toe out to poke him in the side.

"Do you have any idea where that phrase is from?" Mike asked.

"**Cherchez la femme?** It must be as old as time," I said. "Frenchmen chasing after women."

"Not even close," he said. "The phrase comes from a lousy crime novel that Alexandre Dumas wrote."

"You can't be serious," I said. I knew Mike was just chatting me up to get my blood pressure down before the doctor appeared. "Dumas? A crime novel? What do you know about Dumas?"

"First of all, how could I not love the guy who wrote **The Three Musketeers**?" Mike said.

"I'll give you that."

"And his old man was the commander in chief of the Army of the Western Pyrenees, too. Then later, chief of the Army of the Alps."

"A military connection, of course. I should have known," I said, leaning back and resting my head on the pillow. "That's why you read his books. But I didn't know he'd ever written a crime novel."

"**The Mohicans of Paris,**" Mike said. "Detective Jackal suspects a woman was the criminal, so he tells his guys, **'Cherchez la femme.'**"

"And I've always thought it was a line grounded in romance, not in a cop's directive." I laughed. "Look for the woman."

"I did exactly that for years, Coop," Mike said, bending over to kiss me, "and I wasn't going to lose you in a dead-end subterranean tunnel tonight."

"There goes my blood pressure again," I said, sitting straight up. "Just get me out of this place, will you?"

"I promise, kid," Mike said. "Not a blood oath, just my word of honor."

ACKNOWLEDGMENTS

When my great friend—and for twenty-five years my fantabulous literary agent at ICM Partners—Esther Newberg set out to sell the first ninety-six pages of my debut crime novel, **Final Jeopardy**, one of the bidding editors asked whether I thought I could write a second book, to start a series. I told Esther I thought I could write ten. I have always loved serial thrillers, waiting for my favorite sleuths to reappear in tale after tale. So it is astounding to me—and such a distinct honor—to be publishing my twentieth Alexandra Cooper novel, **Blood Oath**.

I got to this point in my career because of loyal readers, knowledgeable librarians, and the best booksellers in the country—like Barbara Peters of the Poisoned Pen Press, who has believed in me since reading the galley of my first novel.

Esther has been my North Star, guiding me wisely and with great good humor through the pleasures and perils of the publishing world. I ran out of words to thank her long ago.

Dutton has been my happiest literary home, with true believers at the helm—Christine Ball, especially, and John Parsley, too. Stephanie Kelly is my editor, and it is a dream to put a manuscript in her hands, knowing she will help make it a better book. Emily Canders sends me out into the world and is my lifeline to the mother ship. I've also got Carrie Swetonic, Elina Vaysbeyn, Lee Ann Pemberton, and a lineup of Dutton heavy hitters at my back. Thanks, too, to illustrator David Cain for the map in the beginning of the book, and to the good people at Little Brown UK, who cover me abroad.

Laura Rossi Totten is the most amazing social media guru and genius, and it is her boundless creativity that spreads the word about Coop and her sidekicks.

Every now and then, one gets extremely lucky. Two years ago, I had the great pleasure of sitting next to Jesse Ausubel at a dinner party. Not only did I have a marvelous evening, but I was captivated by his accessible brilliance and infectious excitement about his work.

Jesse invited me through the elegant gates of the Rockefeller University and, in ways that he never expected, **gave me** this book. I spent hours with Dr. Sarah Schlesinger, who introduced me to the history and significance of this unique institution. Michael Murphy and Jim Rogers, who are both former NYPD supervisors, guard the gates and secrets of Rock U. Mike also led me through the underground tunnels, knowing the way to the heart of a crime writer.

In every book, I acknowledge my real-life heroes—the women and men of the New York County District Attorney's Office and their courageous counterparts in the NYPD.

It was Justin Feldman who introduced me to his beloved friend Esther Newberg. Bones Fairstein, whose DNA passed on to me his love for reading this genre, and Bobbie Fairstein, who believed in everything I wanted to try to do. I carry them all with me, along with Karen Cooper—whose husband's name I stole to create my protagonist.

Jordan Goldberg gets major thanks for gifting his father with a bottle of small-batch Bourbon called Blood Oath.

Michael Goldberg is my rock, my first reader, my most gentle critic, and the man who makes me laugh every day. Laughter and love—a magical combination he has given me for which I am forever grateful.

ABOUT THE AUTHOR

Linda Fairstein was chief of the Sex Crimes Unit of the district attorney's office in Manhattan for more than two decades and is America's foremost legal expert on sexual assault and domestic violence. She is a regular contributor on criminal justice issues to magazines, journals, and online publications like **The Daily Beast**, and does on-air commentary for all the major television network and cable news shows. Her Alexandra Cooper novels are international and **New York Times** bestsellers and have been translated into more than a dozen languages. She lives in Manhattan and on Martha's Vineyard.

LIKE WHAT YOU'VE READ?

Try these titles by Linda Fairstein,
also available in large print:

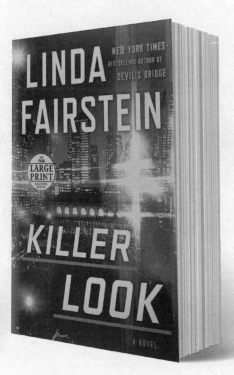